REVENGE DOWN UNDER

REVENGE DOWN UNDER

SIMON ERRINGTON

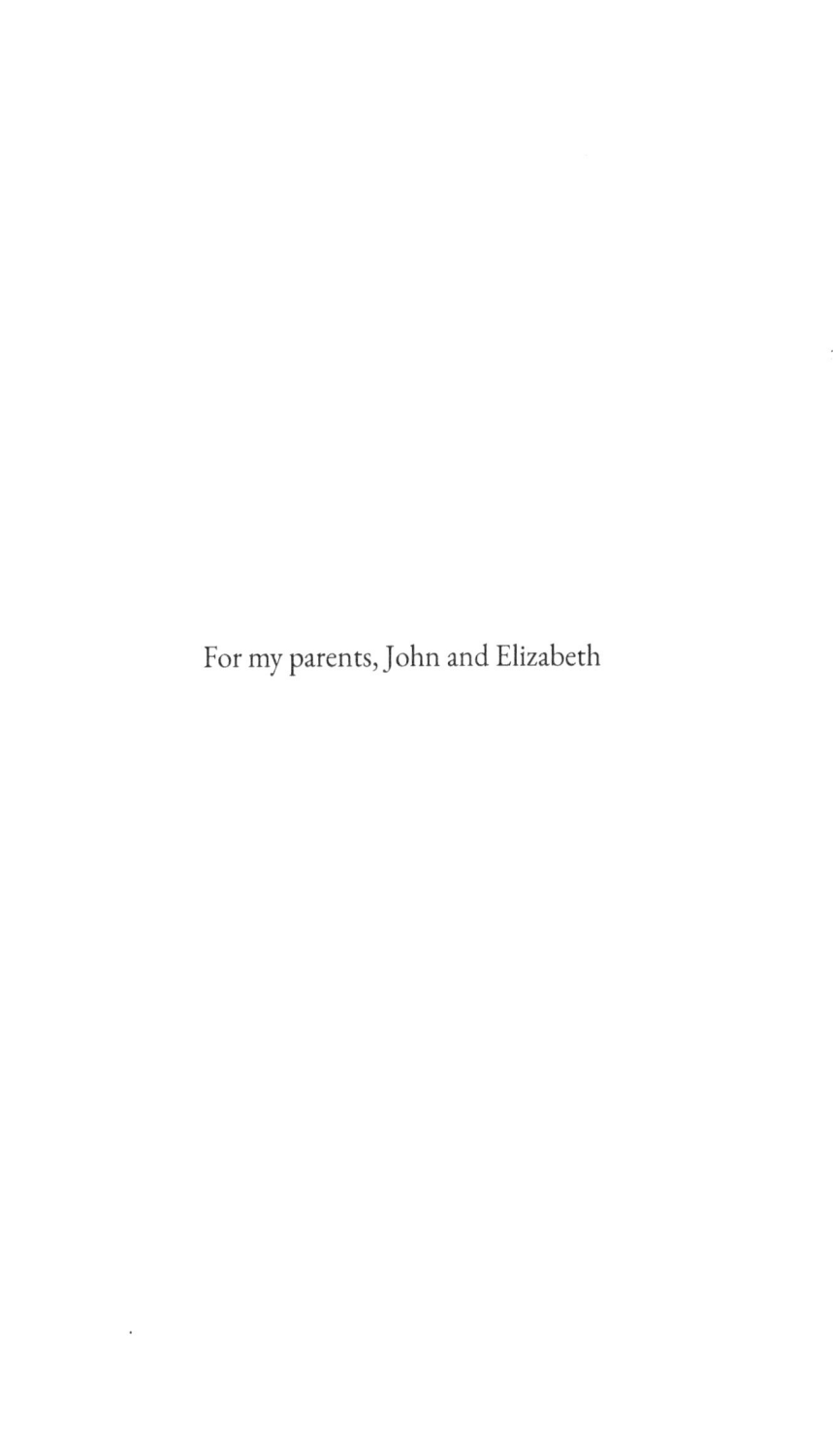

For my parents, John and Elizabeth

The year is

2016

CHAPTER 1

He knew that she knew but had to be certain. In life, he took no chances and would not take one now. She was scared and so she should be. He felt very calm, as he always did. Even as a child, when adults would ask how he was feeling, he never really understood the question and had to learn how to show feelings. And learn to show them he did, so he could appear like everyone else.

Elizabeth was terrified, confused, disorientated, and starting to shake. She had left work late as usual. After making her way to her car in the secure underground company car park, she remembered approaching her car and then nothing. Nothing at all until she realised that her wrists and ankles were tied, head covered, mouth taped, and she was lying down being rocked back and forth, while the humming sound of a car engine made its way into her consciousness.

He had planned this exceptionally well. It wouldn't have been planned any other way. He had been waiting for her in the car park. She was in her normal routine and not even looking at her surroundings as she headed for her vehicle. He learnt that most people are caught off guard when they are following a normal, boring routine. Hence, why most car accidents occur close to home. It was rather simple and easy. As soon as she unlocked and opened her car door with the remote button on the keyring, he jabbed a stun gun into her side and pushed her over onto the passenger seat. He then calmly placed himself into the driver's seat and proceeded to take the car key from her gripped hand as she convulsed and slumped in the seat.

Starting the car, he drove to an area of the car park where there was no security-camera coverage. There was a slim chance he had been seen by a security camera initially but, with a baseball cap and generic clothing, it would not matter. A necessary but reduced risk. Once there, he proceeded to tie Elizabeth's hands and ankles with zip ties, tape her mouth, move her to the back seat and place a blanket over her. Then he searched her handbag and located her mobile phone. He removed the back, took out the battery, and placed the parts back into the handbag. Police can easily go back and trace the movements of a person by their mobile phone, not that this was a huge risk for what he had planned, but always good to keep the police guessing. It was already dark outside so the risk of anyone seeing the back seat was reduced. Slowly and sedately, he drove out of the underground car park and headed out of Melbourne city towards the West Gate Bridge. He knew he would be able to find a spot up at the Westgate Park with privacy and enough traffic overhead to not be heard.

He loved this time of night. Weekday, heading towards midnight, when you could be alone with your thoughts. But he had to get back to the job at hand.

He knew that she knew. Elizabeth was still tied up in the back seat but the blanket and tape across her mouth were removed. Twisting his body, he remained in the driver's seat and kept asking her with a pistol pointed squarely at her face. She was still shaking and had remained quiet for the journey with a few reminders that any sound would result in death. Now she was slowly finding her voice. Words of denial were followed by an almost whimsical recollection of certain facts that may or may not have been relevant. It was hard to hear through the tears, shaking and laboured breathing that often comes with finding oneself in a situation reserved for only the worst nightmares.

"I swear I don't know what you're talking about," Elizabeth nervously answered. "I saw some things like you mentioned, but I wasn't sure what it all meant. Please, you have to believe me."

He was beginning to believe her but needed to be sure, so he made a point of emphasising the pistol in his hand by twitching it as he asked again. But before she could answer, he smacked her in the side of the head with it. Now, while she was stunned and had blood trickling down her face from a cut above the eye, he asked again. She didn't answer for a few seconds and he wondered if he had hit her a bit too hard. But then the same response came out of her mouth again.

Next, he asked if Elizabeth had mentioned anything to anybody else, while also making sure she was seeing the pistol twitching and realised another blow to the face could follow at any time.

"I swear. Oh, my god, I swear that I haven't told anybody. How could I when I didn't know what I was looking at? Please. Please, you have to believe me."

After an hour, it started to dawn on him that Elizabeth knew some facts but had not pieced enough together yet to be a true threat. However, these facts could have easily led to assumptions and then conclusions. He was feeling rather pleased that he had caught it in time. He was also now convinced, which he was even more pleased about, that she had not told anyone. Yet, he couldn't let her free. It was too risky. In fact, he never intended on letting her go free. He placed tape across her mouth once more, in case she decided to scream, dragged her out of the back seat and placed her into the car boot. With the boot still open, he grabbed the blanket from the back seat and placed it over her, not so she couldn't see him but to stop the splatter of blood. He fastened the silencer from his jacket pocket onto the pistol and fired two successive rounds into her head. He then threw the pistol onto her dead body, closed the boot, got back into the driver's seat and wondered if he would feel any remorse for this killing. None came. He reached over to her handbag and removed her mobile phone, battery, and wallet, and placed these in his pockets.

In his jacket pocket was a small wireless detonator. A mobile phone activated this. All he needed to do was dial a number and it would cause a spark to ignite anything flammable it was in contact with. Rather a simple device, like what so-called terrorists were using in the Middle East. A friend had shown him how to make it and how to make it waterproof. He reached down with his right hand and pulled the lever to release the fuel cap of the car. Then he walked around to the rear, unscrewed the fuel cap, and dropped the device into the tank. After he closed the cap, he went back to the driver's door, where he removed his gloves and threw them in, before closing the door with his hip. He then proceeded to take off his jacket, turn it inside out and put it back on, as it was a reversible design, and then did the same with his baseball cap while walking off down to Todd Road, where he could catch a bus back into the city.

He waited about twenty minutes for a bus, and during that time, no one else joined him to wait at the bus stop. As the bus arrived, he made sure his baseball cap was still on to obscure his image in the security camera located above the driver. He tapped on with the Myki travel card that he had purchased from a small convenience kiosk. He wasn't sure if the cards could be traced but, even if they could, the kiosk had no cameras and he paid in cash. He sat down on the bus and discreetly observed that there were five other passengers in it. Going by their industrial hardwearing workwear and nonchalant manner, they were heading home after a late shift at work from one of the many industrial businesses nearby. He fitted right in with his nondescript jeans, mass-produced plain polo shirt and run-of-the-mill jacket. They didn't even give him a second glance. To them, it was just another day that was already blurring into yesterday.

Once off the bus in the Melbourne CBD, he removed the prepaid phone from his jeans and proceeded to dial the number. He heard it ring twice and then go dead. He knew the car would have made a loud explosion as there was just over half a tank of petrol. Even if it had been nearly on empty, the fire still would have done the trick of burning any evidence and DNA traces. It would take at least five minutes for a fire engine to arrive and start extinguishing the burning car.

There was about a fifteen-minute walk to his hotel. Passing a rubbish bin, he removed Elizabeth's battery and sim card from his pocket and placed the phone in the bin. At the next rubbish bin he passed, he threw out the battery, and the next, the sim card. Then checking her wallet, he saw a hundred and twenty-five dollars in cash, along with credit cards, loyalty cards and other wallet paraphernalia that people tend to carry. He saw some homeless people down the street and calmly dropped the wallet, not breaking his stride. What a great night. Everything went per the plan. Better than per plan, as he was now confident that no one else knew anything. He felt in control, powerful and that he was master of his domain. He would have a peaceful sleep and fly back home in the morning, concluding a very successful business trip.

CHAPTER 2

Jacob had finally finished a night shift at Monash Hospital. The sun was already up on what was looking like a beautiful spring morning. He checked his watch, which displayed eight thirty, so he was finishing a bit late but liked to check his patients before leaving. It had been a relatively quiet night. He was on call and had needed to come in. He didn't mind being called in, as it was a teaching hospital and he enjoyed sharing his knowledge and experience with doctors in their intern and residency years. Making his way to the locker room, he said his good mornings to the nurses and those interns that were still hanging around.

Jacob Conway was an intelligent man. He was thirty-eight years old and had studied hard to get through medical school with top grades. After his residency, he had been accepted into the specialist field of cardiology, where he had worked his way into a respected position and had earnt an enviable reputation both locally and nationally. He had a slightly geeky look about him. His hair was in-between ginger and brown, depending on the light. He wore frameless glasses and liked to look presentable at all times, with his hair side-parted and neatly combed. He was clean-shaven every day and liked to wear a shirt and tie when consulting with patients. With his five foot ten inches tall frame and seventy-one kilograms, he wasn't ugly, yet wasn't overly handsome. But although he was what you would refer to as average in looks, with his good career and intelligence, he certainly came across as above average once you got to know him. Which was how he managed to get the girl of his dreams and become happily married.

The shower can wait until I get home, he thought. Opening his locker, he took off the usual doctor attire and put on his motorcycle gear—blue Kevlar jeans, boots, and his new Alpinestars leather jacket that his wife had bought him recently for his birthday. He packed his work clothes in his backpack, placed it on over his shoulders and tightened up the waist and chest strap so it was nice and snug. He grabbed his red full-faced helmet with the gloves tucked inside as he closed his locker and headed off to the basement car park.

This was Jacob's favourite part of the day, especially on a spring morning, when it wasn't too hot or too cold and the sun was shining. Perfect riding weather. One advantage of riding a motorbike was the ability to park it anywhere and not pay for parking. He placed his helmet in his left hand while he put the key in the ignition with his right. Turning the key, he could hear and see the electronics and gauges whir into life on his Honda Fireblade sports bike that was red like his helmet and matched the black and red of his jacket. Pressing the starter button, the four-cylinder engine roared to life with a sound that was always a joy to hear. He placed the helmet on his head, tightened the chinstrap, slid his hands into his gloves, and tightened them with the Velcro straps. This made him feel like a fighter pilot preparing to get into an F-14 or whatever else fighter jets were called, not that he had ever been in one. He loved the preparation before going for a ride.

He swung his right leg over, sat down and felt the power underneath him. He flicked up the side stand with his left heel and then used the same foot to push the gear lever down into first, hearing the pop as the engine engaged. Slowly he released the clutch with his left hand as he made his way out onto the streets, where he could open up the throttle and enjoy the ride home. He derived a great satisfaction from the methodical approach to being on a bike and how every limb was used along with the body and head to get from A to B.

Jacob cruised up Springvale Road, enjoying the feel of the bitumen and the sound of the motorbike purring along in fourth gear at a steady eighty kilometres per hour, which was the maximum the speed limit allowed on this long, three-lane stretch of road. He headed towards his house in Glen Waverley thinking that he should take the bike for a good run on the freeway to get it up through all the gears. Maybe a ride through the Dandenong Ranges on the weekend would be good. Today was Wednesday, so he'd need to check the weather when he got home. Looking at the clock on the instrument display, he saw that it was two minutes before nine. He should be home in ten minutes, he calculated, and he could have something to eat, watch a bit of TV and then have a sleep with enough time to wake up and prepare dinner for when his wife got home. They could spend some time together before he headed off to work again. They missed dinner together yesterday as she was working late.

Pulling into the driveway of their three-bedroom townhouse, he saw a car parked on the road with two men in it looking straight at him. It dawned on him that it was an unmarked police car. It was a dead giveaway being a Ford Falcon with extra aerials and the glint of the red and blue lights under the grill and by the rear-view mirror. Maybe there had been a burglary, but surely normal uniformed police would attend to this. He had learnt a thing or two dealing with the police as a doctor. Maybe they needed to question him about one of the many assault victims he dealt with when working the ER, but usually they would do this at work or over the phone. His mind was still going over these scenarios when he parked up his bike, made sure it was in neutral, turned the ignition off and placed the kickstand down with his left foot. He swung his right leg over his bike and stood facing it as he removed his gloves. He then placed them on the seat to free up his hands to remove his helmet. Once his helmet was removed, he stuffed his gloves inside it while still holding it with his left hand before removing the keys from the ignition with his right and placing them in his jacket pocket. He turned around to face down the driveway. Sure enough, the two men were walking up the driveway towards him.

"Good morning, sir. My name is Detective Senior Sergeant Zhang. This is my partner Detective Constable Moskil. Are you Doctor Jacob Conway?"

"Yes, I am. How may I help you?"

"May we go inside? There has been an incident and we have some questions. If that is okay with you?"

Jacob looked closely at the detectives and saw that they looked very serious even though they were trying to appear friendly and relaxed. A sinking feeling was beginning to descend into his stomach. Why, he was not sure, but it did not feel like this conversation would end well.

"Um, certainly. Follow me," Jacob replied after what felt like a very long pause but was probably only a second or two.

Jacob left his bike on the driveway by the garage door and walked towards the front door. He removed the house key from his pocket and unlocked the door. He walked in first and held the door open for the two detectives. Once inside, he stood facing the detectives with his helmet still in his hand. He gestured for them to go through to the open-plan lounge and kitchen.

Jacob placed his helmet on top of a shoe rack, removed his backpack and placed it on the floor by the stairs that led up to the three bedrooms, took off his leather jacket and hung it on a coat rack. He turned and saw that the detectives had stopped in the area between the lounge and kitchen and were waiting for him.

"Please take a seat," Jacob said as he made his way towards them. "Would you like a cup of coffee or tea?"

"No, we're fine, thanks," replied Detective Senior Sergeant Zhang as he and Detective Moskil sat down on the couch.

Jacob took this as his cue that he should also sit so he placed himself in one of the two armchairs that faced the couch, with a large coffee table separating them.

Detective Senior Sergeant Zhang was obviously in control. Jacob hadn't seen too many Chinese police officers in Melbourne. Come to think of it, this would be his first encounter with a Chinese detective. He knew Zhang was Australian from his accent. Jacob realised he shouldn't be looking at him any differently, especially since Melbourne was full of Chinese, especially in his suburb of Glen Waverley due to the good schools. He got along well with the Chinese community, and one thing he liked about Glen Waverley was that it had an order about it, with many Chinese kids studying hard and showing respect to their elders and their community. Not to mention the great Chinese restaurants. But, still, he had to look twice at a Chinese Australian detective. Detective Senior Sergeant Zhang looked to be about thirty years old and had dark short hair and the type of dark eyes that made it difficult to distinguish the pupil from the iris. He was the same height as Jacob and, strangely, looked like a young Jet Li in a suit.

Detective Moskil was Caucasian and looked like a typical police officer. He was forty-eight years old, so older than his boss, Detective Zhang. He was a bit on the heavy side, with receding light brown hair but, at six feet, he was taller than his boss. He had a friendly face with light brown eyes and wrinkles that looked like they had formed out of laughter rather than age. He was a career police officer and had finally made it to detective after two attempts at the exams. What he lacked in intelligence, he made up for with experience.

"As mentioned, I am Detective Zhang, and this is Detective Moskil." Adam Zhang had left out their rank on purpose to put everyone at ease.

The detectives already knew who Jacob was. He had confirmed it verbally in the driveway and they had obtained a photo before making their way over. Easy enough to do through Google for someone who was a medical doctor, as all photos and professional details were in the public domain.

"Have you just come home from work?"

"Yes, from Monash Hospital, where I was working the nightshift as an attending surgeon."

Detective Moskil excused himself and, holding his phone, walked towards the front door. This was pre-planned, so he could call the hospital and confirm Jacob's whereabouts last night.

"Is your wife Elizabeth Conway, maiden name Paxter?"

"Yes, she is. Why? What's happened?"

"I'm sorry to have to inform you but we found her car burnt out in Westgate Park under the West Gate Bridge in the early hours of this morning. There was a body in the boot of the car. Can you confirm that your wife has a Honda Civic?"

Jacob was stunned. Numb. Speechless. His eyes began to glaze over, and tears started to make their way to his eyes, but he was not crying. Looking through Detective Zhang, he muttered, "What do you mean 'a body in the boot'?"

Detective Zhang looked straight at Jacob to try to hold his attention as it was critical for them to move on this case as quickly as possible. He had already mobilised as many police officers as possible. Yet he did not want to push him too hard and get nowhere. In an even, calm tone, he proceeded.

"We have identified the car through the engine number and what was remaining of the registration plates. It is your wife's car. Can you please tell us if she was driving this last night and her whereabouts?"

"Well, of course, she was driving it. She went to work as per normal yesterday and I know she was going to work late since I was working. What the hell is going on?" His tone was starting to become angry and frustrated.

Detective Zhang knew that he could lay out the facts with Jacob. He moved slightly forward in his seat, maintaining eye contact.

"Okay. I'll be straight-up with you. Yes, we found your wife's car burnt out in Westgate Park. A body was in the car boot with cause of death being two gunshot wounds. We have already obtained security footage from the underground car park at your wife's work, and it showed your wife walking up to her car and then being forced into the car by a man we cannot identify, as his face was not visible. Our forensic team is with the car as we speak. The car was likely alight for an hour and a half before the fire was extinguished so damage is extensive, and the chances of DNA and fingerprint recovery are looking slim. We cannot get you to formally identify the body due to the fire and this will need to be done via dental and DNA records."

Jacob didn't move as he continued to look through Detective Zhang. Tears now came through his eyes, down his cheeks and into the corners of his mouth. But there were no sounds of crying. "It might not be her?"

"That is true. I don't want to raise your hopes as the evidence we have obtained so far indicates it is likely to be Elizabeth."

Detective Moskil returned to the room and subtly gave a thumbs up to Detective Zhang that was not visible to Jacob. He then sat back down beside his colleague. They both now knew that he was working all night at the hospital. To make it official, they would send a junior detective down there to get this in writing.

Detective Zhang waited for a few seconds to see if Jacob would say anything. Realising that he should continue, he said, "We obtained Elizabeth's phone number and have tried calling it but it goes straight to voice message." He held up his phone with Elizabeth's number on the screen for Jacob to confirm it was correct, which he did.

"Would it be possible for you to give us Elizabeth's dentist's details, and can we please take some DNA samples from a hair or toothbrush? This will assist us in identifying the body."

Jacob had eventually made eye contact and was now looking at the detective rather than through him. He wiped the tears from his face and attempted to pull himself together.

"Of course, you can. Sure. Give me a minute."

It was like autopilot had set in. Jacob knew that he now had to do something even though his knees felt weak and a fog was descending through his brain. He had to be productive. Like when an operation didn't go to plan, and he had to remain calm and work methodically through the scenarios to get a positive result. As he walked to the kitchen, he got his phone out of his pocket and dialled Elizabeth. Sure enough, straight to voicemail. Reaching the kitchen, he opened the fourth drawer down, where all important cards were kept, including cards from tradesmen. He found their dentist's card and walked back to the lounge and passed it to Detective Zhang.

"Hairbrush is in the bedroom, if you want to follow me."

They both walked upstairs and into the master bedroom. Jacob went into the ensuite bathroom and handed Elizabeth's hairbrush to Detective Zhang, which he placed in an evidence bag.

Detective Zhang saw that Jacob was doing his best to remain focused and started to admire the man. Looking at him straight in the eyes, he asked, "Do you have anyone that can come around and be with you while we run the DNA and dental records? A family member or friend?"

"I have no family in Melbourne, but Elizabeth's parents live nearby. I'll give them a call once you've gone. I'd like to be alone if you don't mind."

Jacob planned on calling them as soon as the detectives were gone. He didn't want them to hear or see him break down. His mind started to race as he looked at the ground and thought about who else should know. He thought of her brother, Roman, whom he had never met. Maybe her friends at work, her friends outside of work.

Detective Adam Zhang saw Jacob's mind wander and brought him back to the present. "Certainly. I should have an answer for you by the end of the day, if not within a few hours."

With that, Jacob walked Detective Zhang back down the stairs to where Detective Moskil was waiting. As they reached the front door, Detective Zhang turned to Jacob and handed him his card.

"If you have any questions or anything, please call me any time. My mobile number is there. We have your phone number, but I will personally visit when we have some news. If you are going to be somewhere else, please let me know. A text message will be fine. Once again, call me any time."

Jacob saw that he was sincere. He took the card and just nodded his head as his throat had closed up due to the array of emotions. The detectives left, and he closed the door behind them. He made his way back to the lounge, sat on the couch and stared at the blank television screen. Just stared at it and through it at the same time, with his body feeling numb and his mind stunned.

Outside, as he walked towards the police car, Detective Zhang pulled out his phone and organised a plain-clothes police officer to keep an eye on Jacob's house. As in every investigation, he needed to cover all bases, even though his instincts were telling him Jacob had nothing to do with it. His gut was giving him a bad feeling about this and little did he know how right his gut would prove to be.

CHAPTER 3

Roman was finding it difficult to control his emotions. For the last four days, he had been feeling equal amounts of grief, sadness, and anger. Now it was mainly sadness as the funeral started for his beautiful, full-of-life sister. His only sibling and the one that did their parents proud. He felt sadness that he had not made an effort to spend more time with her when it was not her fault that he didn't get along with their parents. He had spent the last fifteen years with little contact with her or their parents, with only the odd phone call at Christmas time, and often he would forget to do this. Now there was no more time to have those chats, or the eventual catch-up and reconciliation that he always thought would happen.

The church was small, with high cathedral ceilings that were in keeping with expectations when you walked through the thick wooden front doors. A beautiful huge lead-lined stained-glass window was the centrepiece behind the old marble altar. The odd bit of sunlight sneaked through the clouds to light up the colours of the mosaic that depicted Jesus on the cross with his disciples at his feet and heaven waiting for him in the clouds above. A ray of sunlight now shone through and gently touched the coffin, as if to accept Elizabeth to eternal happiness and peace. Then the clouds came over again, as though in a sign of respect, demonstrating that it was not just those gathered there that were in mourning.

It had taken three days before his parents had managed to contact him to inform him that his sister, Elizabeth, had died. He was still in shock that she had been murdered. They had informed him of the events and how they had been spending time with her husband, Jacob. Jacob, her husband whom he had never met. Elizabeth had sent him an invite to their wedding, but he had turned it down, using work as a convenient excuse. What an idiot he had been. Hindsight always messes with the brain in times of turmoil.

The church was overflowing with people he did not know. Roman stood at the back, listening to the kind eulogies people were giving. Friends of Elizabeth, and now her husband, were describing the sister he knew and the wonderful and accomplished adult she had become. He found it difficult to concentrate as his mind went back to the phone call from their parents. His dad had mentioned that the body was identified through dental records and later confirmed through DNA. His stomach tightened at the thought that someone had shot his sister and then burnt her in her car beyond recognition, no doubt to destroy any evidence. *Why, why, why* was eating away at him and now the anger was starting to override the sadness.

Roman started to reminiscence about his childhood with his sister, who was two years older than him. They had plenty of fights with each other as kids and, boy, did she pack a mean punch. She always won in those early days when she was bigger and, looking back, it certainly taught him how to take a beating and harden up. At a playground when he was about five years old, he was getting picked on by an older boy to the point that he had started to cry. Elizabeth ran over and gave the bully a humongous shove, sending him to the ground, and forcefully told him to "leave my brother alone". Roman still remembered the look of shock on the boy's face and the stern look her sister gave. The boy ran away, and Elizabeth took her younger brother by the hand and walked him up the road to their house, telling him that she would always have his back. When they got home, neither of them mentioned the incident to their parents, and he realised that even though she would beat him up, outside of the house, she was always on his side.

When Roman was ten years old, and was starting to get taller and bigger than Elizabeth, they still had arguments at home, usually around what television program to watch, but now it didn't result in a physical confrontation. His parents had drilled into him that boys did not hit girls, also that Elizabeth shouldn't hit him—not that she ever listened. They went to the same school but walked home separately with their own friends. One day he had said goodbye to his mates and was walking across a park to their street when he saw her talking to two older boys. It wasn't until he was a bit closer that he noticed the distressed look on her face and that the two older boys, whom he did not recognise, were hassling her and starting to touch her and prevent her from leaving. What they were saying, he still didn't know to this day, but clearly, she was not happy and was trying to get away. Without giving it a second thought, he dropped his school bag and ran over to her aid. Running straight into the first boy, he knocked him over, and then proceeded to punch the other boy as hard as he could in the head. It didn't take long for the first boy to get to his feet and strike Roman in the face, with the second boy joining in to give him a right old beat-down. Roman remembered just holding his ground and throwing punches left, right and centre and managing to keep them at bay while taking a real walloping. Elizabeth, in the background, cried and yelled at them to stop. They did stop, and they grabbed their schoolbags and ran for it.

Roman remembered how he dusted himself off. He felt blood trickle from his nose and face, and his body felt sore and bruised. Elizabeth once again took his hand, but this time said, "Thank you." Together, they walked home. They told their parents what had happened, and he remembered being confused at how they had to tell him off for fighting but were proud of him for looking after his sister and standing up to bullies. It was then that he felt appreciated and honoured to be able to look after his older sister rather than the other way around. From that day, he continued to be bigger and stronger than her, and bigger and stronger than most boys his age. Into his teenage years, he started to excel at sport and boys realised they had to treat Elizabeth with dignity and earn her brother's respect, and on top of that, all her brother's friends' respect as well. It was an unspoken rule between him and Elizabeth that he had her back no matter what. An unwritten rule that he had now failed to follow, and looking at the church full of her friends, it dawned on him that he had forgone that unwritten rule many years ago.

Roman Paxter was always in trouble as a teenager, and right into his early twenties. He had put his parents through grief with constant fighting at high school and being disrespectful to teachers. Somehow, he still passed all his exams. The teachers always told his parents that he was intelligent. Yet, he didn't feel intelligent or that he really belonged at school. He didn't know what he felt at that time, apart from anger towards everything and everyone who told him how he should behave and act. Looking back, he could acknowledge that the school never expelled him and always tried to work with him. Countless meetings with the headmaster, teachers and his parents resulted in empty promises from him. He realised that being good at sport and a key member of the school's first fifteen rugby team helped him not get expelled.

After he passed his final year and graduated from high school, he could have gone to university, but, instead, he decided to work manual jobs in Brisbane, and then travel north up Australia, while drinking, dabbling in drugs, and partying hard every weekend. It was an excuse to get as far away from home and his parents as possible, which also resulted in little contact with his older sister. After a couple of years living this lifestyle and becoming known to local police, luckily without getting arrested, it dawned on him that his life had no meaning. The next step in his life was a very bold move based on a documentary he watched on television in the early hours of the morning after coming home intoxicated from the pub.

The sound of soft crying and the sniffing back of tears jolted Roman back to the present. Jacob's moving tribute to Elizabeth had just ended, and Jacob was being assisted from the lectern by his parents, who had joined him in the tears of mourning a loved one. As they returned to their seats, the priest proceeded to conclude the funeral.

As he felt his throat tighten and tears well up in his eyes, Roman made his way outside to wait for the funeral procession to exit the church. After closing the door silently behind him, he felt eyes on him and scanned the small church grounds, where he saw a girl that appeared to be in her late twenties standing under a pine tree drying her eyes. Walking over to her, he noticed that she was looking directly at him as if they knew each other.

"Hi. Sorry. I had to get out to get some air. I couldn't help but notice you. You wouldn't be Elizabeth's brother, by any chance?"

"Yeah, I am. Sorry, I do not recognise you. Have we met before?"

"No, we haven't. I'm Moya and I worked with Elizabeth. We were quite close friends and hung out a lot. I thought I recognised you from an old photo she kept on her desk that showed the two of you laughing."

"Oh, well, that must have been an old photo as I hadn't seen her for many years. Which was no fault of her own."

Roman sniffed back the last of his tears and deduced from Moya's puffy eyes that she had also been crying. Moya was attractive, with long, wavy, red hair, pale skin, green eyes and a slim five-foot-six frame. Obviously the Irish name matched an Irish ancestry.

"I'm Roman, and it's a pleasure to meet one of Elizabeth's friends."

He didn't offer to shake hands and, sensing this, Moya reached out hers. It was more of a brief hold than a shake.

"So, Roman. I gather you don't live in Melbourne since I've never seen you before. Elizabeth spoke of you a couple of times and said you were the black sheep of the family. It's really nice to finally meet you." Moya was also noticing Roman's six-foot-two, stocky, muscular build, his chestnut-brown hair colour and warm, brown eyes like his sister's.

Roman had so many questions, but it was not the right place or time. What was Elizabeth into? What were her favourite foods? Did she still have a great sense of humour? So many questions.

"Yeah. I now live in Wellington, New Zealand. I flew in this morning. It took a while for my parents to contact me as I haven't exactly been good at keeping contact and letting them know where I live or even my phone number."

"Well, I'm glad you're here. It's been a horrible few days and I still haven't gotten my head around what happened. It's so sad." The tears started to roll again from her puffy eyes.

"I feel the same," said Roman as he tried to comfort her by placing his right hand on her upper arm. "If you'd like to talk, I'd love to catch up with you and hear all about Elizabeth."

"That would be nice. I appreciate it. I haven't been back to work yet so any day or time is good for me."

The sun was starting to shine and the pine tree was providing welcome shade as the day started to heat up. The music from the church suddenly grew louder as the doors opened. Roman recognised the song as Linkin Park's "Shadow of the Day", as the lyrics floated through the air. *And the shadow of the day. Will embrace the world in grey. And the sun will set for you.*

Roman and Moya both got caught up in the moving and appropriate song as the congregation shuffled out into the sunlight. Roman caught the eyes of his parents and turned to Moya.

"Nice to meet you and I'll be in touch. Do you have a phone number I could contact you on?"

"Certainly. Have you got your phone?"

Roman removed his phone from his trouser pocket and passed it to Moya. After a few strokes and presses, she informed him that he now had her number in his contacts under "Moya Connor". Roman gave her a warm smile and headed towards his parents.

As he walked over, his parents made a detour off the church path to meet him. Roman noticed that they had appeared to age since the last photos he had seen via the occasional email from Elizabeth. His mum was an attractive woman nearing her sixtieth birthday. She looked after herself and stayed slim, with skin that could make her pass for ten years younger. Her hair was cut to a neat, wavy bob with dark-brown dye keeping most of the grey away. Roman's dad had now gone completely grey, with an increasingly receding hairline that made him look distinguished rather than old. A slight belly could now be seen under his shirt and jacket, but overall he looked to still be in good shape, and was no doubt continuing those weekend runs and rounds of golf. The look of grief was etched into their features and tired eyes despite an unnatural look of composure.

No one spoke as they came face to face. They could all see the look of pain and grief on each other's faces. Roman gave his mum a big succouring hug and immediately felt the warmth, security, and comfort that he had long forgotten. They embraced for what seemed an eternity before releasing and looking again at each other. With his mum still holding his hands, she broke the silence with three simple words. "We missed you."

While still holding his mum's hands, he turned to face his dad. Roman had never seen his dad cry before but now he looked like a broken soul, for whom shedding a tear was part of life. His dad looked through glazed eyes and muttered, "It's good to see you, son. Really good to see you."

Roman's mum let go of his hands and, with that, he reached out to his father and gave him a hug that was fifteen years overdue. All those arguments, disagreements, shouting matches, and hurtful words seemed to soften, thaw, and diffuse. Roman lifted his head while still embracing his dad and in a chocked-up voice uttered, "I'm sorry, so sorry, for everything."

While they stood a few metres from the main church path, other mourners began to usher past slowly, giving comfort to one another. Roman's parents sensed that they needed to join them. His dad unfurled his hug and said, "I hope you're going to stay with us for a while. We would really appreciate it if you did."

"Of course, I will. Thanks. I've got a rental car for at least a week and would like to stay a bit longer. This has come as a huge shock to me and I don't want to be a stranger anymore."

"Excellent," his mum replied. "Now come with us and meet Jacob, Elizabeth's husband." And with that, they all turned and walked back to the church path, where Jacob was trying his best to hold it together in the presence of all the friends and family that had come to show their last respects. Roman glanced over his shoulder and saw that Moya was gone, no doubt sharing fond memories of Moya with their group of friends.

Jacob looked just like the photos Elizabeth had emailed him a few years ago when they had moved into their new house. Along with the photos was an open invitation to stay with them whenever he wanted. An invitation he thought he'd eventually accept at some stage but now it was too late. Jacob held out his hand and Roman shook it. "I'm so pleased to finally meet you, Jacob. I know my sister was very happy with you and I'm so sorry for your loss."

"Thanks. I'm also sorry for your loss. Elizabeth spoke very fondly of you and I'm so glad you're here."

"Your eulogy was very moving. I needed to get some air afterwards. There is so much of Elizabeth's life I have missed, and your words did her proud. I'd really like to hear more stories about her and everything you accomplished together."

Jacob gave a nod of his head and said, "Of course. We're all on our way to the church hall and I'll introduce you to some of her friends."

Roman had a well-developed ability to sense a person's character and he got the impression that Jacob was a genuine, straight-up person who kept his word and would not let friends or family down. He had an air about him that he could cope with much pressure and maintain his professionalism when it counted. Roman knew he was a successful doctor, so no doubt this came with the job, or he already had those qualities, which made him an excellent doctor. Jacob obviously had a superior intelligence but he appeared humble, not flashy, which was in keeping with Elizabeth. In photos, they always drove sensible cars rather than BMWs or Mercedes, and the last photo he saw from Elizabeth was Jacob on his new motorcycle—a Honda when he could have easily afforded a Ducati or Aprilia. It was generally people that were not comfortable in their own skin or their own abilities that felt the need to project superiority over others with opulent possessions that, most of the time, they couldn't afford. Jacob came across as having neither of these shortcomings.

Roman turned to his parents and offered his arm to his mum, which she accepted. She placed her arm through his and rested her hand on his forearm, and they all walked together in the warm sun to join everyone in stilted greetings and small talk about his sister.

They did not see Detective Adam Zhang in the distance.

CHAPTER 4

Detective Senior Sergeant Adam Zhang was driving along Flinders Street and turned right into Spencer Street as he headed to the Melbourne West Police Station, which was the biggest police station in Melbourne and housed over a thousand staff in a modern twelve-storey complex. It was also home to the state of Victoria's biggest crime investigation unit, which had a wealth of resources and experience. Adam had transferred there when he made detective and quickly established himself as a hardworking, tenacious, intelligent officer, and moved up through the ranks. Now he had been given his first lead detective role in a homicide—the case involving the murder of thirty-five-year-old Elizabeth Conway (nee Paxter). It was a case that had gained media attention, which added to the pressure of achieving a quick resolution.

Adam had driven back from Elizabeth's funeral that morning. It was a Saturday and he had made plans to meet with Detective Constable John Moskil to go over parts of the case in preparation for Monday. John had passed his sergeant's exams, and after this case would hopefully be given the title and promotion to take more senior roles in murder investigations. Adam had worked with him for just over a year and was glad that this case was a chance for him to demonstrate those leadership qualities that would be expected in the future. Adam had given a briefing of the case the day before to his superintendent, in which he put forward the progress made, complexities of the case, and the resources required moving forward. He had been granted two junior detectives to assist, along with forensic and admin staff as required. Adam and John now needed to prepare for Monday morning, when they would bring the team up to speed and allocate clear duties and expectations.

The funeral that morning had been a moving affair, as all funerals of murder victims were. Adam had asked permission from Elizabeth's parents and husband before attending. It was a sign of respect to attend the services, and a courtesy expected of all detectives, but it was also a time to observe all those attending, as often the murderer is someone close to the victim and carries on in that role to not raise any suspicion. Adam had seen Elizabeth's brother, Roman, enter the church and stood at the back not far from him. He had recognised him from an old photo he had obtained when considering Elizabeth's family, but details of him were extremely limited and he had yet to ask the family about him as he preferred to talk to Roman himself.

Before the funeral ended, he watched Roman leave the church in a state of sorrow and suffering, and after the funeral, witnessed him speaking to a girl under the shade of a tree before leaving her to join his parents. He subtly took a photo of her with his phone, and looking at it now, identified her as Moya Connor, a close work friend. Adam had kept his distance and did not introduce himself, not wanting to inject a police presence into this time of grieving. It was his duty to bring closure, and with that in mind, he returned to his car, took out a notebook and wrote down everything he had observed at the funeral before he could forget, no matter how trivial it had appeared at the time.

Adam Zhang was the only child to immigrant parents. He was born in Melbourne and remembered a childhood immersed in Chinese culture. His parents still lived in Melbourne and socialised within the tight-knit Chinese community of Box Hill in the inner eastern suburbs, where they had bought their first and only house many years ago. It was a house they would not be able to afford nowadays if they were a young couple, due to the rapid expansion in the population of Melbourne and the pressure that put on housing that resulted in prices beyond the means of most couples, unless they moved to the newly created suburbs on the outer fringes of the city.

His parents arrived as a newly married couple and quickly got low-paid, unskilled jobs, but with their strong work effort, progressed up the pay scales and saved as much as they could to have a child and give their son everything they had lacked. They were not wealthy but comfortable, and could afford to take a nice holiday if they wished, but they still had the mentality to not waste money, which was very common in the older generation of immigrant couples. This ethos was something they had instilled in Adam from a young age.

Adam excelled at school and studied exceptionally hard to please his parents, who sacrificed a lot to send him to a good school and expected good grades in return. He had plenty of Chinese friends that were in the same position, so it didn't feel abnormal. Towards the end of high school, his parents pushed him towards choosing a degree in medicine, law, or engineering. He had the grades to attend any university and, to please his parents, chose to study law at Melbourne University, which was ranked the top law school in Australia. He also didn't want to move away from home. Throughout his degree, he undertook internships and vocational roles within a prestigious law firm specialising in criminal law. Before graduating, he already had a position within the firm lined up, which made his parents extremely proud and raised their social standing within the extended family back in Nanjing, China. He passed the bar exam and worked at the firm for two years but was never happy being a lawyer. He kept this from his parents as he worked twelve-hour days to accelerate his career. His parents had paid for him to go to good schools, to get a good career, and there was a cultural expectation that he would conform to his parents' aspirations.

One day, Adam decided to sit his parents down and disclose his true feelings about practising law. He had prepared for this talk for many weeks and outlined everything that was making him unhappy. To his surprise, his parents listened tentatively and did not like the idea of their son going to work every day miserable. But Adam knew they still required a suitable profession for him to undertake. Adam, being well prepared, outlined how law favours people with money and how his real interest was in problem-solving and providing the courts with concrete evidence rather than being one of those lawyers paid to debate every subsection and clause of law to provide reasonable doubt to get their clients off. Adam wanted to join the police force and took his parents through the career path to becoming a detective and explained how his law degree and work experience would benefit him in this role and his career progression within the Criminal Investigation Branch. His parents took some convincing, especially in the notion that he would make less money. In the end, they gave him their blessing, but couldn't help emphasise that he needed to do them proud and become the best detective out there. Adam thanked them and promised to study diligently and work tirelessly to establish himself in his new profession. It was a profession he was now excelling in and this case was a defining point—his first as lead detective—and one his parents would be keeping a close eye on.

Adam exited the elevator and made his way to his desk, where he saw John already seated, sipping a takeaway coffee, and tapping away on his laptop. John greeted Adam with a nod and raise of the eyebrows as he sat down at the desk beside him. Adam placed his bag on the floor beside the leg of the desk and retrieved his laptop.

"How was the funeral?" John asked.

"I'd like to say like any other funeral, but this was pretty moving, with the church packed with decent folks that don't deserve a tragedy like this in their lives."

"Anything of note?"

"Nah, mate, but I caught sight of Elizabeth's brother and I'd like to personally speak to him and reinterview this girl he was talking to. Lots of other people that we need to get the team to take statements from. Anyway, are you ready to go over what we know and what we need to do?" Adam looked back down at his laptop as he entered his password and brought up the folder containing everything about the case.

"Ready as ever," John replied. "I'll take notes and then write up tasks for the two detectives that'll be working the case with us. Do you know who they are?"

"Yep, sure do. It's Olivia and Noah. Both young and keen."

"I know those two. Had a little bit to do with them a few months back when helping on that domestic murder case. They both seemed on to it."

Adam got off his seat and dragged a spare whiteboard over. There were many dotted around the walls of the open-plan office, waiting patiently on their wheels like dogs waiting to be of service. After taking a whiteboard marker off his desk, popping the top off and placing it on the other end, Adam turned to John and proceeded to go through everything they knew.

"CCTV footage showed Elizabeth being forced into her car at eight forty-four by an unidentified man that appeared to use a stun gun as Elizabeth opened the driver's door. This subdued her and enable him to push her into the car, all the way to the passenger seat. He then drove off, with no more CCTV footage available. We got a record from the telco on her mobile phone and it appears it was turned off around this time, so there is no trace of where they were between the two hours of this happening and the time of death. I think we can safely concur that this man disabled the mobile phone straightaway as he knew we would be able to trace it."

Adam turned to the whiteboard and wrote as he spoke: "What happened in the two hours from being taken and then murdered?" He underlined the "two hours" to emphasise this critical time.

"We know at that time of night it only takes about twenty minutes to get to Westgate Park and, assuming this man knew what he was doing, he would have wasted little time finding that secluded spot under the bridge. Was she taken someplace else first or did they drive straight there? There was no sexual assault, so what the hell did they do?" As he wrote, he tapped the whiteboard, making many full stops after the written questions.

Adam continued, glancing between the board and John. "She was shot twice, fatally in the head. The pistol used was found burnt beside the body, with no fingerprints due to the fire and any serial number filed off. This man knew what he was doing. We have the initial CCTV footage of him wearing a cap, jacket, and jeans but, so far, no other CCTV footage showing this from shops and cameras around the city. We must widen our search and try public transport near Westgate Park at around that time. Perhaps another car picked him up, which would then involve more than one suspect. Then again, he could have changed clothes, so we need to check all available cameras."

Adam wrote this last comment on the whiteboard, with John taking notes to assign this task to junior detectives Olivia and Noah on Monday. Adam took a long step from the board and reached down into his bag. He pulled out a water bottle, took a sip and, while still holding it, continued.

"Elizabeth's wallet was taken and that was recovered yesterday when a homeless person tried tapping the credit card at the supermarket on Swanston Street. We identified the homeless man from CCTV and that ended up being a dead-end when we located him on the same street. He got it off another homeless man, who he introduced us to, who found it on the footpath, removed the cash and passed the rest on. Therefore, we can assume the suspect took the wallet for something or maybe for nothing more than to waste our time. We need Elizabeth's husband to go over the wallet to see if anything significant is missing."

John made more notes. Adam didn't pause and continued. "You and I agreed that the homeless guys were telling the truth as they had nothing to hide, with statements taken and filed. We must check all CCTV cameras around this vicinity in the city for anybody dropping a wallet. Another job for Olivia and Noah." He put his drink bottle down and wrote that up on the whiteboard, even though John was already onto it.

John stopped typing and said, "Before you got in, I started compiling a list of all city council cameras for Olivia and Noah to go through that are in that area. I just finished going through the few cameras from the roads to and from Westgate Park and have found nothing except one shot that could be

Elizabeth's car, but you cannot see the occupants or plates, so basically nothing. I've started going through public transport cameras from the buses that go from the industrial buildings near the park. So far, nothing to match the suspect's description. Also, camera footage on the West Gate Bridge came back negative on licence plate recognition for Elizabeth's car, so we can assume he didn't head west out of Melbourne and then backtrack before killing her. No cameras with licence plate recognition between the city and the park, but I also checked the tollway cameras around the city and they also came back negative, which adds to the assumption they drove straight there. All this is documented and added to the case files."

Adam was impressed and let John know with "nice work".

Adam turned back to the whiteboard and tapped it with the marker as he continued. "Forensics are still working on the car and at the scene of the crime. So far, nothing of note has turned up except that an incendiary device was likely used to set fire to the fuel tank. My gut feeling is nothing substantial will come from the scene except that this was meticulously planned. It was not a robbery. It was not a sexual assault. So, that leaves us with trying to find a motive."

With the whiteboard marker, Adam wrote in big capital letters "motive" and underlined it numerous times.

John gave Adam a discerning look and said, "If you don't mind my French, boss, this person is fucking with us. I agree that we need to find a motive and then gather the evidence from this. I bumped into someone from the organised crime unit and Elizabeth is not known to them. For this kind of murder, or should we say 'hit', the victim is almost always known to these guys."

Adam nodded his head. "I totally agree with you. That reminds me, and I've also mentioned this to the organised crime unit, on Monday we have a meeting with them to go over this case. You and I will focus solely on establishing a motive. This means going over all of Elizabeth's and Jacob's tax returns for the last ten years. What are their assets? What is their lifestyle like? Does one plus one equal two? I've contacted her manager from work and am seeing him on Monday afternoon, when I'll be requesting all information on what she was doing. She was a financial accountant. If he refuses or is legally bound to not disclose certain information, I will then consult the financial forensics department and obtain a warrant. Actually, come to think of it, I'll get in touch with them anyway to see if Elizabeth's company or any companies she has done business with are known to them." Adam wrote all these questions up.

"John, we have a lot to do. I want everyone on this case to not take any shortcuts. We need to make sure everything is done to the letter of the law 'cause if we do end up with an arrest, no doubt whoever did this or planned this has resources and, with that, comes expensive lawyers."

Adam took his phone out from his pocket and took a photo of the whiteboard. Turning to John, he said, "Email me what you've written up and I'll put together the plan of attack for Monday, so we hit the ground running first thing."

Adam sat down at his desk and looked at John as he finished what he was doing on his laptop. "Thanks for coming in today.

I want you to lead Olivia and Noah in their daily tasks and I'll always be available for any questions. Go home, rest up and enjoy some family time as I can guarantee there will be some long hours with this case. Speaking of family, how are the kids?"

"Yeah, they're good, thanks. The wife is happy for me to do long hours. My two teenage girls basically live their own lives and I have no idea what they think or do. All I know is that their grades are good, and they stay out of trouble." John closed his laptop and reached for his bag. "Just letting you know that I'm also available at any time."

"One more thing. Have a think about a possible motive," Adam said. "Any idea is welcomed, and nothing is off the table. You've got plenty of experience in the police so trust your instincts. Use any contacts you have on the streets but keep me in the loop. I can't do this without you."

John picked up his backpack and headed for the lift.

They both knew this was a complex case. They both had a feeling of trepidation that would be justified in due course. They also both felt for Jacob and the grief he was going through.

CHAPTER 5

It was mid-morning on Tuesday as Jacob walked along Bourke Street, heading for Parliament Station to catch the train from the city to his suburb of Glen Waverley. He had arrived in the city for an early morning meeting with his lawyer to go over Elizabeth's will. He was named as executor and it was a straightforward meeting, one meeting that he never thought he would have. It occurred to him that he thought he would die of old age before Elizabeth, and that this type of meeting should have been the other way around.

Jacob had done nothing for the past two days since the funeral. He had moped around the house making excuses for not meeting people when they phoned offering their support and assistance. He was grateful for their concern but was in no mood for visitors. He knew brooding didn't solve anything, but it was necessary in the grieving process. He cleaned the whole house from top to bottom as if Elizabeth would notice and be pleased. This was their home and he would continue to treat it as such. He had dusted all the beautiful furniture and ornaments that Elizabeth had chosen. She liked to visit antique shops and it was only as he dusted that he noticed how elegant, well-crafted, yet understated these items were, just like his beautiful Elizabeth. Her clothes were still neatly folded in her drawers and hanging crease-free in the wardrobe. The book she was reading was still on her bedside table. He knew at some stage he would need to move on but there was no hurry, and when that time came, their house would no longer be a home.

Jacob strolled along the footpath looking like everyone else who had places to go and people to see, even though the only place he wanted to go was home and to see nobody. He reached into the leather satchel he had over his shoulder and took out his headphones, which he plugged into his phone, and then positioned the buds into his ears. Selecting the album *Paranoid* by Black Sabbath, he slipped into his own world as he headed down the stairs to the underground station listening to the start of "War Pigs".

Boarding the train, Jacob was glad it was late morning and no longer peak time. He could get a seat. Sitting down, he got lost in his thoughts about being alone without his soulmate in life beside him. He concentrated on the music, blocking out all other passengers. The train started moving and soon the blackness of the underground tunnel turned to light as they emerged into the day. As the train made its way past the huge stadium of the Melbourne Cricket Ground, Jacob thought that this winter he should make it to a few games of Aussie rules football as it had been a few years since he had been to a game, especially at the great stadium that could seat over a hundred thousand fans.

Jacob noticed a girl in her late teens sitting in front of him. He looked at the back of her dyed blonde hair that had obviously been coloured at home, with the blonde looking like a dirty yellow that had been dyed repeatedly and in parts was looking like a white-grey. The hair was falling past her shoulders and, with a swipe of her hand, she ran her fingers through it from front to back, dragging it over one shoulder. With this movement, the glimpse of hair extensions became visible for a split second, which probably explained the different colours of dirty yellow to white-grey. With the other hand, she was busy biting her fingernails as she leaned against the window. On a closer look, he could see that there was nothing left of her fingernails as she alternated between tips looking for something to chew. She turned her head as something rushed past the window that caught her eye, then turned back to gaze out the window at nothing in particular. With the turn of her head, Jacob saw that she had a thick layer of make-up on over the top of fake tan. Why people caked on fake tan was beyond him as it looked obvious and not like a tan at all, rather an attempt to look different shades of orange. Elizabeth had beautiful, soft, smooth skin that required very little make-up and definitely no fake tan. He also noticed the girl in front was wearing fake eyelashes that were stuck on and looked very unnatural. She turned her head again as something caught her eye out the window, before returning once again to look blankly out the window, trying to find a slight trace of a fingernail to chew. Jacob observed that she was no doubt a very attractive girl that had tried to look a certain way to feel more comfortable in the never-ending need to conform to the glamor models that appeared in men's magazines, for blokes that liked those types of girls. He would have loved to tell her to relax, be herself and not be so anxious. He could not help but study her to the soundtrack of Black Sabbath as the train pulled in and out of stations. The train arrived at Mount Waverley Station and she got up and made her way out onto the platform. Jacob returned his gaze out the window as the train made two more stops to his destination of Glen Waverley.

Getting off the train, Jacob took off his headphones, unplugged them from his phone and placed them back in his satchel. It was nearing midday and his body started to remind him that he hadn't had his morning coffee yet, so he walked along Kingsway, which was lined with Chinese, Japanese and South East Asian restaurants, along with top-quality European cafés. Nearing his and Elizabeth's favourite café, he noticed her brother, Roman, and friend from work, Moya, sitting at an outside table. A wave of panic flushed over him as he had been avoiding people for the last couple of days and remembered Roman giving him a call to catch-up, which he had declined.

Should he turn around and walk back? Before he could make up his mind, Moya recognised him and waved, and with that, Roman turned around and did the same. Both gestured for him to come over. He had no choice now other than to put on a smile and head their way. As he got closer, he could see that they were halfway through brunch. He hadn't even realised they knew each other.

Roman stood up. "Hey, Jacob. Good to see you. What are you up to? Hope you can join us?"

Moya also stood up and wrapped her arms around Jacob and in a soft voice whispered, "Good to see you."

With all of them standing, Jacob briefly told them what he had been doing that morning. He agreed to join them and ordered a long black coffee from a nearby waiter. Sitting down, Jacob broke the silence. "I see you two have obviously met. Sorry, I have been avoiding everyone since the funeral. Just don't feel up to socialising just yet but good to see both of you."

It didn't take long for his coffee to arrive and they all spoke of Elizabeth like a bunch of close friends enjoying a leisurely morning in the warmth of the spring sun. Jacob learnt how Roman and Moya had met at the funeral, and he felt comforted with stories of Elizabeth from work and childhood that he hadn't heard before.

With coffees empty and plates cleared, Moya mentioned that she should head back to the city, where she lived in an apartment she purchased last year. She invited them all to visit if they happened to be in the city. Roman asked Jacob if he wanted a lift home as his car was parked across the road. Jacob agreed and they all stood up from the table, wishing each other well.

Reaching the car with neither talking, Roman unlocked the doors and they both sat inside, not sure what to say to each other. The conversation had been rather superficial at the café and, now alone, it felt like it was time to get to know each other properly. Jacob knew that Elizabeth was the more social one in their relationship and now yearned for her to be there to smooth over this awkwardness of getting to know her brother.

The car was heading out from Kingsway when Roman spoke. "Look, I really want to start off by saying sorry for your loss. But more importantly, sorry for not coming to your wedding and sorry for not being around."

Roman indicated to turn and before Jacob could say anything, he blurted out, "I've been such an idiot and none of it was Elizabeth's fault. I'm not sure what she told you about me, but I loved my sister and my stupid pride and stubbornness will be my regret for the rest of my life. I only heard good things about you and I knew she was extremely happy being with you."

It struck Jacob that he wasn't the only one grieving. He replied, "Thanks for that. Elizabeth spoke very highly of you and I know she was looking forward to the day when you would visit. She mentioned to me the issues you had with your parents and how you needed to go out in the world and find yourself. She mentioned you were happy and now working in private security, or something like that." Jacob then motioned for him to take the next left to his place.

"Yeah, my life has turned out okay." After a brief pause, he continued. "Hey, I'm staying with my parents and am in no hurry to fly back to New Zealand and would really like to get to know you better if that's okay?"

Jacob felt at ease with Roman. It dawned on him that Elizabeth would have loved him to get to know her brother and that Roman was the closest thing he had now to Elizabeth. With that in mind, he replied, "I'd like that. Glad you're sticking around for a while. I'd love to hear more about Elizabeth's childhood days. What are you doing for dinner tonight? I know a great Korean barbeque place in Surrey Hills that Elizabeth and I would frequent a fair bit."

Pulling into Jacob's driveway, Roman agreed. "That would be great. I love Korean barbeque. I can pick you up at seven if you like?"

"Okay. I'll make a booking as it's pretty popular. See you at seven."

Jacob got out of the car, waved goodbye and entered his house. He made his way to the fridge and got out some cheese, meat, pickle, and spinach to make a sandwich. Once made, he took his lunch to the couch and turned on the television, where he went online to access the many home-movie clips from the cloud. He had already watched many of them in the last week and selected a clip from their last holiday in Hong Kong. He watched his lovely Elizabeth down by the harbor taking in the light and sound display with a light breeze playing with her long auburn hair and a look of happiness and innocence on her face. Jacob remembered how the narration explaining the amazing light display on the buildings was not in English that night, and how they made their way back to the viewing place the next night to listen to it in English.

There were clips of them eating that night and then the next morning having yum cha in a huge restaurant. Next was them on the cable car and around the huge Tian Tan Buddhist statue on top of the mountain. Elizabeth was wearing a blue T-shirt with a cool gecko print on it that she had bought the day before from one of the many shops they popped into. A tear started to form on the outside of Jacob's eye as he sat in silence taking in the moment as if she was beside him again. Her beautiful image moved to the next scene that showed them browsing through the Stanley Market for souvenirs.

The movie clip from Hong Kong ended. Jacob realised that his lunch was still sitting on a plate on the coffee table. Eyeing the sandwich, he picked it up, looked at it and put it down again. Once again, he had no appetite.

CHAPTER 6

Roman pulled up to Jacob's house at seven. He was about to get out of the car, when he saw Jacob already closing the front door and heading over to him. They greeted each other as Jacob got in and they headed off to have Korean barbeque, with Jacob giving directions.

Once there, the waiter led them to a wooden table with bench seats. Above them, a pull-down chimney extractor was hanging from the ceiling. They sat down and were handed menus as the waiter left to see to another group of four customers that had arrived.

"So, what's good here?" Roman asked as he opened the menu.

"Everything," Jacob said with a slight smile. "How about I order for us? The beef banquet is great and, of course, the Korean beer."

"Sounds good. Can't wait. I'm starving."

The waiter arrived back at the table with little individual bowls of kimchi and pickles. Jacob ordered and they both handed back the menus.

"What have you been up to this afternoon?" Roman asked, sensing that Jacob was finding it difficult to face the days without Elizabeth.

"Not much. Just doing things around the house," Jacob lied. He didn't want to let on that he had spent all afternoon sitting on the couch watching home movies while choking back tears. "What about you?"

"Spending some time with the parents. They want you to come over for dinner if you're up to it. They're glad we're out together tonight."

"Yeah, me too. Hope they don't think I'm being rude. It's just that I haven't been up to seeing people."

"Well, you're seeing me."

"True," Jacob replied with a small laugh. He was feeling more comfortable around Roman.

The waiter brought them over two Korean beers in cans with ice-cold glasses. They both said "thanks" and proceeded to pour the beer into the chilled receptacles. Raising them, they clinked them together with a "cheers" and took a sip. It didn't take long for the food to arrive and the waiter to start cooking the strips of beef on the barbeque at their table.

Both felt relaxed and were enjoying the good beer, great food, and excellent company. They talked about Elizabeth, sharing funny and warm stories. Jacob felt the best he had since that fateful morning and could see certain mannerisms and characteristics of his wife in her brother. With the barbeque beef going down a treat, Roman mentioned that Detective Senior Sergeant Adam Zhang had seen him the previous day and asked him many questions about him and Elizabeth.

"Adam admitted that they have gotten next to nothing about her murder from the crime scene and it sounded like they are fishing for motives and suspects." Roman felt that he could now talk to Jacob about the case and was also fishing to see if Jacob was as curious about it as he was.

Jacob was quietly glad Roman had brought it up as he was feeling that he had no one to talk to about it. He didn't feel comfortable talking about it with Elizabeth's parents or his friends. It was a personal matter and he didn't want to come across as interfering with police matters, while also wanting to maintain a professional and composed manner in the wake of Elizabeth's murder.

"I get the same impression. This was a planned murder and, of course, whoever did it would not leave a snifter of evidence. I've been asked questions about her work and personal life. Naturally, they are or have been looking at me as a suspect and I wouldn't expect anything less if they were doing their job properly. No doubt they will also look at you and her friends in the same light until they can eliminate suspects," Jacob replied.

"Well, I didn't give him much. He can consider me as much as he likes but he should be looking at motives rather than questioning me for ages when I wasn't even in the country and any check of my passport would verify that."

"If you don't mind me asking—what were you and Elizabeth's friend Moya talking about the other day over brunch?"

Roman paused for a moment as the waiter cleared their plates, leaving their nearly empty glasses of beer. He then leaned in slightly, rested his elbows on the table, and looked Jacob in the eye. "As you know, I met her at the funeral. We were talking about Elizabeth's work and the clients the company deals with. I wanted to know if there was anything out of the ordinary with her clients or the company because, as far as I can tell, you had nothing to do with it, neither did her close friends. And we all know it was not a random carjacking or robbery."

"So, did she tell you anything of interest?"

"As far as she knows, there was nothing out of the ordinary with Elizabeth's clients or workload. They talked a lot, had lunch together often and after-work drinks from time to time. She did mention that they do accounting work for the Esposito family, which has links to the Melbourne underworld."

"I've heard of them. They are mentioned in many documentaries with regards to the historical underworld battles in Melbourne but have not been convicted of anything. Sounds like a very smart family that treads a fine line between criminal and legal activity. Well, that's how they are portrayed but I get the impression they are not a family you would cross. There was even an assassination of a prominent businessperson outside a café in Lygon Street in the early hours of the morning a few months back, and their name was mentioned in the news. I can't remember what the link was, but it was something like a joint business venture a long time in the past. I think the press were trying to pad out the story. Anyway, I don't think they were charged."

Roman drained the last drops of beer from his glass. "Moya gave me a brief outline of their businesses and it sounds like they have their fingers in many pies. Everything from cafés and construction, but their main money earner is the importing/exporting of consumer goods. I couldn't help myself and even did a bit of digging online. You are right in that they were as dodgy as. They have a large warehouse in Port Melbourne that seems to be their main business hub."

"Well, that may be true, but how does that tie into murder? I'm sure the police will be considering all these angles," Jacob replied a little more defensively than warranted, as he also took the last sip of his beer.

Roman softened his voice. "I'm sure they are. I'm sorry for bringing this up. I just can't help it and want to get involved. I'm not that stupid and realise that the need for me to do this is me psychologically wanting to make up for all the lost time and guilt I feel for not being there for my sister. However, even though I know this, I still want to do something."

Jacob was impressed by this self-realisation. "Roman, you're not the only one to feel like this. Of course, I feel like this every second of the day. Why wasn't I there? Was there something she told me that I didn't listen to that might have helped? Why do I feel so empty and useless? Your parents also feel like this. It doesn't mean we have to get involved in a police investigation, apart from answering any questions they have and providing them with anything they request." Jacob's voice lowered down into a whisper as the waiter came over and took their empty glasses away.

They declined any more drinks or food and asked for the bill.

With the waiter away from the table, Roman asked Jacob, "But what if we could do something and help the police? I'm not talking about breaking the law. Don't you think people would open up to us more than the police if we were to ask a few questions? Like the Esposito family—they won't say jack shit to the police, but they might to us. I'm just using them as an example, but can you see where I'm coming from?"

Jacob ran his hand across his mouth and chin as he considered this. Also, to buy some time as the waiter placed the bill on the table.

With the table to themselves again, Jacob answered. "Look. I understand where you're coming from. I'm just a bloody doctor. I have no experience in these things. I know you can handle yourself but I'm a geek who struggles to open the twist top of a beer bottle. I want to do something, as I'm just sitting around the house, struggling to eat or sleep. You're the only person I've really talked to since Elizabeth was murdered and I'm grateful for your company. I've also noticed that you are a lot like Elizabeth. She would be wanting to do something as well. She was the social one in our marriage and really brought me out of my shell. But there is nothing I can do."

The last sentence came out as more of a question than a statement. Roman picked up on this.

"Mate, there is plenty you can do. For one, you are a hell of a lot smarter than I am. Two, you talk to patients every day, asking questions, and reading body language to determine what is wrong and how to emotionally manage them. Three, you knew Elizabeth better than anyone in this world. I'm sure I could keep going with this list."

"Okay, okay, you have a point. But what can I actually do? Looking at your face, I can see that you've given this a fair bit of thought."

"Let's get some fresh air and talk," Roman replied as he picked up the bill and shifted his bottom to get off the bench seat.

Jacob made his way off his seat as well, while reaching out and taking the bill off Roman. "I've got dinner. Least I can do since you drove."

Once dinner was paid for, they both headed outside and walked towards the car. Roman turned his head to Jacob. "I'm going to start looking into this myself anyway. I am in no hurry to get back to New Zealand and I've let the people I work with know that I will not be taking up any contract jobs in the near future. But, like I mentioned before, I would appreciate your help. I just want to start asking questions and maybe observe people of interest. If I come across anything, I'll inform the police. I know what I'm doing but can't do this alone, and you knew Elizabeth better than anyone."

"Okay, I'll give you a hand. I know Elizabeth would do the same if the tables were turned. But we tell the police anything we come across," Jacob emphasised. He knew Roman was playing up the fact that he was the closest one to Elizabeth. Yet he felt the need to be doing something, rather than wallowing in the useless sensation he constantly felt when at home.

They reached the car, opened the doors, and got in. Roman hesitated to start the engine. Rubbing his hands over his face as if contemplating a deep thought, he said, "It's not that late. Why don't we start now? I have the address of the Esposito family's warehouse in Port Melbourne. Let's just go there, park up and observe the place for an hour or two. It may be nothing, but we also may see something. We'll take some photos of anyone we see and then put names to faces later. From this, we can then ask some questions of these people. Straightforward, boring stuff but it may be of assistance to the police. What do you say?"

Jacob took a few breaths and contemplated what was a crazy, yet logical proposition. "Okay, I see no harm in that, and I have nothing else to do. But we are just going to observe and that's all?"

"Of course. You have my word."

Roman started the car but before putting it into gear, he looked at Jacob again with a serious expression. "Before we head off, I just want to say one thing... That Korean barbeque was fuckin' good!"

Jacob couldn't help but laugh. He felt the tension leave his muscles and instantly relaxed.

CHAPTER 7

Parked up on the side of a street in Port Melbourne opposite the Esposito warehouse, with the car off but radio on, they took off their seatbelts and settled in for a long stretch of sitting and watching. They could see some activity in a couple of nearby warehouses but most, including the one their eyes were on, were dead quiet with no sign of anyone working. The road was quiet and the night still, with a slight chill descending as if the night was trying to distinguish itself from day once the light diminished. Roman wound his window down to let in some air and so they could hear any sounds, as it was on his side the warehouse stood.

To help the time go by, Roman enquired about Jacob's childhood. He had heard from Elizabeth that he was raised by foster parents and had no real family and no idea of who his biological parents were. This was a subject that Jacob skirted around. He had become very skilful at diverting conversations away from any topic relating to his family or childhood. Not that he was ashamed—quite the opposite. He just couldn't be bothered explaining and having people feel pity towards him.

Especially when he didn't pity himself and felt it condescending when people had this reaction. He was more than happy to discuss it with Roman as he was curious about Roman's life, which was very different from his.

Jacob was in foster care from the moment he was born. He found out early in life that his biological mum was not up to raising a child, both financially and mentally. Apparently, she was young, alone, and no father was ever disclosed. She waived the rights to any contact with him and asked for details to remain confidential. He had never tried to find out who she was and had no desire to do so. Many foster or adopted children feel the urge to track down their biological parents, and he had briefly contemplated it, only to conclude that his life was good and this would only complicate it and not enhance it in any way. Even on the plus side, if she happened to be a lovely, warm, stable person that welcomed him with open arms, he knew that the mother-son bond could never be fully established. So why bother when he had found others to give him a sense of belonging and worth?

He found out later in life that he was placed in short-term foster care at birth, and even though his mother wanted to give him up, she was in no mental state to formally do this. She then had second thoughts and couldn't decide but made no efforts to represent to the court that she could look after her son. Eventually, after thirty-four months of being apart, her parental rights were terminated. From this date, Jacob could go up for adoption and was moved to another short-term foster care. He had memories of moving from this one at the age of five to a permanent foster home with no one showing any interest in adopting him. He was now getting past the age at which most families would want to adopt a child.

Permanent foster care was a happy place. He was adequately looked after and had plenty of other kids to play with that came and went as the years went by. Many children were there due to court orders because of an unsafe home environment that the parents could not get into a condition the courts deemed safe for raising a child. He heard many horrific stories of abuse and neglect—most kids were unable to live a normal life and struggled with routine and rules. However, some kids did adapt and thrive, and these were the ones he hung out with.

Jacob showed signs of intelligence at an early age and worked hard at school. He knew life could be better and the only way for him to have a better life was through hard work. The only one he could rely on to deliver this was himself. He obtained entry into a top selective high school with a full scholarship, where he continued to study diligently. He made a few friends even though he continually felt like an outsider with no family in the traditional sense. It was an enjoyable time and his foster parents were very proud of him and constantly used him as a positive example for the others.

In his last year of high school, he knew that he wanted to be a doctor, and this gave him an extra incentive to study harder even though he knew he could easily get the grades. He could not afford medical school and a full or partial scholarship was the only way to make this happen. He already had a part-time job at a supermarket, but this did not pay very well. The careers counsellor at high school was a tremendous help to him and she put many in hours on his behalf and was always there when he needed a chat. There was always the option of taking out a hefty student loan, but she was confident he could at least get a partial scholarship. He wanted to stay in Melbourne, and together they applied for all available scholarships. He eventually got a full first-year scholarship at Monash University. He would never forget the day he found out as it was one of his happiest, and he knew from that moment, if he continued to apply himself, he would have the life he dreamed of.

He continued to work at the supermarket during his first year to cover his living costs. It was a relief to be out of the foster care system and be sharing a flat with other students. He knew that after school age, he would no longer be bound to foster care and he saw many kids move out when they reached this age with no idea which direction they were heading. He was different. He was enthusiastic and confident about his future. He didn't party like other students and was careful with his money, always saving up to cover some of his next year's fees. Fortunately, he managed to get partial scholarships for the remaining years at medical school and worked part-time as a tutor, which paid a lot better than a supermarket job. He finished medical school with only a small student loan, and to this day, he always gave regular donations to charities that supported the development of underprivileged children.

"Mate, you're a credit to society and my sister was one lucky girl to find you," Roman quipped after they had been talking about his past for the last hour or so.

They had taken a few photos of the warehouse with their phones but there was no one around and it looked like their stakeout was a waste of time. Jacob was enjoying the chat, though, and wanted to find out more about Roman.

Bang, bang, bang. Jacob's muscles all tightened with fright at the sudden banging sound against the car.

They both looked out of the windows to see four guys in their late teens walking around the car while banging their fists along the side. One of them walked to the front of the car with one standing behind the rear while the other two stopped outside each of their passenger doors. Jacob was glad his window was up. Roman appeared relaxed and calmly looked at the young guy through his open window, waiting for him to talk.

"Hey, faggots. What's two fuckheads doing parked up here, aye?" spoke the guy beside Roman, looking at him with an overconfident swagger.

Roman still had the keys in the ignition and contemplated starting the car and driving off but that would mean running one of them over. His window was down, so he also knew if he tried anything, the ugly looking guy beside him would have ample time to reach into the car to stop him. He ran through his mind every scenario along with some self-deprecation on how he had not heard them approach or seen them in the rear-view mirror.

"Just having a chat before we head to work," replied Roman to try to make out that they worked at a nearby warehouse.

"Well, that's fucken bullshit. We've watched you for a good twenty minutes and you don't look like you work around here. Looks like you're a couple of bum chums, and now you're going to hand over your wallets and phones and be grateful we don't steal your fucken car."

Jacob was frozen in his seat, trying not to make eye contact with anyone. In his peripheral vision, he saw Roman turn his head, look at the guy in the eye and say, "Look, we don't want any trouble. We'll give you the cash from our wallets."

"Your whole fuckin wallets and your fuckin phones," replied the ugly guy while he removed a knife from his pocket, making sure Roman could see it.

Roman glanced at Jacob and saw that he was terrified. He couldn't see knives in the hands of any of the other three guys surrounding but that didn't mean they didn't have any. He did not mind departing with the little cash he had but did mind handing over his whole wallet with identification and items that showed his personal details like full name and address. This also went for his phone. He could quickly cancel it, but if they were smart enough, they could steal his identity for all manner of crimes and access his emails, photos, and basically, his life. He held the same concern for Jacob. Nowadays, crime wasn't so much about a quick buck, and, increasingly, street crimes were for a bigger purpose with greater and longer-term effects. Information was key. One thing he learnt is that you never give away your personal details and information. One positive in this whole situation was that it looked like they didn't have guns, which was usually the case in street crime in Australia due to the tough gun laws.

"Okay, okay. Relax, mate. Here, you can have our wallets and phones," Roman said calmly, making it clear that one hand was heading to his pocket while the other remained held up in a sign of surrender.

Whack! As quick as a flash, Roman opened the car door and slammed it into the ugly guy, temporarily destabilising him. In one swift movement, he was out of the car, blocking the hand that held the knife and driving his fist squarely into his face. The ugly guy went down like a sack of potatoes, with Roman still holding his arm with the knife. He wanted to get the knife from his grip but saw the others making their way towards him and didn't have time, so gave the arm a vicious shake, causing the knife to fall onto the road. At the same time, he lifted his leg and put all his weight behind a kick into the stomach of the next closest guy. He also went down in a crumpled heap, severely winded and with a cracked rib or two. Roman then distanced himself from the remaining two that were left standing. He did this to rapidly gather his composure and assess the situation.

Jacob had no idea what had happened at first as it happened so fast. He was getting ready to follow Roman's lead of handing them his wallet and phone. Before he knew it, Roman was out of the car and the ugly guy by his window was knocked out and on the ground. That was when Jacob felt his heart start to pound, his breathing become laboured, and a tingly sensation start to work its way across his body, starting from his hands and moving towards his head.

He felt like he was having a stroke or a heart attack. He couldn't move, but he knew from past experiences that this was the start of a huge panic or anxiety attack. He hadn't had one for many years and thought they were a thing of the past. The tingly sensation had now moved to his whole face and his vision was going. He placed his hands on the dashboard in front of him, concentrating on controlling his breathing and felt totally useless as his sight went completely blurry and all he could see was a black and grey haze.

He remembered the first time he had a panic attack. It came out of the blue while at home in foster care when he was fourteen. He thought he was dying and freaked out. He didn't know if his heart would stop, his brain would shut down, or if he would throw up or pass out. Luckily, his foster mum guided him outside, sat him down and calmly told him that it was likely a panic attack and nothing to be worried about. She held his hand and breathed with him while softly speaking comforting words until it passed. She then walked him to his room, so he could lie down and fully recover. He would never forget that day as he believed he now had a mental condition and was not as strong as he had thought. Fortunately, he discovered that it was not uncommon and not a sign of weakness or an underlying mental health issue. He could count on one hand the number of times it had happened since that day.

Roman had managed to kick the knife on the ground away from anyone's reach and, at the same time, stomped his foot onto the winded guy's knee as he lay on the ground and heard the crunch of bone and cartilage. He was now safely out of the equation as a threat, as you cannot fight if you cannot stand. The ugly guy was still down and looked like he had been sufficiently knocked out. That was another one out of the equation, and even if he started to come around, he would not be a threat to anyone for at least half an hour.

The other two descended on him at the same time, with fists flying. One punch glanced off Roman's head as he ducked and swerved while keeping his guard up. He needed some space and managed to grab one of their wrists in the flurry of punches. Roman wrapped his hand around the back of the guy's wrist and hand, applying pressure with his thumb between the guy's thumb and index finger. He implemented a sturdy wristlock and pulled the guy around, using him as an interim shield and pushed him into the other guy with enough force for them both to stumble backwards. He now had a second or two to regain his composure. He caught a glance of Jacob still in the car and then, to his horror, saw one of the guys pull out a switchblade from his rear pocket.

Jacob was still struggling to control the panic attack. He felt like he was going to vomit, and his vision was continued to be impaired. His heart rate was slowly returning to normal, but his face remained numb and tingly. His hands were still on the dashboard and he could hear grunts and groans, punching and movement, and see the outline of hazy figures fighting. He wanted to be a million miles away, and if he could move, he knew he would start running as far away from the car as possible, even though he knew he should be out there helping Roman.

Roman had no time to try to get the ugly guy's knife that was on the ground. He kept his eye on the switchblade and, luckily, the two guys approached him side by side rather than splitting out, so he could see them both easily. The guy swiped at him with the blade, aiming for his chest, with Roman having enough time to rock backwards, ensuring that no contact was made as it whooshed past. His eyes remained locked on the blade as he caught the guy's forearm and, using his momentum, spun him around and landed a punch to the back of his head, which was not his best strike and not enough to knock him out.

Roman was preparing to land a second, when he felt a blow strike him cleanly on the temple, which knocked him off balance and caused a ringing in his ears. He let go of the guy's forearm and directed a forward front kick with all his might in the direction the punch came from. This only made glancing contact with the guy's hip and was not enough to slow down the attack.

The fight was deteriorating for Roman. He hunkered down with arms held up to guard his midsection and head, just like a boxer against the ropes. He threw out sporadic punches to make sure they couldn't grab him and take him down to the ground, which would have resulted in definite doom. The blade the guy was holding was a major concern, and he wasn't sure if he had managed to shake it loose from the punch he landed on the back of his head. He was losing touch with how

many punches were hitting him and how many he was landing. He was now in survival mode, with adrenalin masking the
pain that was beginning to seep through him. Not knowing
how much longer he could sustain the onslaught, he was getting ready to throw caution to the wind and open up with
some wild throws of his fists, hoping that the removal of his
guard wouldn't spell a certain knockout. It was then that he
heard a muffled yelp and the hard landing of a fist or kick onto
skin, but not his skin, and the flurry of punches to his head and
body ceased.

Jacob's heart rate was almost normal. He still had the tingly
sensation all through his head, but this was starting to retreat
from his hands. His vision was still blurry, but he could make
out the outline of images more clearly. The sound of fighting
was the only thing he could hear. He could make out three figures well enough to tell that one of them was getting a beating by the other two. He knew this must be Roman. He could
also see another two rocking on the ground and he gathered
one was the ugly guy Roman took out before the panic attack
hit, and the other must have been taken down by Roman as
well. Taking deep controlled breaths, he was psyching himself
up to open the car door and lend what little assistance he could
offer. The thought of fighting was making him extremely anxious and not helping with the panic attack. Maybe if he could
just open the car door, shout that the police were there and
run, he could avoid any physical confrontation, and the two
guys would make a run for it, taking the two on the ground
with them. From experience, he knew his vision would return

to normal very soon. The time that had passed since the beginning of the attack felt like an eternity when it had probably been only a minute or two. It was then that he saw the fuzzy outline of another person come from nowhere and produce a flying kick into one of the guy's heads, toppling him to the ground, followed by what looked like a punch or grab, sending the other one to the tarmac.

"Let's get the hell out of here now!" the new person shouted as he opened the driver's door and pushed Roman into the car.

CHAPTER 8

While all this was going down in Melbourne, across the other side of the world, a different fight was raging.

The sun was breaking the grey of the sky as it rose over the hills in the distance, spreading a yellow and orange glow through the valley. Where there was once lush green trees and productive fields, now lay rubble and dirt. The seeds in the ground were too afraid to germinate in this cruel new world. A beautiful landscape was destroyed and the outside air was no longer fresh and crisp in the morning light, but heavy and stale.

Mustapha Fakhri woke up after another restless, uncomfortable sleep in the abandoned and bombed farmhouse that had become his temporary home for the last two days. There was one room that still had a waterproof roof, which he gathered had been the main bedroom as the remains of a bed were scattered across the floor, while the rest of the house had been pilfered of the little possessions of value that would have adorned this humble family home. He shuddered when he thought of what may have become of the occupants, and hoped that they had left of their own accord to seek a better life, like his wife and child were trying to do. He was planning to join them by making his way from Syria to the Lebanon border and, hopefully, catching a place on a boat to Greece to seek asylum or travel further into Europe. The only contact he now had with his family was via an email account where they could leave messages.

Mustapha still had some food supplies on him but would need to venture to a market sooner rather than later. He was not feeling hungry and could wait until later in the day to eat. There had been some troop movement in the distance that had made him unwilling to venture forward. He would spend today waiting and observing to make sure there was safe passage before he moved on.

He thought of his wife and their seven-year-old son. He had worked, or technically still did work, for the government. They had assumed that he was assisting the rebels even though this was untrue. Officials started spending more time monitoring him, and conversations with his boss became more and more awkward. There were questions around every detail of his day and who he had talked to and was planning to talk to. He dismissed this at first as paranoid induced by the current climate, but it didn't take long for his suspicions to be proven justified. The day he saw a colleague arrested, he knew he needed to take action. In hindsight, he knew that there was bribery and backdoor deals going on at work, but he ignored it, hoping it wasn't true as he loved his job. Ignorance, in the end, was not bliss.

He arranged for his wife and son to make their way to Lebanon with friends that were also looking for a way out. It was the worst day of his life having to say goodbye to them, not knowing if he would see them again. There were many stories of people being arrested without trial and then their family paying the price and even being arrested as well. On top of that, there were also terrorist groups making their way through the country, like a virus taking advantage and killing off weak cells in a body. So many stories circulated in Syria of missing loved ones.

Once his wife and son had left, he continued going to work to give the illusion that they were still at home. This gave them a head start before the inevitable would happen and troops would start to track them like hounds following the scent of a fox. Everyone knew what happened to the fox once caught. He managed to keep this up for three days before he also had to make the move and leave his home and the city he loved. After yet another colleague was arrested at work, he knew they would come for him the next day, if not that night. He knew too much to be allowed to carry on under the radar of the government.

Mustapha focused back on the present. He sat on a torn cushion beside a smashed window, making sure that he was not visible but still able to look out into the distance. He was as comfortable as he could manage, but even if he was on a bed of pillows, he would not be relaxed. The troops in the distance had moved on, and he was contemplating making further progress to Lebanon once the sun went down. His stomach was starting to rumble so he got out the last of the leavened flatbread and dried dates and ate small mouthfuls, washing them down with bottled water. His mind wandered off to memories of the old city in Damascus, which he loved to visit nearly daily.

There was his favourite café, where he would frequent for hot sweet tea and shisha. There were many cafés, often with wooden tables and wicker chairs outside, in the city's small laneways, which bustled with locals and tourists. Now the tourists had gone, and the locals were few and far between. His favourite café had beautiful lanterns outside that reminded him of the streetlights you would see in English period dramas. Beautiful mosaic tiles adorned the walls, inside and out, the windows were lead-lined, and leafy creepers grew up the support poles to the overhanging roof that provided shade for the patrons. Many hours had been spent there without a care in the world, in one of the oldest continuously inhabited cities in the world, as he observed the thriving markets and architecture steeped in history.

Memories of the Umayyad Mosque in the old city also crept into his mind. It was in the top five holiest places in Islam, and one of the oldest and largest mosques in the world. It was his favourite place of worship, with its beautiful marble floor tiles that made the huge courtyard shine and radiate light as if the prophet welcomed its existence and all those who ventured within its four stone walls. The main dome, Qubbat an-Nisr, rested on an octagonal structure, with two beautiful arched windows on either side. Alluring curved pillars lined the outside of the courtyard, which was covered with mosaic tiles. Many tourists and people of all religions took photos at the significant landmark, with young Muslim girls often giggling at the sight of Westerners, not knowing how they should behave. He imagined this is what it would be like for Muslims when they visited the mighty significance of the Vatican City. Such a holy place of worship, tolerance, and acceptance was now partially ruined, which brought tears to Mustapha's eyes. How could anyone, in the name of Islam, even put a scratch on such an angelic and spiritual site?

Checking out the window and still seeing no activity, he got off the cushion, stretched his stiff legs and made his way over to the other side of the house, peeping out of broken windows as he went. He knew that just over the hills there was a small village that he had visited once with his wife in better times. There were market stalls where he could get some food, and from there, it was less than half a day's walk to Lebanon.

Mustapha decided it was time to move, even though he did not have the cover of darkness. Darkness gave cover but also suspicion if seen, as no one should be out at night. It was mid-afternoon, and he would be able to reach the village by the early evening. There was still no activity from rebels or troops, so he packed up what little belongings he had into his backpack, left the security of the farmhouse and stepped out onto the barren fields to begin the long walk.

One hope he had was running into a foreign soldier, but it was difficult to tell who the foreigners were fighting for. Was it the various terrorist groups or rebels, or those forces that were backed by the United Nations? He cared deeply about his country. In his government position, he knew many terrible things that were going on that were causing irreplaceable damage to the fabric of Syria. He had thought long and hard and concluded that he had nothing against the government and nothing against the rebels trying to overthrow the government. He just cared about his homeland and wished for peace from whoever was in power. But one group of people he utterly detested was the terrorist organisations and various cells that cared little for Syria, cared little for human life, cared little for religion, and only cared about power.

Trudging across the dirt and mud, he neared the top of a hill, from where he would be able to see down into the village. A light, cool breeze was drifting across the landscape, signalling that winter was on its way and, with that, the wet season. The sun was periodically peeking out from the increasingly overcast sky. He hoped there would be no rain tonight as he wanted to get some food and then continue his walk under the cover of darkness.

On top of the hill, he saw the village and estimated it would be another hour's walk to reach it. From the distance, there appeared to be no shooting, fighting or heavy armoured vehicles in sight. That didn't mean that there were no forces in the village. What side those forces were on would not be known until he got there. The government had tried to keep Damascus and the villages nearby under control and portray a sense of normality to the foreign press, but this façade was starting to slip. Control of the capital was paramount for the government. He had learnt of the horrific human abuse in the other large city of Aleppo and the constant fighting and struggle for authority. It was due to this that few people ventured to the northern parts of the country and the border of Turkey. The safest route for escape was now Lebanon and maybe Jordon or Israel in the south.

Mustapha made his way down the hill and briskly walked towards the village, whilst keeping just off the roads. Once nearer, he blended in with the locals that were walking towards the village for food, and no doubt some, like him, were planning on walking further but no one would admit this or talk openly, as an informant or soldier could easily be amongst the people. He kept his eyes down to not draw attention to himself and used his peripheral vision to keep an eye on what was going on around him. His heart was racing but he focused on remaining calm and fought the urge to look around. Maintaining this stance, he carried on putting one foot in front of the other, and before he knew it, he had arrived in the heart of the village.

As he made his way to the food stalls of the open market, he bent down in the motion of doing up his shoelaces to subtly take some money out of his sock. With the notes in hand, he finished tightening his laces and proceeded to buy some hot meat in a basic falafel. Without directly looking, he saw soldiers in partial uniforms holding machine guns and assault rifles. They looked relaxed and were taking advantage of the hot food on offer. He gathered they were government soldiers, but he could not be sure. Luckily, they did not appear to be looking for anyone. The afternoon was drawing to a close and he managed to fill his water bottle. He felt the urge to go to the toilet, but this could wait until he was clear of the village and darkness set in. A group of others were making their way out of the village in the direction of Lebanon, so he decided to blend in with them until it was safe to go alone.

After a short walk, they were clear of the township and the sun was starting to set. Everyone seemed relaxed as they headed off towards their homes in the hills. Some were even chatting about the weather, potential crops they were growing, businesses they were running and what their children were doing. Mustapha kept his head down and the others appeared to not even notice him. People started to splinter off from the group, but he stayed with the main cluster of twenty or so, all men. They continued down a road in the direction of Lebanon. The border was still about ten kilometres away and he knew that most of this group would be gone in the next kilometre or two and then he would be alone to navigate the rest of the journey.

The chatter within the group of men abruptly stopped. He raised his eyes and saw why. A group of six men had walked onto the road in front of them, with machine guns raised at the hips. Everyone was frozen, not sure who they were or what they wanted, but straightaway it was made clear.

"Everybody! Hand over all your cash now! Hurry up! You need to pay taxes for protection in this area!"

Mustapha guessed that they were a terrorist cell or loosely connected to one. This is how they raised most of their revenue, through self-imposed taxes and extortion. He didn't want to part with all his money. He had a little bit in his pockets and most was still tucked away in his socks. He looked like a poor farmer, so he assumed they would believe that the little he had in his pockets was all the cash he had on him. He raised his hands like everyone else and slowly reached into his pocket to retrieve the change that remained from the trip to the market.

Out the corner of his eye, he noticed that one of the men in the group he had been walking with was starting to look nervous. He was standing two people across from him on his right, just off the road. Mustapha wondered if he was a government soldier undercover, which would spell certain death if he was searched. Mustapha did not dare look directly at him and instead concentrated on getting the money from his pocket.

Suddenly the nervous-looking man burst into a sprint, and ran into the adjoining field, which took everyone by surprise. The armed men were also taken by surprise. After a quick heated chat amongst themselves, one raised his assault rifle to his shoulder and calmly lined up the sight. With a loud crack, he fired, and the running man fell to the ground about twenty metres away. This was followed by another two shots that ended in a thud as they hit the lifeless body. The gunman then ambled over to the shot man while swinging his rifle in an arrogant swagger.

Mustapha stood in stunned silence along with the remaining members of the walking party. The armed men reiterated their demands with a raised tone, with the farmers in no doubt about their intentions. They all obediently retrieved any available cash from their pockets.

The armed men motioned for them to place the cash on the ground just in front of them, as they raised the rifles in their direction. As Mustapha and the others started to place their money on the ground, there was a series of loud rifle cracks. Mustapha immediately thought that he and the farmers were being shot at and instinctively dropped to the ground, only to see that the armed men were now lying lifeless on the road, with blood visible in the fading light of dusk, and the smell of gunpowder drifting along in the cool breeze.

Rising up from a slight mound thirty metres in the distance, across a newly established field, was a group of four soldiers in full camouflage gear, matching backpacks, and what looked like night-vision goggles raised on their foreheads. The soldiers made their way towards them with rifles raised and their vision focused down their sights. Mustapha stood stunned like everyone else, not knowing who this new group of soldiers were, only that they looked like a highly organised and well-equipped unit—unlike the dead militias they had just disposed of.

The lead soldier lowered his rifle with his right hand and raised his left with an open palm, signalling that they meant them no harm. In English, he said, "Everything is okay. We will not harm you. Pick up your money and go on your way." He stretched his left palm out, indicating they were free to go.

Mustapha and the others took in this internationally recognised signal and cautiously gathered up any money they had laid on the ground. A soldier moved over to one of the freshly killed and quickly searched him before he made his way to the poor fellow that had tried to run away. While he did this, another covered him, with rifle pointed, while the third aimed his rifle at them. The group, not knowing what had happened, started to disperse towards their homes. Mustapha, who occasionally spoke English at work, had understood what the soldier said and also recognised the British accent from working with an English counterpart the year before.

Mustapha walked up to the lead soldier with his arms down and palms showing.

"Please, help. I have information for you." He spoke in English.

"Move on, please. We cannot help you. Move on," the lead soldier replied, while the other pointed his rifle at him.

"Please, I mean you no harm. Please take this."

Mustapha slowly started to put his right hand down the front of his pants with his left partially stretched out with palm still showing.

"Stop! Stop what you are doing!" the lead soldier shouted while raising his rifle.

With two rifles now pointing at him, Mustapha stopped and very slowly lifted his hand out of his pants. He was holding a folded piece of A4 paper. Slowly, he extended his right hand and offered the folded paper to the soldier.

The lead soldier lowered his rifle and extended his hand, taking the paper. He unfolded it without taking notice of anything on it and folded it back up again, ensuring that it was just a piece of paper. He undid a front pocket on his jacket and placed it inside.

"Now be on your way. Others may have heard the gunfire. Staying around here puts yourself and us in danger."

With that, the lead soldier signalled to his comrades and they quietly moved off into the neighbouring fields in single file, placing their night-vision goggles down over their eyes as darkness took over the day.

Mustapha watched them quickly disappear. Conscious that he was now alone, and everyone had moved on, he quickly looked around to confirm that there was no one else in sight. He then swiftly made his way off the road and headed towards the border.

Little did he know, he would play a major role in a murder investigation in Melbourne, Australia. And little did he know, he would prove invaluable to British intelligence.

CHAPTER 9

Roman was driving. Jacob was still in the front passenger seat and Detective Senior Sergeant Adam Zhang was in the back seat.

Jacob had finally recovered from his anxiety attack. Feeling embarrassed, he turned to Roman.

"Sorry. I, I, I don't know what to say."

"Mate, no worries. All good." Roman looked into the rearview mirror to check no one was following and caught Detective Adam Zhang's gaze.

"What the fuck are you doing here?"

Adam sat back and replied, "I could ask you the same thing. But for now, can you turn left up here and drop me off at my car. Then we need to talk."

"Okay. Let's meet up somewhere as things got a little bit fucked up back there."

Jacob had noticed that Roman swore a lot. This was not his first impression when they were being more formal and polite towards each other. Turning to say hello to Adam, he realised that Roman was bleeding from his upper left arm.

"Hey, Roman. You're bleeding from your arm." He pointed to the wound. "Let me have a look at it."

"Yeah, in a sec. Adam, is that your car?" They turned left and approached a lone car parked on the side of the road.

"That's it. Just stop behind it."

Roman pulled in behind the car, then turned off the ignition and swivelled in his seat to face Adam. As he did this, a fresh stream of blood started to run down his arm and he gave a slight whimper as the adrenalin started to subside and the pain registered.

"Stay still," Jacob told Roman and looked at the wound through his shirt. "Looks like a stab wound but not that deep. Put some pressure on it and I'll drive you to a hospital to get it stitched."

Roman placed his right hand onto the top of his left arm, stemming the bleeding. "Okay, you drive, but I'm not going to a hospital. I'll be right, and my tetanus shots are up to date."

Jacob replied, "I have a comprehensive first-aid kit at my house. Adam, why don't we all meet up at my place? I'm sure we've all got lots of questions, and I need a coffee."

Adam leaned forward from the middle of the back seat. "Sounds good. I have a lot of questions as to what you guys are up to."

"Yeah, and I want to know why you're following us," Roman wisecracked back.

"Let's just get back to Jacob's," said Adam, as they all opened their doors.

Adam made his way to his car while Jacob and Roman swapped sides. The two cars started, and they headed back to the suburb of Glen Waverley for coffee, stitches, and some answers.

After a twenty-five-minute drive, Jacob pulled into his driveway and noticed that Adam was already waiting in his car on the side of the road. On the way, they had both been quiet, with the radio playing an eighties throwback segment to fill the void. Jacob was still embarrassed and Roman was deep in thought as he kept the pressure on his laceration.

Once inside, they made their way into the kitchen, where Jacob gestured for them to take a seat on the stools around the island bench. He filled the kettle with water and turned it on.

"I'll go and get my first-aid kit and clean and stitch that wound of yours."

"Thanks. That bastard must have got lucky with his knife."

As Jacob made his way upstairs to the bathroom to get the first-aid kit, Adam said. "Just to let you know, I was listening to the police radio on the way over and that fight of yours hasn't been called in. Thank god, as I probably should have called it in before coming to rescue your arse."

"Once again, thanks, but what were you doing there?" Roman asked.

Jacob returned to the kitchen and started to set up the first-aid kit to attend to Roman.

Adam got up and made his way to the boiled kettle. "I'll make the coffees. Just point to where things are." Jacob did so with a loose gesture as he started to focus on his brother-in-law.

Jacob, without diverting his gaze, added, "Use the ground coffee, and the plunger filter is beside it. I'll have mine black."

"I'll have mine black with one sugar," Roman said. "Maybe some whiskey instead of the sugar?"

"Just stick to the coffee," said Jacob, while he started to cleanse the wound. He was used to patients that tried to be funny.

Adam continued, "I was going to see you, Roman, as I wanted to ask you a few more questions. I saw you leaving in your car, so I followed you. You picked up Jacob and had dinner, so I stayed in the car eating some Chinese noodles I got from a takeaway place nearby and waited for you to leave. Then I followed you both to Port Melbourne, and the rest you know."

Roman gave a brief grunt as Jacob dabbed the wound and prepared it for a few stitches.

"But why follow us?" Roman asked.

"To be honest, I wasn't that happy with the answers you gave me when we first chatted. You seem to have something to hide or just don't like the police. I had finally got some information about your past, which, I must say, was a bit difficult to get. This made me even more curious about you."

Adam finished making the coffees and placed them on the island bench. He took a seat opposite the others, blew across the cup and took a small sip before continuing.

"I found out that after you left Australia, you went to France. From there, you applied for the French Foreign Legion, passed all the physical and intellectual requirements, and were accepted. From this point, I needed to call in some favours as your records naturally stop. Correct me if I'm wrong, and I won't go into full details. You were in the French Foreign Legion for nearly ten years, which more than qualified you to become a French national, but you did not take this up. Your record is exemplary, and you even did joint training with special forces units from various countries. You were deployed in Afghanistan, but what you did there, I could not find out, and I will leave it at that, as I'm sure it is not public information for a reason. You left the French Foreign Legion with full honours. You now work private security for an international syndicate, which no doubt pays very well."

Roman inspected the three stitches that Jacob had just done on his upper arm, took a long sip of his coffee and gave him an approving nod. He returned his gaze to Adam.

"You've basically got my life after leaving Australia in a nutshell. I don't talk about what I did in the French Foreign Legion, and nor will I answer any questions about it, which I hope you'll understand. My current job also requires a high level of secrecy. So, let's leave it at that. While we're being honest, I can understand your suspicions about me, but believe me when I say I know nothing about why my sister was murdered. I want to know why, and I will do my best to find this out. I've never had a good relationship with the police and do find it hard to confide in others that have not earnt my trust. Having said that, you did just save me from a beating tonight, so that trust you are earning."

They all sat back a bit more relaxed. Adam enquired why they were parked up in Port Melbourne. They explained how they found out that Elizabeth's firm did work for the Esposito family and that their business appeared to be the only dodgy client she had anything to do with. Hence, the reason they were observing their main warehouse on the off-chance they saw something. They admitted that they were going to follow this up by maybe chatting to anyone they saw, as they assumed that people like the Esposito family were more likely to talk to them than the police.

Adam informed them that he was liaising with the organised crime unit and they were aware of the family's link to the firm Elizabeth worked for. He outlined that they were key figures in the early gangland wars in Melbourne but were never convicted of anything. "The police have and do keep tabs on them," Adam explained, "but the family business is now run by the two children. The old man stepped down and is now enjoying retirement. The son and daughter, who were university educated, run the business. From what we can tell, it is one hundred percent legitimate now, and the word on the street is that the daughter is the main brains behind this business, which is very successful. Their main income is derived from the importing and exporting of consumer goods, and it is probably the most scrutinised business in Melbourne, given the family's history. So far, nothing untoward has surfaced."

Adam cradled his coffee in both hands and took a long sip. He placed his elbows on the bench and continued in a firm voice.

"I get it that certain people do not like talking to the police and that they might be more likely to talk to you than me. I cannot tell you what to do. However, I cannot condone interfering with a police investigation. So, let's keep everyone informed and make sure no boundaries are crossed. Like I mentioned before, the head of the Esposito family, Carlos, has fully retired. He loves playing golf most mornings at the Royal Melbourne Golf Club and hanging out with his friends and family in a café he part-owns in Lygon Street."

They finished their coffees and Jacob began to clean up. As he closed the dishwasher door, he addressed the elephant in the room.

"Hey, guys. I know you two are used to what took place tonight but I'm not. I had a panic attack for the first time in ages. I want to help but I'm not like you guys. I'm sorry I didn't get involved and you got cut with a knife and..."

Roman stopped him mid-sentence. "Mate. You've got nothing to be sorry about. I mean that. I never asked you to join me in taking those dudes out. I've seen many guys bullshit about how tough they are and then freeze when push comes to shove. You are who you are, and you don't need to try to be anyone else, and for that, you have my respect. You can go into an operating theatre and cut someone open like you're having a Sunday roast, whereas I'd be as queasy as shit and want to get the hell out of there."

Jacob felt a bit better and returned to his seat. He asked Adam, "So, who were those guys tonight and will we get into trouble?"

Adam replied, "They were just a street gang—that's all. I saw them get up off the ground, so they will be sore but have no permanent damage. I can guarantee that they will not go to the police. Their pride will be dented so they will probably keep what happened amongst themselves. Like I said before, there were no reports made to the police, so no one was around. As far as I'm concerned, they got what they deserved, and that's the end of it. However, Roman, I gather your car is a rental, and if I was you, I'd hand it in tomorrow and get another one, just to be on the safe side."

"Will do," said Roman. He didn't question how Adam knew it was a rental—no doubt he had run the plates.

"Also," Adam added, "I am doing everything I can to find whoever was responsible for Elizabeth's murder. My boss has given me plenty of resources, and we are chasing down every lead. I hope you understand that we need to do everything by the letter of the law. So please let me know if you find anything, or have a hunch about anything, hear anything, or even want an update."

Roman and Jacob agreed, and they all made their way to the front door. Roman let Jacob know that he'd pop over in the morning so he could check up on his wound.

Roman opened the front door and paused. "Just one thing, Adam. Where the fuck did you learn to fight like that? I saw a foot and fist fly through the air like fucken Bruce Lee was there."

They all gave a laugh and Adam replied, "What do you expect? I am Asian." Laughing, he continued, "Like any good

Asian, I learnt karate from the time I turned five, and I still train. But, Roman, it looks like you can handle yourself, and hopefully I won't find myself in that situation again."

"I hope I don't get into a situation like that again either, but if I do, you're more than welcome to be by my side. Plus, I don't need any more scars on my body."

Roman turned to Jacob. "My arm feels better already. Thanks, and I'll keep it dry until I see you tomorrow."

"That would be good, and try not to lift anything heavy."

Giving a partial wave and thanks for the coffee, Roman and Adam made their way to their cars. Jacob closed the front door and, with his back leaning against it, took a moment and looked at himself in the small mirror that hung on the entrance-way wall. Tonight had been like nothing he had ever experienced before. Did he like what he was seeing? He was not sure. He liked Roman and trusted him. He believed Adam was doing everything he could. He wanted to contribute. He needed to think how he could contribute.

Taking his back off the door, he made his way upstairs and walked into his bedroom, where he gazed at a framed photo on their dresser of him and Elizabeth on their wedding day. He spoke aloud, as he held the photo frame.

"Honey, I'll do everything I can to find the person responsible for taking you away from me."

Releasing the photo frame and making sure it was positioned exactly as before, he headed to the bathroom for a long, hot shower.

CHAPTER 10

Jacob arrived at Elizabeth's parents' place at two in the afternoon. He had phoned Roman to let him know that he had a few things to do, and that he would drive over and see him later. This also gave Roman time to return his rental car.

After parking in the driveway, Jacob got out of his white Volkswagen Golf. The car was nearly seven years old and a basic model. He had thought of getting the souped-up version but had read reviews that turbos can cost money to maintain once the car gets older, so he had gone for the standard option. If he felt the need for accelerating quickly and being a boy racer, he had his motorbike for that, which, in his opinion, was more fun than any car.

Elizabeth's mum opened the front door and gave Jacob a big hug.

"So nice to see you, Jacob. You know that you are welcome here anytime."

"Nice to see you too, Mrs Paxter. Sorry I haven't been around more, but I needed some time."

"We totally understand. We will never get over what has happened. Please remember that you are very much like a son to us, so you are not alone."

Ending the embrace, Jacob gave a slight nod and his eyes let her know that he understood. They headed to the kitchen, where Mr Paxter and Roman were clearing away dishes after a late lunch. Mr Paxter put the last dish on the drying rake, dried his hands on the tea towel that was hanging on the oven door, and leaned over to shake Jacob's hand.

"Good to see you. Do you want anything to eat?"

"Thanks for the offer but I've already eaten."

"Roman said that you two are hanging out this afternoon, but please come over for dinner tonight.""That would be nice. I think Roman and I will take in some sights and it would be great to end the day with a home-cooked meal."

Mrs Paxter blushed in the background at Jacob's response but made sure no one saw her. It was a silent victory that her much-loved son-in-law was starting to spend some time with them.

Mr Paxter, oblivious to his wife's reaction, clapped his hands together. "Excellent. It's great having Roman at home for a while and he knows that you have become like a son to us. Would you like a coffee or tea before you head out?"

"No, thanks," Jacob replied.

Roman headed to his bedroom to grab his wallet and phone. It was a hot day outside and there wasn't a cloud in the sky. Summer was on its way, with spring in Melbourne known for being warm one day and cold and raining the next, as if the seasons were in a tug-of-war game, with winter not wanting to give way to summer.

They said their goodbyes and made their way to Jacob's car. Getting in, Roman asked, "So, what have you been up to this morning?"

"First, how's your arm?" Jacob replied as he started the car and pulled out of the driveway.

"All good. No bleeding and looks clean." Roman pulled up his T-shirt sleeve to confirm that the wound was healing well with no infection. "Now, what are we doing this afternoon, as I have some ideas?"

Jacob put the air conditioning on to cool the car down and then explained what he'd been up to since last night.

"I gather you read between the lines after our talk with Detective Senior Sergeant Adam Zhang. He made it clear that he didn't want us breaking the law but also said that he didn't want us to stop asking questions. He even told us that Carlos Esposito likes to play golf most mornings at the Royal Melbourne Golf Club. Well, I happen to know a surgeon who is a member of that club, who schedules his appointments around his love of golf. So, I gave him a call first thing this morning to see if he knew Carlos. I told him that I would like to meet Carlos and would be grateful for an introduction. He naturally asked me why I wanted to meet him, so I explained what had happened to Elizabeth, which he knew. I then explained that I needed to know why she was murdered as it looked like an organised hit and that Carlos may be able to shed some light on it.

"My colleague said that he knew of him and had once played a round of golf with the guy. He also knew of his past and how he was often mentioned in the old gangland wars but was never charged with anything. I then explained that I knew Carlos's family business was legit now and I was not looking at him or his family as suspects. I just wanted to talk to someone that may be in the know to put my mind at ease that Elizabeth was not tied up in anything, and if she was, then I need to know."

"Nice work," Roman replied and nodded in approval. He noticed that they were not heading to Jacob's house and asked where they were going.

Jacob, with a pleased grin on his face, continued, "Well, the best part is that my colleague called me back and told me that Carlos was teeing off this morning in the group behind him and that he would have a chat to him at the end of the round in the clubhouse. About five hours later, I got another call. He had spoken to Carlos and explained who I was and how I would like to have a chat with him. He told me that Carlos had heard of the murder of Elizabeth and would be more than willing to talk to me to put my mind at ease."

Jacob indicated and changed lanes. "You ask where we are going. We are going to have a coffee with Carlos. He told my colleague that I could meet him at his café in Lygon Street at three o'clock."

They entered the freeway to get to Carlton, on the northern fringes of Melbourne city. Lygon Street boasted a very popular strip of cafés and restaurants with an Italian flavour, and was a place that had seen its fair share of controversy. It was famous for its coffee, pasta, and pizza, and infamous as the stamping ground for the underbelly of organised crime. Men in expensive suits could be seen at all times of the day and night sitting outside cafés sipping espressos out of tulip cups, greeting other well-dressed men for short meetings accompanied with handshakes and the occasional double kiss on the cheeks.

Turning into Lygon Street, they scanned the area for a car park and eventually found one that was about a ten-minute walk from the café. Not ideal but they had just enough time to get there. The last thing they wanted was to keep Carlos Esposito waiting. Roman checked that it was okay that he was tagging along, and Jacob let him know that it should be fine. Jacob wanted him there as two heads were better than one.

Entering the café, a front-of-house staff member greeted them, and Jacob informed him that they were there to meet Carlos. After asking them to wait, the staff member wandered over to a table at the back of the café where three older gentlemen were seated. After a few seconds, one of the men looked over at them and motioned with his hand for them to come over.

As they arrived at the table, Jacob made the introductions.

"Hi. I'm Jacob. Thank you for meeting with me. This is Roman, who is Elizabeth's brother and good friend of mine. I hope you don't mind that he has come along?"

"No, not at all. Please take a seat. The other two here are friends of mine that may be of assistance."

Carlos made no attempt to introduce his friends by name. Jacob and Roman gave them a courtesy "hello" and sat down at the table. The men at the table were in the middle of having a coffee and Carlos asked them if they would like a drink. They both replied that a long espresso would be great, which appeared to be what the others were drinking. With that, Carlos waved to a waiter and placed the order with only a hand signal.

Carlos looked older than in the photo Roman had googled on their drive over. He had aged well, however, with a full head of grey hair that was combed back. His face was wrinkled but tanned and healthy. He was dressed in an expensive, ironed, white shirt that was open at the neck and had sleeves that were rolled partially up the forearms.

"So, from what I understand, you are the husband and brother of Elizabeth, who was found murdered by the West Gate Bridge. Looks like the police are getting nowhere, and you want to know from me if she was tied up in anything that could have led to this? I hope you don't think I had anything to do with it?" Carlos said calmly.

Jacob answered. "Thank you for seeing us. In no way do we think this had anything to do with you. The reason we want to talk to you is out of respect and we simply do not know who else to turn to. We understand that you are probably aware of what goes on in this city, and we would like some peace of mind that Elizabeth was not tied up in anything that could have led to her death. And if she was, then this knowledge would give us some closure."

The coffees arrived for Roman and Jacob. The café was only half full after the lunch rush, and the tables next to them empty, which was no doubt not an accident.

"You are correct that I do know a bit of what goes on in this city. The two gentlemen with me also know a fair bit so that is why I asked them to stay and chat with you also. Let me re-assure you that we had nothing to do with this. We are businessmen and not criminals. We have only agreed to meet with you because we feel for you. We get the police asking us questions all the time and we are not in the business of being informants. We have a certain standing in the community. We love Melbourne and do not like to see innocent people harmed. So, let me start by telling you that we have no idea why Elizabeth was killed. The most likely reason for anything like this is drugs or weapons. The biker gangs have made huge inroads into this territory and, from what we can ascertain, this had nothing to do with them. We would like to ask you some questions, if you don't mind?"

Roman and Jacob both took a sip of their long espressos. They signalled their agreement with an "okay" and a nod of their heads, feeling like they were now two little boys being quizzed by elders.

"We gather you know more from the police than what they are telling the media. This murder has us, and the community, concerned. Can you confirm that this was not a robbery, or anything sexual, and that the crime scene has yielded no clues?"

Jacob replied, "That is correct."

"It is because of this that we want to also chat with you. I told you that we had nothing to do with this, obviously. I can also tell you that we have not heard anything as to why this would have happened. We are just as much in the dark as you are. If you talk to the police, you can let them know this. So please take some consolation that Elizabeth was not tied up in anything that we know of. This murder is causing a certain degree of unrest as it appears to be an organised hit that was not sanctioned by anyone we are aware of. Is this the impression you are getting from the police?"

Roman answered this time. "That is the impression we are getting. It looks like this is also concerning the police. Elizabeth was a straight-up, honest person, and thank you for confirming that you know nothing to contradict this. We can tell you that, as far as we know, the police have no leads. To them, it has come across as an organised hit with no known motives."

Carlos looked at his two friends, who had not said a word. He then finished his coffee and continued. "Okay. Outside of work, what was she into?"

Jacob also took a sip of his coffee and answered. "Elizabeth was fully committed to her career and was doing very well. This consumed most of her time. As far as we can tell, she worked for a reputable company, which also does work for your family business. The police have and will continue to go through all her work and it appears to be giving no clues, as far as we are aware. When she was not working, we would hang out together, doing normal couple things. When we were not together, she liked to shop and hang out with friends. Her only hobbies to speak of were going for runs and following the footy with me."

Carlos replied with a steely gaze. "Okay. It looks like you are as stumped as we are. It sounds like Elizabeth was a lovely girl, and please be reassured that we know nothing as to why this happened. If you come across anything and would like to chat, then please feel free to contact me."

With that, Carlos slid a card over the table with his contact details on it.

Sensing that it was now time to go, Jacob and Roman thanked Carlos for his time and extended this thanks to his two friends, who remained silent and just nodded. They got up from their chairs and Carlos stood and shook their hands. Turning to leave, Carlos added, "If you two are going to be looking into this, might I suggest that you focus on her friends and what she did when she was not with you. I'm not saying she was involved in anything, but my hunch is that she likely stumbled onto something or knew somebody that was involved in something and unwittingly became entwined in something untoward."

"Will do. And once again, thanks for your time. It was really appreciated," Jacob replied.

Walking to the entrance of the café, they passed the front-of-house staff member and pulled out their wallets to pay for their coffees. The staff member glanced over at Carlos and then informed them that this would not be necessary.

Jacob and Roman walked out onto the street and squinted their eyes as they got used to the bright sunlight. The day was getting hotter and it looked like the temperature would continue to climb into the early evening.

Walking back to Jacob's car, Roman asked, "So, what did you make of that?"

"Interesting. Glad to hear that Elizabeth was not tied up in anything they are aware of. However, it appears that they wanted to get information from us. No idea who the other two men were, but obviously they have their ears to the ground of what goes on in Melbourne."

"I agree. On the other hand, Carlos might be lying and just wanted to make sure that the police have not connected any of his mates to what happened."

"True. But I think he was being honest. If anything, it sounds like they are worried someone is playing on their turf."

"Yeah, I think you may be right. Shall we tell Detective Senior Sergeant Adam Zhang about the meeting?" Roman asked.

Jacob thought for a while. "Adam did drop us the hint to chat with him, and Carlos did say it's okay, so maybe we do mention it. It's not like he told us anything of value."

"Cool. Sounds like we're on the same page."

Reaching Jacob's car, Roman continued, "Let's catch up tomorrow and decide what to do from here, if you're keen? But right now, let's head back to my parents and enjoy a couple of cold beers before dinner."

Jacob opened the car door and replied over the roof, "I could definitely do with a cold beer. I will need to head back to work at some stage, but I think there is more we can do."

Jacob got in, started the car and wound down the windows. With the radio on and the spring breeze in their hair, they headed off to enjoy a beautiful spring evening with Elizabeth's parents, unaware that one of Elizabeth's friends would indeed prove to be very valuable in their investigation.

CHAPTER 11

Moya Connor had finished work a bit early since it was such nice weather. The days were getting longer, and everyone was gravitating to the green public spaces throughout the city. She was struggling to cope with the loss of Elizabeth, whom she had grown very attached to over the time they had worked together. She had considered Elizabeth a best friend and being at work now was not the same. Moya often reflected on how much more enjoyable it was in the workplace when you sat beside someone you got along with—someone you could share your day with, laugh with, have lunch with, and chat about things outside of work. Elizabeth's desk was now empty but soon someone else would sit beside her, and it just wouldn't be the same.

Moya lived in a refurbished one-bedroom apartment on the sixth floor of an old building. Old as in it had character, not old as in run down. It was in Flinders Lane at the southern edge of the city. Her slice of real estate faced the morning sun, which, in summer, spared her the late afternoon oven effect. There were numerous alleyways shooting off Flinders

Lane, filled with cool graffiti-covered brick walls that framed the trendy cafés and restaurants. All this came with the added bonus of being within easy walking distance to her office.

After work, she changed into her running gear and went for a jog along the walking tracks that lined the Yarra River. The late sun was beating down on her and she could feel the warmth through her light running top, and the sprinkle of sweat that was building up. The tracks were abuzz with walkers, joggers, cyclists, and the odd tourist holding a walking map that was obtained from the many information kiosks that dotted the city.

Making her way back, she checked her watch to make sure her heart rate was in the "fat burn" zone. When she was closer to home, she would increase the intensity, and move her heart rate into the "cardio" zone until she ran out of breath, and then walk the rest of the way to cool down. She could see Melbourne Park ahead on her right, with the huge sports stadiums and tennis arenas where every year the Australian Open tennis tournament was held. On her left was the Royal Botanic Gardens and she contemplated extending her run through the manicured flower beds that lined the walkways. But maybe next time. She liked to let her mind wander when running and allow the endorphins to do their thing and turn any negative thoughts into positive ones. Sometimes during summer, she and Elizabeth would take a long lunch and go for a run. Her thoughts returned to Elizabeth and all the good times they had.

The last time they did something together was when they went out to get lunch the week before her death. They went to

Chinatown and found a new dumpling place that had opened. The dumplings were delicious but the service average, which was common in Chinatown during the lunch rush, when the staff try to turn the tables as quickly as possible. They chatted a bit about work and plans they had for the weekend. Talking to Elizabeth was so easy. Conversations would flow naturally, and time would fly by. After lunch, they ambled back to work, passing a boutique home-furnishing shop that had lots of interesting ornaments that ranged from trendy novelty items to aged pieces that would give a home an "old money" feel, as if expensive items had been handed down by past generations. They decided to enter the shop and have a look. Moya remembered the giggles they had over some pieces and how they both liked some of the more understated items, while they discussed where they would put them in their homes. They had very similar tastes and she would miss hanging out with someone so like-minded.

Thinking of Elizabeth made her think of her brother, Roman. Her heart had skipped a beat when she saw him. *Wow*. He certainly was extremely good-looking with a rugged, boyish charm. He looked exceptionally healthy and probably had a chiselled, toned body. She enjoyed meeting up with him for brunch and would love to meet him again. Was it wrong that she was having feelings for her friend's brother when she should be mourning the loss of her friend? Would Elizabeth approve of her feelings towards Roman? It was then she realised that she didn't even know if he was single. He didn't wear a wedding ring and hadn't mentioned anyone, but they didn't talk about that. Her mind started to wander off as she imagined being Roman's girlfriend.

Moya had never been lucky in love. There had been boyfriends and only one that she ever truly cared about and loved. Upon reflection, she realised that she was in love with him at the start but then that turned into wanting to still be in love. He was a nice guy and treated her well in the beginning—always holding the car door open and making sure she was seated first when dining out. He spoke calmly and gave genuine compliments about her looks, career, and achievements. Everything seemed perfect. She was not sure when it all started to change as it was gradual. The car door was no longer held open, which she would expect as relationships get older and couples grew more comfortable with each other. The compliments started to decrease, which she also would have expected as they got to know each other. But it was so many things that stopped. His smile when they greeted each other. His listening when she talked about work and her friends. His actions when they were out, and it was obvious his mind was elsewhere. It started to get to the stage where they would dine out and their phones provided more entertainment than each other's company. Moya put up with it, but the spark was gone, and she didn't know if this was normal as it was her longest relationship, nearing the two-year mark.

Then she started to sit next to Elizabeth, and as their friendship grew, they talked about relationships. She was in awe of how much Elizabeth and Jacob loved each other after many years. The romantic evenings, weekends, and holidays they would have. How Jacob would still buy flowers and surprise her with little gifts. When she met Elizabeth and Jacob, it was obvious they were a couple. Moya then registered that this was the relationship she wanted and her current one was far removed from how it should be. She thought that maybe it was her fault, so for the next month she tried to be more romantic, but it fell on deaf ears. Within two months, she decided to break up with him. It had been a hard thing for her to do. It felt like she was admitting defeat and maybe throwing away her last chance for a possible husband—not that she needed a husband, but she did want a family one day. He took the news a little too well for her liking, which only confirmed she had made the right decision.

Moya checked her watch as she was getting past Melbourne Park. Time to up the tempo of her run and move her heart rate into the "cardio" zone for the last five minutes. She needed to get Roman out of her mind. So with eyes forward, head up, back straight, concentrating on the cadence of her strides, she powered on along the Yarra River towards home. She felt the burn in her legs and a trickle of sweat run down her forehead as she pushed her heat rate into the "peak" zone for the last minute.

Crossing the St Kilda Road bridge across the Yarra River, Moya slowed to a walk to cool down. Crossing Flinders Street and ducking down a laneway, she turned into Finders Lane and strode back to her apartment. She still had Roman in her head and was not able to shake the thoughts of the possibility that they could be a couple. Feeling great after the invigorating run, she decided to give him a call and arrange a lunch date. Dinner would sound too much like a proper date and she wanted to play it cool. Meeting up for coffee was a bit too casual. Lunch would be perfect, and she knew just the place with a relaxed atmosphere in the city and plenty for them to do if they decided to hang out for the remainder of the afternoon.

CHAPTER 12

Roman was heading into the city on the train. It was nearing midday, the day was overcast and the temperature mild. Jacob had gone into work for the day, as he wanted to get back and check up on his patients and make sure they were being well looked after by other cardiologists in his absence. Jacob wasn't planning to return to work full-time just yet, and his boss was happy for him to take all the time he needed. Jacob told Roman that going into work for the day would take his mind off Elizabeth. Roman agreed.

Reaching Flinders Street Station, Roman got off the train and made his way to Degraves Street, which was pedestrian-only. It was lined with small cafés on each side and small tables down the middle, which doubled the seating capacity down the narrow alley. Walking up, he spotted Moya waiting for him. They gave each other a smile and a wave as they made their way towards each other.

"Nice to see you, and glad you could make it," Moya said to Roman as she leaned in for a welcome embrace, which Roman reciprocated.

"Nice to see you too."

They ended the embrace, which Moya would have liked to have continued. She had enjoyed feeling his strong arms and his manly, refreshing smell that had a hint of cologne and soap. Like an athlete after a big game. She was glad that he had agreed to meet for lunch.

"Perfect weather for sitting outside. If you don't mind sitting outside?" Roman asked.

"Of course. There's a great little Italian place just over there."

They make their way over to an outside table that was shaded by an oversized umbrella. Roman asked the waitress for a long black coffee and Moya requested water.

"I haven't had a coffee today and really need one. I hit a local gym a bit hard this morning. How have you been?" Roman asked while stretching out his arms by his side, trying to loosen the lactic acid.

Moya noticed this and had to stop herself daydreaming of him working out. "I've been okay. I've returned to work, but it's just not the same. Everyone is shocked at what happened. My boss is being nice and allowing me plenty of time off and to leave work early, if need be. How about you?"

"Yeah. What can I say? I just wish I had gotten in touch with my sister. You don't know what you've got until it's gone. I've been spending a fair bit of time with Jacob, which has been nice. He's a great guy, and I can see why Elizabeth married him."

"Yeah, he is. Are you staying in Melbourne for a while?"

"I think I'll stick around for a bit longer. I'm staying with my parents and enjoying spending time with them. Also, spending time with Jacob, and even with you, makes me feel closer to Elizabeth, like I'm catching up on all those years I wasn't there."

The waitress returned with a full bottle of water and two glasses. She placed the glasses on the table and filled them up, placing the now half-empty bottle of water in the centre of the table. She then turned and left.

"I was going to ask how Jacob is doing. He must be finding it tough?" Moya asked, taking a sip of the cool water.

"He's putting on a brave face, but you can tell he's constantly thinking about her. He's gone into work today, which will be good for him."

The waitress came over with Roman's coffee and took their food orders.

As they waited for lunch, they continued with small talk. Moya desperately wanting to ask if he was seeing anyone but did not want to ask unexpectedly. The conversation did start to turn towards his life in New Zealand, but before she could ask if there was a lucky girl in his life, the food arrived.

Roman drained the last of his coffee and followed it with a drink of water to cleanse his palate before he dug into his delicious carbonara. Moya also took a drink of water and eyed up her tortellini. There was silence as they started their meals. After a couple of bites, Roman congratulated Moya on her choice of venue for lunch.

"I've been meaning to ask," said Roman, "have the police been asking many questions of you and your workmates?"

"That detective Adam Zhang and John Moskil have been in a couple of times. They have questioned everyone. It has been so weird. A meeting room was set aside so they could chat to people separately and in private. I know that they have spoken to our boss and boss's boss and obtained many records. It looks like they are leaving no stone unturned."

"So, do you think it has anything to do with Elizabeth's work?"

"I really don't know. I've told them everything I know about our jobs and what we got up to outside of work. Why do you ask?"

"I've been thinking a lot about her death and it just doesn't add up. I know the police are doing everything they can, and I've spoken to Detective Adam Zhang more than once. But I feel useless just sitting around and want to do something to help."

"I'm sure the police are doing everything in their power to find out who was responsible."

Roman agreed and saw that Moya was concentrating on her lunch, so he followed suit. He wanted to bring up the subject again and try to convince Moya to help him and Jacob. He decided it could wait a little bit longer and they enjoyed pleasant conversations about Melbourne, the weather and funny stories involving Elizabeth.

Finishing their lunch, the waitress came over and asked if they would like anything else. Roman looked at Moya and said,

"Well, it's a lovely day and I did see some nice desserts on the menu but wouldn't be able to finish one by myself. Would you like to share one?"

Moya agreed as she was enjoying spending time with Roman and wanted it to continue for as long as possible. Besides, she still hadn't found out if he was seeing anyone.

Once they had ordered a tiramisu and were alone again, Moya rested her elbows on the table, took a breath to build up her courage, and asked, "So, with you spending all this time in Melbourne, is there a Mrs Roman or girlfriend back in New Zealand that is missing you?"

"That's a very direct question. The answer is no. What about you? I'm not keeping you from a significant other?"

"No, there's no one in my life at the moment."

Roman felt a bit silly for asking but felt it was only polite to ask the same question back. It dawned on him that maybe Moya was interested in him. He liked her but not in that way and would need to be careful not to lead her on. Or maybe she was just making conversation and now he was reading too much into it. She was very attractive and easy to get along with. He wondered if he should say something more, but luckily Moya changed the topic before he could add anything.

"So, do you have any plans for the rest of the day?" Moya asked.

"Nope. Just taking it easy today. And you?"

"Same. Do you want to go and check out an exhibition at the National Gallery after this?"

"That would be nice."

The waitress returned with the tiramisu, accompanied by two forks and a fresh bottle of water. As she left, they both picked up a fork and took a bite. Roman topped up their glasses with fresh water and helped himself to another mouthful.

Moya was enjoying the afternoon. She was glad there was not a girl already in his life, but she was not sure if he had feelings for her. He was very nice, polite, and handsome, yet there was so much she didn't know about him. Elizabeth didn't talk about him much and it did concern her that he didn't try to contact his family more often, although he seemed to be getting along with his parents now. Maybe a tragedy was needed to bring the family together and make everyone realise that once someone was gone it was too late to have "what ifs" and any dispute was petty in comparison.

Roman sat back and savoured another mouthful of tiramisu. He decided that it was as good a time as any to ask Moya for assistance in looking into Elizabeth's death. In a gallery, people tend to be quiet, and spending the rest of the afternoon with her would give ample time to clarify any questions.

"That is one good tiramisu," Roman said, leaning in and looking at Moya. "There is something I want to ask you in relation to Elizabeth's death. Before I do, I want you to know that you can say no, and I will not be offended."

"This sounds serious. Please ask," Moya replied with a mischievous grin.

"Okay." Roman checked the tables beside them. One was empty and the other had a couple that was deep in conversation. "What I'm going to ask will involve you breaking a few rules at work. Are you comfortable with that?"

"Well, that depends on what those few rules are. Why don't you just ask, and I'll consider it? If I say no, you can trust me that I will not tell anyone. If I say yes, then, obviously, you will need to trust me even more."

Both leaned in, with elbows on the table. Roman lowered his voice to an almost whisper.

"What I'm telling you goes no further and stays between us. Jacob and I have obviously been in touch with Detective Senior Sergeant Adam Zhang. The police have no solid leads and are being very thorough with investigating and eliminating any possible scenario. Yet we are sure they are totally in the dark as to why Elizabeth was murdered. It is coming across as a professional hit and not related to a robbery or anything sexual. Jacob and I do have faith in the police and are not blaming them for the lack of progress. We want to assist them in any way we can, and in ways that they may not be able to consider themselves due to the tight laws and procedures the police need to follow. Don't get us wrong—we appreciate these laws and rules our police follow."

Roman had Moya's full attention and realised he was starting to ramble, so he got straight to the point. "Jacob and I met with Carlos Esposito and a couple of his friends. I'm not sure if you know who he is?"

Moya nodded her head. "I know who he is. Our company does accounting and financial work for their family business. I thought the family business was one hundred percent legit. Are you saying it's not?"

"No, that is not what I'm saying. You are correct that it is one hundred percent legit. Adam Zhang confirmed that the police have nothing on them. Anyway, his son and daughter now run the family business. Back to what I was saying. We met with him to see if he had heard of anything or knew anything as to why this might have happened. We're not sure who his two friends were when we met him, but no doubt they have their ears to the ground as to what happens in this city. The interesting thing from the meeting was that they had no idea who did this or why, and Jacob and I believed them. They ended up asking us questions as it appears that what happened has annoyed the 'powers that be' in Melbourne. They know it was a professional, well-planned murder, and obviously they are concerned that something is going on or someone is doing business in this city without going through appropriate channels. At the end of the meeting, he gave us some advice, and that was to consider what Elizabeth was doing at work and in her spare time, as it appears that she may have unwittingly stumbled onto something that led to her death."

Moya started to look concerned as well as interested. Roman continued.

"Jacob has thought about what she, and they, did away from work, and nothing untoward came to mind. We have told Adam Zhang about our meeting with Carlos Esposito as we are not trying to be vigilantes. Adam has asked us to look at everything Elizabeth did in her spare time, and if we come up with anything, then to let him know. He has already taken extensive statements from us and, as you know, from everyone at your work. You are also aware that they have obtained detailed knowledge of Elizabeth's workload. However, Adam can ask us questions but cannot give us full disclosure of all the information they have gathered. What Jacob and I are asking is this—and please feel free to say no and we will not be offended..."

Moya took a sip of water and focused on what Roman would say next. Roman looked around and saw that nothing had changed at the tables next to them, and the buzz of conversation was making it near impossible for anyone to hear their private discussion. He remained leaning in on the table, with Moya doing the same.

He took a sip of water as well, and finally asked, "Is it possible for you to obtain for us all the accounts Elizabeth was working on in the last few months? This will involve confidential client information and files."

Moya looked straight into Roman's eyes and replied, "I can get these as I have all the access that she had. The actual copying of files onto a USB drive for you may not be possible. Client confidentiality is a very serious issue. This could lead to me getting fired, deregistered, and having to find a new career. Not to mention the criminal charges I could face. I'm not saying yes or no at this stage, but I will need to think about it and how it could be done without raising suspicion. It is how I do it that is the hard part. Our computers are monitored, which is industry standard practice."

As if she was thinking aloud, she continued, "I could access them over a period of a week or so with legitimate reasons to do so. I know my boss has temporarily reassigned all of Elizabeth's clients and I suppose I can request to take much of this work since we did work closely."

"That would be very useful for us, and I can give you our word that we will not share any of this with anyone. Also, once we are finished, we will delete everything you have given us. There is one other thing, which will be a lot harder to get. This is something else the police will have but cannot give us full disclosure on."

"I haven't said yes to the first part yet," Moya interjected with a grin.

"I know, and this would be a lot harder. We are wanting a full history of what internal files Elizabeth accessed in the last three months as well as her web browser history."

"How am I supposed to get those?"

"Do you know anyone in the IT department? Or maybe login under her name and copy her browser and Windows Explorer history? Not sure what excuse you would need to be able to do that."

"I'll have to think about the last one. As for the first request, I will attempt to do this but no promises. I can say that I need to work from home and had to copy these files due to VPN access issues. I just need to get a legitimate reason, which shouldn't be too hard. But that second request you'll just have to leave with me to think about."

The waitress came over to collect the empty plates. Roman complimented the food and asked for the bill. She walked over to the counter and promptly returned with it on a little black plastic tray and left them alone.

Roman took out his wallet and told Moya, "I've got this."

"Thank you. I'll get it next time," Moya replied, knowing that there would be a next time if she helped him.

Roman placed the credit card back in his wallet and said, "Let's go and check out the National Gallery."

They left their table and walked back to Flinders Street. The National Gallery was only ten minutes away. They walked in silence as if their conversation had put an uncertain cloud over them, like when the weather forecast is for a chance of showers and you spend the entire day being cautious every time you go outside. Roman broke the calm when they were about to enter the gallery.

"I want to make sure that you know that you do not have to do anything that I have asked. If you have any doubts or feel that you are taking too big a risk, then by all means, do not do it."

"Thank you, but I'll give it a go and let you know. Sorry if I suddenly seemed a bit distant as I'm already thinking about how to go about it."

"Just one word of advice. Whatever you come across, please do not search anything online. It is very easy for people to identify who accessed websites. The last thing I want is for you to be in danger, and I'm not talking about your job. If you feel the urge to follow up on anything, please, please, ask me to do it," Roman stressed.

"Okay. I hadn't thought of that."

They continued into the National Gallery with the tension lifted slightly and enjoyed a nice afternoon in each other's company.

CHAPTER 13

Outside, the morning weather had turned to cold and rain. It was a good day to be working inside, sitting at a desk and staring at a computer. The fickle weather was a reminder to everyone that summer was not here yet and winter could still have some fun.

Moya Connor was back at work. It had been a couple of days since she had lunch with Roman and her mind was drifting into daydreams of how nice it was. He was a true gentleman, and they had seemed like a couple at the National Gallery, taking in the exhibitions and talking about what they liked and did not like, including pieces they did not understand. Their tastes appeared similar and now she was imagining what the décor of their house would look like if they lived together. However, there was no special moment or spark that made them turn a friendship into something more. Was she reading too much into this? If she was, it was nice to dream, and if Roman was the male figure in these dreams, so be it.

Brought back to reality by her desktop phone ringing, she got back into work mode. The caller ID showed that it was from the helpful guy she had recently talked to from the IT department. After she said hello, he informed her that her request had been activated and it would be easier if he came to her desk to show her how to access and sort the information. He sent through a meeting request while they talked and locked in a time at two for an hour.

Yesterday Moya had approached her boss about taking more of Elizabeth's workload as she had worked closely with her on many occasions and, as they sat next to each other, they frequently spoke about what they were working on. It didn't take much to convince him. He seemed pleased that she had offered and agreed that they did need someone who knew Elizabeth's clients and had intimate knowledge of her portfolios. He asked her how she was feeling, to which she replied that she was still finding it hard and appreciated the time he had given her, but she was keen to get straight back into work full-time. He replied that he was glad to hear this, as she was an important member of the company. He even told her that she was more than welcome to work from home if she had no client meetings. Moya was thankful and said that she would no doubt do this and was keen to do a bit of work in the evenings to catch up.

Upon reflection, the meeting with her boss went better than expected. He had promptly emailed through all of Elizabeth's clients and what she had been working on. It also included the names of a few people in the company that had already taken over a client or two, with a green light for Moya to contact them and go over any of these as she saw fit. Feeling pleased with herself, she now had a legitimate reason to access everything Elizabeth had worked on, and if the company noticed her logging in frequently and accessing work files in the evening from home, this would not seem out of the ordinary.

One thing remained, and that was accessing Elizabeth's Windows Explorer and internet browsing history. She had an idea, but it would take a lot of work to formulate the necessary reason for making such a request. After the meeting, she had promptly started working and accessing Elizabeth's clients' records. She worked at home until late in the night, carefully documenting everything that would lead to such a proposal. Finally, at one in the morning, she was satisfied that she had put together an extremely persuasive argument.

Moya turned up to work early that morning after little sleep, feeling a mixture of excitement and nerves. The reason for getting in early was that her boss was an early starter. He was often at his desk at seven in the morning, taking advantage of the peace and quiet before the floor started humming with conversations and muffled footsteps, accompanied by numerous interruptions. Seeing him at his desk, she had asked for a few minutes of his time. He obliged, and she put forward her request. She informed him that she had been going over Elizabeth's work, even working until late last night. She could see that Elizabeth had been searching for financial advice for clients and making enquiries into how best to manage their cash flow with investments. In one case, she was going to give financial advice to a client that wished to diversify their investment portfolio. Elizabeth had mentioned via email that she had researched a viable option that would meet their demands.

Moya had her laptop open and was visually showing all this to her boss in a well-documented presentation. Moya outlined that if she started from scratch, it would be very time consuming and "time was money". Moya's case was rock-solid, and clearly showed that it would be extremely beneficial for her to get the Windows Explorer and internet browsing history for the last two months from Elizabeth's computer.

Moya's boss asked more questions and took some convincing. They went over everything she had prepared twice. In the end, he could see the benefits to the clients and to the company if the request was granted. The planned few minutes of his time had turned into half an hour. He said that he would sign off on the request straightaway and someone from IT would contact her.

Pleased with herself, she returned to her desk, and it was not long before she was contacted by IT. With the meeting now booked in for two, she headed out of the building to get a coffee and to give Roman a call from her mobile phone rather than use her desk phone.

"Hi, Moya," Roman answered.

"Hi, Roman. I've got some great news. The first part of your request has been granted. The second part, I will have by the end of the day."

"Wow. That didn't take you long. Before you go into anything over the phone, would you like me and Jacob to pop over this evening?"

"No. How about we meet up in a couple of days, so I can go over it first and see what I have. I'll give you a call end of tomorrow and let you know."

"Okay. That sounds good. Please remember to not search anything online that seems out of the ordinary. Look after yourself, and I look forward to hearing from you."

After a bit of small talk as to what they were doing for the day, they hung up. Moya went into her regular café and got a takeaway coffee. Hunched over against the rain, with both hands on the cup to keep them warm, she headed back to her building with a spring in her step, feeling particularly pleased with herself. She felt she now had a purpose and could make a positive contribution to honour her dead friend. Spending more time with Roman was a bonus.

Moya had now joined the full-scale murder investigation being conducted by the police, alongside Roman and Jacob. Over the ocean, in the Middle East, operations were continuing with no one the wiser that the heat on them had just intensified.

CHAPTER 14

In Syria, a *whack, whack, whack* sound could be heard in the distance as a helicopter made its way to the landing zone. The British soldiers were tired and cold as they lay in wait in the middle of a freezing night in the countryside. There was slight cloud cover, for which they were grateful, as this would enable a relatively safe flight back to base. The sound grew louder, and they now had visible conformation of the Sea King MK4 helicopter that was fitted with a defensive aid suite that included chaff/flare dispensers. The flares were designed to confuse heat-seeking missiles, and the chaff spoofed radar-guided missiles. These were a major concern with the increased use of the fixed and man-portable surface-to-air missiles that had made their way into the hands of the rebel and terrorist units.

The helicopter drew near and lowered itself so that it was just touching the ground and ready to ascend with full speed. Lying in wait, the leader signalled to his team and they quickly made their way to the open door with rifles raised, covering their designated arc of fire. Heart rates were higher than usual. They made their way inside and, with the door closed, they

quickly headed off. Heart rates started to lower. They were forever grateful to the specialist pilots and crew that picked them
up and gave unconditional support.

Cruising at a fast speed and now out of the dangerous fly
zone, they started to relax and enjoy the luxury of talking to
each other. Theirs was a four-man SAS patrol, which was small
enough to avoid detection but still enabled them to carry
enough stores for their recon mission. This was the smallest
unit size possible, as it allowed for a wounded soldier to be carried out by two others while being covered by a third. They
had been intelligence gathering, which was the bread and but-
ter of the SAS. Being on "hard routine", they were not allowed
to cook or smoke and needed to limit any talking. Now safe in
the helicopter, they were enjoying having a chat and couldn't
wait for a hot meal and shower.

The helicopter reached the British-led training camp in Al-
Quweira in remote south-west Jordan. Descending to a stop,
the soldiers disembarked and made their way to their designated barracks. The lead soldier dropped off his Bergen and
made his way to the officers' quarters to meet his CO as expected. Reaching his open office door, he knocked and stood
to attention.

"At ease, soldier," the CO said when he noticed him. "Relax
and take a seat."

He took a seat opposite the CO's desk and enjoyed the feeling of sitting in a chair.

"So how did it go?"

"As you are aware, we had to engage the enemy. We were observing the informant we were due to meet as he was making his way to the meeting point. He was in a group of eighteen men that were making their way back to their homes after work. We had earlier noticed a group of six armed men that appeared to not be government soldiers or friendlies. They were also keeping an eye on the group. Nearing the point where the informant would need to detour, the six men confronted the group. We could not hear them, but it appeared they were asking for money and, in effect, robbing the group. At this stage, we were observing only with no plans to engage."

The CO motioned for him to continue.

"Then the informant made a break for it. One of the six armed men lined him up in his sights and shot him. He fell to the ground and was then shot again twice. The guy that shot him then started to make his way towards him. That was when everything changed. We could not allow the informant to be searched, which he would have been, given the fact that he had raised suspicion by running. We had no choice but to engage them. There was also a clear immediate threat that the others would be killed. We already had designated targets in our sights, so within a couple of seconds, we had neutralised them. We then quickly made our way over to the group, with two of us focusing on them while one went to the informant as he was covered by the third. The informant was searched and all documents and goods in his possession taken. We also did a brief search of the six deceased and confirmed that they were members of the local terrorist cell."

"And how did you determine this?" the CO interrupted, not wanting a shitstorm to land on his desk.

"They had these on them," the lead soldier replied while taking from his trouser pocket the rough paperwork local terrorist cells carried to enable them safe passage and shelter.

The CO glanced at them as they were placed on his desk. He motioned for him to continue.

"All the documents from the informant will need to be translated and will be included in my written report."

The CO leaned forward in his chair and asked if there was any chance they were compromised.

"The group of eighteen men obviously saw us. They were terrified and soon realised we meant them no harm. They quickly gathered the money that they were going to be robbed of and made their way home. Apart from them, no one saw us. We promptly left the scene and took up observation posts to be double sure."

"Excellent. I have not heard anything about this, so it looks like it was contained. Please cover all details in your report."

"There is one other thing that I would like to bring to your immediate attention," the soldier said as he reached into his jacket pocket. "As you know, we are often handed things by locals who would like us to help them, either by giving them asylum or finding loved ones. The clear majority we ignore. However, this time, one of the eighteen approached me, spoke in English, and handed me this."

He passed the folded paper to his CO, adding, "I did not read it at the time. Only checked to make sure it was safe and placed it in my pocket for later, as we had to disperse and establish observation points."

The CO unfolded the paper and leaned back in his chair as he read it. His brow became increasingly furrowed in concentration. He finished reading one side and then turned the page over and continued to read the other without taking his eyes off the paper. Finishing, he placed it on his desk and ran his thumb and forefinger across his chin.

"I gather you have read this, no doubt more than once. What we have here could potentially yield significant damage to the terrorist groups. There are several facts that we will need to check out to verify authenticity and I will forward this on immediately. What's your take on the source?"

"Creditable. The reason I say this is that he spoke to us in perfect English. He had the paper concealed down his pants, so he knew the risk he was taking. Everything that is written down is in English, which is obviously tailored to be handed over to someone like us, rather than government, rebel, or terrorist troops. Also, I gather that you picked up on the last two paragraphs not being grammatically correct, when the grammar is otherwise perfect. This puzzled me, and I haven't had time to work it out, but I am sure that hidden in this would be his name and possible details on how to contact him. He is obviously a well-educated man, and this adds weight to the credibility of what is written."

"I agree. Who else have you shown this to?"

"Apart from my men, just you."

"Let's keep it that way. I know you guys keep everything confidential about what you do and see, but please reiterate the need for discretion to your men."

The CO stood to indicate that the meeting was over. The soldier pushed himself up from his chair and waited to be dismissed. Before this happened, the CO said, "It may come down to finding this guy. If it requires someone on the ground, would you be interested?"

"Certainly."

"I'll keep you informed. Now go and have something hot to eat, and shower 'cause you stink."

CHAPTER 15

Moya Connor was at Jacob's house along with Roman. It was early evening and they were seated around the dining room table with two pizza boxes in the middle, with three slices remaining. Three beer bottles were opened and nearly finished. Also on the table were two closed laptops, one being Moya's from work and the other Jacob's personal one that he had shared with his wife, Elizabeth. Jacob asked if they wanted any more pizza, to which they declined, patting their full stomachs. He closed the boxes and asked if they wanted another beer, to which they agreed. He picked up the boxes and headed to the kitchen.

Returning with three new beers, Jacob flicked on the light switch, noticing that even though the evenings were getting longer, it was getting dark inside. He placed the beers in front of Moya and Roman, took a seat and reached for his laptop. He looked at Moya and said, "Well, then. From the sounds of it, you have gotten a lot of data for us to go over. I still can't believe that you got all of this and, by the sounds of it, you've spent many hours poring over it. I've been going over the browser history on my laptop and have made a note of everything that was not related to anything I was aware of."

Moya opened her laptop and started it up. She entered a username and password, and while it loaded, she said, "I've had a look at all her Windows and internet history for the last two months. I've documented everything that was not directly related to a file she was working on. By this, I mean accessing any folders or files that would be expected with clients. There are obviously company files and folders that have been accessed that do not directly relate to her clients. This could be simply due to referencing work already done for another client, which, as a business, we often do so as to not waste time reinventing the wheel. Or these were accessed to evaluate advice that was previously given to see if it was still relevant."

Moya took a sip of her beer and tapped away at the keyboard before continuing. "I've documented all this in Excel along with timestamps, so it can easily be sorted and searched. I've also tried to group as many browser history site pages as possible, so if she visited a site, we can see how many pages she explored within that site and how many times she went to it."

Jacob had his laptop open and mentioned that he had also put this information into Excel and asked Moya if she would like him to email it to her. She replied, "To be on the safe side, I don't want to get this as an email as this is a work laptop. I have a USB memory stick and I'll save my spreadsheet on it, and you can open it on yours and combine the files. Safer this way, in case my computer gets audited."

Roman agreed and double-checked that they hadn't clicked on any of these links or gone into any of the sites.

With all this information now on Jacob's laptop, they moved their chairs and gathered around his screen. Moya took control as she was the most proficient in Excel and started to lay out both files, so they could be cross-referenced. As she did this, Jacob and Roman took a sip of their beers with impressed looks on their faces.

Tapping away, she asked Jacob if anything stood out while he was looking at her history.

"Well, there was a lot of online shopping, which is to be expected. I ignored all social media. I know that when she found something she wanted to buy, she would then do research on that item, so a lot of what I've included could be related to that. Nothing really stood out."

"Okay. I'm nearly finished. What I've done is look at all her internet browsing history and taken the domain names, ignoring all page directories after the forward slashes. I've also sorted this by date, so we can see how often she visited a website and when. I've got it separated for her work laptop versus her home laptop. This should give us an initial view of her browser habits."

With this, she moved her finger over the touchpad and made a few clicks here and there and sat back. She picked up her beer and took a long sip. They all looked intently at the screen as the blank tab populated with the most visited sites in chronological order, clearly showing when they were accessed on either the work or personal laptop. This was followed by the number of pages visited on the sites. After a second or two, they were left with a long list of over a hundred thousand rows.

The first domain name they could see was for a news website, with just over a thousand pages accessed. Moya informed them that this would not be unusual as Elizabeth did read her news online throughout the day. Jacob confirmed that Elizabeth had subscribed to this site, and he did a quick calculation in his head to add that if she looked at twenty pages of news a day, this would easily bc over a thousand pages over two months.

Roman looked on and added, "Can we get a summary list of counts visited by domain name with the most visited page within that site? I think we should not ignore news pages and, depending on what we find, we can reference back to this."

"I totally agree on both. Saves time scrolling through this long list," Moya replied. She then leant over her laptop and set about doing this.

Roman and Jacob watched on with their beers in their hands as if they were watching the dying moments of a footy grand final.

Moya finished, and they could now see a summary count of pages visited. They looked at the ranked list and could see that the news site was number one, followed by eBay, and then other shopping sites. They recognised the shopping websites, but the items looked at were too numerous to go over manually so they continued down the list. After shopping sites was her bank website, and then many others, ranging from television shows to Wikipedia.

Roman placed his beer on the table and suggested they highlight any sites that seemed out of the ordinary, and of these, to make note if they were accessed on either the work or personal laptop, or both.

Moya scrolled down the list and she and Jacob quickly highlighted about a dozen sites that seemed out of the ordinary. Looking at these, they could not see any relevance. There were sites involving travel destinations, and Jacob said Elizabeth would always be looking for possible future holiday destinations without him knowing. Other sites were product-related, which could have constituted research on possible online purchases. They looked closer at these as they involved an eclectic range of goods. There was no clear pattern in terms of what was looked at on the work or personal laptop.

Jacob leaned back and stretched his arms out, letting out a sigh while he looked at the ceiling. He returned his sight to the screen, thought, and then said, "It would be great if we could click on these sites to see what she was looking at because in these product pages we could see exactly what she was viewing. Also, with the destination sites, the pages listed after the domain name are not clear. How are we supposed to make sense out of the list without clicking on them?"

Moya agreed as they both turned to Roman.

"I know you think I'm being pedantic, but we cannot take any risks. You know I work for a security syndicate and a lot of what we do is not just providing muscle, but also information to minimise risks for us and our clients. Information that you cannot get with a Google search. This can be information gathered from people on the ground, but we also have amazing computer geeks that work for us that can sort metadata and tap into systems undetected. Once we get a list of sites we would like to explore further, I will pass this on to a very good friend of mine whom I work closely with. He can access what we want without leaving a digital footprint. We just need a list of these sites, and he can even dig further, referencing any key words or phrases. You would be surprised at what he can do, but we need to give him a starting point."

"Well, I'm glad we have this resource," Moya replied.

Jacob agreed and they all had a long swig. He then said what they were all thinking.

"Well, we had better get on with this, so your friend can help us. But just to clarify, why would he want to help us when this is not related to your job? Also, does this friend have a name?"

Roman looked at them. "Good questions and I'm glad you asked, as it shows that we are all taking this seriously and the risks involved. His name is Joel and we go back a long way. Back to the armed services, where we did train and go on deployments together, until our commanding officers realised his intellect and put him behind a desk to gather and sort intelligence. I would trust this guy with my life. I've helped him out previously, so he would be doing this as a personal favour to me. He knows I'm in Melbourne because Elizabeth was murdered and has offered to help in any way he can."

Jacob let Roman know that anyone he trusted, he also trusted. Moya agreed.

Returning to the laptop, Moya looked at the summary list, squinted her eyes, pondered, stood up and started to pace the room.

"I think we've been looking at this the wrong way around. We are looking at the sites as products, places, and information. What if we look at the businesses behind these sites? Let's exclude the news sites and eBay. Would your friend Joel be able to tell us what companies own and run these sites right up to their parent companies? From this, we can group together the pages accordingly. If Elizabeth's murder was due to something she stumbled upon and started researching, then I'm sure it would be the companies behind these sites rather than what the sites represent."

"I totally agree," Jacob replied, in awe of this revelation. "Let's compile that list right now."

Moya returned to her seat and opened another file on her laptop.

"We also need to give Joel some direction as to what to look for in these companies. I have Elizabeth's Windows Explorer history from work. I've been looking at this and, from what I can gather, the only thing that looked a little bit out of place with respect to her clients was looking at options, for example, for hedging risks when trading in foreign currencies."

She saw that Jacob and Roman looked puzzled, so she emphasised, "This is just an example. For instance, a company might buy or sell goods at an agreed price in American dollars, but not finalise the payment for another month or two or, in some cases, even longer. Obviously, the currency can change in value in relation to the country in which the companies are based. The last thing you want is to finally pay for the goods and have no profit margin left. The US dollar was the favoured tender, and the Euro has gained popularity as a trading currency, but any currency can be used. Like I said, that's just an example, but my professional intuition is to follow the money as there are always documents that can be fudged to maximise profits or even hide profits."

Moya pointed to the screen and showed company file directories for large multinational corporations. She continued.

"Elizabeth was not dealing with any large multinational corporations. Her clientele was small and medium businesses, and most of these traded internationally in some form or another, mainly making goods in China or importing them. However, she could have referenced these work resources as they may have been relevant to her small and medium businesses. What these large corporations are doing could provide benefits for her clients."

Roman took his eyes off the screen and asked, "I don't know what I'm looking at. I like your professional intuition and trust it. However, is this relevant?"

"I think so because what we are looking at may appear to be small outfits, but this could be hiding a bigger picture. Therefore, I think we should get Joel to investigate the companies behind what we found in her internet browsing history, right up to their parent companies. Of the ones that roll up into parent companies, he should look at the dollar value of their sales and the countries they operate in. What is their main source of income, main product groups, etcetera? And, most importantly, if any are based in Australia or have a considerable trade to or from our shores."

Jacob and Roman agreed with her.

"Excellent. How would he like this file, Roman?" Moya asked.

"Encrypt the file and save it with a title of travel arrangements, and we'll email it to him. Oh, and let me type in the password to decrypt."

Since this information was on Jacob's laptop, Moya tidied up the file and passed it over. Roman took over the keyboard, typed the encryption password, saved it and then opened the mailbox, typed in an email address and pressed send. He let them know that he would give Joel a call from a public payphone on the way home to let him know that he had an email and to give him instructions on what to look for.

Jacob shut down his laptop and finished his beer. Moya also packed up her laptop and informed them that she needed to get home to get some sleep. Roman agreed that he should be going home too.

As he turned to leave, Roman said, "I just realised that I have no idea where to find a payphone. I usually find them at transport hubs like airports."

Jacob and Moya looked at each other with lost expressions and said that they didn't even know if payphones existed anymore.

Roman shook his head, as if he was from an older generation. "Well, they do exist and are very handy if you want to

make a call that can't be traced back to you. I will try Glen Waverley railway station. It's a main hub, so it's bound to have
one."

Jacob replied, "But what about Joel, if he is answering the
phone with one listed under his name?"

"No wonder Elizabeth married you. You don't miss a beat.
You are right. We have a set-up for communicating. I'll give
him a call and ask about a sports match, which will seem like a
normal conversation to anyone listening. We have many codes
we can drop into normal chit chat. He will know to check his
email and then go to a designated payphone and give me a call
back. This may sound over the top, but nowadays, organised
crime is extremely sophisticated and it's the geeks that are running the show, not the muscle."

With that, Moya and Roman made their way out of the
front door. Roman promised to let them know as soon as he
heard anything.

Jacob was left alone with his thoughts and headed to the
kitchen to tidy up. He was tempted to make his way to the
couch and watch clips of him and Elizabeth. But he resisted
the urge as this had been his daily routine since her death and
it needed to stop. He knew if she was looking down on him,
she would be telling him to get off his arse and stop moping
around.

Reaching the kitchen, he saw on a shelf at the end of a
row of trendy cookbooks a photo of them looking relaxed at
a beach, with smiles that only reflected the possibility of good
times ahead. Pausing, he felt a sense of achievement. He did

find love. Love that was like nothing he could have imagined. Few people found this in their lives. No matter what happened, he had those memories, and no one could take that away from him. An old saying came to mind: "It is better to have loved and lost, than never to have loved."

CHAPTER 16

Roman was inspecting his scar with his T-shirt sleeve held up. Or, rather, the lack of a scar. Jacob was putting the sutures in the bin.

"Nice work, mate. I know who to come to if I ever get cut again."

Roman had called in to Jacob's place mid-afternoon after he had heard back from his mate Joel in New Zealand. Before he could even start to tell him the news, Jacob had insisted that they take out his stitches first. With this now done, Jacob returned to the kitchen and started to grind some coffee beans to make a pot of French-press coffee. He also went to the pantry and took out a packet of biscotti.

While the kettle boiled, he asked Roman, "Shall we give Moya a call and share all this with her as well?"

"Good point. I'll give her a call now."

Roman pulled out his phone and dialled Moya's number. She answered on the fourth ring and was pleased to hear his voice. Roman asked if she had time to come over. He didn't need to spell it out that he had heard back from Joel. She was at work and couldn't get away, but they promised to meet up that evening for a drink.

With the kettle now boiled and the water in the Bodum, Jacob placed the steeping coffee on a tray with the biscotti and mugs and headed to the outside courtyard.

"Let's sit outside since it's a nice day. I gather Moya can't come over."

"Yeah, she's at work but I'll fill her in on the details this evening."

Both took seats at the outside wooden table. Jacob raised the umbrella that protruded from the middle to provide some shade from the afternoon sun that was beating down with increasing heat.

Jacob lowered the plunger in the Bodum to force the ground coffee to the bottom and began to fill their cups. Roman placed Jacob's laptop on the table, opened it and turned it around for Jacob to enter his password. While Jacob did this, Roman started to tell him about what Joel had said.

"Joel sent me back the file, which he has sorted in alignment with our request and added further information. He started working on this last night and compiled the data this morning. We chatted before I came around and he said that one company stood out from all the rest. This company trades under different names and it seems that Elizabeth was searching goods under all their different entities and domain names. He said that there was no obvious type of good as this company has its fingers in everything from cheap knick-knacks to expensive ornamentals. He's included this in the results. There were other searches Elizabeth had done where two or three domain names were tied to companies that came under the umbrella of a larger parent company. However, it became clear she was focusing on one."

Jacob had the laptop up and running and turned it back to Roman, so he could access his email and open the file. While he did this, Jacob shuffled his chair around, so they could be side by side and view the screen together. With the file open, they saw what Joel was talking about. Clearly, there was one parent company that encompassed many different domain names. They scanned the list of domain names and confirmed that goods ranged from the cheap to the expensive. Jacob did not recognise any of these and he confessed that, unlike Elizabeth, he was not much of a shopper. He opened the original list with the domain names and the extended URLs to see the description of goods. He told Roman that most of these were things Elizabeth would not buy.

"Joel did not have time to get details of where this company traded from and how large it was," Roman continued. "It was not listed as a public company and Google results were awfully vague, which suggests that it may be a front or even part of a larger consortium. However, by the looks of it, this would be very large, and the main source of income would be the trading of goods. Another interesting fact Joel stumbled upon when looking at the complete browsing history was that Elizabeth was also searching these products from their origin as well as the stores that stock them. This is unusual, because if you're looking to buy stuff, rather than a retailer looking to import or export, you would simply search where to buy the items from. I'll check with Moya if this could be easily explained from a work point of view."

Roman added, "Joel will find out if they also manufactured any of the goods they exported, along with finding out where they are based for exporting to Australia and what companies in Australia bought from them. This could be too long a list to go through, so he will focus on those with high volume and dollar values, with the same criteria given to those that distribute them within Australia."

Jacob was cradling his coffee in both hands as if it were a cold winter's day. He took a long drink and asked Roman, "I still don't see how this could be related to Elizabeth's death, do you?"

"Good question, mate. I'm struggling with this as well. I keep thinking drugs or weapons. You keep hearing on the news how they find these things stashed away in normal household goods that are imported in shipping containers."

Jacob, still cradling his coffee like a child with a teddy, asked, "But what are we going to do with all this information from Joel?"

"We could investigate further ourselves, but I think we need to get in touch with Detective Adam Zhang and share what we have, as he might be already investigating along these lines."

Jacob nodded. "I agree. I have no idea what to do from here and we did agree to do a little digging to help the police."

Roman placed his coffee on the table and took a bite of biscotti. Still looking at the screen, he said, "We should probably agree now before we meet with Adam on what we are prepared to do and not prepared to do. Personally, I would like to continue until I feel I can offer no more to the investigation or the killer is found. What are your thoughts?"

Jacob took a second, released his coffee, and did a full-body stretch while still seated. He lifted his arms above his head, then lowered them down, rubbed his eyes under his glasses, and let out a groan as if his body had aged thirty years overnight. He pushed his chair back to fully stretch out his legs and felt his whole body relax in the warmth of the spring afternoon.

"I have a few thoughts," Jacob replied. "As you may have gathered, I don't have many close friends. Elizabeth was my world. I like all the people I work with and do occasionally socialise with them but none of them really know me. I have always been a bit of a loner. The friends I am closest to, I will catch up with every now and then, but we don't communicate every week or even every month. It hasn't been long since Elizabeth was taken away from me, but last night was the first time I didn't feel sorry for myself. I have had the great honour of finding your sister and loving her. I now fully appreciate the massive positive impact she has had on my life. Don't get me wrong, I will miss her until the day I die. I suppose what I'm trying to say is that you have been a big part in helping me finally feel this way. I see a lot of Elizabeth in you and being proactive in trying to understand why this happened is turning out to be great therapy for me."

Roman pushed his chair back and did a full stretch as well, taking in some of the sun as he moved out of the shade of the umbrella. "Cheers, mate. I feel the same."

Jacob continued, "So, to answer your question, I will continue to try to do my part. I'm in no hurry to get back to work full-time. I have so much leave banked up and my boss isn't expecting me to be back to a full-time workload any time soon. I'll give Adam a call and arrange for us to meet tomorrow. I know Moya would like to be involved, but I think we should not get her in too deep for her own safety."

"I agree. I'll let her know this evening what we've found and that we're meeting Adam to pass this on. I'll also let her know that she has been a tremendous help but best if she goes about her daily life as normal from here on in."

Jacob reached forward and turned off the laptop. "As for what I'm prepared to do, I'll do anything except get into fights."

They both laughed.

CHAPTER 17

Detective Senior Sergeant Adam Zhang was returning to his desk after giving an update on progress to his boss. He slumped into his chair and looked across to Detective Constable John Moskil, who had the look of "how did it go, boss?" on his face.

Adam took a sip of water from a metal reusable bottle that was a permeant fixture near his monitor. He knew that John was itching for an update, so he put him out of his misery.

"It's all good. He's pleased with how thorough we are being and the work you are doing. However, we need results. The media is wanting an update and they will only take the byline that 'the investigation is progressing well' for a limited time before they start hounding us for specifics. I let him know that we are catching up with Jacob and Roman in a few minutes. He also let me know that Detectives Olivia and Noah can remain assisting us on a full-time basis. Speaking of them, what are they up to today?"

"They have finished going through all available footage of that night, including any shop CCTV and road cameras. Now they are out conducting an interview that came through the hotline. I'm not that confident of this one as we've had no solid information or leads from this number," John said with a sigh.

Adam's phone vibrated, and he answered it. After listening for a moment, he said, "We'll be right down," and hung up. He stood up, placed the phone in his pocket, and picked up a notepad and pen from his desk.

"Jacob and Roman are here. Let's head down. The front desk has got us an interview room."

John grabbed his laptop and followed Adam to the lift. They were just in time to catch the next one down. A plain-clothed analyst who was also waiting held the door open with an outstretched arm when he saw them approaching.

"Thanks," said Adam. He had met the analyst before but couldn't remember his name.

There were another three people in the elevator with them and everyone was silent. Adam's thoughts turned to the dinner he had last night at his parents' place. They had asked about the case and how his career was going. He'd been feeling very tired and told them that he was working long hours, to which they replied that he needed to work harder. That was his parents. He was pretty sure other parents would have said to take it easy and not work so hard, but not immigrant parents. He respected this hard-working ethos. His parents also hounded him about his love life. They were concerned that he was not seeing anyone and were still devastated that he broke up with his last girlfriend of one year. She was from a good, hard-working Chinese family but there was no spark. He assured them that he would find a lovely girl to settle down with after he finished this case. Hopefully that would keep them off his back for a while.

The lift pinged, informing them they were on the ground floor. The doors opened, and they headed to the reception area, where they saw Jacob and Roman waiting. With pleasantries exchanged, they headed into a nearby interview room.

"You mentioned that you may have something that can assist us?" Adam asked as they took their seats.

Jacob and Roman looked at each other to see who would start talking. Roman took the lead and informed them of how they had researched Elizabeth's computer history with the assistance of Moya Connor and the conclusion they had come to.

John opened his laptop and took notes. When Roman had finished talking, Adam said, "Not sure how you came by all this information and it sounds like you've been busy. We are also going through all of this but are not near the results you have come to. We are considering the possibility that Elizabeth had uncovered the illegal smuggling of goods by one of her clients. However, we have only started considering this and are sifting through all sites searched on her personal and work computers and the companies behind these. It sounds like you are one step ahead of us in grouping these into parent companies. Why have you gone down this route?"

This time Jacob took the lead and answered.

"It was not uncommon for Elizabeth to spend a lot of time online shopping. When looking at the products, most appeared to be something she would not even consider buying. We were at a loss and it was Moya, with her knowledge, who suggested we consider the businesses behind the goods and who owns these. One clearly stood out, and that is why we have now come to you."

Jacob looked at Roman for reassurance and then informed the detectives of the company's name. While doing this, he noticed Roman pull his phone out of his pocket, swipe and press the screen with an engrossed expression. Looking at Roman, he asked, "Everything okay?"

"Sorry about that. I got an important email. Is there a payphone nearby?"

Adam and John both looked at him suspiciously, with John answering, "There's one just outside in the lobby. But why not just use the phone in your hand?"

"I'll explain later. I won't be long. By the way, can I borrow your pen and a bit of paper?"

Adam tore a sheet from his notepad and handed it to him, along with his pen. Roman got up from his seat and headed out the door. The room was left in an uncomfortable silence. Jacob tried to give a reassuring smile that fell flat. Adam broke the silence.

"Until Roman gets back, we have some questions. I realised that you and Roman would be doing a bit of investigating and I'm glad you've kept true to your word and kept us informed. But I'm surprised Moya is getting involved."

"She was a good friend and I've got to know her better. I wouldn't say she is involved. We were just having a chat over pizza and beer and the topic came up," Jacob answered, feeling a bit nervous about telling a partial truth.

Adam seemed to accept this, and although Jacob could tell he knew there was more to it, he seemed to recognise the fact that sometimes you don't need to know all the details.

Jacob looked towards the door with the hope that Roman would walk back in soon. He felt more comfortable with him by his side. Not wanting to answer any more questions, he decided to ask the detectives for an update on the investigation.

Adam filled him in on the progress they were making and how they had eliminated many potential leads and were liaising with many different departments within the police. He gave Jacob reassurance that they were using all available resources and checking all possible avenues.

John was halfway through telling him about all the CCTV cameras they had checked and how they had put together the movements of Elizabeth's car but had found no footage of a passenger in the car, when the door opened and Roman re-entered the room.

"Once again, sorry about that, but I have some good news."

Roman took his seat by Jacob with his phone still in his hand. He placed it on the table along with the piece of paper that now had scribbled writing all over it. He handed the pen back to Adam and placed both hands over the piece of paper as if protecting it in case a bird miraculously appeared and tried to take it away. He glanced at Jacob with a look of "we've got it" and faced Adam and John on the other side of the table.

Roman said, "What I've got written here is the country from where the clear majority of goods are exported to Australia, with Melbourne receiving the bulk of these in recent months. I also have the name of the company that exports these goods from this location and, surprise, surprise, they are owned by this parent company. As a bonus, I have the name of the receiving companies that distribute these goods in Melbourne and, to top it all off, I know that another shipment is due to set sail in a couple of weeks."

They all sat still with eyes locked on Roman's hands, waiting for the revelation that the piece of paper held. Roman moved his eyes, looked at them and took a moment for the pause to build effect. He broke the silence with a question.

"Is this room recording us in any way?"

"No, it is not," Adam replied.

"I will give you the information, but we want to be involved. We want to work together and assist you in areas where your hands may be tied or resources lacking. We have no intention of trying to be pseudo police, but we know that we can be of valuable assistance."

John moved his hands away from his laptop and interlocked his fingers with elbows on the table, knowing that no more notes needed to be taken at this point. Adam drew a clearly audible breath in and leaned back on his chair, placing his hands on his thighs. Jacob remained still and tried his best to look in control to mirror Roman.

Adam thought carefully and answered.

"Interesting. Let's not beat our chests or see who has the biggest dick. You do know that we can get all this information anyway, but since you already have this, it would be a waste of our resources. Also, technically, we could go down the road of you withholding information paramount to this case. Personally, I want you two involved and I never said I didn't. So, let's cut this crap and work together."

John glanced at his boss and quickly returned his glare back to Roman and Jacob to indicate that he agreed wholeheartedly with his boss.

Roman knew that Adam had rightly called his bluff. Impressed, he removed his hands from the paper and slid it over with his left. "Please write this down," said Roman, "as I will need that back."

Adam placed the paper on the table between himself and John. John moved his fingers back to the keyboard and typed up what was written. Once finished, his hands returned to the previously interlocked position, and Adam slid the piece of paper back to Roman's waiting fingers.

"Thanks for that," Adam said. "I'll immediately go and speak to the relevant department that can get us a copy of the manifest for this shipment and any prior. I'll be in touch with customs to try to raise a flag on these shipments and see what happens from there. However, there are limitations on what we can do without warrants and, judging by this, we do not have enough evidence, but I'll see what we can muster up."

Roman and Jacob appeared satisfied. They both pushed their chairs back, ready to get up and leave. Roman paused in mid-crouch, which caused Jacob to do the same.

"Please keep us updated on how it goes. You have our numbers, so feel free to call at any time. If you need any help, just ask, and we'll do the same."

Adam opened his mouth to reply but stopped himself short. It took him a split second to read between the lines. With everyone now standing, he extended his hand and thanked them.

CHAPTER 18

It was the next day. Jacob looked around his house and caught himself thinking of it as *his* house instead of *their* home. He was taken aback. Surely he was not moving on already. He felt a heavy weight of guilt pass over him as he turned off the vacuum cleaner and slumped into the nearest seat in the lounge. With the sound of heavy rain hitting the windows, he focused on a framed photo of himself and Elizabeth. He then looked at the clean, neat, and tidy house.

Elizabeth would have told him that the house didn't need to be so spotless, but he couldn't help himself. An orderly and clean house made him feel relaxed. From an early age, there were few aspects in his life he could control and, therefore, he became fastidious about his own belongings and space. Elizabeth realised this, so didn't complain. Elizabeth was not messy but it would not bother her if the bed was not made or dirty dishes were left on the bench.

He had spent the morning at the hospital, even though his boss had told him it was not necessary. Going to work took his mind off his grief and he enjoyed what he did. He was also enjoying the company of Roman and being in touch with Detective Adam Zhang, but this would end, and the only enjoyable aspect of his life would be work.

Walking over to the power point, he unplugged the vacuum cleaner and depressed the cord button, so it whipped back into place neatly out of sight. He picked it up and put it back in the cupboard, where he looked at the Dyson cordless vacuum hanging on the inside wall. Elizabeth was a huge fan of the cordless, which he also liked, but he still used the super-powerful corded one every now and then as he thought it did a superior job, even though he couldn't substantiate this. He gave a smile as he knew that if she were present, she'd laugh at him but still thank him with a big hug.

With this thought, he felt his guilt dissipate. This was their house and would always be their home. Their photos would remain where they were. Next time he vacuumed, he would use the cordless.

The doorbell rang, and he looked at his watch as he closed the hallway cupboard. Roman had arrived exactly when he said he would.

He opened the front door, and Roman quickly stepped inside to get out of the downpour of rain.

"Holy shit, it's pissing down," he said shaking the rain from his clothes like a happy dog after a swim.

"Yeah. The weather has turned shit this afternoon. However, it will no doubt clear up soon. Typical spring. Four seasons in one day."

Roman was holding a casserole dish, as promised. "Like I said, I've brought around some of the amazing stew I made the other night. Just needs heating up slowly and the meat will be dissolving in your mouth. Let's get the oven warmed up."

"Sound good. I never took you for one that likes cooking," Jacob replied as he took the dish and headed to the kitchen. "I'll put the rice cooker on now as well. Beer?"

"Sounds good. A true man knows how to cook. When I was out and about with the armed services, I couldn't wait to get back to my own place and spend time in the kitchen. I find it relaxing to follow new recipes, and, of course, nothing beats a good home-cooked meal."

When they were both in the kitchen, with the appliances turned on and beers in hand, Jacob asked Roman a question he'd been dying to ask.

"So, you caught up with Moya again. What's going on there?" he said with a cheeky glint in his eye.

"Mate. Nothing. She's a nice person and I consider her a friend. I'm sure she feels the same."

"I'm not sure of that. Be careful there as I've noticed how she looks at you. She doesn't look at me or anyone else like that."

"Point taken. But I don't think that is the case. I'll be careful but it's not exactly something you clarify when you start becoming friends with someone. Have you ever been hanging out with a female friend and asked if she fancies you in a sexual way?"

"Jeepers. That could be taken totally the wrong way and you could end up with a sexual harassment case against you, not to mention losing your job if she was a work colleague."

They both had a chuckle and a sip of beer. Roman looked at his watch and said, "Anyway, Moya and I had a chat about the information we obtained and gave to Adam. But mainly we talked about crap and had a laugh. Nonetheless, like I mentioned on the phone, Adam wants to talk to both of us, and I said we'd call him about now."

Roman took his phone out of his pocket and placed it on the dining room table. They both pulled out a chair and took a seat. He tapped the phone and swiped his finger through the contacts, tapped again to dial and put it on speaker.

"Hello, Detective Zhang speaking."

"Hey, Adam. It's Roman here, and I have you on speaker with Jacob beside me."

"Hey, mate, thanks for calling. I have some good news and not so good news."

"Okay, well, fire away," Roman replied as he shuffled in his seat and got himself comfortable.

"We traced the company you gave us and there were no flags already in place. Looks like a clean business from the outside. Customs have done routine scans in the past on the odd container and they have passed with no concerns. The receiving company that distributes the goods in Melbourne was investigated many years ago but nothing current. So, as you can tell, there is nothing to go on. I have absolutely nothing to go to my superiors with, apart from it's a possible lead that needs many hours of investigation time from various departments. This, of course, is viewed as dollars and the powers that be are currently weighing up how much money they can pump into this line of enquiry. The one positive is that my boss is more than happy for me and John to look further into this. However, our hands are tied without cross-departmental cooperation."

Jacob leaned forward. "Adam, we really appreciate the effort you are making. What are the chances you will get the resources to fully investigate this line of enquiry?"

"I wouldn't hold your breath. I would be more confident if something untoward had come up when looking at the companies, but there was zip, zilch, nothing. On the bright side, my boss wants no stone unturned in this case, so we will continue to investigate. He told me the chances of getting other departments on board with no evidence was next to nothing. They all have huge workloads and just as much pressure to deliver cost-effective results. The big thing now for me and John is to find something, just anything, that could give us some leverage. Customs have told me they will conduct a few more routine checks as a favour. But to put this in perspective, the Port of Melbourne is Australia's busiest port for containers, with over thirty berths for ships, and receives tens of thousands of containers a week. Therefore, what customs can check is only a drop in the ocean compared to volume. They will put on the resources and check more if there is an active, authorised investigation in place. This is usually done discreetly with only a handful of customs officers in the know, and they would be sworn to secrecy."

Roman and Jacob looked at each other while cradling their beers. Both wore a look of defeat. Roman took a sip, calmly placed his beer back on the table and replied, "You said you had good news and not so good news. All we seem to have heard is the not so good news. Are we missing something here?"

"We did say we'd be open with each other. I do have the exact location of where the shipping containers bound for Melbourne will be sent from and the warehouse where they are being prepared for shipping. This was courtesy of a mate in customs that owed me one."

"Can we get customs over there to check them out before they leave?" Jacob enquired.

"You would have better luck winning the lottery. We have nothing to go on apart from a hunch. Good hunch at that but still only a hunch. Also, we have no idea what we're getting ourselves into, so best that fewer organisations know at this stage."

"Still doesn't sound like that much of good news," Roman interjected.

"Fair enough," Adam replied after a moment's pause. "I've had a bit more time to think about this and I have done some positive reflection. We know exactly who the company is and the exact location of where the goods are being prepared for shipment. We know the company that will receive these and when they will receive them. We have full disclosure of the manifests. The manifests for the next shipment are an assortment of goods as expected. I have someone in customs to keep an eye out if anything changes, and he will keep this to himself.

These are the known facts and a very good starting point. We know what we need to progress this further and this is a positive."

Roman and Jacob nodded and verbally agreed.

"I don't have more to add," Adam said. "Our hands are tied, and it would be great to physically check these containers from both ends. We will rigorously pursue this avenue of investigation with the resources we have, and I can assure you that I am constantly badgering my boss for assistance from other departments."

"Can we get the details of what you have obtained?" Roman asked.

"Ethically, I cannot disclose full details, but once I know anything more, I'll let you know. Also, if you stumble across anything else, please get in touch."

They all said their goodbyes. Roman touched his phone to end the call, and left it on the dining room table. Jacob got up and made his way to the kitchen to put the casserole in. Roman reached to put his phone in his pocket, when it made a beep and the envelope icon appeared to indicate he had received a new email. He glanced at the screen and noticed that it was from someone he didn't recognise. He tapped the icon and opened the email.

Making his way back, Jacob saw Roman absorbed in his phone.

"Got a message from Moya, eh?" he jokingly asked.

"Not exactly." Roman paused for a couple of seconds and then lifted his head to make eye contact. "How would you like to go to Hong Kong?"

CHAPTER 19

The humidity and heat were producing constant beads of sweat that ran down their backs and front. They sat on plastic chairs by a roadside café that looked like it got most of its business from the workers in this industrial pocket of the city. Roman and Jacob sipped away on bottles of sweet iced tea. The bus stops were only a few metres away, and they knew exactly who they were keeping an eye out for.

After an early morning start and a nine-and-a-half-hour flight, they had landed in Hong Kong. The three-hour time difference this time of year meant they arrived mid-afternoon and, even though it was later in Melbourne, they had plenty of energy. They had done nothing on the plane, except watch a movie or two, catch up on sleep, and go over their plans. And as it was a short stay and the weather would be warm, they had only brought carry-on bags and didn't have to wait at the carousel for luggage. They caught the train into the city and checked into a hotel that had two rooms available but only one with a view of Victoria Harbour, which Roman let Jacob have. They wouldn't have any time for sightseeing, and Jacob appreciated the gesture. With plenty of time left in the day, they dropped their bags off and took only what they would require. Catching a taxi, they made their way to the area of Tsuen Wan.

Now they waited outside, enjoying the cold sugary drinks as they double-checked the printed photo of Tony Wang, an operations supervisor of the shipping company located across the road. He was not expecting them.

Detective Adam Zhang had emailed Roman after their chat. Using a made-up account, he had shared the exact address of where the next shipment would be prepared, also the load date and the manifest of goods that would be in the three containers. Roman had immediately contacted his business partner, Joel, in New Zealand and asked him to do some digging on who worked there and anything they could use to get inside. The next day, he came through with information that Jacob had no idea how he had managed to obtain. Roman reassured him that they were not breaking the law, rather bending the rules slightly. Jacob was starting to get an idea of the line of work Roman was in, when at first, he thought the organisation he worked for simply supplied muscle to the wealthy. Now he knew that security and protection were equally about information.

Joel had given them a detailed layout of the warehouse and adjoining offices, including security systems. Getting in would be near impossible without someone assisting them from the inside. Roman had laughed when Jacob had suggested they bluff their way in as they did in the movies, where security guards were gullible. Roman then sarcastically suggested they climb over the back fence. Jacob was also getting an idea of real life versus Hollywood. On the plane, they had gone over the plans repeatedly. They had an outcome they wanted and many scenarios on how this could be achieved. Which scenario they would use would be determined by how well they got to know Tony Wang.

Checking his watch, Jacob let Roman know that he should be leaving work anytime now. With eyes focused but looking like they were in a casual conversation, they soon saw him leave the building and make his way to the line of bus stops. Finishing their iced teas, they got off their plastic chairs and looked as nonchalant as possible while they walked to the same bus stop. It did not take long for Tony's bus to arrive and nine people boarded, including Jacob and Roman. They used their Octopus smart cards to tap on with the same swagger as a local. The bus was half full and Tony took a seat near the front, which couldn't have worked out better, for they moved past him and took a seat towards the back, where they could see him dismount the bus without raising suspicion.

The bus headed towards the northern outer suburbs, initially getting fuller until there was only standing room and then slowly emptying as people reached their homes. With the bus three-quarters full, Tony stood up near the front to get off at the next stop. They waited until the bus stopped and disembarked via the back door.

It was now that the crucial part of their plan needed to take place. They followed Tony, keeping their distance, with several people between them. According to the information Joel had gathered, Tony liked to drink. He was forty-six years old and not particularly good-looking. He was single and looked like he had concluded that he had missed the boat of finding someone to settle down with. He spent most of his evenings drinking and this had been noted by his employer, but it had not come at the detriment of his job performance. He also spent a considerable chunk of his spare time online gaming, with his favourite game being *League of Legends*.

Following him, they passed one bar and then another. They gave each other a sideways glance, as they thought he may head straight home, and then they would have to wait until tomorrow. If this was going to be the case, the next day, they would need to wait by the bus stop he got off as to not raise suspicion. Another bar was passed and then he headed into a relaxed, cheap-looking restaurant. Roman and Jacob carried on walking.

Once past the restaurant, they stopped and had a chat. They knew what they were going to do and needed to look like they were discussing where to have dinner. There were many white people in Hong Kong, but mainly around the central city and hotels, not in the outer suburbs. The chances of someone remembering them was high, so they were wearing short-sleeved shirts and chino trousers like many local office workers. Turning around, they headed back to the restaurant.

Tony Wang had taken a seat and was sipping on a bottle of San Miguel beer while engrossed in his phone. They entered the premises and were greeted by an overly eager teenage girl that was still in her school uniform, no doubt working for the family business. They took a seat at a table beside Tony's and ordered San Miguel beers while they studied the menu. It didn't take long before the two bottles were placed in front of them. They informed the girl they needed a bit longer to decide what to eat. Tony had not taken his eyes off his phone. They saw that the place was starting to fill up, with more than half of its dozen tables occupied and the three ceiling fans fighting a losing battle to keep the heat at bay.

They noticed that Tony did not have a menu on his table, so he may have already ordered or was just having a drink. They pondered the menu to stall, making small talk as if they worked in Hong Kong. Jacob was half-concentrating while mentally going over all the meticulous details they had planned and re-hearsed. This was Roman's terrain and the moves came naturally to him. For Jacob, it was like studying for his medical exams, but for this test, a pass rate of one hundred percent was mandatory. He viewed what they were doing as if it was a surgery where you had an end goal, but many different situations that could play out once the patient was on the operating table. Every possible scenario needed to have been studied and practised beforehand by all in the room.

Four minutes passed, and then the teenage waitress placed a plate of noodles on Tony's table. He did not acknowledge her as he continued to stare at his phone. Aware his food had arrived, he placed his phone down and pulled the plate towards him while still looking at the screen. Gathering his chopsticks, he tucked in.

The waitress was greeting a couple that had entered and gave them a menu as they selected a table and sat down. Roman raised his hand and captured her attention. She came over and took their order. They had worried about a possible language barrier, depending on who they encountered. However, their concerns were soon allayed, with most locals having been taught English and education still largely modelled off the British system.

In their peripheral vision, they could see Tony slurping down his noodles while fixated on his phone. The only time he took his eyes off the screen was to take a drink of his beer. They could not see what was on his phone, but it looked like he was watching something rather than interacting with someone. It did not take long before their meals arrived, which was noodles with chicken and an assortment of leafy vegetables on top.

Roman raised his voice slightly, just enough to be heard by the tables immediately beside them. "Last night I got into an awesome team in *League of Legends*. My kit was fully loaded, and I was almost on maximum level, when my team started to fail. Pity you couldn't have joined us."

"Sorry about that. Damn work took priority. This weekend I'm planning to do some serious game time. Do you want to come over to my place or just hook up online?"

"I'll come over and bring some beers. We need to get a regular team together and play onsite as I like it more when we are all in the same room."

"Totally agree," Jacob replied as they both dug into their food, using chopsticks with confidence but not at the dexterity level of the locals.

Out of the corner of their eyes, they saw Tony's attention move off his screen and he made a brief glance towards them as he took a drink.

To not lose the momentum, Roman continued, "We need to find decent players and maybe in the future enter one of those high-paying tournaments. I know a few players that are average, so what do you think of asking online for any experienced players that want to meet up? The pro teams are always in the same room and we need to do the same."

"That's sounds great. Let's try to take this to the next level."

They were aware that Tony was discreetly listening to their conversation while he ate. They continued the small talk about *League of Legends*. Given the limited time they had to read up on the game, download it and become familiar with how to play, they were doing quite well at coming across as serious, dedicated gamers. However, it was becoming apparent that Tony was the introvert they assumed he would be, and the chances of him introducing himself were going to be extremely slim.

Roman stood up to go to the toilet and deliberately bumped into Tony Wang's table, hoping to spill his drink but was unsuccessful. Tony looked up and Roman apologised. It was then he saw the breakthrough they needed. With quick thinking, he asked, "Is that a *League of Legends* tournament you are watching?"

Tony looked a bit hesitant but answered, "Yes, it is."

"You play?"

"I sure do. It's my favourite game."

"Same here. My mate and I were just talking about it. Do you want to join us for a drink?"

"Umm…" Tony seemed hesitant and took a good look at Roman and Jacob. "Okay. I'll just finish my meal."

Roman made his way to the toilet and caught an approving glance from Jacob. In the bathroom, Roman mentally went through what they needed to achieve, spending a few minutes going over the playbook in front of the mirror.

Returning, he took a drink and tucked in to finish the remainder of his meal, noticing that Jacob was nearly done. Tony was cleaning up the scraps on his plate at the opposite table.

"Come and join us as we're getting another beer. Would you like one?" Roman asked Tony as he turned his head with an inviting smile.

"Sure. That would be great," Tony replied and shuffled his chair over to join them.

"Hi, I'm Sam," said Jacob, using his fake name. "You've met Rob," he added, referring to Roman's alias.

"Hi, I'm Tony."

"Pleased to meet you," Jacob said.

Roman drained his beer and saw that Jacob had already finished his. He made eye contact with the waitress and indicated that they wanted a round of beers. She retrieved some beers from the fridge, placed them on the table and cleared away their plates.

They sat around drinking and chatting about *League of Legends*, comparing how often they played and swapping virtual war stories. It didn't take long before they were on their third beers. The gaming talk continued well into the fourth.

With the alcohol lubricating the inhibitions, Roman carefully changed the conversation by mentioning that he and Jacob were temporarily working in Hong Kong but would rather be gaming or doing anything else than working for their current boss. This proved to be a good strategy, with Tony following suit. Tony opened up about his job and how he was not overly happy with his employer. Jacob cottoned onto the tactical change and added how rich their boss was and how big business could probably get away with bending the rules and treating people like crap.

Tony felt comfortable in the company of fellow men that shared the same interests and had the same life challenges. He finished his fourth beer and casually revealed that there was probably some dodgy shit going on at his work.

Roman, wanting to encourage Tony to keep talking, caught the attention of the waitress and got a fifth round of beers. He also noticed that there were only three tables of people left, including them, and it looked like the staff wanted to close soon. He checked his watch and saw that just over three hours had passed since they had first sat down. Roman finished his beer and saw that Jacob's was still half full. He mentioned that they were pretty sure that they had seen their boss meet some rather shady looking people.

Jacob nodded and confirmed that they had, with one guy looking like he was straight out of the movie *Goodfellas*. They all had a laugh. The beers got placed on the table and Roman and Tony drained the last of their fourth and started their fifth. As if on cue, Tony continued the conversation.

"Well, I haven't seen mafia-looking people, but some strange shit does happen." His language loosened up the more he joined in. "I supervise the loading of containers ready for shipment, and it is pretty important to make sure everything is loaded and accounted for. A lot of businesses don't have the space to load up on-site and many businesses share containers, hence sending their goods to us. Anyway, the company has a rule that all staff finish by nine in the evening, but it can vary depending on seasonality of workload."

Tony took another drink and, as if side-tracked, commented that he felt bloated with all the beer and could do with a whiskey next. Jacob, not being a big drinker, was struggling to keep up. He knew he could not keep on drinking and needed to keep his wits about him.

"Yeah, I'm getting bloated too," Jacob added. "So, what's so dodgy about a workplace closing?"

"Nothing. I totally understand from a safety point of view. However, one night I forgot my phone. It was a Friday and I had the weekend off. I went back late at night to get it. There is security there twenty-four hours a day, seven days a week. Naturally the security guys were there and made a phone call rather than just let me in. I thought they would just let me in and maybe accompany me while on premises, which they had done before. It was strange that the guy made a phone call. He asked me exactly where I had left it and informed me that a security guard would get it and bring it down to the lobby. He was very firm that this was the only way I could get my phone. Anyway, it didn't take long for my phone to arrive. As I was leaving to catch the bus, I thought I'd have a look around, as I could hear that there was a bit of activity with machinery running, like forklifts. Well, I only caught a glimpse through a window, and this confirmed what I could hear. The security guard ran up to me and walked me out. I was a little bit drunk and used this as an excuse."

"Mate, doesn't that sound dodgy?" Jacob replied, noticing his Australian accent really coming through, thanks to the San Miguel beers.

"I asked the other operations supervisors if they ever worked after hours, and they confirmed that they didn't, but knew that sometimes work did carry on. They suspected that extra shipments were done and maybe they were urgent," Tony said as if trying to impress Jacob and Roman. Feeling a bit insecure, he added, "Not a great story, I know, but it just seems a bit dodgy to me. However, I've learned to be like the others and ignore it. So, do you want to get together as a team for *League of Legends*?"

Jacob and Roman agreed and got his phone number. They wanted to probe more into what he thought happened after hours.

Tony wanted to talk about gaming and excused himself to go to the toilet. While he was gone, Roman leaned in to Jacob and asked how he was feeling.

"I can't carry on drinking, or else you'll be carrying me back to the hotel. I don't think we'll get much out of him, and I'm struggling to remember our made-up names. I was going to call you Roman before."

"Let's remember our strategies. We'll get another drink or two and try to get more out of him. We'll get some whiskey when he comes back, and if you want, take a sip and then spit it into your beer bottle looking like you're having a beer chaser."

"Good idea, but I think this place is wanting to close up."

"No worries. There's bound to be a bar nearby. I'll make sure we have beer and whiskey on hand, so you don't get too pissed."

There was bar close by. Unfortunately, the part about not getting too drunk wasn't the case, and the night continued well into the wrong side of midnight.

CHAPTER 20

The knock on his door made Jacob get out of bed. He had been lying there with his eyes closed, praying that the headache would go away. He looked at the clock and saw it was late morning, so he knew he should be making a start to the day. He peeled himself off the sheets and shuffled to the door, trying to minimise the impact of his feet hitting the floor and reverberating to his skull.

He opened the door a crack and saw Roman, dressed and looking a hell of a lot better than him.

"Morning. I come bearing gifts," Roman said as he nudged the door open with his foot, holding two cups of coffee and a packet of paracetamol.

"You're a legend," replied Jacob. He freed one of the coffees from Roman's hand and took the paracetamol.

Jacob sat on the bed, grabbed a bottle of water from the bedside table, popped a couple of pills and downed them in one continuous gulp. He held his coffee like his life depended on it as he faced Roman, who had parked his bottom on the swivel desk chair by the built-in tabletop that housed the television, phone, power, and data points, with just enough spare room to place a laptop.

"As you can tell, I'm not much of a drinker," Jacob sighed.

"Either am I. Trust me—I'm not feeling the best, but it looks like you may win in the hangover stakes." Roman raised his coffee to salute Jacob's hollow victory.

Jacob took the lid off his disposable coffee cup, so it could cool down quicker and the caffeine could flow through his body without delay. Blowing and sipping, blowing, and sipping, he felt the warmth and effect take hold like a drug user getting his fix. After the third sip, which was longer than the previous, he started the conversation.

"So, what do we do now? It didn't exactly go to plan last night."

"I wouldn't say that. Sure, we did not get clear-cut answers, but we still learnt a lot." Roman got up as if to start a presentation on an invisible whiteboard. "Let's go over what we found out and then decide where to go from here."

"Good idea. Just as long as the next step doesn't involve drinking."

"Mate, I don't want that either." As if Roman realised there was no whiteboard, he returned to the swivel chair. "The main thing we learnt was there probably is something amiss going on. Tony Wang doesn't know much, or he's not willing to say much, and if that is the case, I seriously doubt he'll open up to us even after a dozen nights on the ale. So, what do we know?"

Roman raised his fist to shoulder height and extended out his thumb to indicate the first fact. "We know that if anything is going on and the goods in the containers are being tampered with, then it is happening at night. We know that security is exceptionally tight, which you would expect, but it seems even more so at night. The operations supervisors sign off the goods once loaded, and since Tony is one of them and talks to his peers, it appears that they are not involved. Therefore, whatever is going on is at a very senior level and kept within a tight circle. We know through Tony that the containers for Melbourne are being loaded today and ready for transport to the docks tomorrow. We also know that he will sign these off, which was a great piece of information you managed to out of him."

Roman finished with all five fingers extended and raised his other fist for points six to ten. He asked Jacob if he could think of anything else. Jacob finished his coffee and placed the empty cup beside the disposable lid on the bedside table.

"Let me think. I believe Tony was telling us the truth and is a straight-up guy. I used all the skills I learnt in my medical training and career on how to control a conversation and get information in a friendly, non-threatening way. I kind of like the guy and don't want him to get into trouble. The only thing I can add is that we only have tonight to figure out what is happening, and even if we do, we need to have something concrete to give to Adam so he can convince the powers that be that it is worthwhile quarantining the three containers when they hit Melbourne, and go through them with a fine-tooth comb."

Roman agreed. Jacob concluded that, upon reflection, the night was relatively successful. They were hoping to get an opening for an excuse to visit Tony at work and have a look around—less suspicious if you enter a workplace during the day and by invitation. This option faded as it became apparent how secure the facility was. They had also hoped to get some juicy facts from Tony, but this hope faded when it became apparent that he knew nothing and had no interest or curiosity in digging deeper.

Jacob was starting to look and feel a bit better after the coffee. The paracetamol had kicked in and his head was feeling less like a construction site. He asked Roman what he thought they should do now.

"I think you are right in that we need something to give to Adam. What we have now is so circumstantial, even I wouldn't act on it. We need to get something. When I initially viewed the information Joel gave us, I saw they have a state-of-the-art security system and it would be near impossible to break in without getting caught or someone knowing about it. It appears that there are limited views into the warehouse, if any. I was thinking of planting discreet spy cameras in the warehouse if we were to make it inside. These could have given us a feed online, but it would have required batteries, and these would only last a day or two, unless we went for bigger battery sources. But, then, they would become too obvious. Another downside to this is that we would need to retrieve the cameras so they're not found later on, and I think we can agree that this would be far too risky. I was still thinking of getting inside by invite or maybe breaking in, but I now realise that this would be impossible without getting caught and I would rather depart Hong Kong leaving no trace, and not end up in jail."

"I agree. We've been so careful, and it would be stupid to risk that now," Jacob added.

Roman leaned back in the swivel chair and drained the last of his coffee. "Why don't you go and have a shower? While you're doing that, I'll review the layout of the premises on your laptop using the file Jacob sent us. I will also go online and look at the area in general, including the buildings nearby, to see if there are any vantage points we can utilise. If there is, we'll do a stakeout tonight."

"Sounds good," replied Jacob as he reached into his bag and pulled out his laptop for Roman. He then continued to the bathroom. "I will be a while as I'll have a shave."

"Take your time. When you're finished, we should go and get something to eat. I'm thinking of a big English breakfast as I need a greasy feed."

"You've read my mind."

Jacob disappeared into the bathroom and closed the door. Roman placed the laptop on the small desk space and fired it up. The first thing he saw was the screen wallpaper, which was a photo of Elizabeth smiling without a care in the world, a look of absolute bliss and happiness on her face with a clear blue-sky background. He had not seen this photo before. He was struck by how content she looked and how many of those moments he had missed. Looking at the photo, he could feel her presence—his big sister who loved him.

Roman went into his email and opened the layout of the factory. He could see the large open space where the containers got prepared before heading to the docks. He also opened a file that showed the specifications of the security system along with the locations of the cameras and motion sensors. He picked up his coffee for a sip and noticed it was empty, so he tossed it into the rubbish bin. He could do with another one but would have to wait until they got something to eat.

Staring at the screen, he went over the plans again and again. It was not the first time he had studied them and he looked at them as if the power of concentration could miraculously make a kink in their security system appear. Unfortunately, no such kink materialised. Recalling their drunken conversation with Tony, the manpower on site overcompensated for the system in place. He went over it again, focusing on the cameras around the perimeter, and as he expected, there were no gaps in the coverage. The coverage included vision all the way to the neighbouring buildings and streets.

Roman opened Google Maps and zoomed in on the area, switching it to satellite view. There was one possibility of obtaining a view from high up and that was on top of one of the many high-rise apartment buildings. He was unsure of how easy it would be to gain entry, and they would require high-powered binoculars, preferably digital ones that could record. He moved the image around and pinpointed the building that would be perfect. It looked to be about thirty storeys high. He tore off a piece of paper from the hotel notepad, got the complimentary pen and wrote down the address.

Roman closed the programs to return to Elizabeth on the wallpaper. A pang hit his heart. He could not take his eyes off his sister and the lump he felt in his throat at the funeral returned. He hadn't been there for her, and a good way to start to right the wrongs was to find her killer. The sound of the bathroom door opening brought him back to reality. Not knowing how long he had been staring at the screen, he shut it down before Jacob entered the room. Back in the present, he got into work mode. They had a bit to do before they could start his latest plan of attack. But first, it was time to get something to eat.

CHAPTER 21

The city lights fought back the darkness of the Hong Kong night. Roman and Jacob were perched on the rooftop of the thirty-four-storey apartment block, confident no one could see them, and they took out the binoculars they had purchased that afternoon. They had a clear line of sight to the shipping warehouse and, as per the plans, there were evenly laid out transparent roofing panels to allow natural light into the workplace. Roman adjusted his binoculars and zoomed in with a smile on his face. He informed Jacob that these panels were see-through and not frosted. Now they needed to wait.

Earlier that day, after they'd had their greasy meal they went shopping. It was in the third electronics shop that they found high-powered digital binoculars with built-in memory. They weren't cheap, and they split the cost, buying one each. Jacob was quite stoked with the purchase, like a boy presented with a cool digital toy. He had always wanted something like this but could never justify the cost. Now he could take them to the footy and sightseeing. Like two kids, they left the shop wanting to play with them straightaway. They caught the cable car up to the top of Victoria Peak and got comfortable with the functions of the binoculars while taking in the panoramic views of the city and harbour.

For the rest of the day, they worked on their plan of how they would gain access to the apartment building and, ultimately, make it to the roof. They came to the consensus that they would stick out too much as outsiders and would need to look like they belonged in the building. They could use the short-sleeve shirts and suit pants they had worn the night before, but they did not feel comfortable with this. They sat in the shade of an outdoor area by a shopping complex and bounced ideas off one another. Drinking ice-cold bottled water, Jacob told Roman he had the perfect idea, while his eyes focused on two guys over Roman's shoulder. He told Roman to turn around and look. Roman did so, and then they went shopping again.

They got to the apartment building late afternoon after eating street food from a nearby stall. There was no time for a sit-down meal. They had packed some snacks and extra bottles of water into Jacob's backpack as they prepared for a long night.

Arriving at the building while it was still daylight suited the image they were portraying. Dressed in high visibility T-shirts, with Roman carrying a toolbox, they tailgated occupants that were returning from work and entering through the swipe-card access front doors.

No one gave them a second look, as no doubt the sight of workman going in and out of the building was a regular occurrence. They both wore caps to be on the safe side against

CCTV cameras and this also blurred their Caucasian features. Well, one girl who looked to be in her twenties eyed up Roman, which Jacob was getting used to. He couldn't compete with his good looks and buffed body that members of the opposite sex were immediately attracted to.

The lift was full, and luckily the occupants did not need to swipe a card to access any floors. Roman hit the button for the top floor and they were the only ones left when it arrived. They made their way to the fire exit and proceeded up the stairs to the roof. The door was locked, as expected. Roman placed the toolbox on the floor and opened it to reveal an assortment of tools required to pick a lock. First, he had a thorough look around the door to see if there were any alarms. There were none. Not that this would have stopped them, as he was prepared for any situation. Within a minute, he had the door opened. They proceeded onto the roof and stayed by the walled structure of the raised exit to conceal themselves. The roof had raised edging around the perimeter approximately half a metre high, which was more than ample for them to stay behind once darkness fell.

With the blanket of night upon them, they were now looking down on the warehouse, trying their best to see any activity through the skylight roof panels. They waited patiently.

An hour went by and they took turns to have a drink and a snack. After two hours, Jacob saw some movement. He nudged Roman, who immediately took up his position. Zooming in, they could just make out people coming and going from their limited scope of vision.

Roman leaned into Jacob and whispered, "I'm pretty sure that the containers bound for Melbourne are through the third skylight panel on the left and four rows up. I'll concentrate on this view and you scan the other skylights. Hit record if you see any goods go in or out of a container."

"Will do."

Twenty-five minutes went by, which felt like an hour and twenty-five minutes, before Roman gave Jacob a tap and depressed the record button. Jacob altered his view and could see three guys taking some packaged goods from an open container. A forklift made its way over to take out something large.

"I've got this view. See if you can follow the forklift," Roman instructed as they both saw the hand-held goods and forklift head off in different directions.

"Got it."

Both were now recording. Roman saw the hand-carried goods placed on the floor and unpacked to reveal what looked like home ornamentals. It was then that Roman noticed similar-looking items that were already on the ground. The vision was not clear as the guys moved around on the floor like worker ants, but it looked as if the items were being swapped before they were repacked and placed back into the containers.

Jacob saw the forklift place a crate on the floor and then pick up another one and take that back to the container.

They observed this happening again in a similar fashion. It was clear that goods were being offloaded and then replaced with others. This happened to four containers, with Roman pretty sure that two of them were destined for Melbourne. He was grateful that Tony had let it slip that the warehouse floor was zoned into different areas depending on the destination. Being from Australia, they had asked where their zone was, and Tony informed them of the large, bold number coding that was used to ensure no mistakes were made. What seemed like an innocent question revealed the number code for Melbourne that was plastered on the side of the containers.

Roman turned to Jacob. "We've probably only got another five minutes of space for recording, but I'd like to still observe once the memory is full."

"I agree."

"Mate, is that your stomach rumbling?" Roman asked.

"Yeah, it is. Not sure if it's 'cause I'm hungover or it's from that food we ate," replied Jacob, placing his right hand on his stomach while holding the binoculars to his eyes with his left.

"Mate, that stinks."

"Sorry, I've been farting all night. My gut is not feeling good. I think we should leave as I need to find a toilet." Jacob held his stomach. He switched off his binoculars and placed them in his backpack.

Roman was still focusing on the warehouse. "Can it wait for a few minutes? I can see a few of the guys more clearly now as they head out of the building."

Jacob felt the stomach cramps come on stronger and was crippled over. Not wanting to waste the time they had on the roof, he struggled to sit still. As his stomach churned away, he felt an intense cramp ease with a thump to his rectum. He knew what that meant and the predicament in which he found himself.

"Fuck. I've got to go now!" he said through clenched teeth, not wanting to be too loud.

Roman heard the desperation in his voice and dumped his binoculars in the backpack while saying, "Vomit or shit?" He wasn't mincing his words as he saw the discomfort on Jacob's face.

"Shit. I can't wait. *Fuck*. Where am I going to go?"

"There's no toilet up here. Go by the corner of the roof where there's a drainage hole."

"*Fuck, fuck, shit*," Jacob half-screamed, half-whispered, as he quickly made his way to the corner doubled over.

Finally there, he dropped his pants in record time and instantly relief came over him as his insides exploded out of his arse like someone had smashed the top off a fire hydrant. It was all over in what felt like a split second and he could feel the sweat on his forehead, along with his racing pulse, start to decrease. After some deep breaths, it dawned on him that he had nothing to wipe his bottom with.

Roman was trying his best to stifle his laughter as he crouched and made his way over to Jacob.

"Mate, clean yourself up with this," he said as he tossed him a bottle of water. "How are you feeling?"

"Cheers. I'm feeling heaps better now. Must have been something I ate. My gut isn't as strong as yours. Now can I have some privacy?" he said as he saw Roman trying to repress his laughter.

Roman turned and made his way back to their observation point to collect their backpack and toolbox. He kept as low as possible in case anyone saw them.

Jacob did the best he could to clean himself with the water, and with it all gone, he had no choice but to just pull up his pants and ride it out until he got back to the hotel for a hot shower. He shuffled his way back to Roman, feeling gross and knowing that his downstairs was not fully clean. But he was grateful that the cramps had gone.

"So sorry about that," Jacob said with a look of embarrassment.

"No worries. Nothing to worry about. I've seen worse and, believe me, I've had to do it myself more than once. Look on the bright side. At least you get to go straight back to a hot shower. I've had that happen to me and still had to wait two days until I got a shower. Plus, I had to do it in a plastic bag and carry it out."

Jacob slowly started to feel a bit better. But only a bit better as he would always be embarrassed by what had happened. He picked up the backpack while Roman did the same with the toolbox.

"Thanks for trying to make me feel better, but please don't mention this to anyone. We can stay a bit longer if you like?"

"All good. We've seen enough, and the memories are full. Let's just hope it rains soon to wash it all away."

They both let out a faint laugh and made their way over to the door. Jacob noticed that Roman was still laughing when they reach the stairwell. Heading inside and down the stairs to the top floor lobby, Jacob finally asked, "What's so funny? You can't stop laughing."

"Let's get back down and then I'll tell you."

Jacob tried his best to concentrate on getting out of the building. There was no one in the lobby, so they were the only ones to get into the elevator. With the doors closed, and a smirk still on Roman's face, he asked again.

"What is it? I don't smell, do I?"

"Nah, you don't smell. Sorry. I'll tell you later. Let's just get out of the building."

The lift stopped on the twenty-first floor and an elderly couple got in. They all rode down to the ground floor in silence.

They made their way out of the building and into a late-night neighbouring mall, where they headed to the toilets and changed out of their high-visibility T-shirts and back into their normal tops. They removed a plastic bag from the backpack and placed these inside, along with their caps. Jacob also used this time to clean up a bit in the toilet.

They walked to the bus stop, where Roman placed the plastic bag in a rubbish bin. The sky started to rumble with distant thunder. Roman let out another laugh and whispered to Jacob, "One good thing about Hong Kong is that you know a heavy downpour of rain is always around the corner. The roof will get a good clean."

"I'm glad. Can't wait to get back to the hotel and have a shower. Please promise you won't mention this to anyone."

"Mate, I promise. Besides, I'd then have to explain why we were on the roof of a building."

As they waited for the bus, Roman giggled as he looked back towards the building.

"Come on. It can't still be that funny? What is it?"

"I was going to wait until we got back to the hotel, but I'll tell you now." Roman raised his voice as heavy raindrops started to fall and crash onto the corrugated roof of the waiting area they were huddled under. The noise was loud and the few others also waiting could not hear them talking. Leaning in, he informed Jacob, "Let's just say that not all of it stayed on the roof. Some of it made the height and distance to clear the ledge." Roman laughed like a schoolboy trying not to raise the attention of the teacher. He added, "It was only a few drops, and I couldn't see anyone looking pissed off when we left, so no doubt it didn't hit anyone."

Jacob was initially mortified but quickly saw the humour in it and broke into laughter that he also tried to muffle like a naughty schoolboy. The bus arrived but the laughter continued.

CHAPTER 22

The phone rang, and Jacob answered it. Detective Senior Sergeant Adam Zhang was returning his call. It was another warm, pleasant morning in Melbourne and Jacob was sitting outside having a late breakfast. He got home late after his afternoon flight from Hong Kong was delayed and didn't land until nearly midnight. They had spent an extra day in Hong Kong due to not getting a flight straightaway. They spent the day sightseeing around the coast of Lantau Island, visiting temples and old fishing villages. They had paid for everything with credit cards, leaving as much of a digital footprint as possible. They also did this when they got the tram to test the binoculars and anything else that was remotely touristy. This was Roman's idea, to make their trip look like a holiday.

Jacob told Adam to hold the line while he went inside. He did not want any neighbours to hear what he had to say. Once inside, he thanked him for returning his call.

"Roman and I would like to meet with you, if that is okay. We have some information and evidence that will assist."

"Of course. I have back-to-back meetings in the afternoon. How about I come over now? I am already kind of out that way as I've been visiting a colleague at the Box Hill station."

"Yeah, that would be good. I'll get in touch with Roman and tell him to come over."

With that, they hung up and Jacob immediately phoned Roman. Jacob knew that it would take about ten minutes until they got to his place, so he headed back outside to finish his breakfast. His coffee was still warm as he took his seat. He picked up his knife and fork and finished his poached eggs on an English muffin, while music from Led Zeppelin's album *Houses of the Holy* came from the speakers in the lounge.

He reclined back in his chair under the shade of the outdoor umbrella and lost himself in the hypnotic melody of "The Rain Song". He thought of Elizabeth and the many lazy mornings they had spent outside over late breakfasts.

The doorbell chimed and woke him from his tranquil thoughts. He got up, gathered his plate and cup, and headed indoors. He placed the dirty dishes on the kitchen bench, picked up the remote and turned the stereo off. The doorbell chimed again as he made his way down the short hallway. Turning the handle, he saw that Roman and Adam had arrived at the same time.

"Sorry about the wait. Come in."

They headed inside, where Jacob and Roman informed Adam of their trip to Hong Kong. If Adam was surprised, he did not show it. They inserted a USB memory stick into the television and showed him all the footage they had obtained.

Adam did not ask any questions about how they got onto a roof or how they knew that the operations supervisors that signed-off on the containers were none the wiser. It was best he did not know.

After they finished their presentation, Adam leaned back, placed his hands on his head and let out a big breath. Then he returned to a forward-seated pose.

"As usual, you guys surprise me. What you have is useful but still very circumstantial. Not hard evidence, and I'm not sure if it would even be admissible in court, but we won't go down that road as I don't want to ask questions. However, if you will allow me to show my boss, we may be able to get customs to do a thorough check on the three containers that are due to arrive within a week."

Jacob stood up, retrieved the UBS memory stick and handed it to Adam.

"You can keep it. We have copies. Any questions, just give us a bell."

Adam thanked him and leaned back and slightly to the side as he placed it in his trouser pocket. He checked his watch and said, "I have to leave soon, but before I do, I have some questions. I hope this amounts to something, as every theory and lead we have chased down has amounted to jack. If this is the break we are looking for, the question needs to be asked as to why Elizabeth was looking into this. The forensic accountants are still ploughing through the company she worked for and I have instructed them to consider anything and everything that relates to this trading company. There must have been a red flag somewhere that alerted her. If it is illegal goods, then this can easily be hidden in financial records. Maybe they made a mistake and she came across it? How they knew she had done this is beyond me, and the big question of who pulled the trigger is a whole other kettle of fish."

Roman agreed with him but reminded Adam that a motive was a bloody good place to start. Roman didn't really care if they were smuggling class-A drugs, weapons, or noodles with high salt content. He only wanted the person that killed his sister.

Adam reminded him that this was a police matter and he would make any arrests, not him. "The last thing I want is to have to put you in handcuffs. While I appreciate the help, you need to be careful. Evidence needs to be obtained lawfully. We don't want whoever did this to walk free on a technicality."

They all nodded to show they were in agreement.

Checking his watch again, Adam stood up and excused himself. He reiterated that he was extremely thankful for the assistance they were giving him, but to be very careful and keep him informed. "I'll show myself out and let you know how it goes," Adam said as he disappeared down the hallway.

Jacob and Roman heard the front door open and close. Jacob then asked Roman if he wanted a drink. He declined but asked Jacob, "How do you feel about how this is going?"

Jacob was taken aback by this open question and thought for a few seconds before he replied. "I have no idea how a murder investigation normally goes. I can see that Adam is doing everything he can. We should remember that it is one thing to know who killed Elizabeth but another to get a conviction. I get the feeling he has a lot on his mind and is no doubt keeping some things close to his chest."

"Yeah, I agree. I think we did bloody well in Hong Kong. I'm itching to know what they find in those containers. Are you going back to work anytime soon?"

"I'm going to head in tomorrow and work part-time for a while. Take on a few patients. My boss wants me to be one hundred percent before I return full-time. Well, one hundred percent focused on the job, as I'll never be the same after what has happened. He wants me to see a psychologist to make sure I'm on track and no doubt cover the hospital's arse if I lose the plot."

Roman joined him in a giggle about this but added, "I think it will do you good. Nice to have a caring workplace. I've seen many people say and act like they are fine after a traumatic event and then have a breakdown or never fully get back into the real world. I'll let you in on a secret."

Roman paused to build the anticipation before he continued. "I've seen someone a few times since her death. I find it useful to get things off my chest and get some guidance on my feelings. Don't want to destroy my tough-guy image but you'd be surprised how common this is nowadays."

"Wow. I would never have guessed. Thanks for telling me. I'll make sure I turn up to my appointment. Are you heading back to New Zealand and work soon?" Jacob asked.

"I'm getting along really well with my parents and they want me to stay on for a while. I've told them I will. My work is cool with me taking time off." Roman stood and looked out the window. "It's a nice day. Got any plans?"

"None."

"Do you want to catch up with Moya for dinner? She's a nice person and we can find out how her work's going."

"Sounds good. We could head into the city and have dinner outside somewhere by the Yarra River."

Roman agreed and headed towards the door. He told Jacob that he'd call her and then let him know. "Best if we don't tell her everything about Hong Kong. Just say we went for a holiday to get away from it for a while. Saw some sights, ate lots of food, and sweated enough to fill a paddling pool."

"Sweet. The shitting myself story won't come up then."

They laughed and Roman left.

Jacob returned to the lounge and put Led Zeppelin back on. Then he picked up his phone and headed back outside to chill out and read the news.

CHAPTER 23

Sitting at his desk, he looked out his window at the Hong Kong city landscape as the morning sun peeked out over the tops of buildings, making its way higher in the sky. He was not in the tallest building, but he was on the top floor. The view did not really interest him. It was more about the status symbol of being on the top floor of a building with a view. One thing he did like was being able to watch others from a great height, as if he was a king looking down on his kingdom.

He looked back at his computer and eyed the new Rolls-Royce Phantom on the screen. He had the previous model and needed to upgrade before others noticed that he was not being driven around in the latest. Being British, he took pride in being chauffeured around in the best you could buy from his home country. He picked up his desk phone and told his personal assistant to make the order.

Five minutes later, his personal assistant knocked on his door and entered, as he did every morning at the same time when his boss was in town. The personal assistant took his coffee cup and saucer from his desk, which he'd made sure was placed there moments before he arrived, so it was still hot from the café located in the lobby of the building. He informed his boss of his schedule for the day and asked if there was anything else he would like him to do.

Thomas Rayner asked his assistant to arrange a lunchtime meeting with the head of their security company and to make sure it was in a private room. He trusted him to pick an appropriate restaurant, like he always did.

He thanked his assistant and waited until he had left the office before making his way from his desk to a nearby burgundy premium full-grain leather three-seater Moran sofa with hand-studded curved arms. Sitting down, he picked up his tablet from the recycled-wood coffee table and started reviewing the documents for his first meeting of the day.

Thomas had started his company straight out of university, where he studied business at the University of St Andrews in Scotland. He set up in London in a tiny office and negotiated trade deals on behalf of small businesses. He enabled these small businesses to work together to lower their costs and improve their buying power. The fees he charged were easily offset by the savings he offered them. His contacts grew and, after a year, he needed new offices to employ staff to help maintain and grow his expanding enterprise. This type of business was being done by many other companies, but what set him apart was his ruthlessness in getting the deal. As his global contacts and clientele grew, he knew his power at the negotiating table was also growing, and he took full advantage of it. However, he was also a fair man and those that treated him well were also treated well, and were often given expensive gifts and incentives, which could also be brought up at the negotiating table, if required.

After twelve years based in London, he made the move to Hong Kong to expand his empire into the ever-increasing Asian market. He still had an office in London to manage the Europe side of his company, but his move to Hong Kong proved to be a stroke of genius. He quickly established strong relationships that couldn't have been forged over the phone or through fly-in, fly-out meetings. The Chinese believed in strong personal connections and dealing with someone locally based. He made regular trips to Beijing, Shanghai, and many other cities on the mainland. He had arrived in Hong Kong at a crucial time to make the most of the Chinese economic boom. Now at the age of fifty-seven, and having been in Hong Kong for twenty-three years, he had amassed a fortune, had hundreds of employees and traded in anything from cheap plastic goods to high-end collectables. He had expanded into freight companies and logistics. His company was a powerhouse for businesses wanting to import or export goods within Asia and Europe.

Thomas Rayner loved the money but to him, that was just a scorecard. He had seen many businesses come and go and often had a hand in the failure of those that didn't make it. The more money he amassed, the better he felt, and it felt even better if he had control over others to make that money.

He was briefly married once and, looking back, he only married because he thought he should. He was never at home and always had escorts visit him in hotel rooms. He never understood the whole concept of love and wanting to spend all your time with one person. To him, work was life and sex was sex.

Thomas got up from his couch and made his way to his closet to retrieve his suit jacket. He put it on and picked up his tablet from the coffee table. His office assistant knocked, popped his head in and informed him that a private table was booked for lunch at one, and all details were in his calendar. Thomas thanked him and made his way to the elevator. He used to have female assistants, mainly because they were pleasant on the eye. However, he grew tired of them trying to have personal conversations with him, the raised eyebrows when organising the transport for hookers, and the fact that they often got emotional when he was having a stressful day and taking it out on all around. He had an extremely wealthy and successful friend who had a male assistant. Over their long alcohol-fuelled lunch, he was told of all the advantages of a male assistant, and with that, he was converted. Times had changed—male assistants were considered normal and female executives commonplace. He made sure that he had a fifty percent ratio of female executives and senior managers. Initially, he had done this to make his company look progressive and caring, which attracted business, but it did not take long until he realised that they carried their weight and were equal to, if not better than, their male counterparts.

He exited the lift on the trading floor and took the long way to the meeting room so he could pass as many people as possible and say hello. He only did this because he had read that it helped promote employee satisfaction and improve productivity. Everyone seemed to like it and he'd even got better at remembering names.

Entering the meeting room, he greeted the head of sales and said hello to all ten senior managers by name. He took his seat and savoured the air of superiority that he felt sure he brought to the room. His hair was always slicked back, with the grey showing on the sides. A tailored shirt, silk tie and slim gold watch with a dark-brown leather strap enhanced his observant, dull-blue eyes set in a tanned, clean-shaven face, which had wrinkle lines of wisdom rather than age. He was only five feet, eight inches but carried himself with purpose and authority. He leaned forward and placed his tablet squarely on the boardroom table. He quietly told them to begin.

The head of sales was nervous as his boss did not normally attend these meetings, and when he did, it could go in one of two ways. The senior manager chairing the meeting plugged in his laptop to the visual display and proceeded to go over the presentation that everyone had received a day prior. He gave insights behind the numbers and the forecast for the next three months. No questions came from the room. Once finished, he passed on to the next manager for the presentation on her department. She gave a brief in the same format and, once again, there were no questions from the room. The next manager stood and began his introduction.

Thomas Rayner reclined in his seat and firmly spoke.

"Yeah, yeah, yeah. I've read all this before the meeting. Results are not good, people. Yes, sales are up, but only just, and our growth has continued to slow. Forecasts are not good and soon we will have zero growth. Yes, this is the market trend in the current climate." Roman paused. "Sit, please," he told the manager that had remained standing.

Thomas moved forward in his seat and looked around the table, focusing on everyone's eyes. He continued. "Have we followed markets tends?"

The rhetorical question remained unanswered and four seconds went by as if Thomas was daring anyone to answer. They knew better.

"Since I started this company, we have always exceeded market trends." His voice was raised in a controlled, even tone. His steely eyes appeared not to blink.

"All I'm hearing is excuses for mediocrity. This company was not built on mediocrity! Has anyone got anything for me apart from the bullshit I have read and the crap I am hearing?"

Everyone remained silent as they dared not poke the bear when he was in one of those moods.

"Well? Are you all just going to sit there like idiots? I'll tell you what I want. I want double-digit growth for this year! We will allow others to go with market trends and eat them for breakfast! Am I clear?"

Everyone nodded in agreement, yet everyone knew that this was next to impossible and the presentations had outlined very clearly why this was the case. Yet, once Thomas Rayner set his mind on something, they knew it could not be changed. They silently prayed that next month his focus would be on another area of the company, and they also prayed that the meeting would be over soon, and he would decide to not pick on one of them.

"Roger!" Thomas barked across the table. Everyone else held their breath in trepidation as he asserted his power by singling one out and breaking their strength as a collective.

"Your sales for exporting fast-moving consumer goods to the southern Asia-Pacific region are pathetic. These are easy commodities, and we do it better than anyone. We have the logistics, contacts, and market domination, and I expect forecast results to be greater than predicted. Revised results will be given by the end of the week!"

Roger agreed, even though he had clearly outlined why this would not be possible and he had even told the head of sales last month and had received feedback that Thomas had concurred. However, this was not the first time he'd seen the boss change his mind or ignore the facts put in front of him. It was not the first time he had come after him. He knew to go along with it after witnessing others that had challenged him being reduced to tears.

Thomas stood and instructed the head of sales to use the remainder of the meeting to revise targets, and stressed that he looked forward to seeing them. A calm, relaxed expression now came over his face as though a switch had been flicked. His brain had reminded him to leave on a positive note, even though he wanted to vent his frustration even more. He thanked them all for their time and exited the meeting room.

On his way back to the lift, he again put on his charm and chatted to those in the open-plan workspace.

Once in the elevator, he checked his emails and saw the one he had been waiting for. Opening it, he read it all the way to his office. Once there, he closed the door behind him and placed the tablet on his desk. He sat down and clicked his mouse to waken his two desktop monitors. He checked the time. He had two hours before lunch. He brought up the email he was reading and dragged it onto the monitor on the left and clicked "Print" on the attachment. He started a new email on the monitor on the right and proceeded typing "To Mac Hawkins", the head of security he was meeting for lunch. Using the email on the left as a reference, he clearly outlined that they had important matters to discuss, without disclosing any sensitive details. He wanted Mac to be prepared before the shit hit the fan.

CHAPTER 24

Mac Hawkins arrived for lunch and was escorted to a private room by a lovely waitress. Thomas had not arrived yet. As he took his seat, the waitress asked if he would like anything to drink. He declined as she filled up his glass with chilled, still water. As she turned and left, he couldn't help but check out her tight, young arse. He would wait for Thomas and let him decide on the wine.

Mac was forty-six years old and six feet tall. He was of solid build but not solid as in muscle-bound, more a natural solid build, like there was plenty of strength hidden under a healthy layer of fat. His hair was combed backwards but not slicked back, and had sufficient length for its weight to hold it in place. Tufts of hair were visible behind his ears but did not reach down to his shoulders. The grey was starting to come through in uneven streaks. His face had a three-millimetre stubble but his lower neck was cleanly shaven. The greying whiskers matched the amount of grey in his hair. He had dark-brown eyes and the weathered face of a bushman. He wore a black, open-neck shirt and gave the impression that he was equally comfortable in the city as in the country.

Mac had known Thomas for over five years. Mac had started his own security firm designed for providing security to high-profiles and executives. They first met in London when Thomas had contacted him for personal security due to some threats he had received from a Chinese company he had put out of business. They hit it off immediately and Thomas requested that Mac provide his personal protection. Not someone from his security firm, but him personally. Money was not an object and Mac could not turn it down.

Their bond grew one night in Shanghai when they returned to Thomas's car in the early hours of the morning after a late-night function. The driver opened the rear doors for them in the underground parking lot. The car park level was deserted except for two other parked cars in the distance, and there was no sign of their owners. Thomas entered behind the driver's seat and Mac behind the passenger seat, as per protocol. Once they were inside, the driver took his seat, locked the doors, and proceeded to turn in his seat and face them with a black pistol clearly pointed at Thomas. It was then they noticed that two other Chinese men in suits were standing either side of the passenger doors with their jackets partially open, exposing pistols that were gripped and ready in their right hands.

The driver proceeded to inform them that he had an important message. Mac felt the comfort of his Glock pistol in his shoulder holster under his jacket on his left side. His hands were already placed on his stomach and he slowly slid his right hand into his jacket, so it was touching the butt. He contorted his face into a look of fear to put the men at ease, but his mind was running through various scenarios at the speed of light.

Thomas replicated the look of fear. They had practised for hostile situations at Mac's request. Mac had learnt that the threats were very real. Thomas remained quiet and would wait for Mac to take the lead.

The driver continued, knowing that they were listening and aware of the lose-lose situation they were in. The message was clear. Thomas was not welcome in China. Mac knew not to react as if it was just a message and they could go on their way.

The driver started a new sentence with, "To make sure you understand..."

That was all Mac needed to hear. With the speed of a lightning bolt, he swung his back to his window, his front facing Thomas. His left hand pushed the forearm of the driver holding the gun, and his right hand followed through at the same speed, gripping the Glock. Mac's Glock connected with the driver's temple in a backhand flowing motion that finished aiming out of Thomas's window, as Mac pulled the trigger, releasing a deafening sound as the bullet smashed through the glass and slammed into the chest of one of the Chinese men, sending him to the ground.

Another gun fired but it was not Mac's. The man outside the passenger side window had unleashed a bullet that shattered the glass and hit Mac in the side of his back. Mac had taken out the immediate threat to Thomas and shielded him from the other.

The impact bashed him into Thomas. Still conscious and using the adrenaline to mask the immediate pain, he swung around and fired twice, knocking the man over, stone-dead.

Lifting himself enough to see out the windows, Mac confirmed that both men outside the car were dead, with pools of blood starting to seep out around them. Next, he checked the driver, who was starting to regain consciousness. The driver's gun was safely on the floor of the back seat where it had fallen. Mac hit him again on the side of the head with the butt of his Glock to ensure he remained unconscious and to buy him some time. Finally, he checked Thomas.

The ringing in Thomas's ears was decreasing in pitch. He had quickly regained his composure and his eyes displayed the rapid firing of neurons as he assessed the carnage and started formulating plans of revenge. Mac asked him calmly if he was okay, to which he replied that he was. Thomas returned the question.

Mac was struggling with the pain and transferred the Glock to his left hand as he ran his right up and down his side and back. Checking his palm, he saw no blood, and let Thomas know that his bullet-proof vest had just paid for itself. He knew some ribs were broken as the impact was like being hit with a sledgehammer. However, he needed to concentrate and get them out of there. Lesser men would have passed out.

Mac checked the driver and saw that he was still out cold. They departed the car and made their way up to the street, where they caught a cab back to the hotel and chartered a flight immediately back to the safety of London.

Mac remembered on the flight Thomas being hell-bent on unleashing a torrent of fury against the man who was behind the attack. It had taken him some time to convince him that you may win the battle but could very easily lose the war. Once they landed in London, he stood with Thomas while he phoned the man behind the incident. They agreed to meet in London in a private room at a public restaurant. Mac was there, with another two associates keeping an eye from outside. The man behind the Shanghai incident turned up with a similar security detail. At the meal, only one bodyguard each was allowed in the room.

For the first time, Mac got a very in-depth insight into the world Thomas Rayner played in. The meeting was very polite and civil, with the tension of two matchsticks playing nice on a powder keg. Like two poker players, they knew when to raise, call or fold. After an hour and twenty minutes, they shook hands, with both giving a little. It was a win for everyone, and Mac knew then and there that Thomas was the smartest man he had ever met, and it's the smart ones that live to fight another day.

While still waiting, Mac took a sip of water and checked his Rolex Explore watch, which was a gift from Thomas after the Shanghai episode. The door to the private room opened. Thomas entered, and they greeted each other with pleasantries. The waitress took Thomas's jacket and hung it in a nearby coat cupboard.

Once they were seated, the chef entered, a personalised touch that was only for important guests who spent a lot of money. He knew Thomas well and informed him of the in-season dishes he could prepare that were not listed on the menu. They took his recommendation and let him work his magic in the kitchen.

With the room to themselves, they got down to talking about the side operation they had going. Thomas only trusted Mac and could not do it without him.

"How's the latest shipments going?" Thomas asked.

"All on track. I've upped the security, as discussed, and no issues. Any update on our exit strategy?"

"Leave this to me. This is not going to be easy, but we are on track. Our associates have agreed on cutting ties with the moving of the goods within the next six months. They are aware of the potential risk and are not stupid. They know a good thing cannot last forever and appreciate that we know when to walk away to protect not only ourselves but them as well. However, I need to provide a smooth transition, so my business dealings may very well continue past the next six months."

They discussed Mac's responsibilities during the transition stage. The food arrived, and the conversation continued until Mac knew exactly what he needed to do in the coming months.

Finishing the meal, Thomas informed him that there was one more thing. He stood and went to the closet, where he reached into his jacket's side pocket and retrieved a folded A4 piece of paper.

As he went back to his seat holding the paper in front of him, he had Mac's full attention.

"I did some extra digging on our Melbourne situation. I know you did a full background check on Elizabeth Conway. Has there been any suspicious activity from her work, friends, husband or police?"

"None. I have the best tech guys money can buy, and I can assure you that online activity is normal. We are monitoring her old work and no links are being made. The police have forensic accountants and they are none the wiser. Our tracks have been covered. Her husband and parents are getting on with their lives."

"What about her brother?"

"As discussed, her brother has little to no contact with the family. Information was limited, and we needed to contain the situation pronto."

"Yes, I know, and we agreed together to act swiftly. However, I did some digging myself on Roman Paxter."

With that, he pushed the folded piece of paper across the table. It contained a photo and brief bio.

Mac opened the paper and the expression on his face said it all. He muttered, "That little fucker."

Thomas did not need to say anything more. He only added, "I need you to do a thorough check on him. We need to know everywhere he's been and talked to since her death. We needed this yesterday. Once we have this information, we'll decide if we need to alter our plans."

"Of course. I'll get onto it immediately and keep you informed."

"Remember. This is business. Personal matters take a back seat, and feel free to keep that photo."

With that, they wound up the lunch and said their good-byes.

Mac walked back to his office and could not help but look at the piece of paper on the way. This was more personal than Thomas realised.

CHAPTER 25

The conditions were far from what they were used to. One room and a shared tap, sink, toilet, and fridge. A constant air of unrest hovered over everyone's heads, penetrating all thoughts, whether they were awake or asleep. Mustapha Fakhri could not complain. He had his wife and son with him. Things could be a lot worse and he kept reminding himself of this.

Once he reached Lebanon, it took another three days before he made contact with his wife via email. She had made the crossing safely with their son and got as far as Beirut, but like an estimated two million other Syrians, she had been unable to move on. Mustapha told her to stay put. What she had done was correct. Beirut was a safe haven, and he would make his way to them.

They had been together for three weeks, and he spent that time talking to many other Syrian refugees. He always lied about his profession as rumours circulated of undercover government agents. Most Syrians were caught between a rock and a hard place. At least they knew on one side was a rock and the other a hard place, which was better than the unknown and open doors for persecution, assault, rape, or death. Syrians were safe in Lebanon but were not free to work and found themselves living as second-class citizens. The terrorists were kept at bay, or the undesirable terrorists kept at bay, as Hezbollah protected Lebanon. Many talked politics but Mustapha would remain quiet as he had seen the worst from all sides. All he cared about was his country, which was being pillaged, abandoned, and crumbling down, with the risk of his son and son's children not being able to enjoy the fruits of their heritage.

His family was with him now, and that was all that mattered. They had money to get by for a few months, and he was sure he could get some cash-in-hand jobs. His seven-year-old son was starting to get an education again, with makeshift classrooms being set up. This was their life and they were beginning to accept it. He was optimistic things would improve. History told him that they would. He missed his former life, as his passion for what he did could not be extinguished, but at least he once had a chance to do something he loved for a living.

Mustapha arrived back at their one room for a late lunch with his wife and son. His wife had laid out a few basic dishes on the floor, and they sat on the ground and gave thanks for the food they had.

Halfway through eating, two strange men entered the room and remained by the door. Mustapha could still hear noises of chatter and normal life in the neighbouring rooms, so obviously it was not a raid by soldiers. Startled, however, they looked up and noticed that while the men were trying to look like locals, they had Western features. Sitting in apprehensive silence, they saw the men hold out the palms of their hands to show they meant no harm. One of the men spoke in English.

"Are you Mustapha Fakhri?"

Mustapha had a moment of deciding whether to lie, tell the truth, or avoid the question. He decided upon the latter and replied, "Who, may I ask, is enquiring?"

"We mean no harm. As you can tell, we are British. Maybe you recognise this man?" As the man spoke, he gestured to the man on his left, who removed his hat and gave Mustapha a clear look at his face. Then he spoke.

"We met briefly about four weeks ago. Are you Mustapha Fakhri?" As he spoke, he removed a folded piece of paper from his pocket.

Mustapha studied the face and recollected what he had been doing four weeks ago. It then dawned on him who the man on the left was and the significance of him holding a folded piece of paper. He faced his wife and gave her a reassuring smile, which his son also saw.

"Yes, I am. Can you please clarify who you are?"

With that, the two men did a check over their shoulders and, realising that there was no door, only an old sheet hanging down from the doorframe that was tied back on the side, they took a step closer into the room to minimise the chances of being overheard.

"Pleased to meet you again, Mustapha. Thank you for the note you gave me. It took us a while to decipher your hidden message. I am SAS and the man on my right is MI6, called Agent Jones. You can call me Smith."

Mustapha was certain those weren't their real names, but he was overwhelmed that his note had elicited a response in person. His wife immediately understood what was happening as he had relayed his journey in great detail. His son looked confused but was at ease when he noticed the tension disappear from his mum and dad.

"Hello, Smith and Jones. This is my wife and son."

"Honoured to meet you. I'm glad you recognised Smith. We do not have much time so let me explain why we are here," said Jones.

"We have been trying to find you for the last three days. We have been monitoring the email address you gave us. We traced the activity to an internet café in Beirut and needed to be sure it was you before making contact. To cut a long story short, the British government is very keen to utilise your knowledge. We are here to take you, your wife, and son to England right now. There you will have a new life if you are willing to work with us. Will you come?"

Mustapha looked at his wife and saw hope in her face, which he had not seen in a long time.

"Yes. Yes, we will come."

"Excellent. We leave now. You don't have time to pack so please pick up anything important. We have a car outside to take you to the British Embassy."

Smith removed from his pocket what looked like a cross between a walkie-talkie and a mobile phone. He depressed a button and informed whoever was on the other end that they were ready. He then placed his other hand on his ear and asked for them to repeat what was just said. Jones also placed his hand on his ear. A look of concentration spread across their faces, and then turned to concern. They both moved to the sides of the door, Smith on the left and Jones on the right. With their backs pressed against the inside wall, they removed pistols that had been tucked into their lower backs under their loose shirts. Smith motioned to Mustapha to act normally.

There was a commotion outside and raised voices in the adjacent room. Then silence. The tension in the air could have been cut with a knife. They were acting as naturally as they could by proceeding with their lunch. One man entered their room with an assault rifle in hand and voice raised. Smith immediately took him from behind in a chokehold while slamming him into the ground, causing the rifle to dislodge. The man, in shock, froze as Smith knelt on his throat, with his pistol firmly pointed into the side of his head.

Two more men entered the room and their focus was immediately drawn to their colleague on the ground. Jones moved in from the other side and slammed the butt of his pistol into the side of the first, knocking him out cold. The other man, who was raising his rifle at Smith, was distracted by this and turned around to find Jones swinging his left boot into his weapon, which caused a round to fire into the concrete ceiling. Jones followed this through with a fist squarely planted into his face that resulted in the sickening cracking sound of his nose breaking.

Smith and Jones took stock. One man was still concussed, one holding his face with blood pouring between his fingers, and the other still pinned on the ground with a pistol to his head. Mustapha and his family had retreated and were sitting with their backs against the far wall, with Mustapha in the middle holding his wife and son tight.

Jones asked Mustapha if he recognised any of the men. He shook his head and answered, "No." Smith asked the man under his knee who he was, but he muttered words that were not in English.

Jones grabbed the man who was still holding his broken nose and placed his pistol between his eyes and asked him the same question in Arabic. The man removed his hand from his nose and in Arabic told him that he will fuck his mother. Jones asked the man under Smith the same question in Arabic, to which he got the same answer.

Jones removed a small knife from his ankle while holding his gun to the face of the man with the broken nose. He stabbed the blade into the guy's leg. This was simply to show he was serious before he asked the question again. However, the answer was the same, which was no surprise.

While Jones was busy trying to get answers, Smith used his free hand to take out his walkie-talkie and told whoever was on the other end to get in position and hold.

Jones lowered his weight onto the bloodied man on the floor, copying Smith, as his knee applied pressure to his neck. Jones lowered the tip of his blade towards his eye while he kept his pistol firmly pointed to his head. He told him that if he didn't answer, he would pop his eyeball and then smash his teeth out. The knife was a millimetre from his eye and the guy tried to look brave and spat out the word, "Daesh."

Smith and Jones looked at each other, as this was the Arabic term for ISIS or ISIL. This was what they wanted to hear as it would not have gone down well if they had taken down Lebanon soldiers on their home soil.

The man with the broken, bloodied nose had a look of superiority on his face, as if what he had said should put fear into their hearts. Smith repeated the man's answer into his walkie-talkie and said they were ready to go.

Jones calmly told Mustapha to take his family outside now, which Mustapha did. As soon as Mustapha and his family were outside the door, Jones moved the knife away from the guy's eye and took the smug look off his face by plunging it into his throat, causing him to drown in his own blood and die quietly.

Smith lifted his weight off his guy's throat while putting his walkie-talkie in his pocket. He then grabbed the man's hair with his freed hand, so he was looking up at him. Then, in a flash, Smith placed all his weight on his knee and slammed down onto his exposed neck, crushing it, killing him instantly.

Jones was out of the room and leading Mustapha and his family to the front door, with his pistol inconspicuously at his side. Smith followed at the rear after taking out his knife as he exited the room and slitting the throat of the unconscious guy.

Reaching the front door, Jones did a quick check outside and motioned to Smith that the coast was clear. On the footpath was an old Toyota LandCruiser, with the rear passenger door open and, behind that, an old Suzuki van with a man by the open rear sliding door. Both engines were running and had men behind the steering wheels.

Smith and Jones ushered Mustapha, his wife and son quickly into the rear of the Suzuki van. Smith jumped in after them, followed by the man holding the door as he slid it closed.

Jones jumped into the rear of the Toyota LandCruiser and noticed a dead man already in the back seat. Doors slammed closed, and with both vehicles moving, the driver informed Jones that they had taken out the fourth man before he entered the building. Jones leaned across the back seat and opened the car door. He pushed the limp body out as they turned a sharp deserted corner.

Following in the Suzuki van, Mustapha was comforting his shaken wife and son. He asked Smith if any more men were after them. Smith reassured him that they were not being followed, but let Mustapha know that those men had probably followed him and Smith. In a soothing voice, he told Mustapha to relax as they were on their way to the British Embassy and would be on a military flight to England by the end of the day.

CHAPTER 26

Detective Senior Sergeant Adam Zhang and Detective Constable John Moskil were sitting back in their car after a long morning at the ports. The sun was up in the centre of the sky and the midday heat in the car park was stifling. Adam was in the driver's seat and started the car to get the air conditioning going. They both had sombre looks on their faces. They had spent four hours with customs going over the three containers that had arrived into the port the day before.

Adam looked at John. "What a morning. Let's go and get some lunch. I need a greasy feed and a strong coffee. There's a diner not far from here."

"Sounds like a great idea."

Adam put the car in gear, and they headed out onto the road. John leaned forward and put the radio on to give them some reprieve from the thoughts racing in their heads with no finish line in sight.

John started wobbling his head up and down to the sound of Taylor Swift. "Man, my daughter loves her music," he broke out, trying to sing along. "*The haters are gonna hate, hate, hate, hate, hate.*"

Adam couldn't help but smile. One thing he liked about John was that he knew how to lighten the mood, which was important in their line of work. There was a lot of political correctness in the police now, which was a good thing, but he appreciated the humour of the old-school officers, as long as it was done behind closed doors. Humour could go a long way to help you cope with bad situations.

They reached the café and got a park directly out front.

Sitting down in a booth at the end with high-backed seats, they both ordered coffees and the house big breakfast, which should have had a health warning beside it.

Adam reached into his laptop bag and pulled out his tablet along with printed copies of the manifests for the containers.

"So, what are we missing here? Give me anything. Nothing is off the table," Adam said.

John saw that Adam had placed the tablet on top of the manifests to the side of the table. John knew they would look at these again a bit later. Time for a brainstorming session. Before John could answer, their coffee arrived. He opened a sugar packet that accompanied the teaspoon on the saucer, emptied it into the cup, and gave the coffee a stir before he started talking.

"Well. Something is going on. That's clear from the footage Roman and Jacob obtained. We went through everything with customs. They had the dogs and all. How we came away with nothing just makes me think that these guys are more on to it than we give them credit for, which makes them even more dangerous. Maybe they got a tip-off that we were going to inspect them?"

"I initially thought the same. But we only decided to do this after they had left Hong Kong. On top of that, this search didn't go through official channels. It was a mate owing me one that made it look like a random inspection," Adam replied as he lifted his coffee and blew over the top of it.

"What if they knew Roman and Jacob were watching them, and what they did that night was just for show?"

"That is a possibility. However, I don't buy it. No one knew Roman and Jacob were doing that. I mean, we didn't even know."

"True. What if this is drugs? I find it hard to believe it is weapons as we would have come across those. What else is worth smuggling into Australia?"

Adam took a sip of his coffee. "The big three are drugs, weapons or money. Money can be easily hidden. I remember watching one of those border control programs and someone was trying to smuggle thousands of dollars tightly packaged into the soles of shoes. You'd be amazed how tightly you can compact money. But—there is a big but here—we had one of the best dogs sniff everything for this and it came up with nothing."

John was about to say something when the waitress arrived with their plates, which were overflowing with everything that could possibly be fried. Even the token mound of spinach looked like it had been fried in bacon fat. They both leaned back so the waitress could place the meals in front of them on the table.

Both starving, they picked up their knives and forks and tucked in. After a few mouthfuls, John spoke up.

"We can say the same about drugs then. They can be packaged just as tightly as money and that black Labrador they brought in didn't even bat an eyelid. But who's to say they haven't designed some drugs to fool the dogs? I also saw on one of those border control programs where they tried to bring in cocaine in its liquid form in vodka bottles. The main difference between those and normal vodka bottles was that they weighed a shitload more. I know dogs can still detect these, but who knows what they've come up with now?"

"That is true."

"What about the actual shipping containers themselves?"

"The dogs also sniffed the outsides. They were also scanned." Adam mopped up some egg yolk with a slice of bread and washed it down with coffee. Trying to not speak with a full mouth, he continued.

"Let's go back to what Roman and Jacob saw. Why would you move goods out of a container late at night when they had already been signed off and replace them with goods that obviously still matched the manifest?" he said while tapping the printed manifests to his side.

"All I can think of is the big three. What the fuck are we missing here?"

"Exactly. What the fuck are we missing here? I've got to go and see the boss this afternoon and I don't want to be standing there with my dick in my hand looking like a tit on a bull."

They both took a moment and, with their bellies full, leaned back. They both ordered another coffee to cut through the grease that was sitting in their stomachs. Adam slid his tablet to be in front of him and turned it on. He swivelled it, so both could view it. He brought up the many photos they took.

"It appears the items match the manifest," Adam said as he also flipped through the papers beside him and swiped through the photos.

The waitress placed their second cups of coffee on the table with a half-hearted smile as though her shift was about to end and her mind had started to clock off.

"I need something to give to the boss this afternoon," Adam continued when the waitress was out of earshot.

"What about the other documents?" John pulled out his notebook from his pocket and flipped to the correct page. "The Bill of Landing, Commercial Invoice, Certificate of Origin, Shipper's Export Declaration, Insurance Certificate, etc."

"Good point. We have been concentrating too much on the physical goods."

Adam brought these up on his tablet and they both stared at the screen, drinking their coffee, not really knowing what they were looking at. After three minutes that felt like thirteen, they both sat back in their seats.

John started to talk but saw Adam was lost in his thoughts. He watched him drain the last of his coffee and then saw him lean forward again and start flicking his finger across the tablet.

"Holy shit! I've got it!" Having said that a bit loudly, Adam looked around, but no one appeared to have noticed.

"Finish your coffee, John. We need to get back. I have a hunch. A pretty damn good hunch but I cannot substantiate it yet. I'll explain in the car, but we both need to make some phone calls before my meeting. Actually, you need to come to the meeting with me as you will have information."

CHAPTER 27

Thomas Rayner was in his opulent office, standing by the window and looking out at the Hong Kong skyline as another day was about to start. Watching the sun come up made him feel that he had a head start on the competition. His personal assistant had not started yet. He heard a knock on his door, which he was expecting.

"Come in," Thomas said as he made his way to his desk.

Mac Hawkins entered, and upon seeing Thomas sitting down behind his desk, made his way to the two Windsor leather wingback chairs that faced the back of the oversized desk at slight angles to each other. He only sat once he had been signalled to do so.

"So, what is so important you need to see me now?" Thomas asked as he leaned back and crossed his legs.

"I've done some digging on Roman Paxter. It appears that he and Elizabeth's husband, Jacob Conway, were in Hong Kong a couple of weeks ago."

"Appears or were?" interrupted Thomas.

Mac internally kicked himself for using imprecise words, which he knew Thomas hated.

"Sorry. They *were* in Hong Kong. This showed up in their passports and on both their credit card statements."

Mac saw that he had Thomas's full attention, yet Thomas remained calm, with his legs crossed. Mac continued.

"They were in Hong Kong for four days and three nights. They did some shopping every day and went to tourist attractions, including a day tour. On the surface, it appears they were busy and enjoying themselves. I cannot jump to a conclusion that they were here for any other reason, but I still have my doubts, so I got more intel on their online habits since Elizabeth's death. Nothing out of the ordinary was evident."

"They could have been taking a male bonding trip, but I gather you are going to tell me this is not all?" Thomas asked.

"Correct. I thought it prudent to tell you straightaway and would like your advice on what I plan to do," Mac said cautiously. He knew Thomas expected him to already have an answer and obtain an opinion, rather than being an amateur and asking, "What shall I do?"

Thomas uncrossed his legs and smoothed his trousers with the palms of his hands before placing them on his lap. He looked Mac in the eyes as a gesture for him to continue.

"As we know, Roman is not your everyday person. He is too smart to leave a trail if he does suspect us of anything. He also has sophisticated resources at his disposal with the firm he works for. It's enough to use technology and computer power, but to get full intel on someone, you need eyes on the ground. What I propose to do is the same thing as we did for Elizabeth."

"Let me ask you this," Thomas said. "Do you trust the person you used in Melbourne?"

"Not a hundred percent but we didn't ask him to kill Elizabeth. He only gave us intel on her daily routines. No doubt he knows of her demise, but he won't talk as he can easily be implicated in this. I think it's safe to use him again. He's in no position to decline."

"Okay. I agree. I'll try to speed up our exit from these dealings."

Mac pushed himself up from the arms on the seat to leave but then lowered his weight back into the thick leather.

"Melbourne is three hours ahead of us, with them being on daylight saving time. It will be mid-morning. Why don't I give him a call now, so you can hear?"

Thomas did not even need to think about this and told Mac to call him from his own office from a secure line. He let Mac know that he had business of his own to attend to.

Mac again raised himself from the chair and left. He knew Thomas saw right through that. It was worth a shot. If the call came from his office, even with his mobile phone, it would make it harder for Thomas to deny any knowledge of the contact in Melbourne. He needed to be smarter and think about covering his arse. He knew Thomas would already be two steps ahead.

Exiting the building, he began to walk to his office, which was on the twenty-eighth floor a few blocks away. He leased the whole floor and used this as a base for his employees. This got him thinking that he should be more hands-on with other clients his staff had, even though technically Thomas paid him for a hundred percent of his time.

Mac reached his office, closed the door, and sat down behind his desk. It was not as opulent as Thomas's and that did not bother him. He would rather be out and about than stuck behind a desk. He opened the top drawer by his left knee and retrieved his encrypted mobile phone. By using this, the caller could not tell who or where the call came from even if it was traced. He opened his laptop, which was sitting slightly to the left on his desk. From this, he got the number he required and dialled.

When the person on the other end answered, Mac just said, "Cristiano?"

"Speaking."

"Hi, it's your friend that gives you those good deals."

"Hi. How's it going?" Cristiano replied as he got up from behind his desk and closed his office door. His heart was already beating faster from the sound of the raspy English voice on the other end. He had no idea what his name was but knew it was a voice he did not want to hear.

"Good. How's business going? Money come in okay?" Mac asked.

Cristiano knew that his business, or, more accurately, his family's business, was doing very well and in no small part thanks to the English guy on the phone. It was a rhetorical question to let him know that he was indebted to him. A response was required to confirm this, so he answered, "Everything is good, thank you."

"Glad to hear. First, thanks for the information you gave me before. I would like the same again. I have just sent you the details. This is important, and I need a response within three working days."

Cristiano looked at his laptop that already had Outlook open and saw the email from some obscure address. Opening it, he saw it was encrypted and required a password.

Mac waited during the pause in conversation. He knew he had the email and was looking at it. He didn't wait for a reply and added, "You also have a text message."

Cristiano lowered his phone from his ear and saw a text from yet another scrambled source that didn't even resemble a phone number. He opened it and saw one word. Closing the text message, he saw it disappear from his phone. He had no idea how the English-sounding guy did this.

"Thanks, got it," he replied as he typed the word on his laptop. The file opened. Last time he got one of these, it disappeared from his computer after the time was up to deliver the information. He tried to find it but knew his attempts were futile.

"Good. It's straightforward, and like last time, you will be nicely compensated for your time."

"I have one question."

"Go ahead."

"Last time, the person ended up dead. I was not expecting that."

"I don't know what you're talking about. This information is required in the given timeframe. Coincidences are just that. I will be in touch if I don't receive anything."

With that, the phone went dead.

Cristiano reclined back in his desk chair and stared at his laptop screen. He brought both hands up and covered his face. He took a big breath in and then slowly dragged them down while breathing out.

Looking at the email, he had an idea and leaned forward and clicked the print icon, but nothing happened. He tried to save it, but again nothing happened. He tried to forward it and same thing—nothing. *Bugger*, he thought. He then tried a screenshot, snippet tool—nothing. He then had another idea and picked up his phone and took a photo of his screen.

"What are you doing?"

Cristiano almost jumped out of his skin. He looked at the door and saw it was open and his sister, Sofia, was standing half in the room with her left hand still on the door handle.

"Don't you knock?" he replied more curtly than he intended. Trying to hide his blistering emotion, he continued in a more even-tempered tone, "How long have you been standing there?"

"Long enough to know that something is wrong. What's going on?"

"Nothing."

"Don't give me that crap. I know you too well. Once again, what's going on?"

"Nothing. I just needed a copy of an email and my computer is playing up, so I needed to take a photo of it."

Sofia moved into the office and closed the door behind her. She remained standing. In her best calm sister voice, she said, "I heard the end of the call. I'm not stupid. Something is going on. If it has anything to do with the family business, then I have a right to know."

"All good. Some guy is just trying to play hardball with an abusive email, while making it impossible for me to keep it, but he didn't figure out that I could easily just take a photo of it."

Cristiano closed his laptop and sat back hoping that this would be the end of the conversation. However, he knew his sister Sofia inherited the brains in the family and would take some convincing. His doubts were confirmed with what she said next.

"If someone has the technical smarts to make an email impossible to save, forward, print or whatever, he certainly knows you can take a photo of it. The point of all that is to show that he is not your average person, and to emphasise his power. It's as simple as that. Now, please tell me what is going on."

Looking at his sister, Cristiano knew he could not bullshit her and that she was not going to let it go. He looked up at the ceiling for a second to confirm his thoughts, and then told his sister to take a seat.

He told her everything and felt the pressure on his shoulders decrease. He explained that at first it was a straightforward business deal with great commission for the goods brought in. There was an informal confidentiality clause, but everything was acceptable to clear customs. In the back of his mind, he thought it was slightly dodgy, but he wasn't breaking any laws. It also helped the family business, and for once, one of his deals was proving lucrative.

Cristiano then pulled the top of his laptop back up and showed the email to Sofia while relaying the phone call. He also mentioned Elizabeth Conway and how this latest recon information required for Roman Paxter was no doubt linked.

Sofia took control of his laptop, opened the internet, and did a general search on Elizabeth Conway. The leading search result was a newspaper article about her murder. They clicked it open and saw the name Elizabeth Conway (nee Paxter). Next, she typed in "Roman Paxter" but got no results.

"It doesn't take a rocket scientist to connect the dots," she told her brother. "We need to take this to the police."

"No, we can't do this!"

"Why not?"

"For starters, who's to say that these people won't find out and come after me? They may even come after you as well. Let's face it, the police will take ages to find out anything and we don't have any concrete evidence."

"Let's have a look at the next shipments and see if we can get any evidence?" Sofia suggested.

"I've done that already because I was curious, and I didn't see anything untoward. I have no idea what is going on, but there is one more thing I need to tell you. This is the second reason we cannot go to the police. I could go to prison myself."

Sofia gave her brother the type of look that a mother would give a naughty child while waiting for them to confess.

He continued, "Whilst accepting shipments, I have been paying more than the value of the goods by a considerable amount. Someone drops off the overvalued amount to me in cash, which I use to top up the payment."

"Oh, brother, what the fuck have you got yourself into? This is obviously a way for who is sending whatever is hidden in those containers to get paid."

Sofia paced over to the office window and thought for a good ten seconds. She then slowly strode over to the desk and placed both hands palm-down in front of Cristiano.

"There is only one thing we can do. We need to tell Dad. He can help us."

"Shit, I thought you'd say that. Shall we see him tonight?"

"No. Time is not on our side. We see him today. Let me give him a call," Sofia said as she straightened up and took her phone out of her pocket. After a few swipes and presses, she put it up to her ear.

"Dad. We need to see you right away."

After some nods and grunts, she placed the phone back in her pocket.

"We're seeing him at the café in Lygon Street now. We'll take my car."

CHAPTER 28

They found a car park close to the café, which was lucky considering the lunchtime rush was on. The sky was overcast with maybe a thunderstorm due late in the afternoon.

Arriving to see that it was full, they approached a nearby young waiter they didn't recognise. As Sofia was about to ask for her dad, a senior waiter, whom they did recognise, stepped in.

"Sofia and Cristiano Esposito. How nice to see you again. Carlos is expecting you at his regular table."

The young waiter moved away to attend to a table as the senior waiter extended his hand out in the direction of their father, as if to welcome them and part the way, like Moses parting the Red Sea.

Carlos stood and welcomed his children with generous hugs and kisses. They all sat. It was just them at the table and Carlos had already ordered a lunch of various pasta dishes to share, which promptly arrived once they were seated. When their plates were full, he asked what it was that they needed to see him about so urgently.

Sofia and Cristiano looked at each other. She gave him a reassuring glance. He put his fork down and told his father everything.

Carlos did not interrupt. He casually continued to eat as he took it all in. When his son had finished, he picked up the white linen napkin on his lap and wiped his mouth. Roughly folding it, he placed it to the right of his plate and took a long drink of water.

"Well, son, you have gotten yourself into a jam. What's happened has happened, and in my younger days, I would have done the same. As you know, the business wasn't exactly built on the letter of the law. But those days have gone, and I want to make that perfectly clear. I've seen too many friends killed, and it would break your mother's heart if anything happened to you. However, you have done the right thing coming to me. We are a family and we will get through this together. I have a couple of questions."

Carlos got clarification on who could implicate his son in this, and that it was only those around the table that knew about it. He double-checked on the facts and made certain that his son had no knowledge of what was being traded. Carlos did not need to explain the implications of making inflated payments.

Once satisfied with what he had heard, Carlos turned to his daughter and thanked her for getting involved. He knew Sofia was the brains behind the business. She'd always gotten higher grades at school and university. She also took after her mother, with the ability to stay extremely calm under pressure. His son was the opposite but had learnt to control his emotions with age. Cristiano's greatest strength was getting along with people. You could put him in any room, and he would quickly make friends with everyone. People were drawn to him. Together, his daughter and son made a formidable team.

Carlos signalled to a waiter, who came over without delay, took their coffee orders and cleared the table. Then Carlos continued.

"Not long ago, I did a favour for a guy at the golf club and met with Roman Paxter and Jacob Conway in this very café. They wanted peace of mind that Elizabeth was not tied up in anything dodgy. I gave them that peace of mind. I also told them that I would let them know if I heard anything. What I have heard from you does not relate to Elizabeth. Who knows what she did to warrant their attention? I do not want to implicate you in anything. You have my word that this will stay between us. If things escalate, then I will have to involve a few close friends."

Cristiano and Sofia listened intently. They were surprised that he had met with Roman and Jacob but did not ask questions. They also knew in the back of their minds that their dad had his finger on the pulse of what happened in the underbelly of Melbourne.

The coffees arrived, and Carlos added sugar to his espresso, gave it a stir and took a sip in what was more of a sucking motion. He carefully placed the cup back on the saucer.

"Now, listen up, you two. This is what we are going to do. Cristiano, you will do exactly as they have requested and deliver on time. Do not leave anything out, and we will meet to go over the details before you report back. Sofia, you are to help. We need as much information as possible. If Roman gives money to a homeless person, I want a photo of that person and his identity checked out. We need to get a step ahead."

Cristiano and Sofia agreed.

"We need to think of an exit strategy to get out of this business arrangement. We cannot use standover tactics, obviously. Let me think about this until we meet again. If push comes to shove, you both may need to lie low for a while. I will ask around if anyone knows of any dealings that could relate to this. I can reassure you that our community is not involved as I would have heard about it."

Carlos once again reassured his children that everything would be okay, and as usual, he let them know that lunch was on him.

Cristiano and Sofia finished their coffees and left their dad at the table. They saw a waiter bring him a newspaper and he went straight to the back to look at the horse racing meetings and form guide.

As they walked up Lygon Street to Sofia's car, Cristiano started to plan their next moves. Sofia told him that she would drop him back at work where his car was parked. He would then drive to Roman's parents' house and wait to see if he emerged. She would drive to Jacob's house and do the same. Sofia told him to forward the photos he took of the email and attachment.

"If we see anything, we call each other immediately," Sofia instructed.

CHAPTER 29

Detective Senior Sergeant Adam Zhang had arrived at Jacob's place. Jacob was expecting him and had picked up Roman on his way home from work. It was late afternoon and they were sitting around the dining room table. The sky had become very dark and the odd heavy drop of rain was falling, accompanied by the daunting sound of rolling thunder that was getting louder as the storm drew closer. Jacob stood up and turned the lights on.

Adam had not turned up alone. He told them they needed to meet, and he would be bringing someone important to help solve the case. The person sitting beside him was an attractive middle-aged woman, five feet, seven inches tall, with dark shiny hair that was fashioned in a long bob with one side swept behind her ear. She had dark eyes and a broad smile. Half-Aboriginal and half-European, her dark complexion amplified the whiteness of her teeth. Dressed in a smart, skirted, dark suit and white blouse, she radiated authority and competence. Adam had introduced her as Superintendent Bridget Unaipon at the front door. Now she began to formally introduce herself.

"It is great to meet you both. My name is Bridget and I work for the Australian Federal Police in Counter Terrorism and work closely with the Australian Security Intelligence Organisation. You're no doubt wondering why I am here. Well, Adam has done a fantastic job in leading the case of your sister and wife. He has come to a strong theory of what is being brought into Melbourne and has reached out to my department for assistance. Adam is still leading the case of Elizabeth's murder, and I will now be involved as it may involve crimes that affect national security. I'll let Adam explain what he has uncovered."

Adam took over. "Senior Constable John Moskil and I were present when customs methodically searched the latest batch of containers. They used scanners and sniffer dogs and left nothing to chance. However, they found nothing that would prevent them from releasing the containers. After going through the manifests and all the accompanying documents, I came to realise that the containers held various antiques and the paperwork for these was beyond my understanding. John and I got into contact with an antiques dealer I know and forwarded him the photos of these and paperwork. He justified my concerns by telling us that it was very easy to forge antique documents, like details of historical ownership and origin. He could not verify these items and stated that few would be able to do so. The items imported could be exactly as they were, or something completely different. He said that paperwork could even arrive later to contradict the manifest and no one would be any the wiser."

Adam paused and Bridget continued.

"Adam got in touch with us and we also had a look. He also explained to me the information you passed on to him. Naturally, I did background checks on you both. Adam also mentioned Moya Connor from Elizabeth's work, and how she also helped. The main reason I am here is to explain that while Adam has a murder case, I hope you can understand that national security needs to take precedence. By no means does it mean that we will hamper the investigation, but it may mean that we delay an arrest if more information can be obtained to secure this country of ours."

Roman and Jacob diverted their focus from Bridget to each other. This was not lost on Bridget and she gave them a second. Roman was first to speak.

"First of all, it's a privilege to meet you, Superintendent Unaipon. Are you here to tell us to stop meddling?"

"Let me be clear," Bridget replied. "I do not think you are meddling. From what I've heard, you have been cooperating. We hope your cooperation will continue. I'm sorry if I've come across differently."

Roman nodded his head and looked at Jacob to see if he had anything to add. Jacob shuffled in his seat and scratched his nose. He took a pronounced gulp to clear the lump in his throat and started to speak.

"Sorry. Elizabeth's death is still very raw. My thoughts are spinning trying to think of what she got herself into. I gather she came across something in her job. It is now dawning on me that she appreciated antiques. I wouldn't say she knew a lot about them, so when I say 'appreciate', I mean she loved the idea of an object that came with a rich history. I'm sure she innocently stumbled onto something."

Bridget leaned forward with elbows on the table and, with a reassuring expression, she let Jacob know that they were one hundred percent certain that this was the case.

Roman asked what the next step was and emphasised that they were very keen to be kept in the loop and to cooperate.

Bridget answered, "I'm glad you're on board. The last thing we want is for us to be working against each other. I'd be naïve to think that with your background and employment you couldn't add value to this investigation. The Australian Federal Police does outsource if necessary, and what you have both done has been vital. We would like to reimburse you both for expenses incurred with getting the footage from Hong Kong. We would also like to have eyes in Hong Kong and would like to engage your company to do this. Unfortunately, it cannot be you, as you no doubt understand. We don't want federal agents in Hong Kong at this stage, as it would raise too many questions."

"Sure. I'll engage the team straightaway. It appears to be just evenings that this activity takes place, so two guys would be enough. I'll forward you the contact details."

"Thank you," replied Bridget as she handed Roman a business card.

The rain was getting heavy outside. Jacob stood up and closed the window, so they could hear each other better. When he sat down, he said, "I still don't really understand the whole antique story. Is this a case of people not filling out paperwork correctly, or stolen goods? And if stolen, from where, and wouldn't someone have reported them stolen?"

Bridget leaned back in her chair and informed them that she would give them a run-down of what she strongly thought was happening.

"What I'm about to say is nothing new. If you do enough research online, you will find many articles published by respected journalists on this topic. The Middle East is rich in archaeological value. It is where the first cities were built and contains numerous treasures from the Roman, Byzantine, Greek and Islamic periods. In Syria alone, there are over four and a half thousand published archaeological sites. There has always been stealing and bribes in the permits given, also under-the-table taxes on the trade of these goods. This has been done through government officials, tribal authorities, and terrorist organisations. What we are interested in is the terrorist organisations. In particular, ISIS, which has taken the looting of these artefacts to a whole new level, one which has never seen before."

She had Jacob and Roman's full attention. Jacob asked, "When you say 'a whole new level', just how big a role does this play in financing them?"

"That is a very good question, and many experts have tried to put a dollar figure on it. To cut a long story short, no one knows because it is hard to monitor a trade that does its best to remain hidden. Some estimate the overall trade to be worth hundreds of millions and others estimate it in the billions. It depends on how much of this money ends up in the pockets of

ISIS. They can obtain money through bribes and taxes, along with the actual stealing. The consensus is that this is up there with the two big income streams—the access and control of oil, and the taxes they impose on the people and businesses they occupy."

Roman responded that he knew it was big but not that big. "Why Australia? Why bring them all the way down under," he asked.

"Another good question. The big market for antiquities trade from this region is London. It is easy for them to get them into Europe through Turkey. But we have seen them diversify their market and take advantage of countries with a strong economy. Asia is seeing more activity and Australia has had a very strong economy during and post the global financial crises. One thing to remember is that these artefacts can be sold in one country to a buyer in another. Or sold to a dealer that will sit on it as an investment. There has been a crackdown on these goods in London, New York and other major trading cities, so it is no surprise they will look elsewhere to trade."

Jacob took a turn to ask a question.

"I gather there is a big market for antiquities. But how can it be so easy to get these artefacts to other countries to sell? Are there international rules and regulations around this? I mean, it's hard enough to sell a car without all the proper paperwork."

"Some objects are so distinctive that they could only have come from a certain part of the world," Bridget continued. "But you need to know your stuff and it is the likes of professors that have studied for years that can tell this. The United Nations Educational, Scientific and Cultural Organisation does monitor the illicit trafficking of cultural property, working closely with foreign ministries, intelligence agencies, World Customs Organisation, and Interpol. They regularly seize and return stolen artefacts. Investigations are opened, and arrests are made. Think of this as like the drug trade. Many are stopped and caught but many more slip through the net. The demand is huge."

Bridget thought for a while. "I've taken a particular interest in this area over the last five years. Not just with stolen goods coming into Australia but also protecting the illegal sale of Aboriginal artefacts. You'd be surprised how easy it is to make the paperwork appear legit. You can state that you never had any paperwork with the chain of ownership or origin unknown due to it being a family heirloom that was inherited. You don't need records of goods and there is a strong element of trust within the industry. Antiquities can make their way through Europe, changing hands through dealers to create a paper trail that can be used to sell the objects at auction houses."

Roman asked, "So I gather there will be players in Melbourne or other places in Australia that are in on it? Certainly, the people accepting these would know about it?"

"Not necessarily. From what we can see, the paperwork is sufficient to be called legal. We are considering this, as I know Adam has been. So far, we have found nothing to justify an arrest. Even the antique dealers may be perfectly innocent. We need time, resources, and thorough investigating. We have the resources. That is why we have come to you. Roman, we will use your resources, as we want to keep this to people we can trust. Once we have sufficient evidence, we will engage international bodies. Jacob, you are a smart man and we want to give you peace of mind that the murderer of your wife will be brought to justice. We will also bring to justice those that played a role in this murder."

Adam leaned in on the table and asked that they keep this conversation private. To finish, he let them know that the forensic accountants had been all through Elizabeth's work and had not found anything that would indicate any illegal business conducted by them or their clients. That is why it was suspected that the importers receiving these containers may be none the wiser. His theory remained that Elizabeth spotted something, which may have been in a shop or online, that sparked her interest enough to do some research.

"So, does this tie into her work?" Jacob asked.

"My gut instinct is that it does, but, like I said before, it does not mean that anything illegal was happening at work or with any of her clients. There is a client that is an importer of the containers we are looking into, but nothing to indicate foul play. We are looking closely at this company."

Jacob thanked Adam and Bridget for taking the time to visit them. Roman concurred.

They made their way to the front door and could hear the rain pelting down before they turned the handle. Bridget and

Adam bid them a good evening, ducked their heads, and ran to their parked car on the side of the road.

Roman closed the door and asked Jacob how he was.

"I'm as good as can be expected. It's all becoming very real, and now I don't just want her killer found, I want her legacy honoured, and what she was looking into brought to light and all those involved prosecuted."

"Mate. I totally agree. If you need to just talk, I'm available anytime."

"Likewise."

Jacob handed Roman the keys to his Volkswagen Golf. "I know I was going to give you a lift home, but just take the car as I'll ride my motorbike to work tomorrow. It's going to be a nice sunny day and I need to blow some cobwebs away."

After Roman left, Jacob locked the door, turned off the downstairs lights and headed upstairs for a hot shower. Reaching his bedroom, he sat on the foot of his bed, took off his glasses, and broke down in tears. His head flooded with thoughts of what his lovely wife had discovered that could have deserved death. He wanted the murderer to pay. Now all he could think about was the arseholes that were making a dollar and not giving a shit about who got hurt in the process. They would pay. Oh, boy, would they pay.

The tears subsided. He felt better having let that out. The tears were different this time. Rather than tears of grief, they contained an element of relief that progress was being made.

CHAPTER 30

The twenty-four hours since she'd left Jacob's house had been hectic for Superintendent Bridget Unaipon. She'd only managed four hours of sleep, which was caught in the office breakout room on a couch. Looking at the mirror in the workplace bathroom, she ran her fingers through her hair, splashed her face with cold water, patted it dry with a paper towel, and applied lipstick and a touch of mascara. The reflection staring back looked presentable.

The sun had set, and she had one minute before a secure WebEx meeting with London. Seated back at her desk, she noted that the office was basically empty, with only a couple of others working late. She mentally went through her list.

The WebEx window came to life. She put on her headset and accepted the call with, "Good morning."

"Good morning. Or should I say, 'Good evening'?" the well-dressed man from MI6 answered back.

"Thank you for taking the time to meet," Bridget responded.

"Not at all Bridget and I'm Sawyer by the way."

"Nice to meet you Sawyer."

"Likewise. I'm glad to meet you, as MI6 is more than willing to cooperate. This is an international issue and we have extensive overseas human intelligence on this matter."

"That is pleasing to hear."

"Now, I understand you believe that stolen antiquities are being brought into Australia from conflict zones in the Middle East, and you are having difficulties in verifying this."

"That is correct. We have experts that can state the origin of the antiques, but as you can appreciate, it is difficult to prove they have been stolen and even more difficult to establish who has stolen them."

"Of course. We are very much in the business of trying to stop the money from this trade funding terrorist organisations. You have been directed to us as we work closely with your intelligence agency. We may be able to help you identify if these antiquities have, in fact, been looted. This will also assist us in stopping the money going to these organisations. I've been informed that this assistance will be reciprocated."

"Of course. This is a global issue with international consequences," Bridget replied. The last thing she wanted was an organisational turf war over information sharing.

"Well, you're in luck. We have been cracking down on the trade in Britain and antiquities are being confiscated. However, prosecuting is extremely difficult, as you can understand, and I must say that we need to be prosecuting the players behind the scenes, who are like ghosts. They easily find more lackeys to do their dirty work and take the fall."

Bridget said, "I understand. We also believe that a murder took place in Melbourne due to this. We are very keen to track down all those associated and send a strong message that Australia is not a place for the illegal trade of goods."

"I'm glad to hear."

There was a pause in the conversation. Bridget was not sure if she should say something or ask what assistance he could give. She could see that he was thinking and decided to remain quiet. Presently, he broke the silence.

"Have you already confiscated these goods or got them held up with customs?"

"No. We have released them and are tracking them. We have documented these antiquities with extensive photos and videos."

"Good. It sounds like you Aussies are onto it. We made huge inroads in doing the same. What I am going to tell you is strictly confidential, and by that, I mean this is only to be repeated to your superiors and not to any partnering departments."

"Understood."

Bridget looked around the office and saw that only one other person was present on the floor and was down the other end. She continued, "I am in an open-plan office with only one other person present and they cannot hear me. As you can see, I have a headset on but please bear with me as I relocate to a soundproof meeting room."

Bridget undocked her laptop while leaving it open and carried it into a meeting room without losing connection. She closed the door, sat down, and stated that she was now alone.

Sawyer appeared to be in an enclosed office. He reached for something out of sight and brought a mug up to his mouth, which he blew into and took a sip.

"Sorry, I've had an early start and busy morning and need a cup of tea," he said with a smile.

Bridget gave a light laugh and felt that the ice had been broken and the conversation was now between two trusted colleagues. She added, "I had a cuppa tea before this call as I worked all through last night. A coffee would have given me the shakes."

He took another sip of his tea and said, "Ah, that's better," and placed it down out of sight. He straightened himself up and continued.

"Like I was saying, we have recently come in contact with someone who has professional in-depth knowledge of archaeological sites across Syria. He is an expert in his field and has witnessed first-hand the illegal trade and the players involved. We have granted him asylum with a new identity. As you can appreciate, there are many factions that would like him silenced or working for them. What I am getting at is that we can help you formally identify these antiquities and determine if they have, in fact, been looted."

"That is excellent news. I can send you all photos, videos and documents."

"Please do. That will help narrow down what it is that he needs to look at in person."

"In person?" Bridget repeated.

"Can this be done?" Sawyer asked in a well-educated English accent.

"Yes, of course. We know the whereabouts of the items. Most are being held in auction houses, with some already sold. Of those that have been sold, we know to whom, but it may be tricky to gain access to view in person. As you can appreciate, a few may have changed hands more than once and have disappeared. We are doing our best to keep track of them, while at the same time not arouse any suspicion. We did consider placing locator bugs in some, but this was deemed too risky."

"We are on the same page," Sawyer replied. "We would have done the same. If you simply confiscated them, then, yes, we can formally identify them and arrest only those directly involved. That is like arresting drug users while ignoring the supplies and manufacturers."

Bridget nodded and reassured him that every attempt would be made to gain access if required. Also, that they had the manpower in place already monitoring, and were doing extensive background checks on all buyers and sellers.

"That is pleasing to hear. We can work well together. It does not surprise us that they are looking at new markets to trade. Australia is a logical choice as we are also seeing increased activity in Asian markets. Please send me everything you have, and I will be in contact if we need to send this person over."

"Thank you," Bridget replied. "How would you like to receive these?"

"Do it via diplomatic pouch."

"Will do. I'll organise that straight after this call."

They ended the WebEx meeting and Bridget closed her laptop, exited the room, and returned to her desk.

Sitting down, she checked her mobile phone and saw a missed call from Detective Senior Sergeant Adam Zhang. There was no voicemail but a text asking her to call him as soon as possible. She thought about waiting until she had organised the diplomatic pouch, but curiosity got the better of her and she returned his call.

"Hi, Superintendent Unaipon," Adam answered.

"Please, call me Bridget. I'm returning your call?"

"Thanks for calling me so soon. Sorry to interrupt you, but are you having Roman Paxter followed?" Adam asked nervously.

"No. Why do you ask?"

"I had Roman call me asking me the same question. I told him that I wasn't and that I'd check with you. He is certain that someone is following him. He noticed it after we met the other night."

"Well, I can assure you that I'm not. How confident are you that he is being followed?"

"I trust him, and if anyone would notice these things, Roman would. He has seen two different cars trail him and even wait for him down his street. He's only managed to see a partial number plate."

Bridget had been trying to multitask by opening her laptop and typing up the request for the delivery by diplomatic pouch. She now swivelled her chair slightly away from the screen to give Adam her full attention.

"Adam. What have you advised him to do?"

"I told him to do nothing until I spoke to you. He promised he wouldn't, even though he wanted to confront them."

"Good work. We need to identify who this is without them knowing. Please ask Roman to get a plate number and a description of the people without alerting them."

"I have already asked for this. Do you think he is in danger?"

"Short answer is yes. However, if we put a plain-clothed patrol on him, I can guarantee that whoever is following him will notice. Who's to say that these people aren't also trailing Jacob Conway, or Moya Connor or whoever? Shit, they may be trailing you."

Adam confidently replied, "That has also crossed my mind and I'm pretty damn sure I'm not being followed, as I'm the paranoid type and always checking. By the way, I want to give Roman until tomorrow to get a plate number and description, and if he can't, I will intervene as I cannot leave it any longer."

"Great. I like your thinking. Have you spoken to anyone else?"

"I also checked with my boss before trying to call you."

Bridget edged her chair closer to her desk so both elbows rested on its surface. "Adam, this has upped the timeline. If they are on to us, then they will shut this operation down

tighter than a fish's arsehole. I'm about to send all the information on the antiquities you and Detective Constable John
Moskil gathered to an expert who can verify origin beyond
doubt. Tomorrow I'll be catching up with Roman's guys to
see what we are getting from Hong Kong. How's it going from
your end?"

"We have been going through the companies that have imported containers from this Hong Kong shipping company.
We are paying close attention to the business that imported the
latest batch that we searched, as their accounting company is
where Elizabeth Conway worked. All we have is circumstantial
evidence that any defence lawyer with half a brain could get dismissed. Having said that, circumstantial evidence can give solid
leads. I'm more confident than ever that we are on the right
track. Also, I have met with Moya Connor as she said that she
and Elizabeth would sometimes look at the odd antique shops
during lunch breaks. She now recalls that Elizabeth was particularly interested in some pottery that was of Middle Eastern
origin. She also remembers that in the week before her murder
Elizabeth was at her desk looking online at an antique oil lamp.
Moya remembers that she jokingly said, 'Why would you want
to spend close to a thousand dollars on such a thing?' Elizabeth
told her she was just looking."

"Please tell me that no one is doing anymore searching online?" Bridget asked.

"No chance of that. Early on, Roman told them to stay of-
fline, and not do any searching at work or even at home. Roman has been paranoid from the beginning that whoever is

behind this knows how to hack computers and monitor traffic. How else could they have gotten onto Elizabeth? I share his paranoia."

Bridget agreed with Adam. She asked him to contact her as soon as he heard anything from Roman. They ended their call.

Rubbing her eyes. Bridget rotated back to face her laptop and punched away at the keys to get the diplomatic pouch off first thing. Time was not on their side.

CHAPTER 31

Jacob had risen early. He no longer felt the need to stay in bed once his eyes opened. After a strong coffee and two pieces of toast, he was in his garage cleaning his motorbike with the garage door up to let the morning sun in. The bike, which was up on a rear-wheel lift stand, was sparkling. The chain had been cleaned and adjusted. He was bent over tightening the rear bolts with a torque wrench when he heard Roman say, "Good morning."

Roman walked into the garage in a T-shirt, shorts and running shoes. He had beads of sweat on his forehead and was breathing heavily. "Now, that's what a call a clean bike," he said.

Jacob stood up and grabbed a rag that was resting on the bike seat. "Good morning to you too. Did you jog over?"

"Yep. Beautiful morning and I needed some exercise. Need a hand?"

"Yeah, that would be great. Do you mind turning the back wheel while I lubricate the chain?"

"No worries."

Jacob gave the torque wrench a clean with the rag and placed it back on his small workbench. He reached up and got the chain lubricant from a shelf and returned to the bike. With the wheel turning, he sprayed the chain and returned the can it to its place, with the label facing forward. Roman did not miss the fact that the garage was orderly and neat just like the house.

"Need a hand getting it off the stand?"

"Yeah, cheers."

Roman raised the handle of the stand and that, in turn, lowered the rear wheel to the ground, while Jacob held onto the handlebars. Jacob pushed it forward to the side of the garage and rested it on its kickstand. Rolling the rear-wheel stand to its designated position in the back corner, Jacob asked him if he wanted a drink.

They headed inside, and Jacob poured them both a large glass of water. Sitting outside on the patio under the shade of the outdoor umbrella, Roman asked, "Have you noticed anyone following you?"

"No. Not that I probably would. Why?"

"I've got someone following me," Roman said in a matter-of-fact tone, like it was an everyday occurrence.

Jacob put his glass on the table and, with a concerned look on his face, asked him if he was serious. Roman also put his glass on the table.

"That's why I jogged over here. Pretty hard for them to re-main inconspicuous that way. Do you mind walking to your letterbox like you're getting the morning mail and looking down the street to see if a red Audi hatchback is there?"

Jacob hesitantly got up from his chair, walked through the house, out the front door and down the short driveway to the letterbox. He opened it and saw a postcard flyer advertising another real estate agent that claimed they could get you the best price. He looked at the flyer while he took a glance up and down the street.

Sitting back at the outside table, Jacob confirmed that a red Audi hatchback was indeed parked down the road with a guy in the driver's seat. Roman thought for a while, sucking in his lips.

"Fuck it. I'm going to confront the prick."

"Wait a minute," Jacob quickly replied. "Maybe we should phone Detective Adam Zhang."

"I already did, end of yesterday."

"Well, I'm pretty sure he told you not to go and punch the dude's lights out."

Roman, who was pushing himself up with hands on the table, sat back down with a sigh, like a kid that knows his parents are right. "Yeah, he told me to phone him back with a licence plate number and, if possible, a description of the person, while at the same time remaining inconspicuous."

"Okay, we'll do that."

"We can't just walk down your drive and stare at the car. Maybe we walk up and ask him to smile while we take a photo?" Roman said with a cheeky grin.

Jacob saw the funny side and laughed. He thought for a while and then came up with a plan.

"Look. I'll jump in my car and drive away down the road past him. You leave at the same time and start jogging in the other direction. I'll get the plate number and a look at the guy without making it obvious. Let's see who he follows. There's a path down the road that's a shortcut towards the mall. Only for bikes and pedestrians so cars cannot go through. Cut down there, and I'll meet you on the other side."

"Sounds good to me. Let's do it."

They jumped up, headed inside, and placed their glasses on the kitchen bench. Jacob grabbed his car keys and they both headed out the door.

Jacob reversed out of the garage and headed off. In the rear-view mirror, he saw Roman jog the other way. Sure enough, the red Audi hatchback took off to follow Roman. Jacob got the plate number and a good look at the driver.

Driving down the street, he made his way to the back of the shortcut path. Roman was there less than a minute later and hopped into the passenger seat, panting for breath. He grabbed his seatbelt and said, "Let's go. He drove past me and I'm sure he's going somewhere. Quick, quick. We may catch up to him. Let's follow the bastard and see where he goes."

Jacob threw the Volkswagen Golf into gear and they took off, with Roman leaning forward and giving directions.

After only fifteen seconds, they spotted the red Audi hatchback. Roman instructed Jacob to pull back and remain at least two cars behind. He obeyed and, before they knew it, they were on the Eastern Freeway heading to the city.

After a further twenty minutes, and the red Audi hatchback appearing to not know it was being followed, they turned into Lygon Street and watched the car take a park on the side of the road. Jacob, as quick as a flash, turned down a side street. Like a Formula One driver pit stopping, he spun the car into a roadside car park.

Both jumped out of the car and power walked up to Lygon Street to see the guy exit the red Audi hatchback. Slowing to a casual pace, they kept their distance and followed.

What they saw next made them both stop with a "fuck me" look on their faces. The guy had headed into the same café in which they had met Carlos Esposito. Jacob immediately suggested they call Adam, while Roman wanted to head into the café. They decided to weigh up the pros and cons.

Jacob outlined the cons. Firstly, they should notify Adam like he requested, and, secondly, this was the Espositos and not a family you stick your nose into. Thirdly, he didn't want to get into any confrontation that could jeopardise the whole case.

Roman had one pro that was very convincing. Adam had confirmed that the Esposito family business was technically doing nothing illegal or anything to invoke an arrest or search warrant. Maybe they knew what was going on, but obviously they would not talk to the police. So, if they talked to them now, they could be doing the police a favour.

Jacob tried to debate this argument but knew he was fighting a losing battle. Roman's mind was made up. With resignation, he followed his brother-in-law down the street.

Reaching the front entrance, they saw the café was half full, with the brunch crowd starting to leave before the lunch rush commenced. They were greeted by a pleasant young man, who grabbed two menus and started to walk them to a table. Roman stopped him.

"Sorry, mate. We're actually here to see Carlos over there," he said while pointing to a table down the back.

Carlos saw and heard this. He stood up and walked over.

Jacob felt his stomach tighten and concentrated on his breathing. Roman opened his stance, ready for a confrontation.

"Well, I'm not surprised to see you here. We need to talk. Please join us," Carlos said, laying a hand on the back of Jacob's shoulder to indicate the direction and that they did not have a choice.

They reached the table and there was one spare chair, so Carlos grabbed another from a nearby setting and gestured for them to sit. With everyone seated and the air so tense you could cut it with a knife, Carlos smiled and told everyone to relax.

"Jacob and Roman, let me introduce you to my daughter, Sofia, and son, Cristiano."

They exchanged pleasantries, with Cristiano looking uncomfortable.

Carlos continued, "I gather you followed Cristiano here. As much as I love him, he is not the subtlest. In a way, I'm glad you're here. Believe it or not, we are on the same side."

The tension in the air dissipated. Cristiano looked a bit embarrassed but smiled as though he knew and accepted what Carlos had said.

Carlos went on, "Please let me clarify something. When we first met, I was totally honest when I said I knew nothing of Elizabeth's death. It was only a couple of days ago that my kids came to me with some serious concerns about a customer. We have met here today to discuss our next move, and after this meeting, I would have probably got in contact with you."

Roman was about to say something when Carlos signalled for a waitress and told her that they would all have coffees and to bring over a selection of nibbles.

"Thank you, Carlos," Roman responded. "And it's a pleasure to meet you, Sofia and Cristiano. I think we all need to cut through the crap and tell each other how we're connected to all of this."

Sofia and Cristiano remained silent, waiting for their dad's lead. It was obvious that he commanded respect, even from his children. Carlos took the opportunity and informed Roman and Jacob about his son doing a deal with a company from Hong Kong that, while legal, his son should have asked more questions about. He told them about the phone call Cristiano received to obtain the movements of Roman. He told them about the extra payments Cristiano started to receive from an anonymous source in Melbourne, who was to reimburse him for overpayments on the consignments.

After the coffees arrived, Carlos continued and let Roman and Jacob know that his son knew something was wrong, but threats started to be made. He told them that Cristiano confided in Sofia and they came to him as soon as the request was made for information about Roman.

Jacob looked at the coffee in front of him and took a sip. He struggled to swallow as his stomach was tightening. He knew this was getting too much for him, so he concentrated on his breathing.

Roman sensed this and gave him a reassuring glance before asking, "What about Jacob?"

Cristiano replied to this question with, "Jacob was mentioned, but the man I spoke to was more interested in you."

"What man?"

Cristiano got the nod from his dad to continue. "I wish I knew but the number he calls me from is untraceable. He sent me an email with your name, photo, and basic details, including where your parents live. However, this email address is always different and generic and, no doubt, also untraceable. He also has a way of making emails disappear."

Roman, not missing a thing, quickly asked, "So more than one email? What are these other emails?"

Cristiano had noticed that his dad had not mentioned any previous communications relating to Elizabeth. He kept his composure but could feel his dad's glare at this slip-up. In the back of his mind, it registered that Sofia wouldn't have made this mistake.

Cristiano said, "Sorry, what I was meaning is that any email or phone call I got that was not business-related, like the reimbursement payments."

Roman accepted this and asked what information they had about him and what he was going to do with it.

Carlos interjected and let them know that Cristiano had only just told him what he had seen. Carlos let Roman know that he was aware that he and Jacob were in contact with Detective Senior Sergeant Adam Zhang and his partner, John Moskil. He also knew, through what Cristiano had just told him, that they had met with a lady at Jacob's house, which Sofia later found out was Superintendent Bridget Unaipon from the Federal Police.

Carlos took a sip of his coffee. "We were about to decide what information to relay back. Then you two showed up."

Roman also took a sip of coffee. "Tell whoever this is whatever you want. It is obvious to me that this person is behind Elizabeth's murder. You have not mentioned my sister, but I can tell that you've connected the dots. But before you pass on any information I'll let you in on what we know."

This had their attention. Roman outlined that these people were suspected of importing stolen antiquities from the Middle East and supporting terrorist groups, like ISIS. He informed them that he and Jacob were cooperating with the Federal Police as they wanted to get the people behind all of this. He informed them that the Federal Police knew about their family business but did not have any evidence to suggest they were involved. He informed them that this was bigger than any of them, and that they were dealing with extremely dangerous people. He informed them that he and Jacob appreciated their honesty and none of this would leave the room.

Sofia, who had remained quiet, spoke. "So, Roman. How much danger are we in? I don't think we should inform this person that the Federal Police are involved."

Roman answered, "Yes, you are in danger. Yes, we would prefer you to leave the Federal Police out of this. Let whoever it is know that I am speaking with the cops. Let them know that I am hanging out with my brother-in-law. There is nothing unusual with that."

Sofia looked at her brother and father. "One more thing, Roman and Jacob. It appears that these people do not want to do business with us anymore as we have no more orders. No doubt we were not the only ones they used, and if they are as smart as they appear, they would have hedged their risks. Also, we will not be talking to the police as we have too much to lose if they investigate us with a fine-tooth comb. We would appreciate it if you left us out of this and, in return, we will keep you informed of anything else."

Roman glanced at Jacob and then across the whole table. "Agreed."

Roman's phone buzzed. He got it out of his pocket and looked at it under the table. His face drained of colour. Carlos noticed and asked if he was okay. Roman told him he was and thanked him for the coffee. Jacob did the same. They both got up from the table and said their goodbyes, but before they could head for the exit, Carlos got a business card out of his wallet and handed it to Jacob, letting him know to call him if they found anything or needed a hand. Jacob thanked him and asked Carlos if he wanted his phone number, to which Carlos replied that he already had it.

"What was the message?" Jacob asked once they were outside.

"It's not good. I'll explain on the way back to your place."

CHAPTER 32

Back in the suburbs, Jacob waited in his Volkswagen Golf on Kings Way by the Glenn Waverley railway station. Roman had explained the message on the way back and asked to be taken to a public phone box. The message had been from his partner, Joel, in New Zealand. The same Joel who had supplied them with the intel leading them to Hong Kong. The Joel that was now actively involved, thanks to the Federal Police.

Once they had gotten into the car, Roman had told Jacob that the guys doing surveillance in Hong Kong had spotted a guy that used to be in the French Foreign Legion. He informed Jacob that this was not a nice guy and would sell his own mother for a dollar. He also told him that this guy was in the warehouse after hours helping in the movement of goods in and out of the signed-off containers. He outlined that he needed to phone Joel to find out more as this person's name did not come up when they researched the staff employed in Hong Kong.

After fifteen minutes, Roman returned.

"How did it go?" Jacob asked as Roman hopped back into the passenger seat.

"Fuck. This is worse than I thought. Let's head to your place as I need to figure out what to do next," Roman said, looking a tad flustered, which was unusual for him.

Jacob started the car and drove home. Roman was silent the whole way back. Jacob did not dare engage him as he could see that he was busy in thought.

Once inside, Jacob went straight for the fridge and gave Roman a cold beer. He had one himself and they slumped onto the couch in the lounge. Roman took a long swig and said, "I suppose I had better explain."

Jacob took a long drink and waited while Roman placed his beer bottle on the coffee table. He slightly turned his body, so they were facing each other.

"The guy in question is called Mac Hawkins. We knew each other in the Legion. To cut a long story short, he was an arsehole. In fact, he was the arsehole's arsehole. We were in the same unit, along with Joel. We never gelled with Mac. He was one of those guys that seemed to only be in the armed forces to legally kill someone. He had an oversized ego and liked to torment anyone he came across. On a tour one day, we had to escort two captured fighters. Mac decided to bash them around a bit and call them every name under the sun. We had no idea who these fighters were. They could have been simple foot soldiers or higher up. We had no idea, and nor did we need to know. You treat captured fighters according to protocol. We just needed to escort them."

Roman picked up his beer and had another drink. He placed it back on the table in the same place, licked his lips and continued.

"Anyway, Mac went way too far. He beat one of them so badly that a couple of his teeth came out. I had to pull him off the poor guy. In turn, we started to have a fight that was quickly broken up by the other guys in the unit. We covered for him when we dropped them off and said he had fallen while trying to make a run for it. When we got back to base, Joel and I went straight to our CO and reported Mac."

Jacob nodded and asked if Mac got dishonourably discharged.

"Well, not exactly. He got transferred as he strongly denied it and said he was only restraining the poor guy. I think the 'powers that be' didn't want a scandal. He did, however, threaten me and Joel for being snitches. The rest of the guys that were there had our backs. That was the last I heard from him, apart from someone telling me that he had left the French Foreign Legion a year later as more complaints were being laid and he got out to avoid an investigation."

"So, the million-dollar question—is he still dangerous?" Jacob said. "And has he been to Melbourne recently? Also, how is he tied up in all of this, because didn't Joel do a pretty comprehensive check on all staff and associates?"

"You're on to it," Roman replied. "I asked Joel the same question, and being the thorough guy he is, he had already checked on Mac's travels, and there is no trace of him coming to Australia in the last twelve months. He's done regular trips to England and other holiday destinations but none to our end of the world. As for him being dangerous, I would say that he was and, no doubt, still is. Joel also did a background check on Mac and he is definitely not employed by this company. It turns out he has his own security firm, which is very successful, and he is employed by this company as a contractor, which is a bit strange but not unheard of. Usually a large company outsources all its security, and some do it in-house, but most will contract others when specialist services are required. The interesting part is that Mac's company is not contracted for security. However, Mac is employed as a 'contractor'," Roman said, emphasising "contractor" with hand-gestured quotations. "Joel is still investigating this."

Jacob had that thinking look on his face. "Okay. No doubt the police also have this information?"

"Yeah, he said this was included in the latest report they had just sent to the Federal Police."

"Well, first things first. You need to phone Adam and let him know about the car following you. I suggest you say that you have not seen anything today to buy us a bit of time with the Esposito family. Next, we need to see if Moya Connor is okay. The last thing I want is for her to get tied up in this mess if the shit hits the fan."

"I agree. I'll call Adam now."

Roman pulled his phone out of his shorts and rang Adam. He told him that he was certain that he was being followed but had not seen a car today. He also told him that Joel had informed them of the latest developments in Hong Kong, which

Adam was already aware of. Adam asked him for his personal opinion of Mac Hawkins, and Roman was straight-up with him. Roman ended the call and placed his phone on the coffee table.

"Well, Adam knows it all and believes me that I'm probably not being followed any longer. I made it clear that these are professionals we are dealing with, not only in business but also in covert operations, and they can make people disappear and stay disappeared."

Jacob looked at Roman with a concerned look. "What if they were listening in to your phone calls? I mean, are you very careful when talking to Joel?"

"No flies on you, mate. This is a burner sim card I picked up. I change it every day and keep my phone clean. Unfortunately, you cannot make international calls with these cheap burners."

"But I can still call you on your usual phone number?"

"Yeah," he pointed to his phone. "This has dual sim card capability. Not your standard phone."

Jacob looked at Roman's phone, nodded and asked him if he wanted to call Moya. Roman dialled her number and put his phone on speaker.

"Hi, Moya. It's Roman and I'm on speaker with Jacob."

"Hi, guys. What's up?"

"Just wondering if you've had lunch yet, and if not, you want to meet up?"

"That would be great, but I'm just about to leave work and meet Adam for a late lunch. You're more than welcome to join us."

Roman and Jacob gave each other a glance that conveyed their mutual question. Roman asked, "Is that Detective Adam Zhang?"

"Yes, it is. He's being really nice, and we meet up regularly."

Jacob and Roman exchanged a glance.

Roman replied. "That's all right. It's a bit late for us to make it into the city. Say hi to Adam for us."

"Will do."

"Just one more thing, Moya," Roman said in a serious tone. "Not sure how much Adam has told you about the investigation, but Jacob and I think it would be a good idea if you took a holiday and laid low for a while."

There was a slight pause before Moya replied, "What are you talking about? Adam keeps me up-to-date on what is happening. Why would I want to go on holiday?"

Jacob had a thought and answered. "Roman and I are just being cautious. Don't worry about it. Have a good lunch with Adam, and let's catch up again soon."

"That would be great. I miss you guys."

They ended the call on a positive note, and as Roman picked up his phone, he looked at Jacob and said, "What do you mean 'don't worry'? I have no doubt Mac is involved. More than just involved, probably part of running this whole fucked-up operation."

Jacob leaned back and replied, "Look. The last thing we want is for her to panic and feel like we are telling her to do something she doesn't want to do. I am taking this seriously and right now you will call Adam and ask him to also suggest this to Moya. I think his suggestion will carry more weight than ours, and then hopefully she will want to do it."

Roman also leaned back and sighed. "Yeah, you're right. I suppose I'm just used to telling people what to do. Hadn't thought of it like that."

"Besides, Joel told us that Mac hasn't even been to Australia."

"That doesn't mean one of his lackeys hasn't, or someone contracted from his bloody dodgy company. Or, come to think of it, he could have just hired an Australian hitman."

Jacob was taken aback at the thought of someone killing Elizabeth as a paid job. He asked Roman what he thought.

"What I think is that if he did hire someone, it would have been someone he absolutely trusts. But I find it hard to believe that he would trust anyone. This whole operation would be contained in a very tight, small circle of trust. We need to re-member that even though it hasn't been confirmed, they are helping terrorists move stolen artefacts, and, therefore, their clients are extremely dangerous motherfuckers, and, to them, life is disposable. So, Mac and whoever would be shit-scared of fucking up. So, to answer your question, I don't think he would have hired a random local to do the job."

Jacob looked confused. "So, you think bloody terrorists could have killed her?"

"That is a possibility. Let's not kid ourselves that we live in a safe country. I would bet my last dollar that our national security department knows of many confirmed terrorists in Australia and just monitor them to get to the bigger fish. They would foil a lot more plans than they disclose due to this reason."

Jacob gave it a second thought and agreed. It dawned on him how much of a bubble he lived in. He had a nice life and didn't give a second thought to what went into giving him his comfortable, safe lifestyle.

Roman jumped up and said, "I'm bloody hungry. Let's get some lunch. Are you working later?"

Jacob was relieved at the sudden change of subject and felt his stomach rumble. "Lunch sounds good. Let's go to a local café in Kings Way. I'm not working until tomorrow and then I have some days off. Not back full-time yet."

Jacob picked up the two empty beer bottles and put them in the recycling bin. He looked at his watch and saw it was nearly mid-afternoon. As they headed out the door, he reminded Roman to call Adam.

CHAPTER 33

Detective Senior Sergeant Adam Zhang was with Detective Constable John Moskil as they drove to the Federal Police building on La Trobe Street. It was a short drive from the West Melbourne police station where they were based, but the traffic was bad as usual. They were in the morning rush hour that seemed to be more than an hour these days as Melbourne continued to grow faster than any other Australian city. They were driving a totally unmarked car. It didn't have any tell-tale under-the-grill lights or extra aerials on the back.

Adam drove and thought about the case. He reflected upon how he wanted to solve the case for the good of Melbourne, Elizabeth's family, and positive recognition from his superiors. However, he found himself thinking that he really wanted to solve it for recognition from his parents more than anything else. It was funny that, even as a grown man, he still had an overwhelming desire to make his parents proud. He wondered if John beside him also felt like this or if it was just a Chinese trait that was hardwired, even if he was a second-generation Australian.

They pulled into the underground car park and stopped in a space where Superintendent Bridget Unaipon was standing waiting for them. Last night, she had told Adam that she would have someone with her that could formally identify the origin of the antiquities they had been tracking and would be able to confirm if they had been looted. Adam had asked where this person came from, to which he was told not to ask.

Adam turned the car off, wound down his window and greeted Bridget. She leaned down so she could also see John. She pointed to her car, a non-descript white Toyota Corolla, and told them a guy by the name of Mustapha was in the passenger seat. She handed Adam a piece of A4 paper and informed him that they would visit these places to look at the antiques, starting with the one at the top of the page. She and Mustapha would be going in as buyers. Adam and John were to remain outside in their car to observe anyone that went in or out and to provide backup if anything untoward should happen.

Adam and John nodded and stated that they understood. Adam passed the piece of paper to John.

Bridget made her way to her car. Adam started up his engine and waited to follow her to the first location—an auction house that contained three items of interest, located in the pricey suburb of Richmond. John looked at the list and saw six locations they were to visit today with a total of twenty items. He remembered there being at least thirty items of interest but obviously they were targeting items that were at auction houses rather than those already sold.

With Adam driving, John asked who he thought Mustapha was and if that was really his name. Adam focused on the road ahead and replied, "I have no idea. We are only looking at these items with him today, so I assume he is not from Melbourne. He must know his stuff and I wouldn't be surprised if he is someone that has obtained political asylum. As for the name Mustapha—that is fairly common, so it might be correct or false. I would guarantee his last name has been changed. But whatever you do, don't ask any of these questions unless Bridget brings it up."

"Mate, I may look stupid but I'm not that stupid," John said.

"Ha. You know I don't think you're stupid. I hope we all have lunch together, so they can tell us what they find out. I don't want to spend all day cooped up in this car. But we must remember our job, which is to keep an eye on the places and take photos of anyone that comes or goes. Write everything down, as you never know what could prove to be useful in the future."

It did not take long before they were in Richmond. Adam and John pulled up a short distance from the first auction house. They saw Bridget and Mustapha get out of their car and make their way in.

Nothing much happened during the forty minutes they were inside. John took photos of five people that entered, with two lots being pairs and one male by himself. Of these, one pair and the lone male exited during this time. The other pair never came out.

Bridget gave Adam a call once she and Mustapha were back in their car. She did not tell them anything, except that they were moving on to the next place on the list.

This process continued all morning and into the early afternoon. At one fifty, after Bridget and Mustapha had left the fourth auction house, Bridget told Adam over the phone that they were going to stop for lunch at a place just down the road and that they were more than welcome to join them. Adam and John waited until they saw them go inside a café. They made sure no one was following them before they got out of their car to join them.

Once inside, they met Bridget and Mustapha at a table down the back. The tables were in a single row following the side wall, with a long-padded bench seat the length of the café providing seating, and wooden chairs opposite the dotted wooden tables. They were at the last table, with no one beside them, as the lunch crowd was dwindling. Bridget introduced Mustapha to them. They noticed that he had a thick Middle Eastern accent, but his English was exceptional.

They ordered overpriced burgers that arrived after fifteen minutes on small chopping boards accompanied by small, square, wire baskets filled with fries that were made to look like miniature deep-fryer baskets. With their bellies satisfied, and after conversations about the weather and general benign small talk, Bridget final spoke of what they had found.

"It has been a very productive morning," she said as she dabbed away some sauce from the corner of her mouth with a napkin. "There have only been three items that are no longer present from the list, and of the ones we saw, all are from Syria. Of those, we can say that more than half of them were stolen from government-registered archaeological sites. There was also one item that looks to have been stolen from a university in Damascus."

Adam and John simultaneously said, "Wow."

"Mustapha also found one item that was different from how it was listed. Not only that, but it was worth a lot more than what it was being made out to be. When he asked the owner if he was certain the item was as listed, the owner became agitated even though he was doing his best to remain composed. He told us that it had, in fact, already been sold and was being written up to be couriered interstate."

"Interesting. Any idea why?" Adam asked.

"Well, Mustapha and I do not think it was a mistake on the price and label. The owner was packaging some other items at the counter, so he could keep an eye on the shop, and this piece was by the counter. The owner was multi-tasking and probably didn't think anyone would look at it. Mustapha and I think that this was a classic case of a stolen item being sold under legitimate paperwork. Like selling a stolen car using paperwork from another legally registered car of the same make and model."

Adam thanked Bridget for involving them, and Bridget replied that they were working together. This made him and John feel better, and they could see Mustapha start to relax.

Bridget then asked, "So, you are probably wondering how Mustapha knows all this?"

Adam and John waited for the answer to this rhetorical question.

"Mustapha is an expert in his field, and we are extremely lucky to have him assisting us. He cares a great deal about the history of the Middle East and, in particular, Syria."

Mustapha finished eating some fries and spoke. "Thank you, Superintendent, for your kind words."

"Please, call me Bridget, or I will start calling you Doctor," Bridget interrupted with a smile.

"Sorry. *Doctor* does sound presumptuous outside of a university," he replied for the benefit of Adam and John.

Adam could tell by Mustapha's eyes that he was an intelligent man. Mustapha listened intently to everything they said, and when he did talk, his words were measured and well thought out. There was also kindness mixed with sadness in his face. When Bridget mentioned what they had seen, his expression remained stern, but they could tell the passion he had for these antiquities was as strong as the feelings a father has for his child. Adam couldn't resist and asked him how it felt seeing these stolen items.

Mustapha thought for a while, which made Adam and John lean in closer without realising. He glanced at Bridget as if unsure how to proceed. She gave him a nod, not to give permission to talk but to let him know that it was a safe environment.

"I feel sad but also hopeful," Mustapha said. "This is my heritage and the heritage of my family and fellow countrymen that is being pillaged to fund a war that is destroying the beautiful country that my heart calls home. I want to take these items with me straightaway. I must listen to my head and know that this is bigger than one piece. I hold these items and can feel the history. I can feel the significance of what they represent. They are for the people and not the status symbol of an individual."

"I understand," John replied in a sincere tone.

Mustapha continued. "I do also feel hope that there are many people and governments that care as well. I'm not naïve and know that attention is also given because the revenue from these funds a war the West wants to end. However, spending time with Bridget and others that are like-minded makes me appreciate that there is a shared burden to ensure that Indigenous heritage is preserved for future generations, so they can learn about the past and respect the future."

Adam got goosebumps from his words. Mustapha spoke with an educated passion that made you hang onto every syllable.

"We also share this view," Adam said on behalf of himself and John. "This war and unrest in the Middle East is also taking lives over here. I assume Bridget told you that we are investigating a murder?"

Mustapha nodded.

"There are people that do not care about a country's identity," Adam said. "These same people do not even care about the fighting and bloodshed. These people only care about money. These people are helping the terrorist organisations move, sell, and manage their money that is obtained from stealing and extortion. These people will kill anyone that gets in their way. There is another war going on, and that war is supported by the funding of militant forces."

Adam was becoming quite passionate and continued, "These people sit in their fancy houses, drive their fancy cars, and eat at the best restaurants. They are smug because they do not physically have blood on their hands, even though they are the fuel for the war machine engine."

John and Bridget agreed with Adam. Mustapha added, "And they don't lose people that are close to them."

They noticed the sadness that overcame Mustapha. This made it hit home even more that what they were doing was important. They got to go home every night to a cosy house with the knowledge they could get a good night's sleep and wake up in the morning. Kids could walk to school without a care in the world apart from how many likes they got for their latest social media post.

John changed the subject. "So, are you guys going to visit the last two places on the list today?"

Bridget answered. "Yeah, we will. I think we have time, but we had better get going. Have you seen anyone you recognise?"

"Nah, we haven't. Taken lots of photos and made lots of notes, which we'll go over again just in case we have missed something. A copy will be sent to you straightaway."

With that, they got up from the table. Bridget insisted on paying and walked to the counter located in the middle of the café. Mustapha, Adam, and John walked to the front door and waited while she paid. John's mobile phone beeped, and he looked at the screen and placed it back in his pocket.

"Everything okay?" asked Adam.

"Yeah, just my daughter reminding me to pick her up after footy practice," John replied.

Mustapha asked if it was Australian Rules football or soccer. John let him know that she played soccer for the top team at her high school. Mustapha's eyes lit up and he told them that his son loved soccer and had just started playing his first season, and he couldn't wait to get home to watch him play next Saturday.

Adam didn't miss anything and quickly asked what grade he played in.

Mustapha brimming with pride answered, "He is only seven but already has big dreams of representing his county."

Bridget arrived at the door and said that Adam and John had better leave first, and they would follow behind.

Adam and John walked up the road to their car. With Bridget and Mustapha out of earshot, Adam asked, "Did you notice he said his son hopes to represent his county?"

"Yeah, I did. We don't refer to counties in Australia. We'd say region or state. Could be an 'English as a second language' slip up."

"I don't think so," Adam said. "If you ask me, he's been flown in from another country. This thing is bigger than Ben Hur."

"And so it should be. Obviously, the Federal Police have deeper pockets than us. Glad she picked up the tab for lunch. I should have ordered the steak."

They both had a chuckle, even though they were chuffed that they were assisting in the investigation of a global incident.

CHAPTER 34

Thomas Rayner was in his office, looking out at the Hong Kong skyline. This was his favourite place and being up high and looking down on others made him feel superior. He adjusted his cufflinks and turned away from the window to face Mac Hawkins, who was seated on the leather couch.

"So, this had better be good news. I'm getting sick and tired of loose ends."

Mac shuffled in his seat as Thomas sat down in a chair opposite. "I have news on Roman Paxter and some others."

"Well, what is it?" Thomas said impatiently.

"Roman is in contact with the police. Namely, the lead detective, Adam Zhang," Mac said as he referred to some notes on his tablet. "But it appears these are routine follow-ups with family, as Elizabeth's husband, Jacob, was also present."

"Appears? Appearances can be deceptive. You of all people should know that!" Thomas interjected.

Mac wasn't going to take the bait. He hated the way Thomas would cut him off and treat him like an idiot. If it wasn't for him, they would have been caught ages ago. He mentally reassured himself that Thomas needed him as much he needed Thomas. He calmly asserted his authority.

"Please allow me to continue," Mac said, and, to his relief, Thomas relaxed in his chair and remained quiet. "Roman has been hanging out with his parents and Jacob. He has been doing normal everyday activities of jogging, dining out and relaxing. Not once was he seen initiating contact with the police or going out of his way to ask questions, and he has made no contact with Elizabeth's former employer or work colleagues. I have no reason to believe he is conducting his own investigation. I have also been monitoring his phone and internet activity from his parents' house. Nothing out of the ordinary there. I have also been monitoring her brother's and it's the same story. Nothing."

"That is good to hear. Can you trust this information?"

"That I can. This person who followed Roman wouldn't dare cross me. The computer hacking was done by my company, personally overseen by me."

Thomas looked Mac directly in the eyes. Mac was used to this as it was a tactic he used regularly to check if someone was being completely honest. He didn't flinch and continued.

"Besides, the guy who followed Roman got a nice cash reward and knows that his arse is on the line as much as mine."

The truth was that Mac didn't trust Cristiano Esposito. He didn't trust anyone. There was no way he was going to tell Thomas that. He suspected that Cristiano was holding back some information. He couldn't be sure, but he had that feeling. The kind of feeling that had served him well in the past. He knew that Thomas felt the same way and would need further reassuring that he was taking care of his end of the operation.

"Of course, I hedged my bets and had another person also gather information," Mac said, even though it was a half-truth.

"Please continue," Thomas said.

"The other person confirmed this and confirmed that Elizabeth's husband, Jacob, is getting on with life as he has returned to work and stays at home unless hanging out with Roman."

"I won't ask who these people are as it's none of my business. What about her work colleagues and progress on the investigation?"

Mac knew he wouldn't ask about his contacts, just like he wouldn't ask about his. Mac's other contact had been a private investigator from Australia he knew from a security industry conference he had attended many years ago. Mac had helped him out at the time by throwing some work his way for another unrelated matter. It had been legitimate and helped one of his company's clients, who had an office in Melbourne. He had recently asked this person to do some basic background checks on a few people. Background checks that couldn't be done online. The checks included observing who they socialised with and daily routines for a few days. This was normal, but not made public, and was done for those clients that looked to employ or do business with someone and needed to make sure nothing embarrassing or untoward would come out to make them look bad or compromise their empire. This information was not as detailed or specific as what he requested from Cristiano, and that was why it was a half-truth. The reason he chose Cristiano was that he knew his family's business was not totally above board. Mac used another importing company in Australia, but he did not use this one for information or for inconspicuous payments. In fact, they dealt with many importing companies in Australia, as a business the size of Thomas's one would naturally do. Obviously, all of those, bar the two, had nothing to do with the antiquities.

"Elizabeth had only one person from work she socialised with and this person has checked out. The police are still investigating but getting nowhere," Mac lied. He knew that Elizabeth's friend had met up with the lead detective for lunch, but Thomas didn't need to know that. It was in the report outlining everyone she had met within that three-day period. It could have been a social lunch date.

"Excellent," Thomas said as he got up and made his way to a low bookshelf that housed a decanter and lowball crystal glasses. "Want to join me?" he asked as his hand reached the twenty-year-old, single-malt scotch.

"Sure," Mac replied. It was late afternoon and he could do with a drink.

"Water or ice?" Thomas asked as he poured a generous finger for each of them.

"A dash of water, thanks," Mac replied.

Thomas unscrewed the cap off a bottle of water and poured a little into both glasses. He carried the glasses over and handed Mac his as he resumed his seat. They both took a sip.

"Thank you for taking care of the last two shipments. There is only one more to go and then we will step away from this operation. We've had a damn good run and are incredibly lucky we can walk away so cleanly. Let me remind you that even though this has ended, it will never be over. If any of this comes back to us in the future, it is our responsibility to take care of it," Thomas said as he took another sip.

The significance of those words was not lost on Mac. What Thomas really meant was that if anything happened, he would hold him responsible. Mac would need to make sure there were no loose ends. The staff he used in the warehouse were fine. They were none the wiser and thought of it as last-minute changes to shipments that happened from time to time. Doing this after-hours was explained as necessary so as to not disrupt normal day-to-day operations. Using his security staff was his way of offering some overtime to his employees, for which they were always grateful.

"Understood, and thank you for arranging this," Mac said with genuine gratitude.

Mac had no idea who they were doing this for, and nor did he want to know. He knew these antiquities were no doubt stolen and it didn't take a rocket scientist to know who was likely stealing them. He didn't lose any sleep over it. He had made a shitload of money and was planning to sell his company in a year or two and live a life of luxury. Thomas would frown upon him selling too soon. He wondered what Thomas would do. No doubt he had people that wouldn't take too kindly to him packing up shop. Besides, he knew that even though he and Thomas were alike in many ways, Thomas thrived on power that little bit more, and would never retire.

They engaged in loose chit-chat while they finished their drinks. With glasses empty, Mac was about to leave, when Thomas emphasised, "We've had a good run together and I would still like you to be my personal security."

"Of course," Mac said. He would have to bide his time before cutting ties. He knew that Thomas would want to keep him close. Mainly as insurance. Keep your enemies closer, as the old saying went. He was certain that Thomas would dump him in a heartbeat if required. He was also certain that even though Thomas would continue to employ him, he would not be used often. He wouldn't put it past him to have already arranged for him to take the fall if things went wrong.

Mac said his farewells and left the office.

Outside, he said goodbye to Thomas's personal assistant, who looked like he was getting ready to leave for the day. He wondered if he was in on any of it. Was he just a personal assistant? He caught himself in time before his paranoid thoughts ran away on him.

In the elevator going down, Mac knew what his next steps would be. He hadn't told Thomas the whole truth and he needed to make sure that this would not be his undoing.

Little did he know that Thomas was thinking the same thing. Thomas stood back at his office window looking down at Hong Kong city and Victoria Harbour. He had another whiskey in his hand and thought that Mac had done his job exceptionally well, but no one was as good as him. Killing Elizabeth had been necessary. Not to cover up what they were doing, but to buy him time. The police were none the wiser and he had contacts that confirmed this. Not reliable contacts but good enough. He was certain that the police in Australia or in one of the other countries he did this business in would cotton onto him at some stage. It was not thinking your activities would go unnoticed but rather that you had covered your arse so well nothing would stick.

He caught his reflection in the window. He was Thomas Rayner. He had built up a massive business from scratch. He was worth more than 99.9 percent of the world's population. He was smarter than most. He was always going to be one step ahead.

Thomas drained the last of the whiskey with a large gulp and felt the warmth travel all the way to his stomach and then radiate out through his whole body. That had taken the edge off and he felt relaxed. He placed the glass down beside the decanter and checked his reflection in the mirror. He ran his fingers through his hair, admiring the distinguished grey streaks that were carefully maintained. He ran his index finger along his groomed eyebrows. He adjusted his collar and tie even though they were already perfect. He liked what he saw.

He sat at his desk and set to work triple-checking his exit. It was not the first time he had wound up an illegal deal or relationship. This was the reassurance he gave the suppliers. Or should he call them terrorists? No, they were just suppliers. Suppliers that he had made a lot of money for. When he watched the news, and saw the fighting going on in the Middle East, or any part of the world, all he saw was the opportunity to make money.

CHAPTER 35

Roman and Jacob were enjoying lunch with Moya at a riverside Italian restaurant at Southbank. They sat outside enjoying the warm, blue-sky day, with summer officially starting next week. The temperature was perfect under the shade of the awning. Elsewhere along the Yarra River, the sun was getting too hot, and people sought the edge of the concrete walkways to get relief from the leafy trees that reduced the heat to the ground and softened the impact of the buildings on what had been a natural landscape only a couple of hundred years ago.

Moya thanked them both for meeting her for lunch. Her auburn red hair shone with different shades of colour in the natural light as the soft breeze played with it.

Adam and Jacob were grateful that they had reunited. Jacob noticed that Moya was looking healthier than when they first met. She had a glow in her cheeks and her eyes were alive rather than sad. He wondered if he was looking better. His in-laws had told him a few times that he needed to look after himself, which he took to mean that he looked like shit. It appeared that Moya had read his mind.

"You're looking better," Moya said.

"Thank you."

Jacob took it as a sincere comment, even though he was still struggling to live without his rock. There were tears every night. During the day, he kept busy at work, spending time with Roman, or doing jobs around the house, which was now in a state of cleaner than clean. It was when the day was over and the silence set in that the loneliness and emptiness hit home like a freight train. He knew these feelings would lessen over time but never cease.

"How's it all going in your life, Moya?" Jacob asked.

"As good as it can. Work is still work but not the same. It feels like we've been audited multiple times, right down to how we hold a pencil. Of course, I miss seeing Elizabeth every day."

Roman stated that he felt the same, even though he knew this didn't make sense as he hadn't seen his sister for years. Jacob and Moya read between the lines, and reflected that he had seen her every day growing up—something they didn't experience.

They engaged in general chit-chat until the food arrived. A bottle of Pinot Noir from the Mornington Peninsula in Victoria accompanied the fresh pasta.

With the wine flowing and the pasta exquisite, it felt like they were in the company of old friends. Eventually, the conversation had to turn to the ongoing murder investigation. Luckily it wasn't until they had finished their meals and were waiting for the coffees to arrive. It was Moya that broached the subject.

"Sorry, guys, but I have to ask. Have you heard anything more on the investigation? The reason I ask is that I don't believe it was a coincidence that you asked me to take a holiday moments before Adam asked me the same thing."

Roman leant forward and took the lead to Jacob's relief. "You just have people that care about you."

"Don't give me that shit," Moya replied in a playful tone that disguised her seriousness.

"Well, what has Adam told you?" Roman said, echoing her tone.

Jacob wondered if this was flirting. He prided himself on an ability to read people, which was a handy skill to have being a doctor. However, they seemed more like best friends than when he first saw them interact.

"Adam hasn't told me much," Moya said. "He just tells me that the investigation is progressing, but I'm not an idiot, and judging by what's going on at work, it is definitely related to what we found out. I just can't figure out if the company I work for has been indirectly or directly involved in the illegal trade of stolen antiquities."

Roman and Jacob look stunned. They knew that Moya had an inkling that antiques may be involved but not that she knew they were stolen or antiquities, with the term "antiquities" implying that they were from archaeological sites of significance rather than the old items of value that the term "antiques" implied.

Roman again took the lead and asked how she knew this.

"It was not hard. I remembered the items Elizabeth took interest in when searching online. These were not old hardwood writing tables, or dolls your great, great grandmother would have owned. They were ancient items of cultural significance. I told Adam this, and he tried to dismiss it, but I persevered."

"So, I gather he caved in and told you this was the case?" Jacob asked.

"Of course. He was just starting to look stupid after I told him I had seen Elizabeth's browsing history and put two and two together. He told me this was the case and that you both also knew. He thanked me for the work I initially did with you but told me rather firmly to stop snooping, as the best minds in law enforcement were onto it."

"Well, he's right, you know?" Roman said.

"Yeah, I know he is. He said it more as a friend concerned about me than as a direct order from a detective. I told him how it came to me that Elizabeth talked at length one lunchtime about a documentary she watched with you," she said, looking at Jacob.

Jacob was silent and appeared to be lost in thought. Their coffees arrived, and after the waitress left, Roman and Moya waited for him to talk.

He felt the memories stir up in him again. Roman opened his mouth to speak but Moya cut him off. "Sorry, I forget that this is exponentially more difficult for you."

"No, that's okay. It just brought back the time it dawned on me that I should have taken that documentary and the curiosity it sparked in Elizabeth a lot more seriously."

He lifted his tulip cup to his mouth and lightly blew on the hot, strong, long espresso before taking a sip. Placing the cup back on the saucer, he solemnly continued, "I remember that documentary now like it was yesterday. A British investigative journalist did a revealing piece on the extent of the looting in Syria by ISIS. She provided facts that this had always been an issue with many parties involved, but they took it to a level never seen before. I remember pieces had even been found in reputable museums and this had prompted them, galleries, and other institutions to increase their security checks when purchasing. Elizabeth and I were intrigued at the extent of it and the dollar value estimate. Elizabeth mentioned that she wondered how many items made their way to Australia, as the documentary focused on Europe."

Moya reached over the table and placed her hand on Jacob's. No words were spoken. The gesture spoke volumes.

Roman added, "Hindsight lets us see things for what they were, but we must remember all these things shape us into what we are today, be that good or bad. I promise you that Elizabeth's curiosity will be for the benefit of all."

"Thanks, guys," Jacob said.

They all took a moment and focused on their coffees. Jacob changed the subject in his mind, which was a tool he learnt at work to switch off after a taxing day. He wondered if Moya had feelings for Roman as he sensed something when they first met. He was not getting that vibe today. He suddenly felt bad for letting his train of thought be side-tracked when Elizabeth was the most important thing in his life.

Roman looked around and then at Moya. "Moya, sorry to ask, but from the start we were extremely cautious to not investigate anything online. Have you been looking at anything at home or at work in relation to this?"

"Why do you ask?"

"Sorry. It's just that you mentioned looking at Elizabeth's browsing history and I sensed you went into these pages?"

Moya's facial expression became ashen. "I didn't look at many. I thought since the police were involved, a little peek wouldn't matter."

Roman leaned into the table like a headmaster dealing with a troubled child. Jacob and Moya leaned in as well. He spoke in a hushed, stern tone, emphasising every word. "Moya. This is serious. I cannot stress enough how serious this is. When these people sense danger, they do not give a second thought to come out swinging and eliminate any threat to their way of life. Please trust me on this. Obviously, Adam cares for you a great deal, as I know he has been giving the same advice."

The look on Moya's face confirmed that the message was sinking in. Jacob spoke in a more compassionate tone. "Moya, we all care about you. You have been instrumental in helping the police. This is bigger than even Roman and I can comprehend. It would break my heart if anything happened to you."

"I'm so sorry," Moya replied with a lump in her throat.

"No need for apologies," Jacob said. "Your heart is in the right place."

"We have your back," Roman interjected, relaxing his tone a bit to emulate Jacob's. "If I were you, I would take a long holiday. Lie low for a while. Become invisible and let whoever is behind this know you are not a threat."

"What about you guys?" Moya asked.

"We have been careful. I've been having this same conversation with Jacob and he is getting on with work and giving the appearance that he is dealing with the grief of losing a loved one like any normal person. Yes, we are liaising with the police but making sure we are not leaving any digital footprints. It is normal for loved ones to have contact with the detectives leading the investigation. As for me, I'm spending time with my parents and brother-in-law."

"And he is not your average person," Jacob added with a gentle elbow to Moya's arm. "He can look after himself a lot better than you and I."

Moya thought for a while. "But why would I be in danger? I mean, I know bugger all compared to the police and it's not like I am a witness in any of this. I don't even know who's bloody involved."

"You'd be surprised by how much you know," Roman answered. "They could use what you know to get to other people."

"I hadn't thought about me putting other people in danger."

"Also, remember that this is organised crime. A show of force for them sends a message to everyone else."

The penny dropped. Moya had made up her mind that the advice she was being given was to be adhered to. "Shit, I've been bloody naïve. I will take a holiday. Maybe do a road trip up the top end of Australia and see the sights. Do I need to be totally incognito?"

"No. You can still email friends and use the ATMs for money. Go online and enjoy yourself. Post photos on social media if you wish. Make it look like a holiday and like your mind is a million miles away from work. Being totally off the grid may do more harm than good. Just one word of advice. Post photos after you've left the town you've been in. Withdraw money on the way out. If you're concerned about safety, tell the hotel when you leave where you are going."

"Thanks, Roman. First I need to arrange time off with work and wind up a few things I'm working on."

"Well, make it sooner rather than later, and I'll follow you on social media. If I leave you a message saying that you're making me jealous with your long holiday, you know it's all good to come back to Melbourne."

"What if I just want to come back? I can't holiday forever."

"Ha. That would be nice. Let me know when you'll be back, and I'll make sure everything is good. It's about you showing you are not snooping around, as much as being out of town," Roman reassured her.

Jacob lightened the mood by asking Moya to have a drink for him while sitting back and chilling out.

With their coffees drained, they settled the bill and bid each other farewell before they walked in separate directions. Moya went back to work and Roman and Jacob headed to Flinders Street Station to catch a train home.

"I think you should call Adam and let him know that Moya will get out of town for a while," Jacob said after Moya was out of earshot.

"Good idea," Roman replied, getting his mobile phone out. "I also want to catch up with him and that Bridget from the Federal Police, as I got an interesting message from Joel last night. Keen to come along?"

"Sure, I have all day tomorrow," Jacob said. He was enjoying Roman's company, and it felt like if he stopped getting involved now, it would be like leaving a grand final match at half-time.

CHAPTER 36

Roman and Jacob were at the Melbourne West Police Station in a meeting room with Detective Senior Sergeant Adam Zhang and Superintendent Bridget Unaipon. Rather than a casual chat, this was more of a formal meeting but without minutes or any other party. Law enforcement were on one side of the table and civilians on the other.

"You called this meeting, so what would you like to discuss?" Bridget asked Roman and Jacob after pleasantries had been exchanged and everyone was seated.

"Jacob and I have heard from Joel that you are winding down the use of our business for gathering intel in Hong Kong. Do you think this is wise? Everything is pointing to these guys wrapping up their operation, so this is when eyes on the ground are needed."

"We are aware of this," Bridget said, not allowing Roman to start another sentence.

After an uncomfortable two seconds of silence, Jacob spoke. "What Roman is trying to say is that we would still very much like to be involved. We know that time is running out."

Adam interjected as he did not want the meeting to turn into a "them versus us" scenario. "Of course, I want you guys involved. You have been more than generous with your time. On a side note, thanks for helping me convince Moya Connor to get out of Melbourne for a while. Speaking of which, I hear she is planning on leaving in a few days?"

"Yeah, she is," Roman answered. "I would have preferred sooner but she was determined to finish some account she was working on."

Bridget sensed the friendly connection they had and shuffled in her chair. "Sorry, guys. I don't want to be painted as the baddy. However, this goes against all protocol to get a victim's husband and brother directly involved in an investigation."

"With all due respect," Jacob said, "it was Roman and I that got onto the lead of these shipments from Hong Kong, with the help of Moya. It was Roman and I that captured footage of containers being covertly tampered with prior to loading, which then Adam figured out the reason for and kicked off your involvement. It was Roman and I that met with a retired underworld organised-crime boss that helped rule out any involvement from the usual suspects."

"Yes, yes, yes, I get it. I am just emphasising that this is against protocol. I didn't say I was against it."

They all relaxed a fraction and sat a little less rigidly, as Bridget continued. "Okay. Let's start afresh. You are correct in that things are winding down and we do need to move fast. I gather you know a bit more than you should be privy to, and I'll leave it at that. We are tracking all companies that accepted shipments, and they still have consignments on their way, but they are not being sent to the same place as the last few. After this, there is no evidence that containers will continue to be shipped with antiquities on board. Well, not from this company. Who knows if another company will not simply take over?"

Jacob rubbed his chin and felt the stubble from not having shaved for a couple of days. "With all due respect, we are interested in solving the murder of my wife. But we also want those behind it brought to justice, or this added to the charge sheet they will no doubt receive. We feel that we have more to add in assisting you before they vanish."

Bridget looked at Adam and then back at Jacob. "What is it you're not telling me?"

Jacob gave a sideways glance to Roman, who simply gave a nod to indicate that he would take over.

Roman sat up straight, took a deep breath and spoke across the table. "You know how I thought I was being followed?"

"Yes," Bridget and Adam answered at the same time.

"Well, I know that I was, for a fact. I confronted this person and Jacob was with me. The reason we didn't tell you is that we promised this person we would not tell the police. And before you ask why, let me explain. This person has done nothing wrong. This person felt threatened to provide information on what I was doing with my days and who I was meeting. This information was given to someone who goes to great lengths to remain anonymous. No doubt something similar was done to provide information on Elizabeth, and we all know what happened next. Therefore, I know we are getting close."

"This is the Esposito family, isn't it?" Bridget interjected.

"Yes, it is," Roman said as if he was expecting Bridget to say this, while hiding his surprise. Deep down, he was glad she put this out in the open, and also she went up a notch in his books.

"Well, let me tell you, the Federal Police have kept a close eye on Carlos Esposito for many, many years. I know they have been an active importer of these containers and we have investigated them so thoroughly I feel like I know them better than my own mother. Sofia and Cristiano now run the family business, so please spit it out if they have told you something."

"They have confirmed that they have no more orders from that company in Hong Kong. They believe that someone or persons from this company were responsible for Elizabeth's death and are glad they will no longer do business with them. It was only recently that Cristiano and Sofia came to this conclusion and, if you ask me, they looked scared."

"Does Carlos know?" Bridget asked.

"Yes," Roman answered. "He was initially in the dark and reassured us in the presence of his kids that the family business is now one hundred percent legitimate."

Adam leaned in and asked Roman, "When you say they looked scared, do they think these people are tying up any loose ends? This would explain your desire for Moya Connor to lie low."

Roman simply replied, "Yes."

Adam continued. "This makes sense. If anything, they want to buy themselves time. I also agree with this and am glad Moya is taking a holiday soon. She has, without my knowledge, been looking into this company. They will want to send a clear message to deter anyone else from doing the same."

Jacob asked, "But the accounting company Moya and Elizabeth work for is not guilty of any wrongdoing?"

Bridget rested her elbows on the table and made a pyramid with her fingers. "Yes, they are fine. We have assisted Adam with the forensic accounting investigation. They have done nothing wrong. What we have concluded is that this is bigger than the sale of stolen antiquities. We believe this also involves money laundering. They are selling antiquities through Australia and then investing within the country, making a huge profit, and then sending the funds back overseas by overpaying for goods, which is easy to do with antiques as values are extremely subjective."

Roman and Jacob gave each other a look that let each other know that they remembered what Cristiano Esposito said about extra payments for shipments. This would stay between them. No doubt the Federal Police already suspected this but didn't have any hard evidence.

Jacob perceived that Bridget and Adam had noticed this exchange of looks, so he quickly spoke to quell any suspicions. "Yeah, Roman and I were talking the other day about a news item we saw on money laundering and how Australia had become a target due to its strong economy during the global financial crisis. You could have bought a house in Melbourne or Sydney and easily doubled your money in five to seven years, whilst claiming you had spent a fortune renovating."

"Exactly. This brings me to the topic of you guys being in contact with the Espositos," Bridget said. "Like I mentioned, they have done nothing 'technically' wrong." She emphasised "technically" with air quotation marks. "Anything you can tell us would be appreciated."

Roman asked, "Why are you focusing on them, as you mentioned others have been importing antiques?"

"We are not stupid."

"I never said you were," Roman replied, with a little bit of doubt now creeping into his mind about the Esposito family's motives, and whether they were to be trusted.

There was silence as Bridget expected Roman to continue. Roman took the hint and said, "Just trust us when we say they are not involved. The reason we wanted to meet with you is in part to do with them. They have had word that this company is going to stop doing business here and they believe they are in the process of tying up loose ends. You know as well as us that this could end up in more bodies being found and evidence disappearing quicker than you can say…"

"Yeah, yeah, yeah, we know," Bridget condescendingly said with a smile that revealed her perfect teeth and left him confused as to whether he had just received a slap in the face or a friendly remark.

Detective Adam Zhang sensed things were starting to deteriorate. "Look, Roman and Jacob. Bridget and I are working closely. I understand that it must be frustrating to feel that the murder investigation is taking a back seat, but let me reassure you that this is not the case. We are looking at the top down.

Who ordered this? Who stood to benefit from this? Trust me when I say we are getting close. I know you have a personal beef with Mac Hawkins, who is clearly behind these shipments, but this goes higher than him."

Adam looked at Bridget to gauge if he should continue and got a stern shake of the head.

"You mean Thomas Rayner? The owner and CEO of the shipping company, who also has his fingers in every type of business that is remotely linked to global logistics?" Roman said.

Bridget remained composed and weighed up whether to take the bait or remain silent and call an end to the meeting. She decided on the former. "What do you know about Thomas Rayner?"

"I know that he isn't squeaky clean. There are numerous rumours that he is one person you do not cross. He is one very wealthy man, but keeps a low profile. He has been informally investigated by many international agencies but never charged with anything. Shall I continue?" Roman asked.

"No, that will do. I forget that your day job involves gathering intel," Bridget answered. "Please cease looking into him, and this includes your friends. I ask you out of professional courtesy. What I am about to say does not leave this room. Thomas Rayner is very much on the radar and not just with the Federal Police, but also many international agencies that we are working closely with. If he smells a rat, this could jeopardise everything. I cannot go into details as even I do not know all the specifics. But trust me on this. This includes a person by the name of Mac Hawkins, whom I'm informed you personally know. We are monitoring them and if they get on a plane or even sneeze, we will know."

"Okay. I also forget that you are very good at your day job."

Adam's phone rang. He took it out of his pocket and looked at the screen. "It's Moya," he said with a surprised look. He swiped the screen to answer and held it up to his ear.

The look on his face changed from surprise to confusion to concern. "What do you mean? Slow down. What has happened?"

Adam was off his chair and turned to face the wall as if to give Moya all his attention and help him concentrate on what was being said. He listened with great earnestness and then said, "Okay, now listen carefully. Call an ambulance straightaway, stay put, and I'm on my way."

Adam ran out of the room without so much as an explanation or goodbye.

Roman was straight after him.

CHAPTER 37

Roman and Jacob arrived at Moya's place a good twenty minutes after Adam. They need to catch a taxi since they had caught the train into the city. Luckily Moya's apartment wasn't too far away. Their minds raced with anxious thoughts about what could have happened. All that Adam had said as they raced out of the meeting room was that Detective John Moskil had been badly injured.

Roman and Jacob raced up to Moya's floor. There were a couple of uniformed police officers outside her apartment door and they wouldn't let them in. Adam eventually exited with Moya and informed the uniformed police officers to not let anyone in until the crime scene investigators had arrived and declared it safe to do so.

Moya looked as pale as a ghost and stayed close to Adam with her arm looped around his. Her eyes were rimmed by dark circles from crying, accentuating the smudged make-up. She didn't acknowledge their presence and, instead, focused on the floor.

Adam signalled for them to follow him and Moya out of the building. They took the lift to the ground floor and made their way to Adam's car, which was parked directly outside with half the vehicle on the footpath. He opened the front passenger door and guided Moya into the seat. He left the door open, resting his arm on the top. Roman and Jacob moved closer, forming a half-circle around the shaken Moya, who lifted her head slightly to make eye contact.

"How's John?" Jacob asked.

Adam answered, "The ambulance left just before you arrived. He is in a bad way and was still unconscious when they took him away. I've already informed his wife and I will go to the hospital after this."

"So why was he here?" Roman asked.

"I had asked him to spend a bit of today keeping an eye on Moya's place, taking note of any anyone that came and went from the building, including anyone that seemed remotely interested in it as they walked past." He looked at Moya and then back at them. "Before you ask, Moya didn't know."

"But why?" Roman asked again.

"We have a shitload of photos and surveillance footage of everything that's been happening so far, including people going in and out of the antique dealers that have the antiquities we know about. We are doing our best to match anyone we can. With Moya being at risk, we thought it wise to monitor her place."

"Sorry, I didn't mean to be pushy. Now that you explain it, it makes sense. Obviously, you know what you're doing," Roman said. He started to think that maybe Adam cared for her more than they realised? He would keep this to himself. Now was not the time.

"That's okay. Detective work is all about eliminating suspects, and in this case, that list is huge."

"I'm sorry. I'm so sorry," Moya blurted out with fresh tears making their way down her cheeks.

Jacob bent down into a squat position and took Moya's hand. "You have nothing to be sorry about. Detective John Moskil is a tough guy and I'm sure he'll be all right. I'll even go to the hospital myself and talk to the doctors. It could have been a lot worse if you had not come home."

Moya made eye contact with Jacob and could feel the warmth and sincerity in his voice and touch. "Thank you."

Roman noticed how compassionate Jacob could be. It made him realise why he was a good doctor and why his sister had married him. He needed to be more like that but found himself always thinking of the details, the next move, who's to blame, rather than stopping, taking a pause, and thinking about the people involved.

Jacob remained on his haunches comforting Moya and gave Roman and Adam a look that suggested they talk somewhere else.

Adam and Roman moved to the entrance of the building out of earshot. There was still a patrol car out the front that belonged to the two uniforms acting as scene guards. Another car pulled up that was obviously a plain police car, with the red and blue grill lights visible even though they were off. A man and woman exited in police-embossed overalls. They moved to the boot and retrieved two serious-looking large briefcases.

"Hey, Adam, anyone still at the scene?" the woman asked as they made their way to the entrance.

"No one. There were two ambulance staff that saw to John, and Moya the owner who found him. Two uniforms entered and are now guarding the scene for you guys and, of course, me. I'll forward you details soon."

"Cheers. We might as well start." They made their way into the building, leaving Adam and Roman alone again.

"So, was anything taken?" Roman asked.

"I did do an initial search with Moya and we found that her personal laptop was missing. Apart from that, it looks like nothing else was taken, but Moya did think that someone had been through her drawers even though they looked undisturbed."

"Between you and me, what do you think happened?"

"Well, this does stay just between us. I think someone broke into her place and was searching it, being extremely careful to go undetected. I have no idea why John made his way into the building and up to Moya's. I can only speculate that he saw someone or something, as from where he was observing, he could look up and see Moya's windows." Adam pointed across the street to the café where John had been sitting.

Roman took a few steps off the footpath and looked up, as the corrugated awning from the entrance obscured his vision. There were awnings of various designs on most buildings and shopfronts down this end of Flinders Lane. He counted the floors and satisfied his own mind that there was a line of sight, even though he never doubted it. For some reason, he still liked to verify things himself.

"So why take the laptop if you think this person wanted to go undetected?" he asked, making his way back to Adam.

"I'm already speculating it was a man as it is more likely that a man overpowered John and put him out cold. Mind you, a woman could have done it if she was very well-trained. Anyway, my gut is telling me that he didn't intend to steal anything. I think he grabbed the laptop in a hurry when leaving. The game was up. He knew his break-in was compromised. One more thing—I couldn't find John's phone, which he would have used for taking surveillance photos. It might turn up as the apartment is searched or this could also have been taken."

"I see where you're coming from," Roman said. "I also assume you're going to have the apartment searched for bugs?"

"Of course. And get every available CCTV footage from up and down this laneway."

"Going back to your theory that it was a man—how well-trained is John?"

"He's no pushover. He may have gained some pounds over the years, but he's still fit and strong. I've seen him restrain many a big bloke that wanted to take his head off."

Roman thought the same from what he had seen of John. Experience in the police alone will make you more than a match for the average drunk heavyweight-champion wannabe. He looked at Adam's car and saw Jacob still comforting Moya. He still had a couple of questions for Adam. "If this intruder was disturbed by John, and therefore his cover was blown, do you think this was attempted murder?"

"Well, let's pray that this does not turn into a murder investigation. John is in a bad way. You and I are obviously thinking along the same lines. Whoever did this would have wanted John dead and maybe he thought he was. Maybe he left without double-checking 'cause he didn't have time."

Adam's phone rang, and he looked at the screen and answered. It was a short conversation with a few "okays". He hung up and said, "I think we may be right. The crime scene guys didn't take long to discover a listening device hidden underneath the couch."

"Shit," was all Roman could say.

"I'd bet my last dollar they will discover more."

Roman nodded his head. "Another thing. Have you had a chance to talk to Moya about what is on her laptop?"

"Briefly. It was bad enough asking her to go through her place to see if anything was missing. I need to see if she has anywhere to go tonight as I doubt she'll want to stay at her place. I would invite her to mine, but it might not be ethically correct."

Adam turned to walk back to his car, but Roman gently held his arm. "Sorry, but one more thing that is playing on my mind."

"What would that be?" Adam replied, as he adjusted his stance to face Roman.

"Back at the police station, it occurred to me that you and Bridget have the Esposito family firmly in your sights. I am getting the impression that you are not telling me everything. Do you think they are behind what's happened here?"

Adam was taken aback by the question and his face showed it. He thought for a second and then realised that this pause was making him look more suspicious. He should have flat-out denied it instantly, or at least said that it was none of his business. The damage was done and if he said those things now, Roman would see right through it. He trusted Roman and took another second to formulate the idea that speaking the truth may be a good thing and Roman could help him.

"Okay. Now listen carefully, and this must also stay between us," Adam said as he moved closer to Roman and lowered his voice while making sure no one could eavesdrop. "John and I have seen Cristiano going in and out of one of the known antique dealers. We have photos to prove it. We also obtained CCTV footage from neighbouring shops from other known antique dealers that have received stolen antiquities from his consignments. And guess what? He appeared in another recently. That is not all. In one shot, which we personally took, he appeared to go in with a small parcel or large envelope in his hand and exit fifteen minutes later empty-handed. Bridget has also been gathering intel from his recent movements and things are looking extremely suspicious."

Roman saw a group of pedestrians walking towards them from over Adam's shoulder and gave Adam a nod to let him know. They paused and moved closer to Moya's apartment building entrance for greater privacy. With the coast now clear,

Roman asked, "Are you going to arrest him or get a warrant to search his premises?"

"Not yet. We don't have enough to satisfy a judge for a warrant, let alone enough to arrest him. That is why I'm telling you. Can you help me?"

"You want me to do some snooping, so the police don't look bad if they get snapped doing it?"

"No, nothing like that. I was thinking that you could just talk to him, or his dad. They won't give us police officers the time of day. You've already let us know that you and Jacob spoke to him, his sister and dad. That's more than any of us have ever been able to do."

"Okay, I'll do it. I'll make sure Jacob is with me as he has a way of making people open up. I am, however, going to tell them that you guys suspect them and that I can help. You know as well as I do that if I try to bullshit them, they will see right through me."

"Cheers, mate," Adam said as they both walked back to Moya and Jacob.

Jacob saw them make their way over and stood up from his crouching position, shaking his legs to get the blood flowing. "Just to let you know, Moya will be staying with me tonight. Just let us know when it's safe to get a few things from her place."

"It should be fine for her to go up anytime. I'll take you," Adam said.

"Thanks," Moya responded, and she began to get up from the passenger seat.

"I have an idea," Roman said as Moya stood beside them around the open car door. "I know you were going to holiday up north, but I think you should head over the ditch to New Zealand and stay with my partner, Joel. He'll take good care of you. He's a top bloke and there's other guys from our business located there, so you'll be in safe hands."

Moya looked at Adam and Jacob and saw there were no objections on their faces. In a weak voice that sounded exhausted rather than defeated, she said, "I would like that."

"Settled then," Adam said with hope and enthusiasm. "Let's go up to your place so you can pack a bag. I still need to get a statement from you, but I'll send a detective over to Jacob's later tonight. Roman, Jacob, you will need to stay down here as the crime scene team is still doing their thing."

Adam and Moya walked to the entrance, and when they disappeared into the building, Jacob turned to Roman. "Now, tell me everything you guys talked about."

CHAPTER 38

Thomas Rayner was once again staring out of his office window in Hong Kong. It was nearly one in the morning. He held his third whiskey in his hand, having consumed two before a delightful high-end hooker with soft skin had come up and pleasured him on his couch. Security escorted her up and then out of the building, which they were used to doing. She came dressed like a businesswoman, as they often did for their clientele, but who were they fooling? No businesswoman having one-on-one meetings with CEOs looked like that.

His tie and jacket were draped over the back of his desk chair. He had his top two shirt buttons undone, which was about as casual as he got. The city lights from the mass of buildings that hugged Victoria Harbour made him feel safe. Looking down on it all made him feel powerful.

He had spent that day double, triple, and quadruple checking his exit strategy from his latest underworld business venture. This one had been his most risky, but with greater risk came greater rewards. He knew another opportunity would be just around the corner. He had a reputation he was tremendously proud of. Every day, legitimate business had made him successful and rich beyond comprehension, but he had an internal drive for pushing the limits and proving he was smarter than the next. Other CEOs played golf or bungee jumped to get their kicks. Those activities bored him and came across as pointless.

He took a sip of the single malt as he observed a tourist boat bobbing up and down in the harbour. He was feeling proud that he had pulled off this undertaking for the last three years. It had gone better than he initially thought it would and lasted longer than planned. The original agreement had been for a year, maximum. However, the stakes got higher and he couldn't resist challenging his own skills and intelligence. Upon reflection, he had made his clients more money than they could have dreamed of. No other person could have done what he had done. This was a blessing and a curse. He was too good. His clients knew that. They knew no one else could generate the revenue he had. They would struggle without him. They had also made this clear.

Thomas had never feared anyone. He didn't fear them either. He knew what fear was but hadn't experienced it. He was smart enough to know that these people were ones he should fear. The one way to protect himself was to make sure that nothing he did could be traced to them. This was expected and what he excelled in. He was sure this had been done. However, it was not that simple. The curse of his brilliance was that his clients expected their revenue stream to be maintained and looked to him to safeguard this.

He could still smell the perfume from the escort when he lowered his glass. He raised it again and took a long smell of the aged whiskey. He knew her smell would dissipate soon. It's not that he didn't like the smell of expensive perfume, he just preferred that his office got back to the smell of wood, whiskey, and leather. He diverted his gaze from the window to his desk. He found his mind checking things for the fifth time. The only weak link was Mac Hawkins. However, nothing tied them together except authentic security matters. It was Mac that supervised shipments and took care of external contracts that were required to move the goods. His hands were clean of any wrongdoing. There were no discriminating signatures on shipments, with extra payments made through non-traceable aliases and offshore companies with no links to him. He had an accountant at the start of his career hide these extracurricular activities, but he never trusted him. He still didn't fully trust anyone. Thomas learnt how to do all this creative accounting himself, which wasn't hard. In fact, he knew he was doing a better job.

Returning his look to the window and finishing the last of his drink, he contemplated pouring another. He decided against it as he could feel the alcohol starting to take effect, and this was as far as he would ever get. Taking the edge off was desirable but he could never understand why people would get drunk and lose their ability to function to a high standard. The thought of not being in control did not appeal to Thomas. He would never allow it.

Thomas placed the empty glass on the coffee table for his assistant to clean tomorrow. One clause in his assistant's job description was the cleaning of his office. No way would a cleaner be allowed in there.

He got his tie off the back of his chair and took a few steps to his mirror on the far wall. He raised his collar and did up the last two buttons of his shirt. Draping the tie around his neck, he proceeded to tie a double Windsor knot. While he did this, the thought of ensuring a smooth transition with his overbearing clients dominated his mind. He couldn't pay someone to get rid of them, nor could he ignore their demands. He had to give them something or someone that could continue their venture. One thing he knew for certain was that his company and all his intermediary companies would have nothing to do with them. He had some other businesspeople in mind, but he couldn't trust them if they got caught. His best bet was to introduce someone to them in a casual setting that had no knowledge of their history. Also, no knowledge of what type of man Thomas was.

Satisfied with the knot of his tie, he lowered the collar and walked back to his jacket. He put in on and returned to the mirror to make sure he looked presentable. His reflection portrayed an air of confidence. He was happy with what he saw. He stared at himself and gave himself an internal pep talk. He had the intelligence to find this person and the intelligence to provide a seamless transition. This was non-negotiable. Tomorrow he would engage his personal assistant to increase his invites to all the right parties and charity events. Mingling with others was something he despised but was unavoidable in the world of business.

He brushed a speck of dust off his left shoulder, took his phone out of his pocket and informed his driver that he was coming down.

CHAPTER 39

Roman and Jacob found themselves back at the same café on Lygon Street, seated at a table with Carlos Esposito and his son, Cristiano, and daughter, Sofia. They had just dropped Moya off at the airport and battled the ever-increasing Melbourne traffic and roadworks to get back into the city. It was mid-afternoon on another hot day, with the mercury hovering in the mid-thirties. Summer was a week away, when you could guarantee at least two hot spells of continuous days above forty degrees Celsius. This was still hot, and they were grateful to be inside with air conditioning.

In front of them were coffee and glasses of chilled sparkling water. It did not take much convincing from Roman when he called Carlos that they needed to meet. Carlos wasn't surprised that the police were treating this family as prime suspects, as he was used to this in his heyday. However, this was a new experience for his kids and, being a true father, he was protecting and guiding them through uncharted waters.

"Thanks for letting us know the police suspect us of transgressions," Carlos said. "My son may not have dealt with this business relationship correctly, but you have my word and the word of my kids that we did not have anything to do with Elizabeth's murder and nor did we have any knowledge that it was going to happen. Secondly, we are not in the business of trading stolen goods, nor are we in the business of laundering money. It doesn't take a modern-day Einstein to put two and two together and assume that stolen Middle Eastern antiquities and money generated from these are likely to be funding extremists that go against everything I believe in and stand for. For fuck's sake, I have no respect for these arseholes. They stand behind a religious belief to justify their fucked-up actions. It would be like the Italians during the underbelly wars in Melbourne saying they were doing it for Catholics. Whatever the bullshit religion or cause extremists stand behind, it is always about land, control of that land, and the people that reside in it. I go to church, and religion is about bringing people together for the good of themselves and the community."

Carlos took a sip of his coffee. "Sorry, I digress, but I know some Muslims and plenty of others that don't go to my church and they're all good people. There are fucking arseholes in every religion, race, and country. Every sexual preference. That's all they are—fucking arseholes."

Roman and Jacob were seeing the real Carlos Esposito. Gone was the cool, calm front. He was now personally engaged, and this left them with no doubt that he was speaking the truth. Jacob summed it up eloquently with, "Thank you for your honesty. We feel the same."

"Our immediate threat is that the so-called arseholes we are dealing with are just in it for the money." Roman took a sip of the cool sparkling water and continued. "The police know that Jacob and I will be talking to you. They are finding themselves in a difficult situation as evidence is pointing to your involvement."

Cristiano was about to talk but his sister, Sofia, placed her hand on his arm and said, "What evidence are you talking about?"

Carlos appeared to appreciate Sofia taking the lead, and it became apparent to Roman and Jacob that in the pecking order, she came above Cristiano.

"For starters, they have seen Cristiano going in and out of antique dealers where these goods are," Roman said. "Before you ask—yes, the police are doing extensive surveillance. Before you answer, I will let you know that they saw you," Roman continued, looking at Cristiano, "walking into one with a small parcel and then leaving without it, and, yes, they are going through your business with a fine-toothed comb."

Cristiano looked at his dad and sister. "We have talked about this and, yes, I've brought this upon my family. I'm trying to cover my arse and protect my family. To do this, I need information on what the fuck is happening. I have been speaking to these dealers to find out more about the true value of these antiquities and if they are pocketing this money or paying a finder's fee or third-party brokering commission. One dealer was willing to talk about his knowledge of the industry but wanted to be paid for his time. That was what that small parcel was for. I want to be clear that this dealer was not from the antique store I met him in. In fact, he told me to meet him there at that time. Shows how paranoid he was, and I gather he did this in case I was being followed by the police so they would be pointed to a wrong store. However, he did not want to talk then and there, and I'm pretty sure the dealer that owned the store was none the wiser. I met up with him the following day for a walk around Carlton Gardens."

"And?" Jacob asked after a long pause.

This time Carlos leaned in as it was apparent that Cristiano did not know if he should continue. Carlos took a sip of coffee and started to talk. "You'd be surprised at how fucked up the antique business is. These goods have a huge variance in their estimated value. One thing we do know is that most of these goods vary from their description when being imported and obviously, with that, comes a true value that is off the scale in terms of mark-up. We reckon most are bona fide dealers, but some are milking the system. The dealer in question clearly fits into this category. He admitted having a feeling some antiques he traded might be stolen from archaeological sites. He conducts some sales through brokers, who take a substantial fee, and admitted that an anonymous broker seemed to contact him with a buyer as soon as he had signed for the goods. What else would you add, Cristiano?"

"When pushed for more details, he swore he did not know who this broker was and did not want to know. He seemed scared and I could tell that he was having second thoughts about accepting money for information. I pushed him further as, at first, he came across as proud of what he was doing, like he knew who I was and was seeking validation. I played on this and he admitted that there was a side of the industry that was ripe for being exploited and his confidence grew as he was telling me this. He operates with an unwritten rule that you don't ask questions and 'why should he when he's making a bucket load of cash and technically doing nothing wrong'. So what if he knew he was selling these goods at a market value far greater than stipulated, or that they were labelled incorrectly? But when it came across that I was not interested in fuelling this enterprise and wanted specifics, he could not provide any. However, he looked more scared of the people behind the scenes in the black market than of me. Like what my dad said, the money behind this is huge and that speaks volumes for what we are dealing with."

Roman gave Jacob a glancing look that conveyed he was going to mention what happened to Detective John Moskil. They had discussed this on their way there. They would tell them about what happened at Moya's place only if they gave them something in return and confirmed their innocence. But before this, Roman asked if he would be able to pass on the details of this dealer that was willing to speak, and who was obviously tied up in this even if he did have his head in the sand.

Cristiano was dead against this as he had given him his word that he was speaking anonymously. Roman tried to convince him that for the police to lay off them, they needed something as a sign of good faith. Still, Cristiano refused. Sofia and Carlos said nothing.

Roman proceeded to tell them about the incident at Moya Connor's apartment. They had not heard of her but knew of Detective John Moskil. Jacob added that he had been at the hospital last night and spoke to the doctors. John was now in a stable condition, but he had knocked on heaven's door a couple of times, with the dedicated medical staff preventing him from walking through, while his shattered wife sat crumpled in the waiting room wondering what news she would need to tell their two daughters. This morning, he had been taken out of an induced coma and they were now waiting for him to come to in his own time.

Carlos expressed his sympathy and wished him a speedy recovery. Sofia and Cristiano echoed this sentiment. Roman and Jacob were expecting a bit more.

Roman moved his seat back in preparation to bid them farewell. Jacob spoke before he could. "Cristiano, it appears to me that there must be something more driving you to try to gather information on the people we are dealing with. Like Roman just told you, they are serious and have someone in Melbourne. My wife was killed for a lesser involvement. I don't mean to be disrespectful to you, Carlos, or your family, as you have shown an open respect towards us. So, don't take my next comment as disrespectful, but something is missing here. We can help you."

Roman settled back into his chair and was all ears to what Carlos might say. Cristiano and Sofia gave an almost pleading gaze to their father, even though they tried their best not to show it. Sofia then asked her father for a private word.

They both got up, moved to a corner of the café and had a brief conversation in hushed tones with their backs turned. They returned and sat down. Cristiano just swirled his half-empty coffee while they were absent and now tried to look like he knew what was happening.

Carlos drained the remainder of his coffee and then the rest of his sparkling water, as if to build up the importance of what he was about to say. "Sofia has convinced me to share something else with you. These bastards have threatened Cristiano's life if anything goes bad in Melbourne. They want him to assist them in cleaning up any loose ends. He has refused so far but the threats are real. This is apparent with what has happened at Moya Connor's place. I instructed Cristiano to find out more about who we are dealing with. As Sofia has reminded me, we have gotten nowhere. Personally, I am afraid for my son's life."

Cristiano's confident persona crumbled a little as he saw his father express genuine concern for him in front of others. Carlos caught on to this and gave him a nod that spoke volumes for how important his kids were to him.

Carlos followed this up by adding, "I will make sure Cristiano disappears for a while, so please let Detective Adam Zhang and Superintendent Bridget Unaipon, whom I have a great deal of respect for, know that this is for his own safety and not a sign of guilt."

Roman and Jacob caught on that he obviously knew who in the Federal Police was involved. It did not surprise them that Carlos knew more than they gave him credit for.

"We'll pass this on," Jacob said. "If you hear anything more, please let us know. We can help you, as you have helped us."

With that, they said their goodbyes. As they reached the door to head out into the afternoon heat, Carlos caught up to them. He simply said, "There's a nice antique store in Fitzroy." Then he turned and went back to his children.

Roman and Jacob did not try to ask any questions. They let Carlos be and made their way outside, where they walked in silence down the road to Jacob's Volkswagen Golf. They reached the car and got in. No sooner had they put their seatbelts on, when the back door opened, and Bridget Unaipon slid into the back seat.

"I thought we were going to contact you after we had spoken to them?" Roman said as he turned to face Bridget from the passenger seat.

"No time like the present, and I wanted to make sure you guys were actually going to talk to them. By the way, turn the car on and get some AC going."

Jacob turned the ignition on and cool air started to flow out the vents. He wasn't surprised to see her. They did let her know they were seeing Carlos today but did not say when or where. It didn't take a genius to guess where, especially for the Federal Police.

"So, what did they say, as I know his kids, Cristiano and Sofia, were there?"

Roman filled Bridget in on everything that took place and even what Carlos said as they were leaving. Bridget took it all in and appeared to accept it as the truth.

"So how dangerous are these guys?" Jacob asked. "If they are threatening Carlos's family, even I'm getting shit-scared."

Bridget looked like she was going to exit the car and ignore the question. Her hand was on the door lever, but she took it off and positioned herself in the middle of the back seat and leaned forward so that her head protruded between the top of the passenger's and driver's seats.

"So you should be. I suggest you leave it to us. Thanks for all you've done, and I'm certain arrests will be happening in the near future." She patted Jacob on the shoulder. She then prodded Roman in his muscular upper arm. "That goes double for you."

"An arrest for trafficking stolen antiquities or an arrest for my sister's murder? If you say the first, then I might have to go to Hong Kong and beat the truth out of Thomas Rayner and his mate Mac Hawkins," Roman said with a cheeky grin that was nonetheless laced with seriousness, like a pupil challenging a teacher but leaving enough room to not get in trouble.

"I'm sure they both go hand in hand. Since you've helped me out, I'll let you in on something. Thomas Rayner, as you know, is filthy rich. Official worth is in the high hundreds of millions to the low billions. However, when talking with other agencies that have had him on their radar for some time, they estimate his wealth to be well and truly in the billions, multiple billions. He apparently hides it very well so as to not raise suspicion. If you ask me, I think he doesn't give a shit how much he's worth. He likes being on the rich lists but is extremely careful that it is a conservative measure from legitimate business.

What this tells me is that he is enormously careful, has power and is not to be underestimated. In my whole career, he would be the smartest guy I've come across, with experienced people from international agencies holding the same belief."

"Okay, I've got the message to stay well clear," Roman said.

"As for Mac Hawkins, like Thomas Rayner, others are interested in him but he's also smart. Not as smart as Thomas but smart enough. I think you know better than anyone what type of person he is, but if Thomas has his back, then this makes him even more dangerous and harder to arrest and, as with Thomas, it will be doubly hard to make that arrest stick."

Roman nodded his head to show he understood. Jacob remained quiet, his heart racing with the hope that he would never meet any of them. Well, not without Roman by his side at least. He became acutely aware that when it came to physical conflict, he was way out of his league.

Jacob asked, "Any update on their movements?"

Bridget responded, "Interpol has both still in Hong Kong. Passports not used for some time. Credit card transactions back this up."

Roman and Jacob didn't say a word.

With that, Bridget bid them a good day and left.

Roman could see that Jacob was feeling uncomfortable. "Come on. Let's go back to my parents'. There's cold beers in the fridge, and they want you to stay for a barbeque."

"Sounds good. I do have a full-on day at work tomorrow so don't want to waste this glorious afternoon." He put the car in gear and headed towards the Eastern Freeway. He needed to take his mind off Elizabeth's murder and Roman had a knack of being able to switch off, even though he knew Roman, deep down, never took his mind off it. That worried him as he didn't want Roman to do anything stupid. He didn't want to lose him as well.

CHAPTER 40

Detective Adam Zhang was at the hospital. He had slept little that night and was by John Moskil's side as the morning sun rose and the bank of monitors in the room beeped in unison. John's wife and daughters had been by the bed holding his hand when Adam arrived. He insisted they go home, freshen up, have a sleep, and come back in the morning. It took some convincing but, in the end, comforted by the fact that he was there, they agreed.

The staff had been very accommodating and had offered Adam a spare room so he could get a few hours' sleep. He politely refused, preferring to be at his partner's side.

John's chest rose and lowered with each breath. Every other part of him remained motionless. His face was badly bruised, with two black eyes courtesy of the head blow that knocked him unconscious. The doctors had informed him that Adam had suffered extensive swelling in the brain due to the knock and it was now in the hands of time for that swelling to decrease. They had been fastidious and ensured every scan and test was done. There was no need to operate—it would be best to let nature take its course. Chances of any permanent danger were low, but they would not know until he came out of the coma.

Adam had John's hand in his and with his eyes closed was apologising for the umpteenth time. He knew John was strong, and Adam quietly urged him to wake up. He told him his lovely wife and beautiful daughters would be back by his side soon.

The monitors' hypnotic beeps were the only constant sound. He felt himself drifting off to sleep when a change in the rhythm of sounds brought him back to reality. Adam opened his eyes and felt John's hand squeeze his. Adam's heart skipped a beat with excitement. He immediately leaned over John and pressed the big red button to get a nurse or doctor in there.

John's head moved from side to side as he let out a low groan and opened his eyes. Adam held his hand with both of his and told him to relax as tears of relief trickled down his checks. A nurse was first to enter the room, followed by a doctor. Adam let go of John's hand to give them space. The nurse and doctor calmly proceeded to access John's vital signs and spoke softly to him to gauge a response.

John's first words could not be understood, as he tried to find his tongue. Then they heard him ask where he was. The doctor told him that he was in hospital and to try to relax. John raised his hands to touch his face and the oxygen cord under his nose.

"I can't see," John said with his eyes open.

"That is fine," the doctor reassured him. "You've had a nasty blow to the head and your vision will return very soon."

John started to relax and lay there letting the medical staff do their job. He moved his head from side to side and then locked his eyes on Adam.

"Adam. What are you doing here?"

Adam was elated to hear his voice and the doctor was pleased his sight had returned. The doctor took a penlight out of his top pocket and checked John's pupils. He returned the penlight to his coat and let them know all was good.

"Mate. You've given us a massive scare," Adam said as he leant forward and grabbed John's hand again.

The doctor left the room after informing them that he would be back with the specialist. The nurse remained.

John was confused. Adam told him what had happened and reiterated that his wife and daughters would be by his side soon.

"All I can remember is going up to Moya's apartment when I caught a glimpse of someone in her place. I knew Moya was not home. After that, things are a blur."

"That's okay. Just concentrate on getting better. I do have one question. We cannot find your phone. Did you take it up to her apartment?"

"Yeah, I'm sure I had it in my hand recording as I went up, being by myself and all."

Adam never had a doubt that John would have done this. It was nice to hear it confirmed. He asked him if he could remember anything from when he entered Moya's.

John tried his best to remember but he was still a bit groggy. He apologised, and Adam told him not to stress. "You need to concentrate on getting better," Adam reassured him. "The rest can wait."

John closed his eyes as the nurse told him yet again to relax and take it easy. He had suffered a major trauma and his strength would return in time.

Adam did not let go of his hand until he heard the delighted sound of his wife and daughters as they approached the room. He moved away from the bedside and went out the door to give them well-deserved time together. The doctor that was initially there reappeared at the same time with another in tow.

While out in the hallway, Adam took some time to phone his boss and Bridget with the good news. He then called Roman and Jacob, as promised.

Adam watched from outside the room as he caught up on emails and made more calls. He did not want to leave as there was so much he wanted to ask John. However, John needed rest and quality time with family. He knew he would have to return in the afternoon.

Adam stuck his head in the door and wished them farewell and said he would be back in later to make sure John was following doctors' orders. As he turned to leave, John told him to wait, and politely asked the others in the room to give him and Adam a few minutes alone.

John's wife was apprehensive as she naturally wanted him to recover without thinking of work. She knew John loved his job and she didn't hold the job responsible but was protective of her husband. John took a few seconds to reassure his wife that he was fine.

She stroked his hand and led the others out of the room.

"What's up?" Adam said as he quietly closed the door behind him, aware that everyone was still watching through the window.

"Come closer." John moved himself up slightly in the bed as Adam sat in the bedside chair. "My melon hasn't been turned to mash yet and my memory is coming back. I was recording on my phone when I entered Moya's. I remember the door being unlocked, so I cautiously went inside. Then things get a little fuzzy. I remember someone tried to hit me with something, but I managed to half-block it. It was a blur of a fight; however, I remember still having the phone in my hand. Not sure what happened but I recollect knowing that I was losing. This guy was good, and it was only a matter of time before it was lights out. I was by the window on my knees and, for some reason, it was ajar. I pushed the phone out of the gap as I got up to try to stop this guy turning my face into a busted onion. That's the last thing I remember."

"Mate. That is the smartest thing I've heard. You are one tough bastard. Can you remember what this guy looked like?"

"Nah, mate, but he was built like a brick shithouse. I can't remember him saying anything. But if you can find my phone, there may be footage of him."

Adam could have kissed him. Instead, he gave him a pat on the shoulder. "I'll get onto it straightaway. Now, get better, and if there's anything I can do, just let me know."

"Luckily I don't need anyone to wipe my arse," John said while trying to maintain a deadpan face.

"That, I'll leave to the professionals," Adam joked. He was relieved that the beating hadn't diminished John's sense of humour.

Adam made his way out of the room and told the waiting family and medical staff that John was all theirs. He could see John smiling as they entered.

Adam walked in double-time to the elevator, and when he made it to the car park, ran to his vehicle. He started it up and made his way to Finders Lane. He was tempted to put the red and blue lights on but refrained as it was not an emergency that justified speeding. With his phone connected via Bluetooth, he made a call to Detective Constables Olivia and Noah, who had been seconded to him since the beginning. He told them to drop everything they were doing and meet him outside Moya Connor's apartment.

He took advantage of being a police officer when he arrived and parked illegally. He was placing the police sign on his dashboard when Olivia and Noah pulled up behind him. He got out and, instead of going over to them, he took a few paces out into the middle of the laneway and looked up. He knew which windows were Moya's and he could see several awnings sticking out underneath with about twenty-centimetre gaps between them. He glanced down the laneway, even though he knew that if any phone was lying on the ground, it would have been picked up. Seeing it wasn't there, he did the pointless motion of jumping in the hope he had suddenly gained superpowers and could jump high enough to see on top of the awnings.

"What's up, boss?" Olivia asked as she and Noah approached.

"We are looking for John Moskil's phone. He remembers throwing it out of Moya's window. I want you two to go up and down this laneway and see if you can spot a phone. Go into every shop and ask if one was handed in or if they noticed one on the ground. I know you have already questioned them, so they should recognise you. I am going up to the apartment to look out the windows to see if it's on top of an awning."

"Have you got a key?" Noah asked as Adam took off.

"Shit. I don't, and there's no police crime-scene guard anymore."

"Luckily I grabbed it from the boss as we left." He tossed it to Adam, with Adam giving a smile of appreciation at the young detective's forward-thinking.

Adam took the elevator to the sixth floor and opened Moya's door, making his way straight to the window of the open lounge and kitchen that faced the street. He looked out and saw nothing on the outside awning. Next, he went into the bedroom and looked out the window. Again, nothing. No more windows were left in the small one-bedroom apartment.

Cursing, he returned to the open lounge and kitchen. The window was now closed but it would make sense for Moya to leave it open on a hot day, given that no one could possibly get in. He looked out again and caught a glimpse of Olivia and Noah going into the café John would have been seated at. It was then a glint caught his eye from the end of the corrugated awning below him. It was a fair way down, as it protruded from the ground level. There was a small gutter on the end of the lip that he had not recognised at first due to it being covered with leaves. Looking closer, he was sure that there was a phone stuck in the gutter, with only a corner visible.

Adam made a mental note of where it was and raced to the elevator. After three seconds of waiting, he took the stairwell, flew down the six flights of stairs, out the main entrance and across to the café.

Olivia and Noah were in the middle of talking to the lady café owner when they turned at the sound of Adam panting for breath.

"Sorry to interrupt. I'm Detective Senior Sergeant Adam Zhang. You wouldn't happen to have a ladder?"

"Um. Yeah, we do have a small ladder out the back that we use for changing lightbulbs and updating the specials board. What do you need it for?"

"I just need to retrieve something off that awning across the road."

"Certainly. I gather it's in relation to what happened over there. I was just telling your colleagues that we haven't had a phone handed in, nor found one," she said as she turned and went out the back.

Adam noticed that the café was near full and the patrons that were nearby were looking at him. He lowered his voice and filled Olivia and Noah in on what he thought he had seen.

After less than a minute, the lady owner came out with a six-step folding ladder. Adam relieved her of it with a heartfelt, "Thank you."

Adam, Olivia, and Noah went across the laneway and unfolded the ladder. Adam went up the six steps and balanced on the top, with Olivia and Noah holding on to provide support on each side. His eyes were level with the lip but could not see over it. Reaching his hand up and running it along the gutter, his fingers met a slim rectangular object.

"Yes!" Adam exclaimed as he held the phone for Olivia and Noah to see. The screen was cracked but appeared intact.

With Adam's feet on the ground, Noah folded the ladder and took it back to the owner. Adam squeezed the side button, but the screen remained blank. He held it for a few seconds but there was still no response.

"Battery will be flat. I've got a charger in the car."

He headed off to his car, which was only a few metres away. He opened the front passenger door, sat down, and grabbed the end of his charger that was permanently plugged into the vehicle's USB port. Olivia looked on, with Noah already back and standing beside her.

It took about ten seconds before there was enough battery to power up. They all breathed a sigh of relief as the lock screen appeared with a photo of John smiling with his daughters. Adam entered the password John had given him and the home screen materialised with a photo of just his daughters.

Adam tapped the gallery icon and saw the last item was a long video of forty-six minutes. Obviously, it had kept recording until the battery ran out. Starting the clip, they leaned in with bated breath. It started with John approaching Moya's door. Once inside, there was an immediate scuffle. The camera was being moved around and shaken violently, showing only a blur with the odd glimpse of an arm, body, floor, wall, and ceiling. After nearly a minute, the camera showed the phone falling from the window, at which point it went black.

Adam swiped the video back to the beginning, and they watched it again. This time he stopped it before the fall outside and went back frame by frame.

"There!" With a fist pump, he showed a clear partial profile shot of a man. He took a screenshot and emailed it to himself.

"I'm sending this to you guys as well," he said as he took out his own phone and forwarded the image he had just captured to Olivia and Noah. "Now head back to the station and share it with everyone. Get the tech guys to run facial recognition. Cross-reference with all CCTV footage from that day. Pull out all stops to find out who this is. I'll show this to the local businesses around here to see if anyone recognises him."

Olivia and Noah hurried back to their car and took off. They knew everyone at the station would drop everything to help find the person who put one of their own in hospital.

Before Adam got out of his car, he phoned Roman.

CHAPTER 41

Roman was at home. He'd had a difficult morning informing his parents of what he and Jacob had been up to. At first, they were angry about being kept in the dark but soon simmered down and, in their own silent way, were proud of their son and son-in-law.

The previous day, Adam had phoned Roman. The photo he had forwarded him took his breath away. Even though it was only a profile picture, and not a full one at that, there was no mistaking it was Mac Hawkins. Adam was equally shocked, as Bridget had been keeping a tab on him, supposedly along with Interpol.

After the phone call, Roman had phoned Joel in New Zealand. He didn't bother going to a payphone. The game was up. Joel confirmed that Mac's passport had not been used. It didn't take a genius to know Mac was using an alias with fake documents. He had the know-how to pull this off—something Roman and Joel had quietly suspected all along, but they were still surprised by the boldness of the move. Using fake documents and identification was a last resort in their line of work as the risks and consequences of being caught greatly outweighed the benefits. Once caught, you were never going to get out of custody.

Roman looked at his parents sitting around the kitchen bench having a cup of tea with the plain-clothed detective named Noah, who Adam had sent around last night to stay with them until an arrest was made. If anything happened to them, he would not be able to forgive himself.

He had spent yesterday evening in Lygon Street with Carlos, Cristiano, and Sofia Esposito. Jacob was at work and he did not tell him of the Mac Hawkins revelation until early today. Roman left his parents' house and drove around to Jacob's in their car. He had arranged for Adam and Bridget to meet them there.

Whilst driving, he had turned up the radio and listened to Australian legendary band AC/DC. The classic rock station was playing "It's a Long Way to the Top (If You Wanna Rock 'n' Roll)". Roman couldn't help but sing along. Something struck a chord with him in the lyrics. It was all about being an Aussie battler with nothing coming easy. He replayed his plan in his mind again. The song amplified his state of mind and made him feel positive about what needed to be done.

Pulling into Jacob's, he saw that Adam and Bridget were already there. He took a deep breath and went inside.

"Roman," Bridget said as a greeting. Adam and Jacob just gave a nod of their heads.

Roman joined them around the dining table. Jacob had brewed a large pot of coffee, which sat in the middle, accompanied by a small jug of milk, sugar, and chocolate biscuits. They had already poured theirs so Roman took the only empty mug left and helped himself. He did not add milk but took a biscuit.

Bridget said, "First of all, we had alerts in place on his passport and bank accounts. We had no sign he was over here."

"*Is* over here," Roman corrected. "Mac Hawkins is still here and for a reason. I know that reason."

He had everyone's attention. Not even Jacob knew what he was about to say.

Roman finished his mouthful and washed it down will a long sip. "I know Mac, and it bothered me that he would take such a huge risk to come here and break into Moya's. I couldn't put my finger on it. Maybe he was tying up loose ends to cover his arse. But why? He could just carry on with his life. It's not like there is sufficient evidence to tie him to anything. And even if that day came, why complicate it with even more charges?"

"I've been thinking the same," Bridget interjected. "Thomas Rayner could be offering him substantial money to cover his arse. You'd be surprised what people will do for money. Also, we know Thomas has a hold over him."

"Yeah, but I also mulled this over with my business partner, Joel, who also knew Mac back in the day. This theory did not sit well with him either. Mac has a huge ego. Money is a driver but it's not everything. People like Mac only care about themselves and their perceived view others have of them. I believe he would throw Thomas under a bus as quickly as Thomas would do the same to him. They have a self-serving relationship of convenience."

Jacob listened intently. "Sounds like these two guys are sociopaths."

"Exactly," Roman confirmed.

"That's a big leap to make," Bridget reminded them. "But it does hold water. We did background checks, and we have this as a possible profile. Let me emphasise, though, that this is a possible profile. A lot of criminals like to think they can operate in this way, but they crack in time, as it is just an act."

"Yes, but Thomas and Mac have been operating for a long time," Adam said, backing up Roman. "I've arrested a few arseholes in my time, and it's the true sociopaths that don't crack, as they honestly believe they are right. I always get confused between the difference between sociopaths and psychopaths, but whatever—if you're operating that high up in the corporate world like Thomas Rayner and being as dodgy as fuck, then you're no doubt one of them."

Bridget drained her mug. "Thomas I can understand as we have knowledge he displays this type of behaviour at work. But we are talking about Mac here. So, spit it out, Roman. What is Mac up to?"

Roman was quietly amused at the banter that had just taken place. It showed him that others had also been scratching their heads. "Okay. Yesterday evening, I went and saw the Espositos. They may be innocent, but they hold more cards than we give them credit for. They are the ones that can help both of you," he said looking at Adam and Bridget.

"What is it with you and the bloody Espositos?" asked Bridget.

"Well, they have helped us a bit," Adam reminded her.

Jacob spoke calmly to ease the tension. "We all know they have helped us. Personally, I think Roman and I have seen a side to this family that no one with a badge could ever witness. At the end of the day, this is a very tight-knit household that cares a great deal about each other and their community. An example many of us could learn from. I have no idea what Roman is about to say, but let's hear him out."

Roman sat back in his chair and hoped they would let him finish before voicing their objections. "One thing I know about Mac is that he wants to be top dog. I don't think he is here to clean up after Thomas. I think totally the opposite. He wants information. Why does he want information? He wants it because he doesn't want this great run to end. It's no secret that they are winding down their operation, which we agree is incredibly smart. Thomas is the brains behind this. He knows when to walk away and how to walk away with your head held high and reputation intact. We've all assumed that Mac is going along with this."

He had their full attention. No one interrupted as he took a drink. He continued.

"I saw the Espositos because I want them to convince the man they are dealing with that they don't want the relationship to end. In fact, I want them to boast about how they can handle the operation in Australia and assist internationally. I want them to brag that they know how to move money and make it squeaky clean. I want Cristiano and Sofia to leverage off their father's reputation."

"You're assuming the man they are dealing with is Mac?" Bridget asked.

"I'm certain he is. But where's the harm if I'm wrong? Especially for you. Oh, and by the way, the Espositos are a hundred percent behind doing this. They want these guys out of Australia, and it may surprise you that they do have a code of conduct, and financing terrorist activities where innocent children are being murdered is not one of them. Don't get me started on where they stand on the raping of culture and heritage from a country."

This hit a note with Bridget. The penny dropped that maybe she had more in common with them than she liked to admit.

Roman continued. "Cristiano was going to go into hiding but instead has arranged to meet the man he has been dealing with to discuss moving forward in a joint venture. This man has let Cristiano know that he is in Melbourne, which is why I think it has to be Mac Hawkins. He has the meeting scheduled for tomorrow night at their warehouse in Port Melbourne, at eight. He's bought some time to get his affairs in order, as he said he needed to get his father's network on board. The man bought this and has agreed. He just wants Cristiano there. Not his sister or dad. He gave strict instructions that he will know if anyone else is present. So, Adam and Bridget, you've got limited time to set up surveillance, but make sure it's at a distance. You can put listening devices in the warehouse. Get in touch with his sister, Sofia, straightaway and she will plant them." He slid Sofia's phone number over the table, and Bridget palmed it.

"Can we get in touch with Cristiano beforehand?" Adam asked.

"No. We are certain that Mac will be having him followed and monitoring his email and phone. We are also certain he will case out the warehouse prior to the meeting."

"Well, what are we expecting to get out of this?" Bridget asked before Adam could.

"Cristiano knows that, first, he needs to get this guy to confess to the exportation and importation of stolen antiquities. Second, to mention Thomas Rayner as also being involved and, if possible, that Thomas is the mastermind behind it all. Third, to confirm that it is funding terrorist organisations and that money laundering is also involved. Fourth, to name associates already in Melbourne and Australia. And, finally, the most important one—to tell us who murdered Elizabeth and why, and hopefully to implicate himself in this."

Bridget and Adam thought about this for a few seconds before nodding and giving their approval. Bridget didn't need to ask questions as Roman had clearly stated that they were also setting up Thomas.

"We have a lot to do," Bridget said as she and Adam got up. "We will get everything in place, and as for you two, stay safe and remain at Roman's until this is over."

"We will," Jacob said as he and Roman made their way out the front door. Before they left, he asked, "By the way, how's John?"

Adam answered. "He's recovering well and should be discharged from hospital in a few days. Took a nasty beating but all his marbles are in place. He says thanks for stopping by when he was in a coma."

With the door closed, Jacob took Roman to one side. "So, what is really happening?"

"What do you mean?"

"Come on. I happen to have gotten to know you pretty darn well. You are not just going to leave Cristiano and the police to handle it from here."

"Listen, Jacob. The less you know the better. Just go and stay with my parents, who have Detective Constable Noah for protection."

"Fat chance of that. You've dragged me along this far. I can be of assistance."

Roman thought long and hard. He ran the palm of his hand over his face from forehead to chin. "Okay. We don't have much time."

CHAPTER 42

Roman and Jacob were lying down in the upper level of a vacant warehouse. They were looking out a dusty window that they had partially cleaned from the inside, but it was still dusty and dirty on the outside. Jacob had the binoculars they purchased in Hong Kong beside him, and they were fully charged and ready to record. It was early evening and still hot and stuffy, with no air conditioning in the building and hardly a breeze coming through the upper louvered windows.

When their eyes were focused, the view was clear enough through the windows of the warehouse that was located opposite and across the road. Roman had gotten access thanks to Carlos Esposito, who happened to know every owner of every warehouse in Port Melbourne.

After Jacob had convinced Roman to let him in on his plan, and subsequently discovered it was a plan based on assumptions, they had gathered their gear and headed straight to the vacant warehouse. Roman was adamant they had to get there the night before as he was certain Mac would have the place cased out as soon as he got a chance, including neighbouring buildings.

Empty packets of chips and muesli bars, bottles of water and Subway wrappers that they had grabbed on their way were now lying on the ground next to them. It had been an extremely uncomfortable night as they tried to get some sleep with only a faint dapple of light from a nearby streetlamp. They did not risk using torches. Luckily the warehouse had running water, so the toilet worked, and there was even an old roll of toilet paper left in the holder. The nights were now relatively warm, but there was still a chill before the sun rose. Under the cover of darkness, Roman had ventured into the warehouse across the road, thanks to keys and alarm codes from Cristiano, where he had planted his own listening devices. Jacob kept a studious watch to make sure no one was observing.

The day had dragged on as they played the waiting game. Now the daylight was fading and rendezvous time was getting close.

"You sure about this?" Jacob asked.

"Yeah, sort of," Roman replied as he looked through the binoculars. "Mind having a look at the rain radar on your phone? I don't like the look of those clouds over there."

Jacob got his phone out of his pocket and went straight to the app. One thing he found out about people that ride motorcycles is that they always check the rain radar religiously. He was now one of them. With the app open, he saw a heavy rainband coming in from the east. It looked like it was some time away as it was moving slowly. He told Roman this, while also showing him the screen.

"Okay, let's hope it holds off."

Roman then raised an open left hand to request silence as he lowered himself closer to the ground while holding the binoculars to his eyes with his right. "I see a car pulling into the warehouse car park with Cristiano behind the wheel."

Jacob slowly got his binoculars and shuffled next to Roman on his belly. He took off his glasses and gave them a quick clean on the upper neck of his T-shirt. He placed them back on, peered through his binoculars and saw the car parked close to the warehouse front door. They watched for a further six minutes. "Here comes another car. I can't make out the driver."

They both saw it pull up beside Cristiano. Cristiano got out first and walked to the front door. The man got out of the other car and joined him as Cristiano opened the door to let him in. As the man went to enter, he turned around and gave a cautionary scan of the neighbouring buildings. He did not see Roman and Jacob, but they saw him. Roman confirmed the identity under his breath. "Fucking Mac, fuckin' Hawkins."

Scanning the windows of the building, they saw them enter the main floor of the warehouse and, as instructed, Cristiano had them position themselves exactly where they could be seen. However, Mac had a pistol in his hand, raised from his hip, pointing at Cristiano. The audio they had set up worked perfectly and came through the small speaker resting on the floor behind them.

"What the fuck is up with the gun? I told you it's just you and me," Cristiano said in a relaxed, confident tone.

"I need to be sure," Mac said as he moved forward to Cristiano, who had his arms half-raised and palms showing. With the pistol aimed squarely at Cristiano's chest, he patted him down thoroughly, right down to his socks. "Okay, looks like you're clean. No hard feelings but I need to make sure."

"So now that you know I'm not packing or wired and you've felt my balls, you can at least tell me your name."

"My name is not important. If you end up delivering what you say you can, then I'm sure we'll be bosom buddies and go on man dates."

Cristiano already knew it was Mac Hawkins, as Roman had shown him photos. The strong cockney British accent was as he expected. Mac reminded Cristiano of the British actor Ray Winstone when he was about forty. Cristiano hoped that Roman and Jacob were recording clear footage of him, since he apparently didn't want to formally identify himself.

"Okay, understood. But let's be clear, I also like to know who I'm dealing with. How do I know you are who you say you are?" Cristiano calmly asked, remembering the list of facts they wanted Mac to disclose.

"For starters, I got in contact with you. I manipulated your email account to freak the shit out of you and cover my arse. You took extra payments to overpay for goods. Shall I continue?"

"Nah, all good."

"Now, let's cut the crap. Tell me what you can do for me."

"I'll be honest. I've enjoyed the money I've made from helping you move these stolen antiquities. I have an extensive network across Australia and could be a real asset to you."

Roman and Jacob watched on, waiting for Mac to admit to moving stolen antiquities. The words that came out of his mouth were disappointing. "Now, wait a minute. Who the fuck said they were stolen antiquities? Also, why would I need you for a network when I already have one?"

Cristiano thought quickly. His dad and sister had coached him extensively on what to say and when. This coaching had been videoed to make it clear that what he was saying was scripted and couldn't be used against them.

"Come on. I wasn't born yesterday. I visited some dealers where they end up and researched the goods myself. The antiquities are even being washed with new descriptions, source of ownership and history. So, cut the crap or else this meeting is over. Oh, and when I said an extensive network, I was also meaning the ability to wash the money generated and make you a tidy return."

Mac took a few seconds to think. This was the one thing he needed more than anything. Thomas Rayner had the contacts and resources to do this, not him. If he wanted this to continue, he needed someone like Cristiano and his family. "Okay, you have my attention. So tell me more."

Roman and Jacob were disappointed again that he had not admitted to anything.

Cristiano was finding Mac a tough nut to crack, but he continued as instructed. "My dad has been washing money before you were even a glint in your daddy's eye. He has cash-based businesses everywhere and his fingers in investment structures that not only wash money but provide a great return, like property development where you inflate your costs, pay for tradies that never worked and still return a profit. But more than that, we know a lot of people that would pay good money for stolen antiquities as an investment for their dirty money. But before I go any further, I need to know these are genuine antiquities and you're not just ripping people off, that in turn may want to put a bullet in my head."

"Oh, they're fucken genuine all right."

"I know you fake the documentation when exporting them. Why the need to do that if they're not stolen?" Cristiano said, remembering that Mac had not admitted to them being illegally sourced.

"Well, let's just say that they haven't been legitimately acquired and, if that was known, red flags would pop up to alert every fucken agency in the world."

This was more like what Roman and Jacob wanted to hear, see, and record, but they needed more. Cristiano was doing a great job and Mac was feeling more at ease.

"I know one was definitely from Syria," Cristiano probed. "How are you getting them out of there? I need to know who I'm dealing with as I know you personally don't obtain them."

"I've got contacts. There's more stolen antiquities coming out of that fucken shithole country than I can move."

Roman gave a "yes!" under his breath. Jacob continued to watch and quietly asked Roman how much memory he had left in his binoculars, as it was agreed he would fill up his drive first and then Jacob would hit record. "Nearly half full. Now we need Cristiano to get the rest out of him."

Cristiano was feeling pleased that item one was admitted to. He pushed the boundaries. "My family has done checks on the businesses that export these goods. One name concerns us, and that is Thomas Rayner. If you're going behind his back and he knows nothing about his companies being used, then we're out. He is one person we don't want to piss off."

Mac was surprised to hear Thomas's name. He now knew that the Esposito family did their homework but was still taken aback that they knew of Thomas and his reputation. "For fuck's sake. Thomas is all over this shit, so don't worry about pissing him off."

Bingo. Cristiano, Roman and Jacob all thought this at the same time.

Cristiano had Mac on a roll but needed to remember to pander to his ego. "I can see you are an important part of the operation. Looks like you take care of everything. So, who does Thomas deal with and will it be you or him we launder money for?"

"You'll be dealing with me."

"Yeah, I know that, but before I agree to anything and put the reputation of my family in your hands, I need to know where the money is going so we can litigate against any risk and assist you getting it to them."

Mac was thinking fast. He knew that if the money could be moved without him having to touch it, then his arse would be covered. He knew Thomas did this but did not know who he used. All he knew was that he got a substantial cut.

"I'll get back to you on that one, once you've proved you can do it."

"Well, I heard through the grapevine that Thomas was dealing with known terrorists. If this is the case, I need to know now because there will be a few palms I'll need to grease. The last thing I want is you and me being blown to smithereens 'cause we pissed off the wrong people."

Mac still had the gun in his hand, but it was now lowered and held loosely in his hand. "I'll be honest with you. All I know is that these goods come from the Middle East. I don't ask questions and I don't plan to. For argument's sake, let's assume that the people smuggling them are the worst of the worst, but they pay well. So, no more questions about this. We can go our separate ways right now if you wish?"

Cristiano decided to let it go. There was still more information he needed to get. "No worries. Just to confirm, you will want me to accept the antiquities into Australia, distribute them and wash all proceeds from them?"

"Correct."

Roman and Jacob wanted to give each a high five but remained glued to their views. It was then they heard a loud rumble from the sky and a crack of thunder. Both diverted their sight to the sky, and in the diminishing light, they saw thick, black clouds rolling in like an angry wave in slow motion. Cristiano had lights on in the warehouse that were taking effect as darkness slowly descended, and by the look of the clouds, it was going to get really dark.

The sporadic sound of large rain droplets could be heard hitting the corrugated-iron roof accompanied by the sweet smell of them evaporating off the hot tarmac and metal surfaces.

Roman and Jacob remained steadfast in their job, although as the rain intensified there were moments of blindness as lightning flashed followed by deafness as thunder crashed. They could make out Cristiano and Mac talking about money and timeframes, but it was getting difficult to hear clear sentences and visibility was becoming almost non-existent as the rain strengthened.

"Fuck this. I can't see a fucken thing," Roman said as he placed his binoculars down. He turned and faced the speaker. "And I all I can hear is the sound of fucken rain."

"Let's have faith in Cristiano," Jacob reminded him.

"They're just talking business. I want to know who the fuck killed Elizabeth, and I don't think Mac is going to give that up. Also, how are we supposed to protect Cristiano if we can't see or hear him?"

Jacob knew these were good questions. "Shall we call in the backup now?"

"Just tell me this. Do you want to know who killed Elizabeth?"

"Of course, I do!" Jacob raised his voice. There was no need to be quiet.

"Well, down there is the only chance we've got. Look through the binoculars and tell me how much you can see?"

Jacob rolled back to his stomach and faced the window. "I can barely make out details. It's just a blur."

"That's good enough for me. Hit record and if you lose sight of me, call back up."

Roman was already out of the room and running down the stairs before Jacob had a chance to turn and question him, let alone try to stop him.

CHAPTER 43

Roman was soaked through to the skin after his dash to the opposite warehouse. He stood outside the front door under the narrow eave and caught his breath. Mac had a gun—he didn't. This was a gamble, but he had no choice. He took his phone out of his jeans pocket and phoned the "backup". He gave clear instructions for them to wait ten minutes.

Quietly he opened the door and ventured inside with soft steps. The sound of the storm hitting the room gave an ample buffer if he did make any sound. He reached the main area and saw the door ajar. He heard voices and gave a quick glance inside. With his back to the wall and out of view, he had seen that there was no chance of taking Mac by surprise. They were too deep inside the vast room. This could work in his favour. He now needed a lot of luck.

He took three long breaths to lower his heart rate. He then turned and entered the room in the most casual way he could muster. "Gidday."

368 – SIMON ERRINGTON

"What the fuck!" Mac exclaimed as he and Cristiano turned at the same time. Mac raised his pistol with a finger on the trigger.

"Woah. Steady on, mate." Roman stopped and tried his best to take the sting out of the surprise of him just showing up. He had his hands visible, outstretched at about thirty degrees from his hips.

"What the fuck are you doing here?" Mac's question was said directly to Roman but was also directed at Cristiano.

Before Roman answered, Cristiano jumped in. "Who the fuck is this?"

Phew, Roman thought. Cristiano had acted surprised and remained in character. Roman coolly said, "Well, how do you do, Mac? Are you going to introduce me to your friend?"

"You two know each other?" Cristiano growled before Mac could answer. "What the fuck is going on here?"

"Let me tell you." Roman remained still and nonchalantly continued to talk, with even Mac wanting to hear what he had to say. "My name is Roman Paxter and me and Mac Hawkins go back a long way."

"So, your name is Mac Hawkins?" Cristiano interjected.

"Yeah, well, that's pretty fucken obvious now," Mac conceded with a quick glance to Cristiano before returning his sight down his pistol aimed at Roman.

"Me and Mac go back a long way. Don't we?" With arms still slightly raised and looking at Cristiano, Roman did not wait for a reply. "Sorry to interrupt this intimate get-together.

But you should know what sort of person you are dealing with."

"Shut the fuck up!" Mac shouted. "This arsehole is no friend of mine. Now strip off before I shoot you!"

Roman was wondering if Mac would search him. Now he knew he was taking the best option, avoiding getting close. He took his wet clothes off and dumped them on the floor. He didn't wait to be shouted at again and even removed his underpants and did a three-sixty. Being naked was nothing. The dipshit hadn't cottoned on that the room was bugged. But why would he when this was a last-minute change of location?

"Move three metres to the left!" came the next instruction. With his gun remaining raised, Mac crouched down and, with one hand, went through the pockets of Roman's clothes. He came across his phone, placed it on the polished-concrete floor, stood up and smashed the crap out of it with his heel, until the screen went dead, and the battery was visibly separated.

Roman stayed silent until Mac was finished. Another mistake Mac had made, he thought. He should have made him unlock it and looked to see who he called last and when. He should have also checked text messages and all messaging apps. This told Roman that Mac was concerned about someone listening or being recorded, and that he might be in a hurry.

"I'm going to call this meeting to a close. I'll contact you later," Mac said to Cristiano as he headed for the door.

"What the fuck?" Cristiano shouted. "Who the fuck is this guy? He's seen me! You're not leaving me to deal with this mess!"

This made Mac stop. Cristiano's reaction once again impressed Roman. He thought he had blown it by turning up. Now he needed to take control. Roman removed his calm demeanour and said with a sting in his voice, "Mac is a pussy. He's always feared me. He only hits guys that are handcuffed. He's a fucken faggot!"

"Fuck you. I should put a bullet in your head right now!"

"Just like you did to my sister."

These words cut through Mac. He looked visibly shaken as he took a couple of steps back into the middle of the room towards Roman, which was exactly what Roman had hoped for. Mac thought long and hard, with the pistol at full arm's length pointing at Roman's head. "Fuck you and your fucken sister."

Jacob was still lying on the ground in the upper floor of the vacant warehouse. He could barely make out what was happening through the heavy rain, but he stayed focused, recording. The audio was terrible. He knew the hidden devices would be recording okay from where they were but the one he was getting the feed from was not in a good position. He could make out a confrontation and hear shouting. It looked like Mac had a gun and Roman was naked. It was then he heard the loud crack of the pistol firing and the outline of Roman falling to the floor. Thoughts inundated his head. Should he run over there? Should he phone for help? Medically, he might be able to save his life. Physically, he could offer nothing. It was then that his vision went, his heart raced, his stomach turned, and pins and needles overtook his whole body.

"What the fuck did you do that for?" Cristiano asked.

"He's a piece of shit, just like his sister."

Roman tried his best not to scream and remain steadfast as he clutched his right leg, with blood seeping out of his lower quad. The pain was unbearable. He applied pressure and knew he would not be able to stand. He was thankful that Mac had missed his kneecap and, judging by the flow of blood, any major artery.

Cristiano knew he needed to be careful. He didn't want a bullet, and Mac was starting to lose it. He would use this to his advantage. He wasn't as thick as his father thought he was. His sister might have the brains, but he had street smarts. He clicked to everything Roman had said since turning up.

"Hey, Mac. This arsehole said his name was Roman Paxter and asked if you shot his sister. That would be Elizabeth Paxter. That means he's her brother and he personally knows you. What the fuck are not telling me? I don't mix business with pleasure, so unless you can tell me, I'm out."

"That had nothing to do with him. That bitch needed to die for being a nosy cunt!" Mac bellowed.

"Just be straight-up with me. You do that, and I'll finish this prick off and make sure his body is never found," Cristiano said bravely. "Is there someone in Melbourne working for you that takes care of people? If so, I need to know."

"You don't need to know shit!"

Roman knew Mac was rattled and he didn't care if he got shot again—he needed to know. He grimaced with the pain and screeched, "You're too much of a pussy to do it yourself!"

"Fuck you," Mac spat at Roman, moved forward and got into his face as he lay on the ground unable to move. "If I had known it was your sister, I would have killed her slowly instead of shooting her in the head!"

With that, Roman found an inner strength and leaped up onto his good leg and lunged at Mac as fast as a death adder snake. He punched him square in the nose before Mac got a chance to raise his gun and fire. The pistol dropped to the floor in unison with Mac hitting the concrete. Roman rained down strike after strike. The sound was louder than the deluge and thunder outside. Hitting and hitting and hitting again.

Roman was pulled away by the shoulders. It was then the red mist dissipated from his vision. Cristiano was standing over Mac's body. Carlos Esposito had turned up as requested and was standing by his son. Roman also saw the older gentleman he had originally seen at the Café in Lygon Street on that fateful first meeting. Holding him back by his shoulders were two younger, stocky guys he had not seen before. It was then he saw how bloody and battered Mac was. He was withering about with a faint moan.

Carlos took a step towards Roman. "We'll take it from here. Jacob will take you home and clean up that bullet wound."

It was then he saw Jacob enter, soaking wet, running over to check his brother-in-law, his mate. "I came over as soon as I saw the backup arrive. I saw him shoot you. Are you all right?"

"It hurts like fuck, but I think it went clean through and missed the bone. The dumb fuck was never a good shot." Roman winced as the adrenaline started to subside.

"I need to get you to a hospital." Jacob had taken off his T-shirt, ripped it into three and was meticulously applying a compression bandage.

"No hospital. Just help me get to the car and clean me up at your place." Roman noticed that Cristiano had rushed around the warehouse and gathered up the recording devices. He made it to Jacob and handed them to him in a bag that apparently came from Carlos's mate. It was then he noticed Mac was looking at them with swollen eyes. A look that took in the fact there had been listening devices and an acknowledgment that he was fucked.

"Okay. My place it is," Jacob said to Roman. He did not protest as he knew that going to the hospital would cause more trouble for Roman and, subsequently, for him.

Another young man that looked like he lived at the gym entered the building carrying a holdall. He looked at Roman and Jacob. "I've got all your gear from across the road. Let me help you get to the car."

He pulled Roman to his feet and wrapped his arm under his armpit, around his back and through the other, holding his weight like it was just another day at the office.

"What about Mac and all this mess?" Roman asked Carlos as he saw Mac trying to lift his head, with pleading eyes that could barely be made out under the swelling and blood.

"Don't worry about him. You've got all the evidence you need. Mac here will learn the penalty for fucking around with the Espositos. My boys will clean up."

Mac muttered a sound through his broken lips and a tooth fell to the floor. He tried to form a word but was too damaged.

Carlos leaned down with a look that could turn concrete to jelly. "Oh, this is nothing, you piece of shit. Helping terrorists and fucking around in my backyard. You honestly didn't think you'd get away with it?"

Mac tried to move but Carlos just placed a boot on top of him while his "colleagues" circled around like vultures waiting for a feast

Roman turned as he was shuffled out. Jacob was behind him. He saw Jacob was looking pale. "Just focus on me, mate. You've done good."

As they exited the building, the rain ceased, leaving only the smell of water on a hot night, cleaning today for tomorrow.

CHAPTER 44

The curtains were pulled back, revealing a glorious day.

"What time is it?" Roman asked as he woke. Jacob placed a glass of water by his bed with another round of painkillers and prophylactic antibiotics.

"Just after midday."

It was then that Roman noticed they were not alone. Detective Senior Sergeant Adam Zhang stood in the doorway of Jacob's spare room looking rather pissed. Roman shuffled himself up against his pillows to be in a semi-sitting position. He felt the bandage around his right leg, just above the knee. "Hey, Adam."

"You look like shit," Adam said as he remained leaning against the doorframe. "I should be as mad as hell. We waited all night for Cristiano and Mac to turn up. We finally gave up at one in the morning. Don't get me started on the cost."

Roman was unsure what Jacob had told him. Luckily, Jacob spoke before Roman could put his foot in it.

"Adam arrived here about an hour ago. I told him there had been a change of plan. I hope you don't mind but I played him the evidence we gathered."

Roman was itching to ask Jacob if he had edited the recordings. He wanted to give him a look that conveyed that message but knew Adam would notice. Jacob saved him the hassle and added, "I told Adam that due to the bad storm, we lost recording here and there, and the video footage was difficult with the lack of visibility."

Roman knew Adam wasn't buying it. However, he also knew he wouldn't ask questions. He went to speak, but Adam cut him off.

"Before you say anything, let me tell you how pissed off my boss is. I was also fuming. I've been trying to get hold of Cristiano and the rest of his family, but they seem to have disappeared, or are ignoring me. That's why I came around here. I was ready to haul both your arses in, but Jacob calmed me down and told me you had been injured and needed rest."

"I'm really sorry about this," Roman said. "Hope you understand why this was done. Mac would have known you were there. Him getting a last-minute change of location added to the credibility of the meeting."

"Come on. I wasn't born yesterday; you must have tipped him off somehow for him to buy into a last-minute change."

Roman replied, "Yeah, okay. Cristiano sent him a photo of you guys getting into position. And, yes, I instructed him to do so. But, hey, he would have seen you guys anyway."

"Yeah, I get it. I'm still not happy about being out of the loop. Your saving grace is that the evidence does close the case on Elizabeth's murder. We now need to arrest Mac." Adam raised his eyebrows to form the sentence into a question.

Roman knew he was fishing. He and Jacob had gotten their story straight on the drive back last night. "No doubt Jacob told you that he did a runner once he knew the game was up. Obviously, I tried to catch him but had to give up the chase."

"That's what Jacob told me." Adam looked like he wanted to press the issue but knew better. "After I leave here, a warrant will be issued for his arrest."

"I hope you get him," Jacob said. "I think Roman needs some more rest now."

Adam remained where he was and spoke with a deadpan look. "Jacob told me you injured your leg jumping a steel picket fence while trying to apprehend him. Hope you get better soon."

"Will do and say hi to Bridget for us, as no doubt she'll be pleased."

"I hope you guys realise that I've had her yelling at me down the phone. Before I came up the stairs to see you, I called her and calmed her down. I need to see her immediately and will share this evidence. Just be grateful the Federal Police isn't knocking on your door right now, but she will want to see you at some stage."

"Thanks for that," Roman said.

"Well, I suppose I need to thank you guys, but don't expect it in writing."

"Understood."

Adam then moved himself off the doorframe and straightened up his shirt. "I'll show myself out." He turned and made a show of the USB drive above his head that he held in his hand as he bid them farewell with a wave of the drive.

Adam closed the front door behind himself and made his way to his car. He was incredibly pleased with what he had in his possession but knew he needed to smooth out the cracks that would be asked by his superiors. Most of all, he couldn't wait to tell his parents.

CHAPTER 45

"On the floor with arms spread out!" Sawyer, the nicely spoken man from MI6 shouted, with Superintendent Bridget Unaipon by his side. Behind and to the side of them stood fully armed tactical response members courtesy of Her Majesty's Secret Service.

Bridget had flown non-stop to London once she had delivered the final piece of evidence needed to make an arrest and make it stick. Sawyer knew Thomas Rayner was back in London staying at his penthouse apartment in Canary Wharf. He had insisted that Bridget be part of the apprehension, with partial credit naturally being given to the Australian Federal Police.

Bridget had slept well on the plane but was still feeling exhausted from the round-the-clock investigation. They had kept it quiet that an arrest warrant was out for Mac Hawkins, with Adam Zhang keeping it from the press. As far as Thomas was concerned, Mac was still in Australia tidying up loose ends for their imminent departure from moving stolen antiquities from the Middle East.

Thomas lay still on the lounge room floor with his trousers unbuttoned and shirt untucked. He had not said a word since his door had been forcibly opened at just after midnight. Two armed men dressed in black from head to toe were taking a scantily dressed hooker out to the hallway for further questioning. Judging by the labels on her underwear and clothes she had under her arm, she would not have come cheap.

A man and lady in dark suits entered next and picked up a handcuffed Thomas off the floor. He looked at them with utter contempt but remained tight-lipped. He had been clearly informed of why he had been arrested and what his rights were. He had chosen to stay mute. They escorted him out of his apartment, not bothering to ask him anything as they knew he wouldn't talk. They had plenty of time to interrogate him.

"He'll be taken straight to Vauxhall Cross for questioning," Sawyer told Bridget, referring to the MI6 building. He then instructed all others to vacate and signalled for the forensic teams to enter.

At precisely the same time, Thomas Rayner's places of work, and warehouses in Hong Kong and London were being raided, along with Mac Hawkins's offices. Sawyer had worked non-stop while Bridget was in the air to ensure this would happen.

"You're more than welcome to stay behind with me as we search this place," he told Bridget. "Later we'll head back to see if we can get anything out of him."

"I thought you wouldn't ask," she replied. "Are you certain he isn't going to walk?"

Checking that only they and forensics were there, he walked Bridget to the large opulent kitchen, out of earshot. "We have enough on him to sink a ship. But tying him to murder, via his association with Mac Hawkins, is the icing on the cake to ensure any judge keeps him in custody. We know that with his resources he could disappear like *that*," he said with a click of his fingers. "Having Mac nailed for using a false passport and other documents adds considerable weight to this as you've proven that they worked extremely closely together."

"One more thing," Bridget said. "If you don't mind me asking, who exactly is that Mustapha guy you sent over to identify the antiquities?"

"I'm impressed you haven't asked until now. He is originally from Syria, and kind of found us first, but that's a whole other story. He's a professor that worked as a leading archaeologist for the government overseeing many archaeological sites. He had valuable information that the terrorists wanted, and the government was becoming heavy-handed, silencing officials that they even remotely suspected of sharing information for profit. Basically, he was caught between a rock and a hard place. He and his family were doomed no matter what direction he took. One thing I can say for the guy is that he has risked a hell of a lot to protect the culture of his country, and for that, I have a ton of respect for him."

Bridget nodded her head in agreement.

One of the forensic team was making his way into the kitchen to search it. Sawyer politely asked him to give them another five minutes.

"Sorry, where was I? That's right—Mustapha and his family are now living in England with new identities. He has provided our operatives with priceless information, which has allowed us to gain Thomas's trust. It just so happened that Thomas was wanting to pass on the enterprise and approached our undercover agent in Hong Kong, who had been trying for months to get his foot in the door."

"That explains a lot," Bridget said. "Sounds like you have enough to lock him up for life."

"Well, the fun is only beginning. It will probably take about two years to get this thing to trial, and I can guarantee by sunrise there will be a busload of overpriced lawyers knocking on our door, looking for any loophole to release Thomas. Fortunately, we have two busloads of lawyers."

Bridget gave a light laugh. "Can you freeze his assets and funds?"

"We'll try, but he can easily prove he's a billionaire through legitimate means. He'll spare no expense to clear his name."

The forensics man returned to the kitchen. Sawyer indicated that they were finished, and he could proceed. Walking back to the lounge, he asked the lady in charge if they had found anything. She advised that the place was clean so far, with no work items present, but they'd still dust the place down in case they could tie someone else to having been there. She mentioned a safe in the expansive walk-in wardrobe that they had just opened. It had contained only money and expensive jewellery.

"Shall we head off now to see Thomas?" he asked Bridget.

"Sounds like a plan. By the way, I'm to let you know that Australia will dedicate whatever resources are required to stop money fuelling terrorism."

"Appreciated. No doubt we'll be working closely for many years on this. It is imperative that we disrupt their funding. Without money, they become weak and fall, which makes the whole world safe. The knock-on effect from tonight will be huge. Many more arrests will come off the back of this—that I can guarantee."

They exited the apartment knowing that the enormous challenge they had in front of them was only just getting started. But a good start it was.

CHAPTER 46

Jacob and Adam had gotten changed from their motorcycle gear and were now relaxing outside in shorts. They had been for a morning ride through the Dandenong Ranges. Jacob was surprised when Adam told him he had a Yamaha R1 sports motorbike. They immediately agreed to meet up for a ride. The sun was shining, and they had thoroughly enjoyed pushing their high-powered bikes around the twists and turns in the hills. The day was warming up and they were glad to get back as beads of sweat started building up under their gear. In summer, they knew you needed to ride early.

Christmas was only days away. They were sitting with Roman at his parents' place. They were parents to Jacob as well, as they kept reminding him, which he appreciated. Jacob had told them that they were the mum and dad he never had after he had married Elizabeth. Now he also had a brother in Roman.

Roman's parents had organised a huge barbeque as an early festive celebration, in honour of Elizabeth. Also, outside with them, enjoying a cold beer, was Moya and Joel from New

Zealand. They had flown over two days ago, with Moya show-ing Joel all the sights of Melbourne that you would only find out about with local knowledge. They had become great friends, and Moya was extremely grateful for how well she had been looked after.

Jacob enjoyed his company as well. It was good to put a face to the name. He was slightly shorter than Roman but still tall at six feet, with the athletic body of a triathlete.

Walking out onto the patio was Detective John Moskil with his wife. He had been discharged from hospital and told to take it easy. He could return to work in another couple of weeks, but he had already been in, which his wife had turned a blind eye to. Upon leaving the hospital, he was informed that a Detective Sergeant position had become available and was his with immediate effect. He was stoked but his wife was cautious after what had happened and made a deal with him that he would start attending karate classes with Adam, as he was not getting any younger and needed to look after himself.

"I suppose you saw the news?" Adam asked them as they stood around the barbeque watching the assortment of meat cook. Roman's parents were in the kitchen preparing the sal-ads.

"Yeah, we did," Roman replied. "Congratulations on a case well-solved."

Adam decided to state the obvious since it was just them. "Well, it was easy to explain all the bruises and broken bones on Mac Hawkins's body, since it was washed up onto rocks in the harbour. The media accepted that he had escaped capture

386 – SIMON ERRINGTON

and fled into the ocean that night. He shouldn't have underestimated the currents," he said in a dry tone.

"Well, I'll drink to that," Jacob said as he raised his beer to his mouth.

They all joined him.

"I managed to get in touch with the Espositos," Adam said. "They confirmed what you told me. They were an innocent party in the whole fiasco. A little birdie also told me that the Federal Police have stopped investigating them."

"They're a good family," Roman said. "I put in a good word for you and John. I'm sure they'll invite you for coffee when needed."

"Is the meat ready yet?" Mrs Paxter asked as she placed a large salad bowl on the outdoor table. Mr Paxter was placing another in the middle.

They all turned as Roman started to get the meat off the grill and place it on platters.

All seated, they tucked into the magnificent spread before them. Mr Paxter even brought out another round of cold beers, as he and his wife relaxed, soaking in the company and pleasure of having their home filled with laughter, feeling as if all those seated were their family. Roman, Moya and Jacob shared funny stories of Elizabeth, which made her beautiful presence felt.

With bellies full, Mrs Paxter insisted that they all remain seated as she and her husband cleared away. Joel would hear nothing of it and got up and headed inside with a stack full of dirty plates.

"So, I hear you've kept a bloody good secret from us?" Adam asked Roman.

"Mate, I don't have to tell you everything," Roman shot back.

Jacob was enjoying this and added, "Well, you kept me in the dark. I had no idea."

Moya was next to add to the light-hearted ribbing. "I kind of suspected. Call it women's intuition. But I definitely knew once I was in New Zealand, you sly bugger."

"So, when did you tell your parents?" John asked, and received a poke in his side from his wife.

"I told them about a month ago. They were thrilled and didn't seem surprised, which made me feel like a total idiot for not telling them sooner."

Mr and Mrs Paxter came out to get another load of dishes, followed by Joel. They all noticed that Mrs Paxter had a tear in the corner of her eye as she stood there another moment with Mr Paxter's arm around her. They stayed still, taking in the scene before them.

It was then that everyone noticed Joel had walked up behind Roman. Roman turned on his seat as Joel got down on one knee.

Acknowledgments

I would like to thank my parents for all their input. You brought me On Writing by Stephen King which was a great help. I enjoyed debating topics in which you were both mostly right. Thank you to all those people that I asked random questions, now you know why. I would also like to thank my lovely wife Kunkun for giving me the time to pursue this crazy dream of writing a book, it couldn't have been done without your support, let alone your input into many fine details of the story. Thank you, Graeme from The Expert Editor team, for making it flow and correcting all my grammar mistakes. A big thank you to Adam Errington for rebranding the book with a new title and awesome cover.

Lastly, thank YOU for taking the time to read this book.